The Lazarus Ciphers

by William Struse

www.the13thenumeration.com

The Lazarus Ciphers is a work of fiction. Characters, places, events, and names are used fictitiously by the author to challenge the reader's imagination. Any resemblance to real locations, events, or people, dead or living, should be considered coincidental.

The Biblical history upon which the Lazarus Ciphers are based is true.

Dedicated to:

My Father
the late
Dr. William P. Struse, DO

Faith found a way, Dad.

Acknowledgements:

Winnie, my love, thank you for your tireless help and enthusiasm for this project. This story is better because of you. To our children Maranatha, Hope, Hannah, Zane, and Noah, you inspired this story. I know in whom I believe. Your faith will find a way.

Denise Weimer, your editing skills sharpened the dialog, quickened the pace, and improved this manuscript in so many ways. Thank you for your monumental effort.

Jeffrey Mardis, you took the themes of my book and created a book cover that captured the story.

Jorge, Braxton, Dawn, Allen, and Steve, thank you all for your thoughts and criticisms. Each of you had a special perspective that added to the novel.

Last but not least, to you my readers, I thank you for the privilege of sharing this story of faith, failure, and the redeeming power of God's love.

Prologue

The End to a Beginning

Something was off with this mission.

John Plummer consulted the luminous dial of his watch as the Gulfstream G650 banked. Three a.m. At Mach .90, the Mediterranean waters 50,000 feet below would soon give way to the tawny sands of the Libyan coast.

He should be sleeping like the rest of his team. Were these globetrotting forays into third-world war zones his way of escaping his problems at home? At fifty-seven, he no longer needed the money. He could have quit long ago. There were other men, younger men, who could troubleshoot for the firm.

He'd flown into plenty of dangerous places in the past eight years, but this time was different. It wasn't just that the trip had been hastily thrown together. It wasn't that Libya was in the midst of a bloody civil war. No, the problems lay closer to home. Money was missing. Men in the field had turned up dead.

John frowned at the file on the table in front of him. Someone in the firm was dirty. Someone clever was trying to cover their tracks, and John had been sent to figure out who.

This would be his last trip. He'd already told the firm that. He would solve this problem for them, and then he was done traveling the world putting out their fires. John squeezed the plush, white leather armrest of his recliner. He had his own fires to fight. The problem was, he didn't know how.

The ironies of life. Here he was at the top of the world, at the top of his game, in the prime of life. He had it all except …

except he would trade it all to somehow fix his children. He had long since gotten past the self-recriminations. If only he hadn't traveled as much. If only their mother hadn't left. If only he'd done this or that differently. But all that didn't matter anymore. His beautiful children were broken, and he didn't know how to mend them. They both traveled destructive paths that already had a bad outcome, but hopefully not a permanent one. The only thing that kept him from losing all hope was his faith that God still had a plan for their lives.

The moonlit, sparkling waters below gave way to the sands of Libya. Flashes fifty miles to the west reminded him just how dangerous this mission was. Libya was being torn apart. A rogue general controlled half the country and that part of the army loyal to him, while a democratically elected western puppet government ran the other half.

Democratically. Hardly. It was all about oil and the money it generated.

John's firm represented western oil companies with concessions in Libya. With the civil war raging, keeping the oil and the money streaming became increasingly difficult. In the midst of this chaos, some enterprising individuals had decided to stick their hands into the pipeline of money flowing to the clients his firm represented. They were skimming millions of dollars. Larceny on this scale could have only been accomplished by someone on the inside. Someone at their firm.

He should have walked away from this one. Just handed in his resignation and tackled his own problems instead of accepting this assignment. The problem was, he had an obligation … and Eric had asked him as a personal favor. Every time he saw Eric's empty sleeve, he felt the guilt. So here he was half a world away doing penance for an accident that had changed three lives.

John turned away from the all-too-familiar flashes and explosions of battle that lit the sky far in the distance. He'd seen enough of war, death, and tragedy in his lifetime. Pulling his laptop across the table, he tapped the screen and then typed in his password. He scrolled to an open tab and tapped again.

His last will and testament opened. He stared at the words without seeing them. Eric had advised against the unusual instructions he'd requested in his will, and so had several of his friends from whom he'd sought council. In the end, though, he had decided that he couldn't leave his children his fortune in their present conditions. At least not without trying to reach them one last time. In their current states of mind, the money would only harm them further. If they wanted their inheritance, they were going to have to earn it. It wouldn't be easy.

A smile broke the hard lines of his mouth as he thought about the 7 ciphered riddles he had given them to solve. His smile was not because of the difficulty his children would face in solving them. He knew they were difficult. The smile was for the countless hours of enjoyable and fascinating research it had taken to compose them. In any case, if they couldn't or wouldn't solve them, someone else would have a chance.

John studied the first cipher and its riddle. Concealed in those twenty-five letters of the cipher was an astounding claim. That claim was one of the foundational statements of the Biblical texts—a fitting place for his end to find a new beginning. He counted to the 13th letter. Would they see why it was important? If they did, they'd find a key they could use to solve the rest of the ciphers.

You could describe this enciphered Old Testament passage numerically as 39 is 1.

Provide the reference to where it is found in the Biblical texts.

He thought of these Hebrew ciphers as his Lazarus Ciphers. In the event of his death, they would be his hand from the grave, a hand reaching across that great divide. They were ciphered riddles representing a lifetime of research into history's most important claim.

Timbre and Cadence would have to work together, or they wouldn't be able to solve the ciphers. They didn't know it, but both of them had pieces of the puzzle the other didn't.

It was a desperate ploy, but what alternatives were there? He had asked himself that a hundred times. He was broken-hearted to admit they didn't deserve his fortune. But he refused to forfeit his faith. John thought of the words his mother had claimed on his behalf, words of faith that now guided his hopes for his children.

I know in whom I have believed
and I am persuaded that he is able
to keep that which I've committed
unto him against that day.

John placed his reading glasses on the table next to his computer and rubbed the bridge of his nose. More flashes from the window drew his attention. At that moment, he felt so small and insignificant. The world below him went on unaware and unconcerned by his problems. John rubbed his face with both hands.

"Father, please have mercy on them. Please don't let them get away. Keep them, please," he pleaded quietly. "Into your hands, Father."

He looked at this watch. They would be landing in thirty minutes. With a newfound sense of peace, John returned to his vigil. It was darker now. The sands of Libya didn't reflect the moonlight the same way the waters of the Mediterranean had. Ten minutes later, the pilot came over the speaker and advised the passengers to fasten their seat belts. John's ears started to pop as the plane began its descent. Lights came on in the cabin, and his team members prepared for landing.

The city's lights soon appeared over the tip of the Gulfstream's wing. A flash of light shot toward them. Instantly, he knew what it was. John Plummer had three thoughts in the six seconds it took for the streak of light to reach their plane. The first was that he'd never see his children again. The second, he hoped the Lazarus Ciphers would somehow reach them, that in his death, they might find a new life. Finally, that he'd been the final loose end that someone needed tidying up.

The missile exploded on the starboard side of the cabin. The explosion jolted the airplane as if the hand of God hurled it from the heavens. Half the wing disintegrated in the blast, and the plane rolled violently as the pilot tried to regain control. Jagged holes appeared in the fuselage over the wing, and the scream of depressurized air deafened him. Time slowed. A member of John's team who had not buckled in was thrown around. Oxygen masks dropped from the ceiling. Grasping hands flailed unsuccessfully to grab them in the violent gyrations.

The captain's terse voice crackled over the speaker, barely audible in the roar. "Prepare for a crash landing."

Instinctively, John leaned forward and grabbed his knees with his arms. A few seconds later, they hit the ground with a bone-breaking shock that left him gasping for air and his mind screaming in pain. The screech of tearing metal and the violent shaking numbed his senses. The seats in front of him disappeared as the fuselage was rent in half. John Plummer saw his children's faces and then a brilliant burst of orange flame.

The searing heat was the last thing John Plummer felt. The dry Libyan desert air and aviation fuel were the last things John Plummer smelled. His friends' and colleagues' terrified and agonizing screams were the last things John Plummer heard.

I know in whom I have believed, was the last thing John Plummer thought.

Chapter 1

The Ritual

Four Months Later

The imminence of death brought a naked clarity to my life. It wasn't pretty. It shouldn't have ended this way. I had started with more than most, but I'd lost my way. One poor decision had led to more. Now, eight years later, I had reached the terminal velocity of my grotesque life.

I reached for the briefcase beside my desk. It was stained and scuffed. Its once-rich brown had faded into a calico of lesser colors. I laid it flat on my desk. Gently, I ran the palms of my hand over its soft, warm, oiled leather.

Eight years ago today, the briefcase came into my possession due to a youthful act of indiscretion. It marked a crossroads in my life. It was a reminder of what might have been, of what should have been. I slid my hands to where I could reach the combination locks with my thumbs. I rolled the numbered tumbler on my right until it read 514. With my left, I rolled the number 314. A smile broke the tight press of my lips as I remembered the day I had figured out the combinations. It had taken days of fruitless effort, but it had been simple in the end. The combinations had been our birthdays. The left had been March 14th, the birthday of my sister, Cadence. The right, May 14th, the inglorious day five years previous that I had been born.

I placed both hands back on the briefcase, in no hurry to reveal its secrets. With unseeing eyes, I stared out the window of my sparse high-rise office, across the smoggy skyline and urban sprawl of Phoenix, across the barren browns and tans of the wilderness, to the broken, craggy hills that skirted this dusty bowl of desert. In the eight years since that day when my life took on a new trajectory, I had accomplished nothing of any fundamental importance or made any real difference. I had squandered my time and my substance. Worst of all, I'd offended the few people in my life who cared for me. I was alone. I was desperate, and I had nothing to live for.

I pushed the small brass releases on the briefcase. They were cool to my thumbs. The locks opened with a sharp click and snap that sounded ominous in the quiet room. I hesitated before lifting the lid. I brushed my hands over the leather once more. Life wasn't a fairytale—I knew that for sure. This briefcase wasn't a magic lamp and rubbing it wasn't going to get me three wishes. There was only one wish this briefcase could grant me, and it wasn't happily ever after. I stilled my hands. I opened the case.

To the casual eye, it was an ordinary legal case with all the pockets, pouches, and straps that held an array of paperwork, pens, and files tucked haphazardly here and there. I'd thought that at first myself. Only later had I realized there was one big difference. This briefcase was slightly thicker than most and a bit deeper. It was a custom-made job.

My discovery had been an accident. I'd been rummaging through the pens and paperwork at the bottom, and I'd found the cleverly concealed panel. It had appeared to be just a loose ribbon of fabric. But when I pulled it, the bottom panel of the case had lifted, and there, nestled in the warm brown felt, was a collection of my father's treasures. Why he hid them there, I still didn't understand.

I reached into the briefcase and pulled open the secret panel for the last time. As the light from the room revealed its contents, a storm of guilt, remorse, and regret struck me like the scorching blast of an open furnace door. I swallowed the lump in my throat and pushed the lid up until the brass-hinged braces held it open. The smells, real or imagined now, grabbed me like they always did. I was transported back in time to a dozen places and a million memories as if it was yesterday. I removed a packet of love letters yellowed with age. They were tied with pale blue ribbon. I held them up and breathed in the faint scent of a woman's perfume. I closed my eyes and saw a boy and a girl laughing, a beautiful woman spinning, a merry-go-round flashing. Faster, faster, and faster, it turned until all that I could see was a blurring circle and the flash, flash, flash, of my mother's fading face.

I set the letters down in front of me. Two tears followed them to the desk and landed on her name. I whispered the magical name. "Katia." It sounded foreign to me. The only name I had known was Mother. This pack of correspondence had revealed her real name to me. Two letters from my mother's name stood off the envelope for a brief moment, my tears magnifying them. Bigger than life and fading, like my memory of her. Slowly, then faster, the yellowing fibers of the paper absorbed the salty liquid and added it to the hidden words of love and pain inside, a slight stain and the faint wrinkle the only evidence of their passing.

I placed the letters to the side with an empty ache. I reached back into the case for the small black velvet box with a rounded top. With careful fingers, I held the box as I pushed the thumbnail of my right hand into the seam that divided it. I pried the lid partway open, and with a crinkling pop, it flung itself the rest of the way apart. Inside was baby-pink velvet lined with the silky curls of chocolate brown and snowy white. A golden wedding band and matching engagement ring lay in this nest with a glistening, one-carat gem casting sparks of light. I closed my eyes, buried my nose in those soft curls, and took a deep breath. The smell of milky childhood conjured scenes of pattering feet, cooing, gurgling laughter, and the forlorn cry of innocence. A sense of deep regret, missed memories, and shame were followed by the image of my daughter's face. I squeezed the box, and the closing clap pinched off the plethora of memories like a clam protecting its pearl.

The photographs were next. Their curled edges stuck out from the elastic strap that held them against the false bottom of the briefcases. I slid one out, pulling it by one of its brittle edges. The picture showed a Humvee parked on the sand. Deep ruts led away behind the vehicle into the distant dunes. Three men leaned against the hood of the vehicle, their muscled, shirtless bodies shiny with sweat and relaxed smiles on their faces.

The man on the right was of medium height, black hair cropped tight against his bronze scalp. He had a nose bent slightly to one side. It looked broken. A broad smile cut across his lined face. His buzzed haircut made his large ears stand out from his rounded head. Cradled in the crook of his arm was an M16 pointing at the rills of sand.

The man in the middle looked like my own reflection. Five-eleven with dark brown hair just long enough to see the natural wave. The serious brown eyes that stared at the camera told you there was substance deeper than the smile on his face. The tip of his sharp nose was peeling, and his dark brow showed the deep etching of a man who worried. Smoke trailed from his lips. A half-smoked cigarette hung at his side, grasped between the forefinger and thumb of his right hand.

The last man in the picture had fiery red hair, pale, freckled skin, and a smile that split the sky. His rifle lay across his shoulders, his head resting on its stock. Arms extended, one hand flashed the peace sign while the other held rabbit ears behind my father's head. The Irishman was the jokester of the trio.

I turned the picture over. There were three names printed on the back—Eric, John, Rory. Below the names, words were scrawled in my father's hand.

Greater love hath no man than he lay down his life for a friend.

I placed the picture on top of the stack of letters and reached for the other photograph. I stopped myself. I'd save the happier memories for the end. Instead, I slid my hand into a pocket sewn into the secret place. I removed a small purple felt bag with gold embroidery and drawstrings. The bag read *Crown Royal* across the front. Loosening the drawstring, I turned the pouch over and poured its contents into my hand. A purple heart, bronze star, and airborne wings dropped into my palm. Was there some deeper symbolic meaning to the placement of the metals in a bag that once held hard liquor? My father had never spoken about his military service. Were they his? Were they one of the other men's? The big-eared man on his right or the redhead on his left?

I rubbed the cool metal of the purple heart between my thumb and forefinger. The sacrifice, bravery, and honor these symbols represented were words as foreign to me as friendship, companionship, and love.

My most significant accomplishments in life were a failed marriage, a dead daughter, and a mediocre law practice that catered to people I neither respected nor liked. The only danger I'd exposed myself to was in service to my avarice. That expedition had led to a crushing debt of six figures which had now come due. The only thing my circumstances had in common with the sacrifice represented by these metals was that both had to be paid in blood. I set the metads on top of the discarded felt bag on my desk and touched them one last time.

I removed the other packet of envelopes. These were tied with a piece of rough garden twine. All twenty-four of the plain white envelopes had been opened. The postage on each was stamped roughly one month later than the next. All envelopes were empty except the last. Across each envelope, in a beautiful scrawl, were the brutal words, "Return to Sender." Two years of refused letters. Twenty-three times my father had sliced open the refused envelopes, and in some unfathomable expectation that the contents might be read, had repacked the letter and sent it off again.

The final envelope still held its unread correspondence when I had acquired the briefcase. I should have left it unopened, but I didn't. I shouldn't have read the words, but I did. I wish I didn't recall the pleadings my father had written to my mother, but now I knew. I knew what no son should have known. That twenty-fourth letter had been a desperate man's final attempt to reconcile with the mother of his children and the love of his life.

I pulled out that final letter and unfolded the thoughts of a desperate, lonely man. My hands shook with the memory of the raw emotions immortalized on the pages I held. The curls, twists, and loops of ink blurred. I couldn't make myself read the vain hopes and unrealized promises one last time. I refolded the letter and put it back in its empty tomb.

I wiped my eyes with the sleeve of my shirt and reached back into the briefcase for a gift I had never opened. Originally, it had been in the regular compartment of the briefcase. Like a sacred relic preserved in a museum's vault, I'd hid my father's gift in the secret chamber with his other treasures. It was a small box I could hold in my hand. It was wrapped roughly in green-and-white-striped paper, and across the top in my father's masculine script were the words:

To Timbre,
Happy Birthday, my son.
Love, Dad

Today was my birthday and the anniversary of the event that changed the trajectory of my life eight years ago. I suppose he'd meant it as a surprise, and it was. Only it was the worst kind of surprise for both of us. He had shown up unexpectedly with my birthday present. I hadn't opened the gift. I was still too ashamed. So, it lay there in his briefcase as a silent reminder of my indiscretion. A reminder that actions have consequences. A reminder that consequences often shape our lives in ways we could have never imagined. I groaned with regret as I set the gift aside and reached back into the briefcase.

Happy memories now.

I slid out the faded photograph of the three of us. It was summer. We were smiling. Dad was in the middle, his arms around our shoulders. Cadence was on his right, and I was on his left. You could almost feel my sister's enthusiasm and joy. It radiated and glistened like the sun in her golden hair that hung over one shoulder. In her right hand, she held a compound bow. She was shorter than Dad and me, but not by much. My sister was nifty in the best kind of way. She had the natural grace of an athlete and the mind of a genius.

We'd spent two weeks at my late grandfather's cabin on the Mogollon rim of Arizona. Grandpa had passed the old homestead on to my father upon his death in the early eighties. For two weeks, we'd explored the cool waters of Clover Creek as it twisted and turned its way through the sheer cliffs and forested slopes of the Mogollon rim country. We'd fished the deep pools from the bouldered banks of the creek. Each evening back at the cabin, the three of us waged an unrelenting competition with bows and arrows. Late into the night, we would talk about our day's adventures.

Dad was a sportsman who considered a scoped rifle in the same light a skilled surgeon saw a rusty butcher's knife.

"Any armchair weekend warrior can kill an animal with a high-powered rifle and a scope from half a county away," he would say. "Taking any life should not be that easy," he'd always finish in a solemn, quiet voice. His statement had always seemed haunting and unreasonable to me. Looking back, I wondered if he spoke from personal experience—the kind of experience only the tragedy of war provided.

I never asked him about it. Mark it up to another missed opportunity, another life regret. I would have liked to have known my father from a man's perspective. I'd only known him as an admiring son and then a rebellious adolescent. For the last eight years, I'd been stuck in the angry, bitter, uncommunicative stage of young adulthood.

That summer break of my second year of college, Dad insisted that we all needed a break from our regular routine. No electronic devices of any kind—not that it mattered because there was no internet or electricity at the cabin. Just the three of us and "God's wonderful creation," as Dad called it. Cadence had just finished her first year of high school. She was all-in right from the start. I wasn't too enthused, but they worked on me, and I finally relented. Mostly it was Cadence, though. I couldn't resist her enthusiasm.

Growing up, we had a special bond, maybe because we didn't have a mother around or Dad was gone a lot. Perhaps it was a little of both. But we'd been fiercely loyal to each other. I'd always done well in school—at the top of my class more often than not. But Cadence was on a whole different planet where brains were concerned. Her IQ was off the charts. What I loved most about my sister was she never let her intellect dampen her enthusiasm for the action of life. She loved to be outside. She was captain of the soccer team and a champion cross country runner during high school. She always brightened the room she walked into, and people gravitated toward her like butterflies to a glistening pool of water. I was no exception. She provided the sunshine that so many other people in life lacked. Growing up, she brightened my life in so many ways.

I lived in Phoenix now, and she had an apartment near our father in Ashburn, Virginia, but I could use a little of her sunshine in my dark soul right now.

Like my father, my wife, and anyone I might have once called a friend, I'd finally pushed Cadence out of my life. It was not one of my finer moments. At the time, I was up to my eyeballs in debt and out of control after the divorce. A poker tournament was coming up, and I was a few grand short of the necessary amount to enter the game. The bloodsucking lawyers got everything of value my wife hadn't wanted.

I was desperate to play. It was my way of blowing off steam and forgetting my miserable life. My sister knew I loved to play poker. Okay, she knew I was addicted to playing poker. I'd asked her for money that weekend, and she, in an uncharacteristically blunt way, had said she didn't have any to gamble with, said she had her own problems.

In retrospect, she hadn't sounded herself, and I hadn't cared enough to ask if she was okay. Instead, I had made a nasty comment about her being a daddy's girl, and she had hung up on me. That was several years ago. Since then, we'd only had a couple of stilted phone conversations.

If I had been a gunfighter and regrets were the people I had killed, the handles of my guns would have been covered in notches.

I rubbed the photograph's edges with my thumbs and looked at the three of us smiling. Those two weeks had been the happiest of my life. How had I gotten so off track? I used to be a reasonably happy kid. Maybe not a shining star like my sister, but certainly not the life-sucking black hole I'd become. I turned the photograph over. On the backside, my sister had written:

Timmy,

Thanks for going. Best time of my life!

Love,

314514

"I miss you, Caden," I whispered.

Caden was the nickname I'd given her the day she discovered her name's "numerical secret." She was eleven, and I was sixteen. With solemn, glowing eyes, she had revealed to me that the numerical value of the first five letters of her name gave both of our birthdays. She'd handed me the paper where she'd written it all out. I could still picture the two columns of letters and numbers.

C = 3

A = 1

D = 4

E = 5

N = 14

Cadence. Her name meant the balanced, rhythmic flow as of poetry. It described her perfectly. She'd made me swear that I wouldn't tell anyone her secret nickname. I hadn't. It had been one of the few promises I'd managed to keep.

I fingered the nickel-sized, magnetic ladybug and beetle clasped together at the top corner of the photo. I don't know how my father had gotten hold of the photograph, but he must have known our secret because the power of the two symbols of his and my sister's own secret communication held it tightly in his briefcase with his other treasures.

The ladybug and beetle were the emblems of an intellectual battle my sister and father had waged when she became fascinated with numbers. Nearly every day before work, Dad would put a math problem, a riddle, or some brain-teasing puzzle under the ladybug on our refrigerator for Cadence to solve. Her answer could often be found under the beetle when he returned home from work. Along with her answer would be her problem for him to solve. This war of intellect and cunning raged until it changed one day when Candence found a book on cryptology in our father's library. From that day forward, their brain teasers, puzzles, and riddles became cryptograms, ciphers, and codes.

I bowed my head. There was only one item left to remove from the briefcase. It was something I had placed there the night before, one of my possessions, but in some cruel, ironic twist of fate, it had been a gift my father had given me on my sixteenth birthday, sixteen years before. Time seemed to slow. I wasn't ready yet to pull the trigger.

Into my desperate thoughts rose the memory of the only item I had removed from my father's briefcase—years ago. A book. It hadn't been in the secret compartment when I acquired the briefcase. It was right there with the papers, files, and other items he used every day.

I didn't like to think about that little book because it made me uncomfortable. Its golden edges had been faded, its pages wrinkled, its worn condition evidence it was consequential to my father. His other treasures unsettled me in many ways but not like the pocket-sized book had. On the scuffed and tattered black cover, two words and nine letters had been embossed in gold. On the inside front page, scrawled in a woman's neat hand, was a message to my father followed by three lines of verse. It was part of a verse I remembered from long ago and a different life. I was deaf to it now, but I could see the handwritten words in my mind as if I were reading them off the page.

My dearest son John,

I know in whom I have believed and am persuaded that he is able to keep that which I have committed unto him against that day.

May God bless you and keep you.

Love, Mom

By my second year of college, I had no appreciation for the stories and history found in my father's book. I'd also rejected its morals and teachings, as my father had inadvertently learned in stark, naked detail the night the book had come into my possession. I had kept it through those final years of college, but every time I thought of that night or looked at the contents of the briefcase, it was the book that made me the most uncomfortable. The book made me feel shame. The book reminded me of the look on my father's face.

I had no loving mother to write such a note for me, and my college professors had conveniently helped me exterminate my faith in God. So eventually, I removed the uncomfortable, mocking presence of the book. For a short time, I felt liberated. But, in retrospect, I could see that my new master was harsher and less forgiving than any of the words found in the book. I was reminded of that fact every time I stood in front of the mirror and stared into his hopeless, unforgiving eyes.

With a clenched jaw, I reached into the briefcase for the final time and touched the smooth cedarwood box that lurked in its shadows. I still remember the serious look on my father's face when he gave it to me. I remember the lecture on its use and misuse. In the past sixteen years, I had never once broken the rules he had laid down. But, today, I was going to break them all.

With unsteady hands, I removed the lacquered cedar case. I unclipped the brass hinge that secured its fragrant lid. I opened the box. I lifted the cold, blue .22 revolver from its velvet bed and pushed the cylinder release with my thumb. With my free hand, I fumbled open the cardboard box of .22 magnum ammunition nestled in the red fabric. One by one, I fed the six, brass hollow-point cartridges into the cylinder. With a flick of my wrist, the cylinder snapped back into place.

"Sorry, Dad," I whispered into the silence of my office.

With a final look at the memories arrayed before me, I cocked the hammer and placed the barrel of the pistol against my temple. With blurry eyes and a gasping sob, I started to squeeze the trigger.

The phone rang.

My finger froze a hair's breadth before the trigger released its catch and sent the spring-loaded firing pin on its split-second journey into the drop of high explosive patiently waiting inside the end of the brass shell casing. The pistol started shaking, the tip of the barrel rocking back and forth on my scalp. My resolve weakened, and I loosened the tension on the trigger. I gritted my teeth and squeezed the wooden pistol grip harder. The shaking of my hand steadied. I jabbed the barrel of the pistol tighter against my head. My finger took up the slack a final time. The phone rang again, and again, and again.

"Just leave me alone," I growled between clamped teeth.

On its last ring, for some inexplicable reason, with the revolver still pressed so tight against my head that I felt the warm trickle of blood from the gunsight where it was cutting my head, I picked up the phone.

It was my father.

At this bloody crossroads of my life, he had reached from the grave to offer me hope.

Chapter 2

In the Shadows

May 30th – Two Weeks Later

The three-ton black Cadillac Escalade was parked backward in the yellow gloom of the underground garage three spaces down from the stairwell. The Cadillac's 420 HP engine idled with a hungry, muffled rumble. Like a Swiss watch, every thirty-seven seconds, a drop of water fell from the vehicle's underside. Two seconds later, it was gone, evaporated in the dry Phoenix air. That drop of water told the careful observer that the dark, tinted windows hid people that the vehicle's overworked AC was trying to keep cool in the oppressive one hundred and one degrees.

It was 106 above ground, and Phoenix was just a degree away from setting a new record for May. On the north side of the concrete complex, four massive exhaust fans turned with a soft *whoop, whoop, whoop*, their dull silver blades beating the super-heated air three levels down into the subterranean car lot. The 33-foot journey only cooled the air a slight five degrees. Still, the fans accomplished their primary purpose of removing the car exhaust fumes that would have otherwise made the parking garage inhospitable to humans.

Every thirty seconds, a jet of white smoke was ejected from a half-inch crack in the car's rear passenger door window. Inside the vehicle, thin, cruel, pale lips took another deep drag on a cigarette. One, two, three, four seconds later, the lips pursed, and a column of white nicotine-laced smoke, like the hot, bitter waters of Old Faithful, erupted through a gap in yellowed teeth and passed through the narrow slit in the window. The toxic stream floated, swirled, and stirred until the only evidence of its passing was the faint, stale smell of tobacco.

From outward appearances, the ashen, diminutive form in the ebony leather seat resembled a man's, but behind these eyes lay a cruel, rabid mind. The unblinking gray eyes gave him away. Except for flecks of hazel around his irises and a slash of gray across his right temple, Benito Silva was a lurid white ghost. An albino.

Benito waited with the natural-born patience of a predator. He exhaled. Another stream of smoke passed smoothly through the window crack. In the sickly glow of yellow light next to the concrete stairwell, a man paced. Every time the restless man passed the graffiti-covered wall beside the stairs, he looked towards the black Escalade. Benito watched his man. They both waited for another.

Unconsciously, Benito did the math. Thirteen drags on his cigarette, thirty-second intervals, and he'd looked at his watch six minutes and fifteen seconds ago. That would make the time precisely 2:34:37 p.m.

Any moment now.

The man they waited for was punctual. He hadn't varied his routine. At 2:35, he would exit the stairwell and walk the twenty-nine steps to his beat-up blue Volvo. From the two previous visits to this underground vehicular tomb, they had watched the man unlock his car with a remote from three steps away. He would open the door, lean over the driver's seat, and place his briefcase on the passenger side. He would straighten and then remove his sports jacket. After he folded it, he would lay it across his briefcase. Next, he would slide into the driver's seat, lock the door, and start his car. For exactly three minutes, he would listen to Franz Schubert's "Ständchen S. 560" while the AC cooled his vehicle. At 2:39, the serenade still pouring from his speakers like a cooling fog rolling in from the ocean, the man would pull out of his parking place and exit the garage.

Today, Timbre Plummer would not be departing on schedule. The man in the shadows next to the stairwell would see to that. Benito needed to talk to Timbre Plummer about an outstanding debt.

Raul Ramos fidgeted by the exit doors of the stairs. Raul was his bodyguard, muscle man, and fixer. At least, that is how he thought of him now. Once, they had been friends. Friends and partners. But that was a long time ago.

Raul was tough, loyal, mean as a molting snake, and almost as smart. They had been together since they'd fled Argentina nearly ten years ago. *Fled* was not exactly right. He'd left after his father's unfortunate death. Benito's eye twitched.

He took another drag on his cigarette. His hand quivered slightly. He'd been born a freak and practically locked in their villa basement in Bariloche, Argentina, until his teenage years. Then, when his father could no longer hide him, he'd been sent to a private German school in Buenos Aries. Two years later, he was home again, expelled, a little white monster bringing unwanted attention and embarrassment to his father.

Benito's internal clock ticked to 2:35. It was time. Benito watched the stairwell exit door. He exhaled another hoary stream of calming smoke. Timbre Plummer was late. Benito's eye twitched again. He remembered the punishment for being late. He still carried some of those scars. He stared at the steel exit door, ignoring the creeping itch that wormed its way up his back.

His father had a dark past. It was a past his father had spent all his adult life trying to hide. An albino son made this more difficult. An albino was an oddity in any culture, but in the circle of Nazi expatriates who had escaped to Argentina, he was an abomination.

Benito had been blind to it all until one hot, humid afternoon in June when he was thirteen years old. He'd been exploring the rooms and passages of the *verboten*, the forbidden place. It was a large room filled with discarded family heirlooms. There were boxes of books, bales of moth-eaten cloth, three-legged chairs, cracked tables, dusty trunks, misshapen picture frames, and an old armoire.

On the day he had discovered the family secret, he had been cutting, stabbing, and slashing away at the armoire in a frustrated rage, practicing his swordsmanship with a rusty saber he'd found the previous winter in a trunk of the same room. He'd flung open the cabinet doors and thrust his sword inside. This time, though, instead of sticking into the planking, the saber slid neatly between a quarter-inch crack in the shrunken wood. Then, with a metallic *thunk* of steel against stone, it stuck fast.

He had yanked, pulled, and tore at his sword until he blistered his hand. In a frustrated rage, he slammed the doors. Only the hilt of the sword remained visible. Kicking the debris piled on the side of the armoire, he had tried to find a means to overturn it. He scratched and clawed at the corner where it met the wall. It was so tightly set he could find no purchase. He turned his attention to the right side and attacked it as well. After a minute of mad, fruitless effort, he calmed and made a more reasoned assault.

Snapping back to the present, Benito viciously stabbed out his cigarette in the gold ashtray next to him on the seat. It was

2:36. He held the flame of his lighter to a fresh cigarette. He exhaled. Benito looked down at the lighter in his hand.

It had been a fire iron that had done the trick back in the *verboten*, the fire iron buried in a tangle of other implements. It was an ugly bit of twisted iron about a meter in length. With newfound determination, he'd returned to the cabinet and inserted the edge of the poker into the small crack at the back right side, then pried. The rod started to bend, but the armoire didn't move. He removed the rod and kicked the cabinet in a flurry of impotent anger. The pain in his bare feet sobered him, and he inserted the rod again. Sitting on the floor, he placed his injured feet against the wall and grabbed the bar with both hands like an ancient oarsman in a Roman galley.

Benito had bent his slight frame over the bar, and with arms and legs, he pulled until a red film glazed his sight. He screamed with the berserker fury bred into his German genes for ten generations. The armoire moved. With a triumphant growl, he inserted the rod farther and pulled again. The cabinet pivoted from the wall with a deep groan. He could see the rusty sword sticking out the back of the wood planking. Four rusted hinges held the cabinet to the wall on the left. Benito swung the armoire open as far as the hinges would allow and stared at a small wooden door expertly built into the stone wall.

The door was made of thick wooden planks of Argentine Osage orange and banded iron with steel spikes set deeply into reddish granite blocks of its arched frame. A thick metal bar hung across the door. It was secured with a lock. The only part of the door not hoary with age was the brass lock holding the bar in place. He rattled it in frustrated curiosity.

Benito still remembered the feeling when he realized where he would have to go and what he would have to endure to get the key. The pale hair on his arms prickled as he recalled putting his eye to the ajar door of his father's study.

Benito crushed out his cigarette at 2:37. His impatience grew. The hair on his arms settled, but the fury in his mind stirred.

Raul stopped his pacing and stared. Benito followed the direction of his gaze, not toward the stairwell but toward the elevator doors across the garage. Raul faded into the shadows.

The elevator doors slid open. For a moment, no one appeared. Then a man stepped forward and stopped. He looked in their direction. Benito exhaled. He hated lawyers, this one in particular. But it was more than that—there was something about Timbre Plummer that set him off.

Their quarry exited the elevator, took several steps along the elevator bank wall, turned the corner, and disappeared. For a few seconds, both of them just watched the corner where Timbre Plummer had vanished. Then, Raul started to move from the shadows. Benito slightly nodded to the pair of eyes looking at him in the rearview mirror. The Escalade accelerated out of its parking place, its wheels giving a screech of protesting rubber.

Chapter 3

Explanations and Appointments

I stopped at the bank of elevators and pushed the down arrow. As I waited, I replayed the phone call that several weeks ago had saved my life.

"Hello, may I speak to Mr. Timbre Plummer?" a young male voice had asked.

I had said nothing.

"Hello, is anyone there?" the voice had repeated. "Hello?"

Still, I'd said nothing. The line went dead. Before my finger could tighten again on the trigger of the pistol, the phone rang once more. This time I was not silent.

"What do you want?" I yelled into the receiver.

"Mr. Plummer, this is Alex Athanasiou with Layton, Barrett, and Stowe. I'm—"

I interrupted. "Alex, I'm not interested in anything you might be trying to sell." As I lowered the phone, Alex spoke again.

"Mr. Plummer, this is about your father."

With a shaky hand, I lifted the phone back to my ear.

"What about my father?" I asked as I laid the cocked pistol in the open briefcase.

A sigh filtered from the other end of the phone. "Thank you for taking my call, Mr. Plummer. As I said, my name is Alex Athanasiou. I am a legal assistant for attorney Eric Pincer with Layton, Barrett, and Stowe. Mr. Pincer would like to speak to you about your father."

"Listen, Alex, I don't have time."

He ignored me. "Please hold while I transfer you, Mr. Plummer."

A stern, deep voice blasted my ear. "Mr. Plummer, thank you for taking my call."

"What do you want, Mr. Pincer? Your assistant said this was something about my father. If this is some sort of solicitation, I'm hanging up, so please explain."

There was a pause on the other end of the line and a sigh. "Mr. Plummer, I wanted to do this in person, but I'm sorry to inform you that your father has died."

"My father is dead?" My father couldn't be dead. I hadn't, we hadn't—I couldn't process what I had heard. I didn't want to believe it, couldn't believe it. I looked at the briefcase and the memories lying around it. I looked at the gun and recoiled as the horror of it struck me.

"Is this some kind of sick birthday joke?" I yelled into the phone. "Did someone put you up to this? Because if they did, I don't think this is one bit funny."

"No, Mr. Plummer, this is not a joke," the voice said coldly. "I'm your father's attorney. We work in the same office. Your father was a friend, and we were in the military together."

I was quiet for a long time. Hurt and bitterness contended with the love and respect I hadn't been able to kill.

Well, happy birthday to me.

"Are you okay, Mr. Plummer?" Pincer asked quietly.

Of course, I'm not okay, I almost said. I'd just had a pistol to my head only to be interrupted by someone telling me that my father had died. But I couldn't tell him that.

Ironic, twisted karma, or just more bad luck, I didn't have the mental clarity to decide. But it was certainly the cherry on top of a very screwed-up life.

Instead, I just said, "Thank you for letting me know, Mr. Pincer." I hung up the phone and picked up the cocked pistol. Before I could pull the trigger, the phone rang again. I considered the cord plugged into the wall next to my desk. I wouldn't be able to carry through with this if I kept being interrupted. I picked up the phone for the last time.

"Mr. Plummer, I'm sorry for your loss." Eric Pincer again, of course. "I know this is not a good time, but as your father's attorney, we need to discuss his will."

"Listen, Mr. Pincer. I appreciate your call, but my father and I were estranged. We haven't spoken in eight years, so I doubt there is anything we need to discuss further."

"Well, you are wrong, Timbre. There is a lot to discuss. Your father left precise instructions in his will for the distribution of his estate. You and your sister, Cadence, are the only beneficiaries." He let that sink in for a minute before continuing. "I'd like to fly out to Phoenix and meet with you to go over the will. The next couple of weeks are hectic for me. How does the end of May work for you?"

How did it work for me? I laughed bitterly. My father hadn't spoken to me since that horrid night he'd surprised me on my birthday. The next day, he'd notified Harvard that he would not be paying for my upcoming year of law school. I finished that semester and dropped out of the Harvard law program. I was at the top of my class, but I couldn't afford the tuition even if I had worked every remaining hour of the day I wasn't in class.

Every time I looked at the law degree hanging on my office wall from Phoenix State instead of Harvard, the old wound festered more.

He had left me in the will, after all. I had two options, the way I saw it. Hang up and put the pistol back to my head or wait a couple of weeks and see what surprises the comic tragedy of my life held in store.

"Mr. Plummer, are you still there?" Pincer asked into the silence.

"The end of May is fine," I replied.

"Thank you. I'll have Alex call you with the details." With a click of the receiver, my father's lawyer ended the call.

For the first time in months, a sliver of hope had wedged its way into my despair. Was I so messed up that it took the death of my father to give me hope? I eyed the pistol in my hand. Lift and squeeze it my mind called to me. An explosive gasp escaped my lips as I released the revolver's hammer and set it down on my desk.

Somehow, with that phone call, I'd already managed to bury the deeper feelings of regret, loss, and sorrow beneath the new dirty layer of hope that chance had thrown on the rotten tomb of my life. For god's sake, we hadn't spoken in eight years. I had transgressed, a vulgar insult had been given, and he'd responded forcefully in the most painful way possible.

After that, I vowed never to talk to him again. Time had taken the edge off my feelings, but I still resented him and what he had done. Now, eight years later, was I so desperate that I, hat in hand, was going to humble myself at the foot of his grave? Dare I hope that his animosity and resentment towards me were not equal to my own? Was there reason to believe that in his death, he might have thrown a few crumbs of his fortune in my direction? Deep down, I hungered for the love I had once known. Maybe he hadn't totally withdrawn it.

The chime of the elevator door made me jump. As the silver doors opened with a whisper, I looked into the carriage and hesitated. I waited. The doors started to close, and I cursed silently. At the last moment, I stuck my hand between the stainless-steel panels. My hand was released with a slight jerk, and the empty vault was revealed once more. Quickly, I stepped over the crack and into the tiny room that hung over the dark, void below my feet. "Like a matchbox on a string," I muttered. I pushed the glowing button and loosened my tie. The doors closed, and I tensed.

As the floor fell away, I swallowed part of my lunch for the second time that day. I focused on the flashing orange buttons that marked my descent into the abyss. Sweat trickled on my forehead, and I loosened my tie a bit more. As B3 lit, I tightened my grip on the briefcase. The elevator began to slow. The bell chimed, and the floor lurched and settled. The doors slid open, and the ferocious heat hit me.

"Welcome to hell," I muttered.

I wanted to curse the person who had first settled this hellish place. It was only May, and we'd already had weeks of triple digits. Only in Phoenix could you be three stories underground and still have your breath taken away by the oppressive springtime heat.

I moved forward and held the hot stainless-steel doors open with my hand. Before stepping out, I looked to the left and right. I owed one of Phoenix's most dangerous criminals a hundred thousand. I had to see him before he saw me. Peering into the gloom, I cataloged the rows of cars, many of them familiar compact foreign jobs you'd see in an underground parking garage. It was Arizona, though, and here and there, a pickup was rebelliously parked, the top of their cabs narrowly clearing the gray concrete beams of the ceiling. In the far back corner of the garage, barely illuminated by the glow of the exit sign, was the stairwell that I usually used. This was the first time I had used the elevator in six years. I'd only made the exception out of necessity. Today was the day my father's will was to be read, and I didn't want to show up sweaty and smelling like I'd just stepped out of the gym. The trickle on my forehead reminded me that I'd probably failed in this plan as well.

I frowned at my car at the other end of the garage. "Piece of junk," I muttered. I turned right toward the parking garage exit. Rounding the corner, I walked four spaces down and stopped in front of a Hertz rental car. The saleswoman had said it was some sort of hybrid. Great mileage, great for the environment, blah, blah, blah. I just wanted something cheap that would get me from here to there and back without more trouble.

Yesterday had been infuriating. For two hours that morning, my internet connection had been down, and I had sat around waiting for my files to download from the cloud. Where the heck was the cloud, anyway, I'd like to know? Probably the same place where all those angels play their little gilded harps. After the cloud finally found my files on the dark side of the moon, I'd hiked down into this hot hole, and my car wouldn't start. That had cost me a return trip out of Dante's inferno, two blocks in the fierce heat to the rental agency, and the final pennies squeezed out of my fifth credit card—the first four maxed out courtesy of my wonderfully inefficient divorce lawyers.

How had they even managed to fit an engine into so tiny a car? I let out a long, hot breath. As long as the AC worked, I'd be willing to pedal this thing like the Flintstones. "Yabba dabba doo."

I glanced around to see if anyone was watching before I opened the driver's door. I leaned in and placed my briefcase on the passenger seat and then straightened and quickly slid out of my sports coat. Folding it, I draped it over my briefcase on the driver's seat. I locked my door and started the car.

The AC kicked on, and I waited for it to start working. I had tested it yesterday, and it cranked out copious amounts of ice-cold air. At least there was one silver lining to this miserable day. I loosened my tie still further, unbuttoned my collar, then my cuffs, and leaned my head against the steering wheel. The car's Bluetooth linked with my phone, and the sad notes of Franz Schubert's "Ständchen" started to work their magic as I felt the chill of the car's cooling system.

Every time I listened to the song, it made me think of my sister and better times. Times before I'd grown up and learned how messed up the world could be, how messed up I could be.

A metallic tapping on my window brought me back into the present with a jerk. I turned and looked into the dark, gaping hole of a Model 29 Smith & Wesson .44 Magnum.

Chapter 4

The Gamble

My eyes followed the six and a half inches of the pistol's polished nickel finish and rested briefly on the hairy hand that engulfed the grip. I continued past the muscled forearm, the MS-13 tattoo, the bull neck, the smirking lips, and froze when I met the ugly glint in the eyes of Raul Ramos. I was in trouble—the worst kind.

I started sweating again. The vein in my temple throbbed. The pulsing beat was driving a migraine-sized wedge into my brain. A familiar anger kindled in my gut, which competed with my growing anxiety. My appointment was at three. It would take me fifteen minutes if I left now. That meeting would determine my future.

"Not today." I slammed my hands against the steering wheel.

The rubber covering creaked and groaned in my grip. Benito would have demands that I couldn't meet. At least not yet, not until I knew what was in my father's will.

Raul tapped harder on the glass. He made a circular motion with the end of his pistol, telling me to roll down my window. I calculated my odds. We were three stories down in the Phoenix Professional Plaza parking garage. However, Benito had gotten past security, it was unlikely that he or Raul would risk firing a weapon with all the security cameras and gated entry. Maybe a silenced weapon, but not the hand cannon Raul was pointing at me with a tolerant smirk that told me I'd run out of options.

Without taking my eyes off Raul, I slowly reached to put my car in reverse. He tapped harder on the glass. I could read it in his eyes—*Don't even think about it, dumbass*. I glanced in my rearview mirror. A Cadillac Escalade was idling behind me. I gave the hybrid a bit of gas. The thought of ramming the luxury vehicle and ruining its perfect lines brought a perverse thrill. The math didn't work, though. My rental was a third the Escalade's weight, and all it would do is make a terrible situation worse.

I pulled my hand away from the shift lever and looked back to find Raul wagging his head like a parent with an unruly child. I pushed the silver button on the door console and lowered my window a few inches. Raul peered into the car with a condescending sneer.

"Mr. Silva wants to talk to you."

I shook my head. "I don't have time right now, Raul. I have an important appointment I can't be late for." I started to raise the window again.

Raul stuck the barrel of the gun into the window crack. "It wasn't a request, *hombre*. Either you get out of the car now, or I'm going to break this window and drag you out. *Comprende*?"

I turned off the car and grabbed my sports coat and briefcase. Raul removed the pistol muzzle from the window. I opened the door and stood. Raul held my car door and pointed his pistol toward the Escalade. I tightened my grip on the briefcase and walked toward Benito's vehicle. Raul slammed my car door and followed. I hesitated, and he prodded my backbone with the gun.

I stopped at the back passenger side window. It lowered with a smooth hum. Benito Silva peered at me with a cold, snaky smile on his face.

"You've been avoiding me, Timmberr."

I gritted my teeth. The little mobster always mispronounced my name. He must have sensed it bothered me. He said *Timbre* like I was some lumberjack or something. *It's T-a-m-b-e-r, you little albino runt*, I wanted to say, but I kept my mouth shut. He repeated his insult.

"You've been avoiding me, Timmberr."

There was no use in lying to him. I had been avoiding him. I didn't have his money. Maybe after today, I'd have some, but as I looked into those icy, hypnotic eyes, the warming glow of rage heated my neck like magma rising through a dormant volcanic cone. He wasn't getting a cent of it if I could help it. He had set me up. He had played me. He called his nightclub, a two-story building in the seedy part of town, the White Wolf. Upstairs, above the bar and dance floor, a private room next to Benito's office hosted high-stakes poker games.

I played poker by the numbers. I had a good memory, not photographic but above average. I knew the odds of nearly every important combination. I always played conservatively. If I lost, it was never that much.

Looking back, I should've known my run of luck was abnormal. Soon, bigger games and higher stakes required more cash than I could safely carry. So Benito had gradually given me more and more "house credit," as he had called it. He soon had me comfortable playing five-figure games. Poker had been fun for me. It had been how I had paid my way through law school after my father had withdrawn his support. It was how I blew off steam.

But not that night. The minimum to enter the big game with some of Phoenix's high rollers had been a hundred and fifty thousand. The thrill, the risk of it, had given me a rush. But I set myself a limit. I wouldn't risk more than fifty thousand of what I'd won so far. I'd saved every cent of my winnings so I could pay down the debt I'd accumulated since my divorce. But they had sucked me in, played my intelligence against my pride. I had bet big, then bigger, and then I'd made the biggest bet of my life. I lost … a hundred and fifty thousand dollars. Minus the fifty thousand I'd won the past six months, I would still owe Benito a hundred thousand. There was no way.

After fifteen minutes in the restroom splashing water on my face, I'd finally pulled myself together enough to leave. As I walked back into the poker room, no one was in sight. Downstairs, the nightclub was also empty. Just as I'd put my hand out to push the exit door open, a soft voice from the shadows beside the bar had called, "I'll send Raul around tomorrow to settle up our debt."

I'd nearly ended it right there by stepping off the curb in front of a Phoenix metro bus.

That afternoon, a knock on my apartment door had told me my debt had come due. I'd opened the door and handed Raul fifty thousand in cash.

Laboriously, he'd counted the bills with his thick, stubby fingers. "You're short a hundred grand."

"I know. Tell Benito I need a few more days to get his money." Short of robbing a bank in the next couple of days, there was no way I was going to come up with a hundred thousand.

Raul had grabbed the front of my shirt and pulled me in close. "Give me the rest, or I'll beat you half to death." He let go of my shirt, and with the back of his meaty hand, he gave me a vicious blow across the face.

I'd boxed in college. It had always taken a good, stiff punch to bring me to my senses, and then I was fighting mad. Raul's backhanded smack had worked like magic.

I'd shoved the big man out my door. "I said, I need a few more days to get the money. Call the little runt and tell him that." I slammed the door in his face.

Later that day, I drove to my office and put the gun to my head. After the phone call from my father's lawyer, I'd managed to avoid Benito for sixteen days. Today my luck had run out.

As I peered into the black Escalade, Benito Silva sneered. "Not very talkative today, are you, Timmberr."

Chapter 5

Consequences and Collections

I didn't have the answer Benito Silva was looking for. I stood there staring at the little man in the expensive suit, a half-burned cigarette in his hand, his thin lips stretched into a fake smile.

"I don't have the rest of your money yet, Mr. Silva. By the end of the day, I might have it."

Benito took a long drag on his cigarette, turned slightly toward the window, and let a jet of smoke out the side of his lips. He watched me from the corner of his ugly gray eyes.

Finally, he spoke again, his voice sibilant. "I want my money. Right now. Right here."

"I already told you, I don't have it."

"Let me explain to you how this works. You owe me money. I am here to collect. I cannot let your debt go uncollected because it would be bad for business. It would set a bad example for others. It would show that I am weak and a poor businessman. I am neither." He took another drag on his cigarette. "Either you pay me right now, right here, or your debt goes into default. Once in default, the special terms of our contract go into effect."

"We have no contract, Mr. Silva. And if you ever want to see the rest of your money, I need to go and see about getting it for you."

I started to turn away. A crushing hand grabbed the back of my head and shoved my face up against the open crack at the top of the passenger door window. Raul's hand held me there, my eyes and nose inside the crack, my forehead cutting into the frame of the door, and my chin against the edge of the window.

"I don't think you understand the gravity of your situation, Mr. Plummer. How do you lawyers say it? You forgot to read the fine print. Once your debt goes into default, you work for me. I own you until the debt is paid off. During this time, interest on your debt will accumulate at the rate of ten percent per week. So, you will have to work very hard to service your debt."

Benito tapped his cigarette on a golden ashtray and held it as he slid across the seat. He stopped when his face was just inches from mine. "I own you. You work for me now. You will do as I say when I say it. Do you understand?" he said as he took a drag on his cigarette. It flared bright orange and I felt the heat on my face.

I tried to struggle, but Raul just pushed my head harder against the door. I was angry now. Full on, beyond-reason angry. I wanted to reach into that window and pull the little man through the crack and thrash him. The anger washed over me and took away my fear. It took away any thoughts of wanting to end my life. I wanted to live if only to hurt these two men who had trapped me. To hurt them like they were hurting me.

"You can shove the unwritten terms of your contract into that dark, twisted soul of yours, you little albino runt. I'll never work for you, you ugly freak!"

Judging by the look in his eyes, my words had found their mark. He took another slow drag on his cigarette until it glowed brightly again. With exaggerated slowness, he pressed the burning tip against my lip. My mouth exploded in pain. Benito stared into my eyes as he held the cigarette against my sizzling flesh. As the cigarette was extinguished, the sadistic smile on his lips started to twitch.

I roared. My head was pushed harder against the door.

He leaned closer to whisper, "You will pay dearly for that insult. The last person who insulted me that way, I drowned in a barrel of bleach and left hanging from the bridge to the town where I grew up. But, unfortunately, your punishment will have to wait because I need you right now. So … you will work for me. You will do as I say, or I'll make you watch as I carry out your punishment on someone you care about. Your sister, perhaps?"

He must have seen the fear in my eyes. He smirked.

"Yes, that's right. I know all about you, Timbre. I did my research before I chose you. If you don't follow my instructions precisely, I'll send one of my men to find your druggy sister, and I'll make you watch as I turn her into an albino. I might even make you help. Do you understand?"

I said nothing.

"Do you underst—" His hissing words were interrupted by a voice shouting from the other end of the parking garage.

"What's going on over there? Let him go. I've called the cops."

Raul's grip loosened as he turned to search for the speaker. I slid my right foot along the concrete until I felt the toe of his thousand-dollar alligator-skin boots. I lifted my leg, and with all of my anger and hurt fueling my muscles, I stomped down on his foot like a pile driver. His grip on my shoulder loosened further, and I pushed off the car and twisted out of his grasp. I spun away and stepped to the side, I added to the momentum by pivoting and swinging the arm that held my briefcase. As I reached maximum velocity in my turn, the bottom half of my briefcase took Raul full in the face, the seven pounds of leather, paper, legal briefs, and memories toppling him as neatly as a lumberjack's sharp ax might topple a tree.

Then I ran, not in fear but with smoldering determination. I was going to make it to my appointment. Sweating and disheveled, to be sure, but I would be there. I ran back toward the gloom of the stairwell. I jerked open the stairwell door and flew up the steps two at a time, my briefcase slapping against my leg until I reached ground level and burst out into the burning glare of the Arizona sun. I darted right out of the exit of the garage. Halfway down the block, I turned into the service entrance of the Edisson hotel. A moment later, I ducked into the kitchen. The chef hollered.

I ignored him and continued through the kitchen. Strong-arming the double swinging doors, I burst into the dining room. In the glittering glow of the chandeliers, faces turned my direction. Sparkling silver utensils paused mid-arch to mouths. Ruby waves danced and rippled in frozen crystal. Slender fingers and big hands held magenta napkins to gasping lips. Porcelain clattered. Then all was silent.

I padded down the plush red carpet toward the entrance, conscious of the gazes that followed me.

Back outside, I hailed a taxi, yanked open its door, and plunked onto the seat.

"Where to?" the driver asked as he looked at me through the rearview mirror.

"201 Washington." I consulted my watch. "There's a ten-dollar tip in it if you can get me there in less than eight minutes."

He glanced at the meter on his dash and grinned. "Buckle up."

Chapter 6

Taxis and Attorneys

The taxi cut into traffic, and horns blared. I laid my head back against the seat, closed my eyes, and laughed. A couple weeks ago, I was trying to kill myself, and now I was trying to figure out how to keep from getting killed. I felt alive in a way I couldn't explain. I no longer wanted to die. I wanted to fight.

It wasn't every day someone assaulted Raul Ramos and insulted Benito Silva and lived to tell about it. I'd let my temper get the better of me. They would be looking for me now. Before my assault today, I might have been able to get my inheritance and slip out of town without them any wiser. Just disappear. Not anymore. I would be war now. Cadence lived in Virginia so she was safe. At least I hoped so. Benito would have to cross state lines to mess with her, and then it would be an FBI thing. I doubted he'd want that kind of heat heading his way.

The cabbie's horn blasted, and my eyes opened. A guy on a Harley had cut him off. I closed my eyes. Was this really my life? I was a broke fugitive running from one of the most dangerous men in Phoenix. By this evening, there would probably be a bounty on my head. How had it come to this?

I'd been a fool. Benito told me I could work off my debt. But at ten percent interest per week, my obligation would become a permanent occupation. I was conned, pure and simple, and I hadn't seen it coming. If I acquiesced to Benito's offer of employment, I'd likely become one of his mules ferrying drugs into the courthouse or prison. When he was done with me, I'd probably be on the other side of the bars.

"Like hell," I muttered. I wasn't going to jail, and if I had to die, there was one little white freak I would take with me.

I must have spoken out loud because when I opened my eyes again, the cabby was watching me intently through his mirror.

"Just drive," I said.

The cabbie's gaze flitted back to the road.

The briefcase lay heavy on my lap. My father wouldn't be very proud of me right now. I certainly hadn't lived up to his high standards. Part of me was glad he wasn't here to see the mess I'd made of my life. How was Cadence taking our father's death? She'd been closer to him than I, especially the last eight years. Maybe after today, I'd take a road trip to see her. If she wasn't still holding a grudge, we might try to rebuild our relationship.

The cabbie braked hard in front of the Bank of America building. I handed him his fare and tip through the wire mesh that divided the cab.

"Thanks," I said, slamming the door. I stepped to the curb and looked up at the high-rise.

I'd done a bit of reconnaissance the week before. My father's law firm had a satellite office on the 7th floor. Their main offices were in DC, close to where he lived. *Had lived*, I corrected myself. They were a large law firm specializing in oil and gas concessions for several of the world's largest petroleum companies. From what I could gather, my father had been a consultant for their customers' concessions in the more troubled parts of the world. With his military background, they sent him when some mess needed cleaning up.

I pushed through the revolving glass doors that led to the spacious lobby. There was an information desk to my left and five elevators straight in front of me. I followed the sign down the marbled hall to the men's room. I set my briefcase on the vanity and accessed my condition in the mirror.

Not a pretty sight. My lip had blistered like I had the mother of all cold sores. I tried to smile and winced as the cauterized skin tore and started to seep blood. I pulled a paper towel from the chrome dispenser and dabbed my mouth. Tossing the bloodied paper in the trash, I tucked my shirt in and straightened my tie. I leaned over the sink, held my hand in front of the automatic lavatory faucet, and gingerly splashed my face. Straightening, I ran my fingers through my disheveled hair. I wasn't happy about what I saw in the mirror, but it was the best I could do.

Moments later, I stepped out of the elevator and stopped at the double door with a bronze plate set into the dark wood. *Layton, Barrett, and Stowe*. Well, this was it. I turned the brass handle and pushed open the door. A smiling receptionist looked up.

"Good afternoon, Mr. Plummer. Glad you could make it. They are waiting for you." She stood. "Come on, I'll show you the way." With an inviting inclination of her head, she headed to the back of the office. She knocked softly on a door and opened it. "Mr. Plummer is here, sir."

As she stepped aside, a man faced me from the other side of the table. I recognized the crooked nose and big ears from the photograph in my father's briefcase. As Eric Pincer reached his full height, I saw what the photo hadn't yet recorded—he was missing his right arm. I glanced away.

The professional, welcoming look on his face subtly changed for a brief second. When it returned, the room felt colder. I squeezed the familiar, warm handle of my father's briefcase. I thought of the words on the back of the photograph hidden within. “Greater love has no man …” I bet there was a story there.

I stepped toward Eric. Although cordial, he didn’t smile. He was serious.

“Glad you made it, Mr. Plummer.” He walked around the table. But he didn’t extend his hand. “I’m Eric Pincer, your father’s attorney. My condolences on your loss. Your father was a good friend of mine. He will be missed.” His words felt flat, rehearsed.

I said nothing. The door shut behind me. Eric Pincer motioned toward an adjoining door. I stepped through. Floor-to-ceiling windows lit the room with its twelve-person mahogany conference table and gave a panoramic view of metro Phoenix. Eric followed me into the room and indicated a seat beside the only other occupant. I stared at the woman’s long, tangled, unkempt hair and hunched shoulders. A tie-dyed t-shirt with a confusing pink, blue, and yellow psychedelic swirl hung off an emancipated frame like a sheet on a wire clothesline. I looked back at Eric with a question on my face.

“Please have a seat.” He walked around the other side of the room to face us.

I hesitated. I didn’t want to sit next to this—this old homeless person. This was a private matter. I shook my head and stepped toward the table.

The smell of an unwashed body made my stomach churn. I started to steer myself a few chairs away when the tangled head turned. My feet stopped. I squeezed the handle of the briefcase and stared. Wet trails streaked the pale, blotched, paper-thin skin that covered the high cheekbones. As I stood there with my mouth hanging open, more tears cascaded over the dark circles that surrounded the sunken violet eyes of my sister, Cadence.

Chapter 7

Reunions and Repercussions

"C-cadence?" I managed to stammer. "What are you doing here? I thought you were in Virginia." Her violet eyes deepened, and her face shrank. I stepped toward her. She recoiled like a trapped animal. "What happened to you?" I asked softly. "Are you okay?"

A ghost of herself, Cadence just looked at me. Then she turned away from my intent stare. Her head bowed, and she shook and shuddered. I was rooted to the floor.

Finally, Eric saved us from the uncomfortable silence. He cleared his throat. "Why don't you take a seat, Mr. Plummer, and we'll get started."

I sat down next to Cadence and placed my briefcase on the floor

Eric stood across from us. The fingers of his hand were spread wide and rested on one of the piles of papers on the table in front of him. "First, let me say again how sorry I am for your loss. Your father was a friend. I can't imagine the pain you both must be going through. Before you got here, Timbre, Cadence asked about your father's death. To bring you up to date, all we know right now is that several months ago, he died in a plane crash in Libya."

I sat forward. "What was he doing in Libya? Isn't that a war zone right now?"

Eric averted his gaze and arranged the piles of paper on the table. He was silent for a few seconds before responding.

"Your father was the point man for our oil and gas acquisition and stability team. Because of his military background, he would often go to some of the world's hot spots to pave the way for negotiations between our clients and various government and quasi-governments."

"So basically, you are saying you guys sent our father into war-torn hellholes so you could keep the petro-dollars flowing."

Eric flushed and lost some of his conciliatory manner. "It's a bit more complicated than that," he said stiffly. He took a breath and tried again. "Your father volunteered for the position. He was never ordered into harm's way. He always had the final say. If he thought the risk was too great, he would say so, and we would wait or come up with an alternative plan. We've been in this business for over fifty years, and this is the first time we've ever lost one of our people."

"Small consolation," I muttered.

"Where is the body?" my sister asked in a voice just above a whisper. Her cheeks were still wet, but her chin lifted, and her twisting hands hardened into tight fists.

Eric sat down and flicked open a thick folder. His face flushed. He didn't look up when he spoke. "We don't have the body."

Cadence stiffened. Her voice crackled with intensity. "You called us two weeks ago to tell us he was dead, and you still don't have the body?"

Eric nodded. "Right now, Libya is in the midst of a civil war. The plane crashed in a region where heavy fighting was going on. We immediately sent a forensic team to access the crash. For weeks, they waited in Tripoli while the State Department tried to work out a temporary ceasefire. Finally, our team was granted access to the site." Eric's shoulders lost a bit of their rigidity.

"It was a mess. The wreckage was strewn for half a mile. The main cabin had broken into two parts. The front half of the plane was severely burned, the back only partially. No one had protected the crash site, and anything of value had been looted. We were told the bodies had been taken to the local morgue." He paused, his brow furrowing as his throat worked. "Two days before our team arrived, they burned the bodies."

My sister sobbed. I felt for the handle of my father's briefcase. I closed my eyes as I squeezed it. What was I supposed to feel? I loved my father, or at least I thought I still did, but eight years of resentment had taken its toll. A sense of certainty solidified the emptiness I'd felt since our estrangement. While my father lived, he made a convenient target to blame for my failures. With him gone, I no longer had anyone to blame but myself. That was not a pleasant thought.

Eric finally broke the silence. "I'm truly sorry for these unfortunate circumstances. John was a personal friend."

"You keep saying that. What kind of friend sends someone he cares for into harm's way?"

Anger flashed in Eric's eyes. He raised his finger. "The last thing I need is to be lectured by John Plummer's son about sending a friend into harm's way."

I started to stand. Pressure on my arm made me turn. Cadence clung to me. Her boney fingers, tendons white and distended, dug into my arm with surprising strength. I sat back down.

Eric lowered his hand and took a deep breath. "Look, we are not here to talk about your father's occupation. He loved you both very much. So, let's get back to the reason we *are* here. As you may know, Timbre, in most situations like this, we just send the family of the deceased a copy of the will for them to read in the privacy of their home. Then when the time is right, we help them with any pertinent legal issues relevant to the estate. Your father's case is an exception to the rule. You see, he left exact instructions for the distribution of his estate."

Eric slid two copies of the will across the table. I reached for mine and glanced at my sister as she just stared at hers. It was as if she was afraid to touch it, to make it real. She finally reached for it with a shaky hand.

I started reading. I got halfway down the page and looked up at Eric in disbelief. "Is this some kind of joke?"

Eric shook his head solemnly. "No, I can assure you, it is not."

As I continued, heat crept into my face. I looked over at Cadence, who had stopped reading as tears dripped from her chin onto the paper she grasped.

"No, no, nooooo …" I said softly under my breath. I had come for an inheritance, and my father had given me riddles and ciphers to solve instead.

Eric spoke. "As you can see, your father left you two options. To inherit the full estate, you must solve a series of …" He paused as if looking for the right word. "Ciphered riddles. It seems your father had a real passion for the Old Testament trivia, and he has come up with these seven conundrums you must decipher in order for me to distribute the estate. If you solve all seven, then the estate will be split between you evenly. You have 30 days from today. If you fail, the will instructs that the challenge be made public. After that, the first person to solve them will be awarded the estate."

I shoved my copy of the will away. "This is garbage." But I jerked it back and kept reading as I listened to Eric with one ear. Surely, I'd missed something.

"If you do not wish to participate in your father's challenge, I am authorized to distribute twenty thousand dollars to each of you. Your father included a no-contest clause in his will.“ Eric's gaze met mine. “As you know, if you try to protest the will in any way, you will be excluded from any inheritance. Any questions?”

Eric watched me as if he expected the trouble to come from my direction. I couldn't believe what I was reading. My father had gotten the last laugh. This was his revenge—First Harvard Law, now this. If I wanted what he had, he was going to make me jump through hoops like a circus performer. And if I didn't do it in time, he would give the inheritance to someone else. A stranger.

A sob made me turn. I couldn't see Cadence's face because of the tangled hair, but the tears had stopped falling on the paper. She hadn't turned a single page. Her skeletal arms lay limp on the table, her fingers clutching and unclutching the edges of the papers in front of her.

“Is this even legal?” I asked, at a loss for anything else intelligent to say. I was not well versed in estate law. Criminal law was my forte. “I've never heard of someone withholding their estate from their heirs until after they've solved a series of coded riddles. What kind of person does something like that?” I aimed the question mostly at myself. But I looked up to see if Eric had any answers.

He shrugged. “I really don't know why your father wrote his will this way, but I can assure you, it is legal. I can also tell you that your father was in a sound mind when he wrote it.” As he spoke, he flipped through the pages of the original document in front of him. I closed my eyes and massaged my throbbing temple. *What a nightmare.* I grabbed my copy of the will as Eric started to speak again.

“If you turn to the last page and read the signatures of the witnesses, you'll find the names of a retired Virginia Supreme

Court judge, a former attorney general, and the senior partner of our law firm. None of those people would have added their name to any document that wasn't perfectly legitimate. I might also add that your father was well respected in the legal community. In many places, he was admired, even."

Something in his tone made me look up from my perusal of the will. It almost sounded like an admonishment, like Eric knew some of our histories. He stared at me, and it may have been my imagination, but the corners of his lips held a hint of a mocking smile.

I turned back to the will. I flipped past the first ciphered riddle and its instructions. Finally, I got to the page that listed the assets of my father's estate. By my rough calculation, all told, it was well north of nine million dollars. That would certainly solve my financial problems. I felt Eric's eyes on me, and I looked up again. He was watching for my reaction, and his knowing look said it all. I'd found the jackpot, and I was officially in.

My sister clutched her papers in a shaky hand as she pushed herself up from the table. She struggled momentarily with the chair.

Eric asked, "Can I get you anything, Ms. Plummer?"

"No," she replied. "I would like to leave now." She started for the conference room door on unsteady legs.

"What are your instructions concerning the will?"

She looked back at both of us. Her violet eyes were veiled with deep sadness. "I don't want anything. The only reason I came here was to find out what happened to my father." She walked to the door and turned the handle.

"Please stay, Ms. Plummer. I still need you to sign some paperwork stating your intentions." He held out his hand.

Cadence turned once more, and her violet eyes blazed. She screamed, "The only thing I wanted, you can't give me. I want my father back. These"—she shook the papers in her hand and threw them at Eric— "cannot give me back my father." She looked at me then with disdain and resignation. "You can give my share to Timbre. He'll need it more than me." She stepped through the door and was gone.

I should have tried to stop her, but I didn't. I should have followed my sister to make sure she would be okay. Instead, I just sat there. What had happened to the brotherly love I'd once had for her? Was it dead? I peered into my soul, and all I saw was a dark, empty hole. How had that happened?

A numbness settled over me. In my short, miserable life, was money the only thing I had left to pursue? I hadn't known real peace and contentment since that night eight years ago. Would the inheritance finally make me happy? If not, what would?

Eric walked around the table and picked up the papers one by one. With difficulty, he re-ordered and smoothed them. Without a word, he set them down on the table next to me and returned to his chair opposite.

Finally, I reached into my left breast pocket and removed my pen. I signed on the page that testified that I had accepted my father's challenge. I wrote the date, May 30th, next to my signature. The countdown started in my head. I had thirty days to solve the riddles and claim my inheritance—that is, if I could keep a step ahead of Benito Silva. If I was unsuccessful, I also now knew the date of my death.

I stood and slid my stack of papers across to Eric. He rose and took the will. "Your sister needs to sign the document to make her intentions clear. Or at least give me a certified letter stating that she is refusing any remuneration from the estate."

I nodded.

Eric continued. "Why don't you take it to her when she's gotten over the shock of all this? Maybe then she'll change her mind. It looks like she could use your help right now."

I kept my gaze lowered as shame flushed my face. "I don't know where she lives," I finally said. "Last time we talked, she lived in Virginia with my father."

Eric removed a pen from his pocket and opened one of the tan file folders set to one side of the desk. On the notepad, he copied an address. He held the note across the table.

I shoved the note in my pocket and met his gaze at last. "Thank you for all you have done for us. I'm sure my father would have appreciated it. I'll be in touch."

Chapter 8

Legal Friendship

As the conference room door closed behind Timbre Plummer, Eric stood a moment in deep thought. The thin smile faded and a frown replaced it. He flipped open the two file folders and looked down at pictures of Timbre and Cadence stapled to the inside flaps of each. Sean O'Sullivan, the private investigator he had hired, had been thorough. He shook his head. How had John Plummer sired such losers? A drug addict and a compulsive gambler.

Eric tapped his left index finger against the photograph of Timbre. A dead ringer for John, but not even half the man his father once was. Timbre Plummer liked to play the high roller games at Benito Silva's swank club, The White Wolf, in downtown Phoenix. If he was involved with Silva, he probably wouldn't survive to claim his inheritance. Hmm. He smiled and made himself a note. His idea couldn't hurt, and it might even speed things up a bit.

Eric shifted his attention to Cadence's picture. This one he couldn't figure out. She was a gorgeous young woman—or had been. John Plummer had brought her by the DC office several times over the years. The last time was just before his move back to Phoenix. John had said she needed help, and Phoenix had one of the best treatment centers in the country. At that time, to all outward appearances, she'd looked okay.

Eric flipped through the pages of the will until he came to John Plummer's ciphered riddle. From what John had said, this was the first of seven. Once John's kids solved this riddle or its related cipher, they would enter the answer into a website John had set up. If the answer was correct, then the servers would provide the second riddle. John had explained this process was repeated until the last ciphered riddle was solved. Each time they solved one of the ciphers, the firm's servers would automatically notify Eric of their progress.

The first ciphered riddle was a square of twenty-five Hebrew characters. Five across and five down. Below the square of characters was the riddle and five verses he assumed were clues.

You could describe this enciphered Old Testament passage numerically as 39 is 1.

Provide the numerical reference to where it is found in the Biblical texts.

Jeremiah 51:41

How is Sheshach taken! and how is the praise of the whole earth surprised! how is Babylon become an astonishment among the nations!

2 Samuel 24:12

Go and say unto David, Thus saith YHWH, I offer thee three things; choose thee one of them, that I may do it unto thee.

Ecclesiastes 7:8

Better is the end of a thing than the beginning thereof: and the patient in spirit is better than the proud in spirit.

Revelation 1:17

And when I saw him, I fell at his feet as dead. And he laid his right hand upon me, saying unto me, Fear not; I am the first and the last:

Isaiah 46:9-10

Remember the former things of old: for I am God, and there is none else; I am God, and there is none like me, Declaring the end from the beginning, and from ancient times the things that are not yet done, saying, My counsel shall stand, and I will do all my pleasure:

John had always been brilliant. He never made a big deal about it, but you knew. He had an amazing memory, and when Eric reached for a calculator, John already had the answer figured out in his head. One glance at a restaurant menu was enough for him to calculate the entire check for any sized party, plus tax and gratuity. It was annoying, actually. When John was around, there was no question about who the most intelligent person in the room was.

Eric's intrigue with John's ciphers was quickly turning into bothersome preoccupation. He'd already spent more hours than he could count trying to solve the first riddle. How freaking hard could it be if John expected a drug addict and a compulsive gambler to solve it? Eric didn't consider himself an idiot, but he was completely stumped.

Before John's cipher, he hadn't cracked a Bible in his life. In the past few weeks, he was willing to bet he'd spent more time reading the Gideon Bible he'd borrowed from that hotel in Austin than the Bible-thumping televangelist his mom watched every Sunday morning.

Eric reached into his pocket and pulled out his phone. He scrolled down the menu, tapped the screen, and put the phone to his ear. It rang twice. His legal assistant, Alex, answered.

"Hi, boss. What can I do for you?"

Eric glanced at his watch. It was 7 p.m. in DC. "I'm finished in Phoenix. Would you book me a flight out of here for tomorrow afternoon? If possible, I'd like it to be earlier rather than later."

"Sure, anything else?"

"Yes, would you also call the Phoenix *PI* we hired for the Plummer account? I'd like him to stay on the case a little while longer. Tell him to dial it back a bit, but keep us informed about anything he thinks we might want to know."

A pencil tapped on the other end. "That's a bit broad. Would you like me to be a little more specific?"

"No, Alex, just tell him to keep it passive and use his best judgment. He's a professional. He'll know what I mean."

"You got it. I'll call him right now."

"Thank you, Alex. See you tomorrow. Oh, and bring the Pershing Petroleum file with you when you come. I'd like a progress update on our push for their Libyan concessions."

"Okay, I'll have the updated file for you to review. Anything else?"

"No, I think that will be all for right now." He ended the call.

Eric glanced at the photos of Cadence and Timbre once more. A frown tightened his lips. He reached with his left hand to scratch the arm that wasn't there. He gazed down at the empty sleeve sewed closed at his shoulder. His subconscious mind just wouldn't accept the loss of his arm. It had been nearly two decades, and he still had the phantom limb sensations, especially when he was agitated. It was a reminder of how much he owed John Plummer. Someday he'd be able to pay back his brother-in-arms. He looked at the stump arm. Brother-in-*arm*, he corrected himself with a sour smile.

The mind-numbing itch worked its way up from the tip of his missing index finger. He closed his eyes and followed its progress. It crawled and burrowed its way along his forearm until it reached his burning stump, where it seemed to chew and chew and chew and chew and chew and chew like a starving animal that was never satiated. The sensation was exquisite.

A crooked smile twisted his mouth. "Brother-in-arms," he whispered. His stump wiggled of its own accord. The frustrating signals gnawed at his mind. When he couldn't stand it any longer, a broken laugh escaped. A moment later, another. Then all at once, the damn broke, and the laughter came in a cascading, gasping, choking roar.

Minutes later, Eric sank into a conference room chair and laid his head on the mahogany table. He pounded the top with his head. The pain steadied him. The itching stopped. A hoarse voice surprised him.

"John Plummer, I hate your guts."

Chapter 9

Unfinished Business

I stood quietly with three other business professionals as the elevator plummeted to the ground floor of the Bank of America building. I'd been so distracted I hadn't even searched for the stairs. The ground floor bell chimed. The doors slid open with a silky whisper and disgorged us into the glass-and-blue-granite lobby. I made for the spinning doors and stiff-armed them with a frustrated push. Instead of walking out of the building a rich man, I was now further away from that goal than when I'd entered the building an hour earlier.

I plunged into the burning sunshine that reflected off every glittering surface. Heat immediately radiated up through the soles of my scuffed, cognac-colored Kenneth Coles. How I hated Phoenix and its brutal, draining heat.

My fingers tightened around the handle of my briefcase. At the sidewalk, I followed the signs toward the Valley Metro bus station half a block away. Not the most glorious mode of transportation, but I had a complimentary annual pass that would have to do until I got my car fixed. Right now, I just needed to get back to my apartment and start on the ciphered riddles. Or was that riddled ciphers? I guess it didn't matter. If I could solve one a day, then a week from now, I'd be sitting pretty.

Maybe a week was optimistic. My father probably handn't made his challenge easy. But not impossible either. They couldn't be impossible. This was an inconvenience, to be sure, but I would stay sequestered in my apartment until I figured them out. Then I would claim my inheritance, skip town, and start living the good life. Maybe buy myself some nice beach house on the California coast. Someplace where it didn't get so hot. Yeah, someplace where there was water and milder temperatures. Maybe I'd take up surfing, buy a small boat or something. Maybe I'd even learn to fish. How hard could it be?

My plans to spend my inheritance were interrupted by a brutal hand on my arm. A black door opened at the curb. Before I could even protest, I was shoved in. Doors slammed. As the ebony Escalade sped away, I studied the pale face of Benito Silva. *What an evil little wretch.*

A burly, tattooed arm reached around the front passenger seat and prodded my chest with a revolver. Raul glared at me. I couldn't help the smile that crossed my lips as I gazed at his nose, swollen and twisted to one side.

"It's an improvement," I said.

Raul cocked the revolver. I felt a stabbing pain as he jabbed the cold, hard metal into my ribs.

"We didn't get a chance to finish our conversation earlier." Benito shook out another cigarette and leaned down to light it with a gold zippo.

"As far as I'm concerned, the conversation was over."

"Maybe from your perspective, but certainly not from mine." Benito flicked ash from the end of his cigarette. The memory of the sick smell of my flesh rose in my mind, and I could almost feel the burn again.

I shrugged. "I don't give a rip what you think, Benito. I'll get you your money, but you are going to have to wait a little bit longer. You do know that kidnapping is a federal offense?"

Benito's flecked gray eyes bored into mine. They shone with the hypnotic, calculating intensity of a snake hunting its next meal. His manicured fingers started rattling sharply against the door's leather armrest. Maybe he was trying to intimidate me or gauge my resolve. Whatever the reason, I wasn't going to give him any satisfaction. I was in trouble, and no matter how things turned out, I was in for some rough treatment. But I'd been beaten up before and now I was looking at my circumstances from the other side of nearly blowing out my brains. I sat back and folded my arms across my chest.

The rattling stopped. Benito made a motion with his head, and the Escalade started to slow. We were in the older part of town. Vacant commercial warehouses lined the left side of the street, their broken windows barred with jagged teeth of glass. On the right side of the street, lonely storefronts huddled together, their peeling gray plaster falling from their red-brick walls in blotches, like a mangy dog shedding its winter coat. Here and there, a few beat-up old cars were parked haphazardly against the concrete curb. Trash fluttered as we passed.

The Escalade slowed more and turned into a dim alley. We stopped with a slight jerk. The driver and Raul stepped out and walked around to the door where I was sitting.

"Mr. Plummer, I can see that further conversation at this time will be wasted. A more practical approach, I think, is necessary." Benito pressed a button on his armrest, and my window rolled down a couple of inches. He nodded to the men standing outside my door. The door was jerked open. Raul grabbed my arm and pulled me from the vehicle. I didn't resist as the driver seized my other arm. I was just glad to get away from the little reptilian monster.

Benito called from the car. "Mr. Plummer, next week, after you've recovered from Raul's disciplinary instruction, one of my men will be by to drop off a package. You'll deliver that package to the person and place described in the attached note. Failure to accomplish your task will result in a repeat of today's attitude adjustment. Also, each week, I'd like an update on your progress regarding your father's will and your efforts to unlock its fortune."

I stiffened slightly. How did he already know about my father's will? I started to ask but bit my tongue. I wouldn't give him the satisfaction.

"I'll be expecting payment in full, plus interest, when you receive your inheritance. Maybe then I'll end our working relationship." He flashed a thin, evil smile.

Benito lifted his chin, indicating to the men holding me that he was finished. Before they pulled me too far away, he called, "Raul."

Raul turned back toward the car."*Jefe*?"

"Hurt him. But don't kill him, or the debt and punishment are yours. *Comprende*?"

Raul nodded.

The window slid silently closed as I was dragged back into the dim alley.

Chapter 10

Crime & Punishment

The dragging heels of my Oxfords left furrows through the dirt and trash that covered the potholed asphalt. For some inexplicable reason, the progress of those tracks fascinated me. Time and distance were being recorded by shoe leather. Funny, the way your mind works.

I'd offered no real resistance, and the grip on my arms relaxed. As we drew closer to the end of our journey at the back of the alley, I jerked my left arm free of the driver. The momentum turned me toward Raul, my arm swung free with the briefcase in my white-knuckled grasp. I reversed the momentum and launched the briefcase up and toward the slack-jawed driver. He was no novice to a street fight because instead of ducking or trying to back away from the impending blow, he took a quick step inside the arcing swing of the case. I couldn't stop in time, and he encircled my arm at the elbow. With his free hand, he gave me a vicious blow to the kidneys that sent a flash of pain through my core.

The driver kept pummeling me with his boney fist in sharp, vicious, punches. One, two, three, four. When I groaned, Raul turned with a wicked smile. He wanted in on the action too. With his right hand, he landed a punch to my stomach that took my breath away in an explosive gasp. Mouth agape, I tried to catch my breath.

Raul let go of my arm and stood back. With an inclination of his head, he spoke to the driver. "Hold his other arm."

The driver grabbed both my arms and held me upright.

Raul grabbed my hair and jerked my head back so he could look me in the eyes. "Now, amigo, I'm going to hurt you so bad, you'll beg me to stop." His big fist slammed into my face.

Raul let go of my head and stepped back to get some distance. As he did, I lifted the heel of my shoe. It came down in a smooth, sweet release of fury. As the raging piston began its journey down, I raised my head and gave Raul Ramos a crazed smile that made him hesitate with his cocked arm.

Oh, I was in my element now. When I'd boxed in college, my coach had tried to teach me how to control and direct my rage, but I'd never really gotten the knack of it. Never really wanted to. He'd told me it was a weakness because I stopped thinking. I would never make a great fighter, he said, unless I learned how to think and fight. If I ever got in the ring with a seasoned fighter, I'd be taught a lesson I'd never forget. But I liked to brawl too much.

Today, my volcanic rage poured out like a protective force that took away the pain and gave me a vicious lust for the fight I didn't want to control.

My right heel smashed the top of the driver's foot with the satisfying, crackling crunch of dry kindling. The driver screamed and released my arms. They came free a fraction of a second too late for me to completely avoid the four large hairy knuckles heading toward my face. The glancing blow shook every bone in my body. As I straightened, little white sparkling lights danced before my eyes. I came up smiling again, though, and Raul hesitated as he had before. There was a bit of grudging respect and a little fear in his eyes now. But not enough.

Raul's next blow was directed toward my midsection, and I blocked it by raising my briefcase like a shield. As the blow knocked me backward, I aimed a glancing kick between Raul's legs that didn't have much effect. The rage was still on me, and

I wanted more. Palm up, I curled my fingers, motioning him forward.

"Bring it, you big hairy *gorilla*," I said. "What are you waiting for? My sister hits harder than you."

To my surprise, Raul dropped his arms, and a smirk broke his ugly face. I heard the crush of gravel. I felt the explosion of pain. Then nothing at all.

Chapter 11

Homeless Intervention

Benito's driver dropped Timbre Plummer with a pistol butt to the head.

"Timmberrr," Benito whispered.

His heart raced as his men beat the unconscious body. The violence stirred him, calmed him, satisfied him. His eye twitched. He remembered the last beating he'd received. He smiled. It had been worth it. He'd endured it for the key to the hidden door.

His father had come home from a several-week trip abroad and had called for him. He'd already been drinking when Benito had stepped into the flickering shadows of his father's study. The look of revulsion on his father's face at the sight of him was worse than the beating that followed.

Benito reached to still the twitch of his eye.

That night, it had taken his father longer than usual to exhaust himself. But he had eventually collapsed into his leather chair with a final roar of German curses. Benito had crawled out of the study and down the cold stone stairs to his room in the basement. He waited and nursed the blistering red belt marks and black bruises that appeared like the graffiti of an abstract artist on a canvas of snow-white silk.

The old man could hold his liquor, but after two hours of silence, it was usually safe to return. Where the servants disappeared to, Benito never knew. But after the screams, wails, and yelling stopped, it was always as silent as a nunnery at midnight. Still, in his *unterhosen*, Benito shuffled half-naked out of the silent depths of the deserted house like a painted phantom. He approached his father's study as silent as a wraith. Through a half-swollen eye, he peered around the partially open door.

His father was sitting in the leather chair next to the fireplace. A fire crackled cheerfully in the old stone hearth. Head back, nose pointed at the ceiling, his father slept. Benito stepped over and studied the hard wrinkles and deep furrows that etched the strong face. He tried to imagine what lines of compassion and love might look like. A curl of dark hair had fallen across his father's face. With every rumbling snore, the hair would lift and then float down. His lips would twitch, and a slight smile would break the cruel lines of his mouth. Then the rumbling would return.

His father's eyes opened, and Benito stiffened as terror petrified his limbs. Those eyes didn't move but just stared straight at him. A look of pity or remorse appeared briefly, then they closed again. His father's chest heaved, and another snore disturbed the silence of the room.

Benito turned away. He picked up the keys on the table next to his father's chair and left the room. Swiftly as his injuries would allow, he returned downstairs. The slap of his bare feet down the basement hall sounded like large raindrops on the solarium window during a summer monsoon. He skidded to a stop in front of the forbidden room. Pulling open the armoire, he tried the keys one by one. On the fourth attempt, he felt the satisfying turn of the key and the metallic snap of the lock. Benito let go of the lock and headed back upstairs. At the study door, he paused and peered through the crack of the partially opened door once more. His father still sat in the chair. The obscene rumbles still disquieted the room. Benito returned the keys without a sound, careful to place them exactly where he had found them. He took one last peek at his father. What would the old man look like if *he'd* been on the receiving end of a belt and fists?

Benito rubbed the corner of his eye to stop the twitch. The pleasure of the memory evaporated as the vehicle shuddered slightly. He turned to look out the back window. A man leaned against the corner, then moved toward the front of the vehicle. The long, twisted dreadlocks, scarred face, and staggering steps proclaimed him a homeless bum with a drinking problem. Mumbling, he staggered past the driver's side of the Escalade and stopped with a wobble and jerk. He leaned on the hood for support.

For a moment, the bum watched the beating taking place at the other end of the alley. Raul was still kicking Timbre's unconscious body with swift, vicious blows. The driver hobbled on one foot, yelling curses and encouragement. Timbre lay face down and motionless. One arm curved underneath his body, and the other was outstretched with a leather briefcase held firmly in its grasp. In between the curses and yelling, his driver tried to stomp on Timbre's extended arm with his good leg.

"Whassa going on here?" the bum called in a slurred, belligerent tone.

Benito's men glanced up. "Beat it, old man," Raul yelled. "Unless you want some of this."

The bum ignored the threat and headed toward them in a weaving, staggering walk. He drew the filthy blanket around his shoulders tighter as he approached. His shaggy mane of hair partially hid his face. He hollered again. "What are you doing here? Stop kicking him. This is my alley."

Benito's men exchanged a glance, probably thinking, *Fresh meat. No restrictions.*

Raul lifted his foot to kick Timbre again. As he did, he glanced at the bum and said, “Last chance. Beat it, or we’ll start on you.”

The bum stumbled closer, now only four or five paces away.

“I said, beat it,” Raul hissed. He viciously kicked Timbre in the ribs to emphasize his command. Then he raised his foot again and adjusted his aim toward Timbre’s head.

Between the folds of the man’s blue-and-brown-striped blanket, the barrel of a silenced pistol appeared. It wobbled back and forth between the two men. Raul’s foot froze.

“What the…” The driver cursed as he reached for the inside pocket of his jacket.

The bum’s pistol froze like it was an extension of a granite statue. A calm, deep voice issued from the shaggy curtain of hair. “Don’t do it.”

The driver didn’t listen. As the gun cleared his jacket, the bum pulled the trigger on his pistol. At the *pop, pop* of sub-sonic rounds, Benito jerked upright. Two small holes appeared in the shiny shoe of the driver’s good foot. With no leg to stand on, he collapsed onto the asphalt with a scream.

Benito grabbed the seat in front of him and leaned forward as the bum ignored the screams and turned the pistol on Raul, whose hairy hand was halfway to his hidden shoulder holster.

“Drop the gun,” the bum commanded.

Raul looked toward the Escalade. Their eyes met. Benito gave a sharp nod.

With a violent jerk, Raul cleared his big pistol. As his fat finger tightened on the trigger, the bum’s gun popped twice more. The pistol fell from his hand. Raul stared down at his shattered elbow with his mouth agape. He turned malevolent eyes towards the bum, then threw his head back and roared in pain.

The bum kept his pistol out and rigid. He took several quick steps and kicked away his opponents' guns, then moved back, any hint of inebriation had vanished. Indicating the driver with the end of his pistol, he motioned toward the silent Escalade at the other end of the alley. He spoke to Raul.

"Pick up your friend and get out of here."

Raul glared at him. "I'll kill you for this.". He leaned down, grabbed the driver by the arm, and dragged him to his feet. The man screamed in pain as his broken feet bore weight.

"Stop acting like a woman, you useless piece of—" Raul was cut off by another howl as he slung his comrade over his shoulder. They set off toward the vehicle. Bright splotches of blood and the driver's screams marked their unsteady progress.

With a final, backward glance, Raul repeated his threat. "I'll kill you for this."

The bum's pistol disappeared into the folds of his filthy blanket. He bent down, and the discarded pistols disappeared into the folds of his blanket. He stepped toward the fallen man, leaned down, and felt his pulse, then straightened and faced the Escalade. He crossed his arms and stared toward Benito. Raul dumped the driver into the front passenger side. Did the man know who he was?

As the Escalade backed from the alley, Benito glared at the defiant man standing over the body of Timbre Plummer. As they entered the sunlit street, the "bum" knelt and tried to remove the briefcase from Timbre's grasp. After several attempts, he gave up and gently picked him up. The last thing Benito saw was the man walking down the alley, his burden carried lightly in his arms.

Chapter 12

Repercussions

An incomprehensible pain ripped away the dark curtain over my mind. A muffled scream split the silence, cut off by a burning hand clawing inside my chest. The scream came again. This time I felt my lips shutter with the primal cry. The hand released its grip slightly, and my scream subsided. I held my breath, and the pain was not as intense. I took a shallow gasp of air, and my chest rent again.

Throbbing pain in my head brought the events in the alley back to me. Every hammering beat produced a new memory and more pain. I had taken a monumental beating. I remembered nothing after losing unconsciousness, but my body told me what I didn't remember.

Where was I? I tried to open my eyes, but it was either dark or I was blind. As my mind assessed different parts of my body, new pains were added to a growing list. I willed my left arm to move, but it was held fast. After marshaling more mental effort, I attempted to move my right hand. I got some satisfying feedback and tried my arm. That effort brought more pain. I ignored it. As long as it wasn't the fiery talon in my chest, I could manage it. My arm felt like someone had removed my muscles and sinew and poured concrete into their place.

I moved my fingers and touched something soft. I listened. Nothing. I heard nothing at all. I was no longer in the alley. But where was I?

Slowly, I raised my hand to my face. My skin felt foreign, round, smooth, and burning to the touch. Swollen. It had been this way one time before when I'd gotten into the ring with Johnny Velenti. He had a right jab that I just couldn't avoid, and he'd beaten my face to a pulp before I'd been able to knock him out in the sixth round. I laid my arm back down with a tiny breath of relief. I probably wasn't blind—my eyes were just swollen shut.

I groaned, and the pain in my chest spiked. I must have several broken or cracked ribs. My shallow, panting breaths didn't sound like I'd punctured a lung, so that was good. But where was I?

I made an effort to sit up, and the dark curtain dropped again.

Sometime later, I regained consciousness. The pain returned. This time, though, a tiny slit of light penetrated my eyelids. My forehead was chilled. I reached to my face and felt a soft, cool rag. I tried to turn my head to catch a glimpse of my surroundings, but all I saw was a slight crack of dim light between my swollen eyelids. Then the whirring, humming, pulsing sound of my air conditioning told me I was in my apartment.

"Anyone here?" I called out in a gasping whisper. Only the cooling sound of the AC answered.

I don't know how much later, I woke again. It was still dark, but by turning my head, I could see the light to my bathroom had been left on. I tried to open my eyes farther, and the fuzzy edges of my room came into focus.

The pain was not as severe. I moved my arm, exploring the surface upon which I lay. I was in my bed. The tips of my fingers found the edge. I slid my legs toward it and then over. I ignored the stabbing pain in my chest and tried to stand. It took three tries, but I managed it with a firm grasp on the headboard.

As I stood my useless arm was jerked downward, and I collapsed to my knees. The pain in my chest took me back to the edge of unconsciousness. When the haze of agony cleared enough for me to think, I realized I'd been pulled to the floor by my father's briefcase. I almost laughed then at the absurdity of my predicament. I still held onto my kryptonite, only I wasn't superman. I told my fingers to relax, but they wouldn't work. I lay back against the bed and reached over to peel my fingers from the handle with my right hand. I worked on it like a child learning that the little digits attached to his meaty hand were fingers. Finally, I managed to unclasp my hand from the leather handle.

With a grunt of pain, I stood and made my way with short, shuffling steps to the bathroom. Each one sent explosions of pain through my chest. I pushed the bathroom door all the way open and stepped to the cracked mirror that hung over the single white porcelain lavatory bowl.

The person who looked back at me was unrecognizable. My face was bruised and battered. My left eye was swollen shut. A thin line between the eyelids of my right eye was all that allowed me to see. Black bruises which were already starting to turn purple in places rounded the angular lines of my face. My lips were three times their normal size. My shirt had been removed, and ugly black-and-red bruises covered my chest. The jerks must have kicked me when I was unconscious.

With painful effort, I removed the rest of my clothing and stepped into the shower. I turned it all the way hot and stood under it for fifteen minutes. As the water washed over me, I tried to figure out how I'd gotten back to my apartment. I couldn't have walked that far in the condition I was in. If a stranger had found me in the alley, I would have been taken to a hospital. Had Benito returned to check on his investment? Had one of his men brought me here? Surely not, but who, then? Who had brought me back to my apartment and removed my shirt and cleaned my cuts and bruises, then left me with a cold rag on my forehead?

I felt better after the shower, but the effort had cost me. I returned to bed on shaky legs and gently lay back down. What was I going to do now? The briefcase on the end of my bed caught my eye. I had to solve my father's riddles, collect my inheritance, and start over. First, though, I had to find a safe place to stay. Somewhere where Benito Silva couldn't find me. He said he'd send a messenger with a package in a week. So I had a few more days to pull myself together before I had to find a new place.

I lay back and closed my eye. I started to fade.

A *pound, pound, pound* on my apartment door brought me wide awake in an instant.

Chapter 13

The Cipher

The knocking was bold, loud, and insistent. I waited in silence. The pounding was repeated. It wasn't the hard knock of bony knuckles on the metal-clad wood but the open-handed slamming of a large meaty palm. With a grunt, I slid out of bed and padded to the door. There was silence. I stood at the door listening. The door-shaking assault came again. The slapping *pound, pound, pound,* high up on the door, where a big man could reach. A very big man. Silence settled over the room once more. The door handle wiggled like someone was trying to turn it. Then nothing.

I stepped to the door and put my swollen eye to the peephole. The hallway on both sides of my door was visible. At the far edge of the field of vision, a big man disappeared—a big man with a round head atop a bull neck. The Donegal on his head and the tweed jacket stretched around his bulky frame probably meant he was an Irishman. He hunched slightly, and long arms hung at this side. He passed out of sight with a steady, confident plod.

I returned to bed. I tried to ignore the sharp stabs of pain as I straightened out. I knew from previous experience that a cracked or broken rib would take weeks to heal. I'd have to take it easy. I certainly couldn't take another beating. I had to disappear.

I sorted through the possibilities and concluded that the best solutions all required money. Money I didn't have. I'd be lucky if I could find one of my credit cards with enough left on it for a single night in a seedy South Phoenix motel.

I ground my teeth. Why did my father want to make me jump through hoops to get my inheritance? Why couldn't he have just been like other fathers who didn't try to mess with their kids from the grave? The truth was that he probably didn't think I deserved an inheritance. Otherwise, he would have just left a check, and I would have been on my way to a better life, not lying here in bed, beaten to within a half-inch of my life.

Maybe his riddles were just a way of him getting his final licks in. A kind of punishment for my mistakes. A penance that I had to endure to finally stand again in his good graces. Whatever the reason, I had no choice but to play his games. I was out of other options. Well, not totally out of options, but I no longer wanted to put a pistol to my head. I'd burn down Benito's place first.

I laid in bed for another hour, but I was restless. I couldn't sleep. I needed to get busy solving my father's riddles so I could get on with my life. Millions of dollars were there for the taking.

I slid out of bed. I couldn't bend down, so I squatted and reached for my briefcase. I stifled a gasp because it only made the effort more painful. I grabbed the leather handle and stood. I shuffled into the cramped living room off the kitchen, sat down on the ragged tan sofa, and tried to find the least painful position. The sofa springs squeaked. I slid my open laptop out of the way and placed my briefcase on the glass coffee table in front of me. I fumbled with the numbered tumblers. When I had 314 514, I opened the briefcase and removed my copy of the will.

Cadence's copy of the will was stuffed in beside mine. I'd already forgotten about her. If there was anyone in worse shape than me in this world, it was probably my sister. I didn't have time right now to think about her. I had to help myself first before I was in any position to help someone else—if she would even let me.

I closed the briefcase and set it down beside the table. I slid the will in front of me and flipped through pages until I found the instructions on how to play my father's inheritance game.

There wasn't much—a brief riddle, a cipher, and instructions. The words sounded foreign as I read them out loud through my swollen lips.

This enciphered Old Testament passage could be described numerically as 39 is 1.

Provide the numerical reference to where it is found in the Biblical texts.

I studied the square block of twenty-five Hebrew characters. There were five lines of text across and five deep. Below the ciphered text were five passages of Scripture.

Jeremiah 51:41
How is Sheshach taken! and how is the praise of the whole earth surprised! how is Babylon become an astonishment among the nations!

2 Samuel 24:12
Go and say unto David, Thus saith YHWH, I offer thee three *things*; choose thee one of them, that I may *do it* unto thee.

Ecclesiastes 7:8
Better *is* the end of a thing than the beginning thereof: *and* the patient in spirit *is* better than the proud in spirit.

Revelation 1:17
And when I saw him, I fell at his feet as dead. And he laid

his right hand upon me, saying unto me, Fear not; I am the first and the last:

Isaiah 46:9-10

Remember the former things of old: for I *am* God, and *there is* none else; *I am* God, and *there is* none like me, Declaring the end from the beginning, and from ancient times *the things* that are not *yet* done, saying, My counsel shall stand, and I will do all my pleasure:

Enter your answer at the following link:
www.thelazarusciphers.com

I had to hand it to my father. He had a sense of humor. To get my inheritance, I had to solve a Biblical riddle ciphered in Hebrew text, the answer for which had to be entered at a webpage address named after a beggar.

Chapter 14

Indecipherable

I vaguely remembered the story of Lazarus from my youth—something about a rich man wanting to send the beggar Lazarus back from the grave to warn his family about the torments of Hades. The memory gave me a good feeling. Not so much the content of the story itself, but the happier time it brought back when I'd taken the stories of the Bible at face value. I had loved to read my Bible. For the final two years of high school, I'd even taken an interest in learning Hebrew and Greek. Those stories had inspired me with an interest in history and archeology that I'd carried into my first years of college. Then I grew up and became a doubting cynic.

I slid my laptop closer. In the browser window I typed *www.thelazarusciphers.com* and hit enter. The webpage came up and I entered my login credentials provided in my copy of the will. It displayed a duplicate of the instructions, cipher, and verse clues provided in my father's will. At the bottom were three more lines of instructions and a rectangular box with seven spaces to enter the answer to the first riddle. I read the new instructions.

Enter your answer in the space provided.
A correct answer will reveal the next cipher.
Only one attempt allowed per 24 hours.

___ ___ ___ ___ ___ ___ ___

Okay. Straightforward. Solve the riddle and provide the correct answer in the space provided. Incorrect answers will require a twenty-four-hour wait before a new attempt.

Got it.

I turned back to the riddle and instructions. I had no idea where to begin with the ciphers, so I ignored the five-by-five block of Hebrew text. Cadence was the math and cipher expert. She and Dad had spent years solving ciphers together. Had my father ciphered the answers to give Cadence an advantage in solving the riddles? No, my father wouldn't do that. He wasn't that kind of man. He'd never shown favoritism to either one of us. Instead, he'd celebrated each of our strengths and challenged us to overcome our weaknesses. He was a hard, intense sort of man, but he was fair.

In any case, the ciphers wouldn't help Cadence. She wanted nothing to do with them. Even if she had, she appeared to be in pretty bad shape.

Right now, I had to focus on the riddle itself and the verse clues. At least, that was what I assumed the verses were for. They must be some mental prodding or reminder to help solve the riddle. Or were the verses clues to help solve the cipher? Maybe the passages were just false leads meant to confuse. I sighed. If I kept thinking this way, I'd run myself in endless circles.

I'd start with the riddle first. I read it out loud again at a normal conversational speed. Then I reread it slower. Then again and again until I could see the words written in my mind. The first eight words had a satisfying driving flow, but the ninth word, *numerically*, kind of jammed up the sentence. Words ten, eleven, twelve, and thirteen carried the sentence to its numerical conclusion and provided the crux of the numerical riddle. *39 is*

1. My father had specifically written *39* and *1* as numerals instead of phonetically spelling them out. Why?

This enciphered Old Testament passage could be described numerically as 39 is 1.

Provide the numerical reference where it is found in the Biblical texts.

The second sentence was instructive on how to answer the riddle. It was a straightforward sentence. There was little wiggle room for hidden meaning or implied reference. The two sentences totaled twenty-five words, the same number as Hebrew characters in the cipher. Was this intentional? I reread the first sentence.

This enciphered Old Testament passage could be described numerically as 39 is 1.

The meat of the riddle was only 13 words. Of those words, 11 and 13 were the focus. There were 67 letters in the riddle. It appeared to be a numerical riddle or possibly a play on words. I reached to the side of the coffee table and pulled a brand-new legal pad from my briefcase. I ignored the stabbing pain in my side. I was engrossed.

I placed the yellow legal pad to the side of the will. First, I copied the riddle, cipher, verse clues, and other instructions. Next, I wrote out the six numbers that stood out to me: 39, 1, 11, 13, 25, and 67. I studied the numbers for a few minutes and then rewrote them, but this time in two rows. Finally, I ordered them numerically, which arrangement I speculated might be related to their relative importance in the riddle.

1, 11, 13
25, 39, 67

I was making some sort of progress. Next, I reread the passages of Scripture from my pad. I read through them all several times.

Jeremiah 51:41
How is Sheshach taken! and how is the praise of the whole earth surprised! how is Babylon become an astonishment among the nations!

2 Samuel 24:12
Go and say unto David, Thus saith YHWH, I offer thee three things; choose thee one of them, that I may do it unto thee.

Ecclesiastes 7:8
Better is the end of a thing than the beginning thereof: and the patient in spirit is better than the proud in spirit.

Revelation 1:17
And when I saw him, I fell at his feet as dead. And he laid his right hand upon me, saying unto me, Fear not; I am the first and the last:

Isaiah 46:9-10
Remember the former things of old: for I am God, and there is none else; I am God, and there is none like me, Declaring the end from the beginning, and from ancient times the things that

are not yet done, saying, My counsel shall stand, and I will do all my pleasure:

Other than those in its reference, the first verse from Jeremiah had nothing to do with numbers, so I ignored it. The second passage of Scripture was numerically interesting. It contained an equation of sorts. It was about choices. Three bad choices, to be exact. I added the equation *one-third* to my legal pad. One-third of thirty-nine was 13. I circled the number 13. I had no clue whether this was important or not, but it might be. Right now, that was about the only numerical relationship I could find between the riddle and the Scriptural clues.

The last three verses described a type of chronological order. First and last, the end and beginning. In a numerical sense, this might refer to the end and beginning of a sequence of numbers, or maybe letters. I played with my pencil as I thought about the possibilities. These passages might also refer to the ciphered text.

My sister would probably take one look at the clues and know exactly what this all meant. I ran my fingers through my hair. The cheap, analog clock on the wall tapped out its *tick-tock*. With every click of its internal gears, pressure to solve the cipher grew. I only had a few weeks to get this done. I tried to push out the merciless countdown in my mind and refocus on the problem in front of me. I read through the verses several more times. I needed more context. I didn't have a Bible in my apartment, so I slid my laptop closer and typed in, *online Bible*. I searched through the suggestions and settled on Bible Hub.

Over the next several hours, I read the surrounding context of the passages my father had provided. Then the chapters and any related verses. Finally, my ribs screaming at me, I returned to my bed and lay down. Maybe my subconscious mind would magically put some of the clues together in my sleep.

That didn't happen. I woke with a splitting headache, no closer to an answer than when I'd laid down. I stumbled to the bathroom. The swelling had gone down a little bit, and I had a good view of the damage through half-opened eyes. My face looked like I had gone twenty rounds with Mike Tyson. My body felt like I'd been run over by a truck. The dark bruises were fading into a jaundiced yellow color, and some were spreading under my skin.

After twenty minutes under a blistering shower, I felt better.

The kitchen called me. At last, I had an appetite. I locked for something I could eat through a straw, settling on a glass of milk and a packet of applesauce. I searched through cabinets and drawers for a straw. The previous tenant had left silverware, pots, and pans behind. I didn't do any cooking, so I hadn't bothered to inventory the items. Finally, I found my prize buried in the bottom of the drawer with a cornucopia of cooking utensils.

I held up the yellow twisted and swirled crazy straw, with a rather painful quirk of my lips. "Yeah, right," I muttered. "How the mighty have fallen."

I swallowed what little pride I had left, scooted over to the kitchen table, and attacked my breakfast with the crazy straw. I settled on the recipe of two parts milk and one part applesauce. After much sucking and slurping, I got it down. A few minutes later the tremors in my hands and the nervous churning in my stomach made me regret my choice of nourishment. Way too much sugary food on an empty stomach. I had more energy alright. I returned to the living room and renewed my assault on the ciphers.

***

Three days later, I was physically better. Mentally, I was losing my mind. I wandered around my apartment muttering Bible verses and calculating numbers in my head. I'd memorized all the verse clues. I had covered pages of my legal pad with equations and calculations that would have made an insane man mad with envy. I'd even started writing mathematical equations on the living room walls.

I had nothing. I couldn't figure out the riddle or the cipher, and I had no idea what the verses were for. My father was probably up there somewhere laughing his head off. Adding to the pressure was the knowledge that I'd soon be receiving a visit from Benito Silva or one of his knuckle busters. I couldn't stay in my apartment any longer.

There was only one thing I could do. I had to ask Cadence for help.

Chapter 15

Help and the Helpless

I stepped off the Valley Metro with a wince, three blocks from my sister's apartment. With a light backpack slung over my shoulder, I gave the handle of my briefcase a reassuring squeeze. The sun was just starting to warm the edges of the hills over the valley with a glow. Yellow brightened into gold. Pink tinged a few straggling clouds as the cool Phoenix shadows began to fade. The chill of the desert morning lulled the uninitiated with a sense of invigorating anticipation. When the first direct rays of the mighty sun broke the horizon, the laser-like beams of light warned the more knowledgeable that it was time to cover up and seek shelter. In a matter of hours, the temperature would spike fifty degrees or more. The muffled morning metropolitan air would be humming like a colossal hive of bees as the air conditioners tried to keep the invading heat from turning every Phoenixonian's dwelling into an inhospitable oven.

The closest I came to liking Phoenix was in the early morning or late winter.

I stepped off the curb to cross the street. I tried to favor my left side, which was where most of the damage had been done to my ribs. Each time I placed weight on my left foot, a jolt of pain stabbed me. I gritted my teeth. At least it wasn't the fiery agony I'd felt the first day.

I followed Filmore for two blocks and turned on Ninth. Cadence's apartment was in a four-plex halfway down the block. The sidewalks bustled with early morning joggers. In front of me, an elderly couple walked hand in hand. A groggy dog owner's four-legged friend led him in an urgent, erratic zigzag from one side of the sidewalk to another, one landmark to the next.

The man and his dog kept my mind off my growing agony. He was several hundred feet in front of me, the retractable leash making a zipping whir as it was run out like a fisherman's line with a marlin on it. When the white-and-black skunk-like fur ball reached the end of the line, the man's arm would come up with a jerk and a thud. I couldn't help a laugh that escaped. The blossoming pain cut off my mirth and took me to my knees. After most of the pain subsided, I staggered upright.

Cadence's four-plex came into view past a run-down condo. I stopped at the chain-link fence enclosing a small grass-and-gravel yard. The latch squeaked as I lifted it and stepped through the gate. It gave a desolate squeal as I closed it behind me. Four sidewalks led away from the gate like the veins of a fan. I took the second to my right. I stopped in front of the door with a black-and-gold letter *B*. A crooked *A* listed on a bent finishing nail on the door to my left. On the entrance to my right, a similar nail protruded, but no ornamental letter adorned its head. Instead, a clumsy hand had lavishly painted a bright red *C*.

I pushed the yellow doorbell bar, which glowed faintly orange behind the blackened smudge of a thousand fingerprints. I waited. I pushed the grimy doorbell again and held it down. I took half a step closer and leaned my ear toward the door. A television blared in the background. Someone was home. I pushed several times in succession. Absently, I examined the tip of my finger. How many times would I have to push the doorbell before the stain would rub off?

I rapped on the door and then stepped back to make some room. There was nothing worse than opening the door to find someone standing right in your face. Still, no one came. I rapped again, louder. My side was cramping up from the uneven load, my ribs were on fire, and I was getting mad. *Bam, bam, bam*, I pounded on the door with the bottom of my fist.

"Cadence, I know you are in there. Open up, please. I need to talk to you."

Still no answer. My frustration mounting, I reached to the top of the door jamb and felt for a key. Nothing but a layer of Phoenix dust. I searched around the door.

My sister was notorious for locking herself out. She'd locked herself out of her car, the house, her locker at school. Anything with a lock on it seemed to emit some kind of magic that caused my sister to forget her keys. So, to compensate, she'd always hidden a key near where she had a lock. I nudged the pot with a shriveled brown petunia. Cadence loved flowers. By the looks of her petunia, she *was* in bad shape. I felt a small stab of pain. This time it wasn't my ribs but my conscience. My sister was in trouble, and here I was at her door not to give her help but to ask for it.

"You are a real selfish jerk," I said to myself as I looked under the potted plant. Then under the clay overflow dish it was sitting in. I stepped back and studied the faded green letters and numbers that covered the worn doormat. I smiled as I read the inscription.

Mathematics is the key
that unlocks the
door to the sciences.

I lifted the mat, knowing what I'd find. Just dirt. I lifted the mat clean off the ground. Then I saw it. My sister had cut a slot in the thick rubber mat, and a sliver of brass gleamed. I slid out the key and dropped the mat. A cloud of dust rose from the edges. I stepped to the door. The dust tickled my nose. To my terror, a sneeze built, not one of those slight tickles that could go either way unless you turned your face to the sun. No, this was one of those sneezes that would not be denied—like an old dam, with cracked ramparts strained with a thousand-year flood. I wrinkled my nose and tensed my muscles to hold back the growing pressure.

The dam burst. I sneezed a gale of hurricane-force wind. Instead of the usual euphoric release, the blinding pain of a thousand burning swords followed. My head came down hard against the door. Stars swirled in my vision, and the key and my briefcase dropped from my hands. I reached for the door to try and remain upright. Only the fear of adding to my injuries kept me on my feet.

It took me several minutes of shallow, panting breaths to calm the fire in my chest sufficiently to reach for the key once more. I knocked one last time in a weak *tap, tap, tap*.

I slid the key into the lock and turned. I opened the door, grabbed my briefcase, and stepped inside. Then the smell hit.

Chapter 16

Unexpected Encounters

As bile rose in my mouth, I buried my nose in the crook of my free arm, but it didn't help much. The smell of filth, unwashed bodies, and vomit hung thick in the air. The pungent stench of weed added to the putrid mix, like early morning smog over Metro Phoenix. The place looked like a garbage dump after a category 5 tornado.

"Cadence?" I called through the baffles of my shirt buried in my cocked elbow. I removed my face from my arm and called louder. "Cadence, are you home?"

No one answered. I picked my way through the trash and garbage that littered the short hallway and stepped into the midst of the wrappers, bottles, cans, and pizza boxes that littered the living room. How could someone live like this?

To my right lay a short, trash-strewn hallway with three closed doors, two on the left and one on the right. I started to call out again, but the words never came. A single, bony, bare foot was sticking out from behind the wall that divided the kitchen from the living room. I groaned. I willed myself toward the kitchen, afraid of what I would find. As I drew closer, my fears were confirmed.

My sister lay sprawled on the floor, one arm outstretched with a scrap of paper grasped between her slender fingers. The jagged ridge of her backbone showed prominently through her dirty tank. A small circle of yellow-green bile had pooled in front of her parted lips.

I let go of my briefcase and unslung my backpack, discarding both onto the filthy brown squares of linoleum that covered the kitchen floor. I dropped to my knees beside her.

"Caden, are you okay?"

No response. With shaky fingers, I felt for a pulse in her neck. Nothing. A terrible fear washed over me. As gently as I could, I turned her over and put my ear to her chest. The strong, steady beat of her heart rewarded me. I put my face close to hers, and her rotten breath brushed my cheek.

I had never cried much in my life. I'd been raised by a father who I'd never seen cry. I'd learned it wasn't what guys did. But there, on my knees in the grime and filth of my sister's kitchen, the bitter tears welled up in my eyes. What a selfish looser I'd become.

I jumped to my feet and tore at my backpack. I pulled out a clean white T-shirt and wetted it under the kitchen faucet. Kneeling back down beside my sister, I gently wiped the vomit from her lips and face. I returned to the sink and rinsed the T-shirt thoroughly and then placed the cool, wet material against her forehead.

I left my sister there on the floor and headed back to the hallway and the three closed doors. I opened the first door on my left, assuming it was the bathroom. I guessed correctly but quickly closed the door as an even worse stench tried to escape.

Next, I stopped at the door on my right, where the television was blaring. A coarse laugh came from the room within. As I flung the door open, a white sickly-sweet cloud of marijuana smoke poured out. A pair of dark, antagonistic eyes met mine through the smoke. Their owner was six-foot-one and looked to be two hundred and twenty or thirty pounds. His white T-shirt covered a bulging chest and biceps. Thick white hairy legs protruded out of a pair of beige cargo shorts.

"Who the hell are you?" the man asked before I could form a coherent thought.

His insolent tone set me off. This time, it didn't take several stiff jabs or an uppercut to make me fighting mad. It was right there just below the surface like a faithful companion. Just what I needed—someone who needed a butt-kicking more than I. The smug jerk stared at me across the dirty bed. He didn't know it yet, but he had yanked my chain in the worst possible way.

I started to ask, "Who are—" before he cut me off.

"Get out of here, buddy, and close the door behind you." He said it dismissively as he took a deep drag from his joint. He gave me a lazy, knowing smile as he blew the draft of smoke towards me.

That was it. My rage burst its cardboard cage. I took two steps toward the bed and crushed those insolent lips against his crooked yellow teeth with my clenched fist. Bruised fingers never felt so good. His head jerked, and blood trickled through his broken lips.

Before he could react, I hit him again and grabbed his shoulder-length hair with an angry roar and pulled him off the bed. He grabbed for my wrists. I didn't let him get his footing as I yanked him through the door in a dragging, stumbling run. He screamed and then clawed at the hand I had securely buried in his shaggy mop. I propelled him through the house, facedown and off-balance. In two seconds, we were down the hall and into the living room. I picked up speed along the short hallway and through the front door I had left open. With one final, violent yank, I drove him out onto the sidewalk, where he skidded face first for a short distance before coming to rest.

I squatted beside him. As he drew his arms under himself to push off the pavement, I looked him in the eyes. "Stand up." The murderous rage on his face briefly changed to confusion.

“Stand up, you filthy gigolo.” I pointed with a rigid finger, “My sister is lying inside in her own vomit, and you are sitting on her bed watching the Simpsons and smoking weed? Stand up,” I repeated with a choking hiss.

I was smaller, older, and looked like I’d been run over by a bus, but his eyes widened as he took in my expression—one of berserk abandon. I wanted him to stand up. I needed him to stand up. The fight went out of his eyes, and my mad savagery was left unsatisfied.

“You piece of garbage.”

He tried to look away.

I grabbed his hair and jerked his head and then leaned in until my face was just an inch from his.

“You freaking coward. Listen to me. If you ever come around here again, I’ll give in to the part of me that desperately wants to tear you apart.”

He attempted to turn away, but my firm grasp in his thick hair held him fast. I yanked hard, and he gasped in pain.

In a deathly whisper, I said, “If I ever see you again, if you ever try to contact my sister again, I’m going to kill you. Do you understand?” When the fight reignited in his eyes, I shook his curly head violently. “Do you understand me?”

He finally nodded.

“Say it, you dope-smoking piece of trash.”

“I understand.”

I released him and waited. He looked away and didn’t move. I walked back into the house and slammed the door.

Chapter 17

Refuse and Recriminations

With shaky fingers, I turned the deadlock, placed the brass bolt hanging from its chain in the eye slot, and slid it home. I leaned against the door. As my cocoon of invisible rage cooled, the exquisite pain from my ribs blossomed into a full-blown inferno. My gaze followed the stains and spots on the grimy floor to the garbage-strewn living room. That set me off again, and I almost unlocked the door to take it out on the guy I'd left out on my sister's sidewalk.

How could any human live like this? The bums in their homeless camps were cleaner and more orderly. With a sigh, I headed back to the smoke-filled bedroom, opened a window, and stripped the bed down to a single soiled bedsheet. I carried the bedclothes to the kitchen and dropped them beside the double pantry doors that I supposed hid a washing machine and dryer.

I knelt next to the skeletal form of my sister. As gently as I could, I scooped her up in my arms. I clamped my teeth together and ignoring the pain, lifted. A gasp escaped my chest at her weight. All those years of sports and outdoor activity had given her strong big bones. Her flesh had wasted away, but she still had the frame of an athlete. It was her face that kept me from passing out. Etched in lines, blotches, and bruises, I read a story of want, neglect, and excess. It was as if the lifeblood of her personality had bled out, and the body of a stranger remained.

Cadence's head, arms, and legs dangled like a lifeless doll's. Her limp body slid out of my arms as I leaned over her bed. I placed my ear to her chest once more. The steady beat of her heart reassured me.

"What happened to you, Sis?" I whispered. A lump swelled in my throat.

In the kitchen, I scooped my wet T-shirt from the floor where it had fallen when I lifted Cadence. I rinsed it in the sink and returned to her bedside.

I rewashed her face and left the rag on her forehead. A weak smile turned up the corners of her mouth, but her eyes didn't open. I left the room and closed the door behind me. Back in the kitchen, I removed my dress shirt, folded it, and placed it in my backpack. After rummaging through the cabinets to find a bucket, I grabbed dish soap, a rag, a half bottle of bleach, and an unopened package of heavy-duty garbage bags.

I removed the unwashed dishes and garbage from one side of the kitchen sink and set the red bucket under the faucet spout. Filling the bucket with hot water, I added a squirt of dish soap and a cup of bleach.

I shook out one of the black garbage bags and swept all the bottles, paper plates, napkins, and half-eaten food into it. Next, I attacked the kitchen table with soapy, hot water and bleach. My assault on the grimy table slowly revealed its natural honey-colored wood. By the time I finished, the water in my bucket was a cloudy brown color. I started to dump it down the kitchen drain but stopped myself as I looked at the kitchen floor. I could use this water to loosen the grime and dirt. It was going to take more than one washing to get the floor clean. I set the bucket down and reached for my briefcase and backpack. I placed them on the center of the clean table and breathed a sigh of relief. Now I had a base of operations.

I worked my way outward from the kitchen, cleaning my sister's apartment from top to bottom. I kept the door locked but opened the three small windows. The apartment smelled like bleach and Dawn dish soap. Now and then, I'd pause to check on Cadence. Still out like a light.

I found enough meth and cocaine to make me wonder if pretty boy was using my sister's apartment as a distribution hub. All of it went into the toilet and on its way to the city's sewer plant. I must have flushed fifty grand of premium drugs.

That made me think of Benito Silva and his efforts to force me into his gang of drug pushers. I slammed the lid of the toilet and flushed one last time, just for good measure. No way was I going to ruin more beautiful lives like my sister's.

The anger got me through the next four hours. I cleaned the bathroom and then tackled the spare bedroom, a dark little hellhole that had been used as a gaming room. There must have been twenty grand in high-tech gaming equipment in the room. The only thing not filthy was the single cockpit-type chair in the center of the room, in front of three large flat-panel displays. Red Bull and Monster cans lay ankle-deep around the chair like multicolored slag from a volcano.

I saved Cadence's bedroom for last. She lay where I'd left her earlier that morning. Carefully, I slid her to one side of the bed. She groaned but didn't move. The groan was encouraging. I undid the sheet and bed liner and placed a clean sheet on the mattress and scooched her onto it. When I finished making the bed, I scooted her to the center and covered her with a light blanket.

It took me another two hours to clean the bedroom. I filled nineteen garbage bags and stacked them in the front entry. My sister had a serious drug problem. Evidence of it had filled every room.

When I finished, I was wasted—and in so much pain I could barely stand. Counterbalancing the discomfort was a sense of satisfaction I hadn't felt in as long as I could remember. I brought a chair from the kitchen and set it beside my sister's bed, then collapsed into it. I reached for her hand and started talking. I fell asleep pouring out all the miserable events that had taken place in my life over the past several years.

Chapter 18

Starvation and Sustenance

I woke to find Cadence watching me with haunted, sunken eyes. I still held her hand. I gave it a gentle squeeze.

"How are you doing, Sis?" I asked quietly. After a couple of minutes of silence, I added, "Can I get you anything?" A weak shake of her head was all the response I got. "When was the last time you ate anything?"

Beyond Cadence's listless eyes resided a stranger I didn't know. The life that had animated her seemed to be fading like a sunset on a receding tide. The sparkling, bubbling, dancing light had nearly disappeared into the cold, dark, misty night. The tidal waters seemed to reveal the gloomy outlines of her shattered dreams, worn-out hopes, and tangled piles of her fears.

I wasn't going to just sit here and watch my sister fade away. I stood up. The pressure on my hand increased, and her eyes dilated. The violet pools stirred. She didn't want to be left alone. That gave me a little hope. I released her hand.

"I'm not leaving you, Sis. I'm just going to find something for you to eat. I'm not going to watch you starve to death."

After rummaging around in the pantry cabinet, I finally found a can of tomato soup. Might not be the right thing for someone in my sister's condition, but it was unlikely I'd get her to eat the mac and cheese, so tomato soup it was. After the broth was hot, I poured it into a bowl I'd washed. I took a glass from the cabinet, filled it with water from the tap, and grabbed a spoon.

When I entered the room, her face brightened, and a soft breath escaped. I set the food and drink down on the nightstand.

"Let's get you set up in bed," I said as I helped her move. "Can you slide back a bit against the headrest?"

She made a weak effort, but with my assistance, she managed to wiggle back far enough that I could bunch up a couple of pillows for her to lean against. She watched me with solemn eyes.

I grabbed the bowl and spoon. Dipping the spoon into the creamy orange liquid, I raised it to my lips and blew gently. I wasn't a fan of tomato soup, but this didn't smell too bad. Of course, I hadn't eaten anything myself. Cupping the spoon with my other hand, I raised it to my sister's mouth. She wouldn't open her lips. I waited a moment, and when she still didn't take the spoon, I set it back down in the bowl and pursed my lips.

"Come on, Cadence. You've got to eat something. You've already nearly starved yourself to death. Just take one bite for me, please?"

She lowered her gaze. "I'm not hungry, Timmy," she said weakly.

"What happened to you?"

My sister and father had shared a special relationship, yes, but something more than grief hovered in those sunken eyes of hers. What she had done to herself hadn't been done in a few weeks. I couldn't force her to eat. So far, the only thing that had gotten any real show of emotion from her was when she thought I was going to leave her. Okay, then. I'd use that.

One more nice try. "Please eat something, Caden."

She *just* shook her head.

"Okay, then." I sighed and stood. "If you won't eat anything for me, I'm going to call 911 and have you taken to the hospital. I won't sit here and watch you die."

A look of terror crossed her face. Tears welled up in pleading eyes. "Please don't call. I'll try to eat something. But please don't call them."

I didn't understand the terrified look on her face. It was shockingly primal. She was shaking now. She sobbed.

"Please don't let them take me back."

I sat down, shaken. What had made her so fragile, so broken? My heart groaned. Who or what had sucked all the sparkle and joy out of her and left this nearly empty shell of a person? Was this all self-inflicted?

I waited until the sobbing subsided and then I spooned up a little more soup and held it to her lips. "Careful. It might still be a bit hot."

Her lips parted, and she took the spoonful of soup and swallowed. Her wet eyes closed, and the muscles in her throat worked violently—no doubt, fighting a gag reflex. But she kept the liquid down, and I dipped another spoonful and raised it. It was torture to watch her. How long had it been since she'd eaten anything that didn't involve a needle, pill, or straw?

After twelve spoonfuls, I stopped. By the convulsive straining of her throat, I could see that she was barely holding it down. It wouldn't do her any good if she lost the progress we'd made.

I smiled at her. "Good job. Let's see how you handle that. If you can keep it down, we'll try again later." I reached for her hand and gave it a squeeze. "Let me go put this away, and I'll be right back."

She nodded and closed her eyes.

I poured the half-filled bowl of soup back into the pot on the stove and covered it. When I returned, a bit of color brightened her face and brought a smile to mine. Amazing what just a few spoonfuls of food could do for a person. I sat back down beside the bed.

"I need to go to the store and get us some food. Your pantry is empty."

Her eyes came wide open. The fear was back.

"If we are going to get you strong again, your body needs some good fuel. Is there anything I can get you?"

Her mouth worked but no words came. Then, after an uncomfortably long pause, she shook her head. Her fingers grasped the sheet and pulled it up against her chin.

"I'll be back in an hour," I said reassuringly. "Okay if I take your car?"

She nodded. I sat there for a few more minutes. What could I say or do that might lessen Cadence's anxiety? She seemed so fragile.

I smiled big and stood. "All right, then. I'll be back in a little while. I have your spare key from under the mat. I see you are still forgetting your keys." My smile morphed into a corny grin. "Some things never change." I shook my head in mock disapproval.

Her violet eyes flickered briefly. The corner of her mouth started to turn up but didn't quite make it.

A new thought gave me pause. "Does your boyfriend have a key to your apartment?"

After a moment, she shook her head.

Thank God. "You should probably know that I kicked him out of the house."

Her expression settled into lines of gravity that told me she understood.

I hesitated. I couldn't bring myself to apologize for stepping into her affairs that way. So I just shrugged. I didn't look at her as I added, “We exchanged words and I lost my temper. I told him never to come back.” I shifted my feet.

I hadn’t seen my sister in years, and I had no right to butt into her life this way. Worst of all, I’d not come over here to check on her because I had been concerned for her, but because I was being the same selfish jerk I’d been for the past eight years. I had wanted something from her. How was I any different from the gigolo I’d kicked out of her house? The only thing that held my dignity by a thread was that since finding her on the floor of her kitchen, I hadn’t once thought about my father’s will or solving his stupid ciphered riddles. My sister needed my help, and as long as she wanted it, I was going to try to be man enough to help her.

I studied the floor at my feet. “You deserve better than a guy like him,” I raised my eyes and held her gaze. “I mean it, Cadence. You deserve better than all this.” I gestured with my outstretched hand. My foot squeaked on the clean floor as I turned to leave.

I entered the hall, and she called to me weakly.

“Thank you, Timbre.”

I paused, wheeling around with my hand on the door frame. “For what?”

“For caring. For being here.”

I stared at her sadly and shook my head. “I don’t deserve your thanks, Caden.” I turned to leave before she could see the shame on my face.

Chapter 19

New Cadences

Cadence lay in the bed staring at the ceiling after Timbre locked the door. She was only a few steps away from the next life and whatever waited on the other side of that invisible line. If her brother hadn't come, she would probably have taken those final steps. If not last night, soon. But this morning, that self-destructive drive wasn't as strong. She had not been asleep when Timbre had poured out his heart beside her bed. Listening to him tell of his mistakes, pain, and self-loathing made her realize that all the ugly of this world wasn't just following her around.

He would never have told her those things if he'd known she was awake. But she was glad she had heard them. Sure, he'd admitted that he'd come for selfish reasons. But he had stayed and cleaned and taken care of her because he cared. Just knowing that seemed to give her the first bit of hope in a long time. Hope and purpose too.

Cadence shuddered at the image of Timbre holding a gun to his head. Her brother was always strong and level-headed, except when he was wronged. Then he was a holy terror. Yet, from what he had admitted last night, he was a few steps ahead of her in his race to cross into the great unknown.

"Thank you, God," she whispered. "Thank you for sparing my brother's life and bringing him back into mine." Her tears dropped onto her pillow. Maybe God hadn't forsaken her for what she'd done.

Cadence slid her feet off the bed and stood. She held the mattress until her head stopped spinning. On shaky legs, she reached the door frame. A few more steps and she made it to the hall. A stuttered gasp escaped her lips, for the change from dark, ugly filth to clean, fresh orderliness made her realize just how far she'd let herself go. Her house had reflected her heart and soul.

She crossed the hall and opened the bathroom door. Here, too, Timbre had scrubbed away the filth and neglect. Suddenly, she glanced down at herself and tensed. She smelled, her clothes were soiled, and she felt dirty. Dear God, how had she let herself become this filthy animal? She stepped over to the tub and turned on the hot water.

Thirty minutes later, she climbed out of the tub fresh and clean. Most of that time she'd spent washing and untangling her hair. She emerged from the bathroom with a towel around her head and fresh clothes that Timbre had thoughtfully left for her in the bathroom. Feeling almost human again, she wobbled into the living room. Her strength waning, she grabbed the wall and looked around.

She stared in dismay at the black garbage bags Timbre had stacked from floor to ceiling in the hall. Had there been that much trash in her house? How could that be possible? The garbage made her think of Bobby Joe. She'd let him stay because he had been a good source of drugs. She would have liked to see her brother throw him out. She'd tried to get rid of him several times, but he wouldn't leave. Not that she tried too hard. The drugs he supplied kept her mollified.

She pushed off the wall and squeezed by the trash bags to get to the front door. Leaning against it for support, she inserted the extra safety chain. It probably wouldn't keep Bobby Joe from breaking down the door, but it made her feel better. Holding the wall, she headed back to the bedroom.

She got as far as the living room when a noise outside the front door stopped her. On trembling legs, she turned to face the sound.

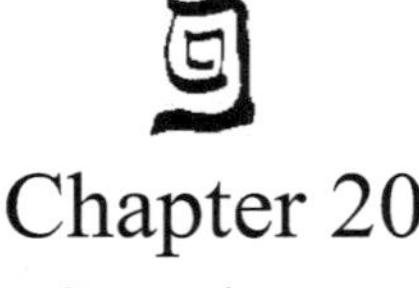

Chapter 20

Commitment

Ten minutes after leaving, I'd parked Cadence's Honda Civic and I was pushing a shopping cart through the local Walmart Supercenter. Forty minutes after that, I was back at the curb in front of her apartment. Having made it to her front door with two armfuls of groceries and cleaning products, I set the paper bags down carefully, but fire still stabbed in my ribs. I leaned against the door as I waited for the pain to subside. Finally, I turned the key in the lock and pushed the door. It came up short on its safety chain.

A wave of dread and anger swept over me. Had Cadence's boyfriend returned and locked me out? Cadence was in no position to resist his efforts. I knocked. Not a sound came from the house. I knocked again, this time louder. Still nothing.

"Cadence!" I hollered through the crack in the door. "Cadence? Are you in there? It's Timbre." I was just about ready to step back and kick open the door when a shuffling sound came from inside. The door closed. After a few moments, a chain rattled. The door swung open.

I let out a long breath. Cadence stood there in the clean sweatpants and shirt I'd left for her in the bathroom. There was more color in her cheeks and relief in her eyes. A large white towel wrapped around her hair. I never understood how girls managed to keep them balanced on their heads.

A nervous laugh escaped me. "You had me scared there for a second, Sis. When the door chain engaged, I thought … Never mind what I thought. I'm just relieved you are okay. And looking better." I clamped my jaw shut before further words could escape, fueled by my nervous energy.

Unfathomable eyes met mine for a full thirty seconds. "I'm …" Her brows drew together as her pale skin flushed with pink. "You…" Whatever she wanted to say, she couldn't get it out. She stomped her foot as tears shimmered in her eyes.

"What is it, Cadence? It's okay."

"Thank you, Timmy. Thank you for cleaning up my mess. I–I–I wish you didn't have to see that. To see me this way."

"We are family, Sis. When the chips are down, family sticks together."

The chips are down? *Really, Timbre?* A gambling metaphor now, at a time like this, in these circumstances? Really. The last time we had talked, I'd been asking her for money for gambling! If she found out that I showed up at her door looking for her help so that I could pay off a gambling debt, I'd lose any credibility I'd managed to salvage.

"Crap," I muttered.

She gave me a funny, penetrating look. But she didn't say anything.

I lifted the groceries. "Probably should get these in."

Cadence stepped weakly to the side. I unloaded in the kitchen and returned to the car for a second and then a third time. As I surveyed the supplies on the table, my insides clenched. This trip had maxed out another one of my credit cards.

Cadence still stood in the hallway. One hand held onto the hall closet door handle, and the other hand was braced flat against the wall where she appeared to be steadying herself. Her legs were shaking. So that's why she was just standing there. She didn't have enough strength to take another step. I cursed myself silently for not noticing sooner. She looked at me with determined, sad eyes that said she would fall before she asked for help. I reached her just as her legs gave out and carried her back to her bed. I stifled a gasp as I set her down. "Sorry, Timmy," she said.

Right then, I swore to myself that, no matter what happened in my life, I would stick it out long enough to help see her better. The decision gave me peace and a direction I hadn't felt in years. I'd lived for myself for so long, I'd forgotten how good it felt to do something for someone else.

"Caden, don't apologize. I've been a crappy brother. I used to look out for my kid sister."

"I'm not a kid anymore, Timbre."

I nodded sadly. She was right—neither of us were kids anymore. We had both made an incredible mess of our lives. By helping her, I was throwing myself a lifeline. I needed to be needed. Maybe that came down to another selfish motive, but I didn't want to see it that way right now. I couldn't see it that way. We both needed each other, and that was good enough.

I reached for her pale, cold hand and squeezed it gently. "I'm here now, Caden. I'll stay as long as it takes until you get back on your feet. Or until you tell me to get lost. Deal?"

She returned the pressure with surprising strength. She gave a slight nod, and her eyelids fluttered close.

Chapter 21

Withdrawal

Over the next three days, I looked after Cadence. I fed her soup and broth to start with. Then I made fruit smoothies for her to sip on. Her color improved, and she was able to walk short distances without help. She smiled more. I started reading *The Great Alone* to her, the bestselling novel by Kristin Hannah about a broken military family that moved to Alaska to escape their problems and get a fresh start. As with most problems in life, they found that they couldn't outrun theirs. We laughed and cried together.

As Cadence slept, I worked on my father's cipher. While I was helping my sister, I wasn't going to ask her for assistance solving the ciphered riddles. She didn't want anything to do with Dad's will, and I would respect that. I was still ashamed about coming to her for selfish reasons. We didn't talk about Dad's will at all—just let it lay there between us like dirty laundry on the floor. We kept talking around it or over it.

Cadence had seen me working on the ciphers the few times she had gotten out of bed and wandered to the kitchen for a glass of water or a bite of food. Maybe she was just looking to make sure I was still there. She'd glance over my shoulder for a moment and then head on to the kitchen without comment.

In my efforts to clean up her apartment, I'd found several of her books on cryptology. I'd tried to read them but quickly found they wouldn't help with my father's ciphers. They applied more to advanced mathematical theory, one of Cadence's many areas of expertise.

By the second day, my sister's improvements seemed to plateau. By the third day, she was no longer eating. The shadows of worry in her eyes became undisguised fear. I asked her what was wrong. At first, she tried to play it off as if the food was not agreeing with her. Then, when the tremors started, she told me.

"I'm going through withdrawal," she said with a growing look of desperation. "I've gone through this before. It's not fun. I waltzed with the devil, and now I have to pay." Cadence gasped and bent forward with her forearm tucked into her midsection.

"Cadence, we should get you some help."

"No," she said firmly. "I can get through this. I've done it before." But the wild look of fear in her eyes told me there was something she wasn't saying.

Throughout the day, the tremors got worse. When vomiting started, I had seen enough.

"Cadence, you need medical attention. Going through withdrawal in a rehab center where they can give you drugs to help you deal with the symptoms is not the same as withdrawing cold turkey.

"Timmy—" She continued with a pleading look on her face. "Please don't call anyone. I can get through this if you are here with me. We can do this together."

I rubbed my face and ran my hands through my hair. "Why don't you want to go to the hospital?" She didn't answer. She gave me an unfathomable look. "Cadence, you were barely alive when I found you on the floor. You can still hardly stand up. You need help."

"Please, Timbre, please don't call them. I can't go back. I can't go back there." My sister spoke with such shockingly primal fear, it made my hair tingle. She was terrified. Truly terrified.

"Okay," I said. "Okay, I'll wait. For now."

And I waited. But the symptoms got worse. Much worse. By midnight, she became delusional and raving, then by turns, unresponsive. I called 911 just after one in the morning.

Five minutes later, the paramedics arrived. I explained to them that my sister was going through withdrawal. They asked why I hadn't called sooner, and I told them she'd asked me not to. The lead paramedic gave me a look that said I'd made a poor choice. And more than that. It was a look of suspicion and contempt. He'd tried to hide it under his professional detachment but couldn't quite manage it. Obviously,

Cadence was a very sick woman who'd needed medical attention several days ago. His raised eyebrow made me feel like an abusive husband caught trying to explain his wife's black eye. I'm sure my own bruised and battered face did nothing for my credibility.

When I requested to ride with her in the ambulance to the emergency room, his curt refusal further clarified what he thought of me. They left me standing there on the side of the street. I watched the flashing red and blue lights take my sister away.

Chapter 22

Bobby Joe

The throbbing in Benito Silva's head grew as he assessed the man in front of him. Bobby Joe's hands were jammed into his pockets, and he shifted from foot to foot without looking up. His dirty white tank top was too small for his bulging frame. His soiled khaki shorts and unlaced Adidas tennis shoes spoke of neglect and a lack of disciple. His pretty face was scratched down one side, and his hooked nose looked like he'd tried to cut a furrow in the asphalt.

Benito made him wait, let the tension build. Every time Benito exhaled a stream of cigarette smoke in the man's direction, Bobby Joe would pull his hands out of his pockets to run his fingers through his thick, wavy blond hair as if he was combing it.

Bobby Joe LeBlanc was one of Benito's dealers. Benito had learned that Bobby Joe was friends with Timbre Plummer's sister and kept her stocked with drugs. It turned out they were his drugs. Benito smiled. It was a small world.

It had taken him several days to track Bobby Joe down. They finally found him holed up in a seedy hotel on Main Street.

"What do you know about the Plummer girl?" Benito asked after sending another jet of smoke across his desk.

Bobby Joe glanced up, brows lifting. "Who?"

"Timbre Plummer's sister. You know the young woman you sell drugs to over on 9th Street?"

Ah, the look of understanding dawned. Bobby Joe's face flushed. Benito read anger and resentment there.

"Yeah, I know her," Bobby Joe replied morosely.

Benito stubbed out the butt of his cigarette in the gold-plated tray on his desk and leaned forward. "I didn't ask if you knew her," he whispered. "I already know you know her. I asked you what you know about her."

Bobby Joe darted him another glance. He quickly averted his gaze like he'd caught an unintentional glimpse of a welding arc in his brother's chop shop. He shrugged. "Just some chick I shack up with when I need to crash in that part of town. She doesn't even know I'm there. We don't talk. She's too jacked up on coke to know much of anything. Has a nose like a vacuum cleaner, if you know what I mean." He gave a good ole boy laugh that died on his lips.

Benito sprayed him with another fog of smoke.

Bobby coughed and continued. "All I know is that her dad is some rich dude who pays the bills. He's not around much." Bobby looked up hopefully at Benito.

Benito's cold, hard stare told him he'd better keep talking.

"Look, man," he said plaintively. "I really don't know much about her at all. We've spoken maybe a couple of dozen words in the three months I've used her place. One day I sold her some drugs and grabbed the couch. She didn't seem to mind. Like I said, she is out of it most of the time."

"If you haven't talked to her more than a few words, how do you know her father pays the bills?"

Bobby Joe shrugged. "I looked through her mail." He paused as if he expected Benito to say something. Instead, the cold stare and silence again compelled him to continue talking. "Her daddy is some big-shot lawyer for some fancy law firm out of DC. I looked them up on the internet. He has an office in downtown Phoenix. Partner or something. I just assumed he is dirty rich."

Benito watched the man. What an imbecile. Benito had learned over the years that silence was often a more compelling force than threats of violence or harsh words. Unspoken words let the interrogated use their own imaginations against themselves. They believed everyone was as dirty, suspicious, and evil as they were, so naturally, they expected the worst.

Sweat beaded on Bobby Joe's forehead. Finally, he blurted out, "I've told you everything I know, Mr. Silva. I swear."

Benito removed his Luger pistol from its shoulder holster.

"Are you willing to swear your life on it, Bobby Joe?"

Bobby Joe swallowed and stared at the floor. Afraid, no doubt, to allow Benito to see the lie in his eyes.

Benito leaned back in his chair and lit another cigarette, inhaled, and fifteen seconds later, sent another stream of smoke to envelope Bobby Joe. "You are lying to me, Bobby Joe. You are holding back."

Bobby Joe looked around like a mouse trapped in a room full of cats. He stared at the big man who stood next to the door blocking his escape. A cast covered his right arm, but he suspiciously tucked his free hand inside his sports jacket.

Finally, Benito spoke again. "What happened to your face, Bobby Joe?"

Bobby Joe laughed nervously. "I got into a fight."

"With whom?" Benito pressed him with a colder edge slithering into his voice. When the dealer raked his fingers through his hair again, Benito tilted his head to one side. "Bobby Joe, playing verbal hide and seek with me is not going to be your wisest choice."

The slump of the man's shoulders indicated the moment he decided to come clean. "With the dumb chick's brother."

"And? What happened?" Benito goaded him

"I was minding my own business, watching TV in her room, when this guy just barges in and attacks me. Grabs me by the hair and drags me out of the house and leaves me on the sidewalk in front like I'm some piece of trash."

"And what were you doing when all of this was going on?" Benito asked sarcastically.

"It happened so fast I—"

Benito held up his hand. He jumped to his feet, circled the desk to face Bobby Joe, and leaned his backside against it. With a sneer twisting his face, he grabbed Bobby Joe's blond locks and jerked his head down. He stared into the bigger man's eyes.

"So you let him walk all over you, didn't you? Just like I'm doing right now." Benito rolled his head and scoffed. "You took it from an older man half your size who I happen to know was beat half to death just a few days earlier." Benito shook the hairy mop—and the attached head. "If I didn't need your help right now, I'd have Raul take you out back and shoot you." He flung Bobby Joe away.

Bobby Joe stumbled back and righted himself with a growl.

"I tell you what you are going to do, Bobby Joe. You are going to go back to Cadence Plummer's apartment. You'll wait there until you hear from me. Find someplace where you will not be seen. Report back to me if you see Cadence or Timbre Plummer. Do you understand?"

Bobby Joe replied without an upward glance. "Yes, sir."

Chapter 23

Loyalty and Ultimatums

Benito resumed his seat as Raul ushered Bobby Joe out of the room. Raul returned and sat down in the chair in front of Benito's desk, his shattered, casted elbow making his movements rather robotic. He shifted, unable to find a comfortable position. His face still showed the damage done by Timbre Plummer's briefcase. Benito didn't attempt to hide his disgust.

He couldn't let this go on much longer. A down-on-his-luck lawyer had beat up his toughest lieutenant, and thrown one of his dealers out on his face. It was beginning to look like keeping Timbre Plummer around was a mistake. Maybe it was time to cut his losses and make an example out of him, so his organization understood who was in control.

He studied his lifelong friend through a cloud of cigarette smoke. Maybe Raul was losing his edge. Perhaps it was time to replace him with someone who could get results. He had some loyalty to Raul, but not if it would cost him credibility. Maybe he needed to clean his organization from the top down. Give them all a refreshing dose of healthy fear and an intimate knowledge that failure was punishable by death. If he killed Raul, everyone would get the message. Benito Silva could not afford to tolerate failure—even from his best friend.

He sighed. After setting his cigarette down in the golden tray, he looked up. He'd give Raul one more chance, for old time's sake.

“I want you to watch Timbre Plummer’s apartment. If he shows, follow him and find out where he is going and what he is doing.” He let anger creep into his words. “You are not to be seen. You are not to touch or interact with him in any way. If my source’s information is accurate, Timbre Plummer is busy earning his daddy’s fortune. We will wait until he has that fortune in his greedy little hands, and then I will convince him of the wisdom of sharing with us.”

Raul’s sour expression and the flexing of his fingers indicated that he didn’t like what he was hearing. “I think we should kill him and make an example,” he said bitterly. “We’ve never let anyone treat us this way before. The men are laughing behind my back.”

Benito stood with a jerk that sent his leather chair crashing back into the wall. In a single violent motion, he grabbed the pistol in front of him and jumped onto his desk. He pointed the barrel at Raul’s head. The click of the safety release seemed unnaturally loud.

Raul froze in his chair.

Benito spoke in a cold, soft, almost sensuous voice. “I don’t care what you think, Raul. I do the thinking for this organization now. It was your incompetence that got us in this compromising position. If it weren’t for our history, I’d put a bullet in your head right now.”

Raul slowly stood until they were eye to eye. Benito raised the pistol to compensate. He expected fear but only saw disdain, then disappointment. Then anger flushed away the other emotions.

“Pull the trigger, *Jefe*.” Raul said. “If you think I deserve to die for giving advice I’ve given you a hundred times before, then pull the trigger. We began this together, you and me. I’ve been willing to do as you’ve said because I know you are smarter and a better planner than me. But just because you've gotten used to me saying 'yes, boss' all these years, don't think for one second that I'm your little *perro.*

Raul leaned into Benito's pistol. "I'm not scared of you, my friend. Pull the trigger and be damned. I would rather die a man than live like a dog on your leash." He emphasized *dog* and *leash* by jerking his head into the barrel of the gun and pushing Benito back toward the edge of his desk.

Raul's passion made Benito waver. Maybe he had misjudged him.

"I will do your bidding, Benito. But because of loyalty, not fear. So listen to me, my friend. We started this as a partnership." Raul took a half step until he was tight against the desk and Benito was standing on the edge. "Our organization has seen unprecedented success because you have been allowed to do what you do best. Do you know why this was possible?"

Benito lowered the pistol slightly.

"The reason you've made it this far is because I stand between you and the rest of the disloyal, conniving buzzards that want to take your place. That's why. Kill me, and you'll never have a moment's peace again."

Raul turned his back to Benito and headed toward the door but stopped halfway. "One more thing. You can shoot me in the back as I leave, but don't you ever talk to me that way again, or I'll cut out your tongue and make you eat it."

Benito pointed the gun at the floor as the door to his office closed behind Raul. He didn't respect much in this world, but fearlessness and loyalty topped his list. His friend had both. And Raul was not afraid of *him*. He hated to admit it, but the man was right. Raul had not put a bullet in his head at some point over the past ten years—and neither had anyone else—

because Raul was, in fact, loyal. True loyalty could not be bought.

Maybe Benito would keep him around.

Chapter 24

The Lawyer

The lawyer watched the activities outside Cadence Plummer's apartment complex from a silver Audi RS E-Tron GT. He glanced at the gold Rolex Submariner on his wrist as the Honda Civic pulled away from the curb to follow the ambulance. The departing ambulance made his heart beat faster, he needed to follow it, but he wanted to get into Cadence's apartment first, and this might be his only opportunity.

The ambulance lights faded into the dim gloom of the city street. He wanted to wait until all the spectators had left, but he didn't have time. He slid from the plush leather seat and stood for a moment beside the car, sweeping the area with his gaze. Left to right, close to far, he memorized every detail and cataloged any potential threat. He closed the door, its cushioned thud sealing the luxury interior from the dirty, early-morning Phoenix air.

With a purposeful stride, the lawyer approached the group of neighbors who'd gathered on the sidewalk to watch the excitement as they started to mill about. He targeted four still standing in the small square of green artificial turf in front of the row of apartments.

They showed neither hostility nor friendliness as he neared, but rather a mix of mild curiosity and city-bred skepticism. While the lawyer's medium build and height didn't usually intimidate, the scar that ran down his face under the dark sunglasses drew their glances. When he was six feet away, he stopped and spoke.

“Hi, folks, my name is John Henry.”

They watched as he pulled a reporter’s notepad from his pants pocket and a pen from his shirt.

“Anyone see what happened?” Nothing but blank stares. The lawyer suppressed a sigh. Not a very talkative group. “Come on, folks. I need some help here. I’d like to get the story firsthand.” He glanced down at his notepad. “Does anyone know Jerry Everson, Candy Blake, Cadence Plummer, or Judith Carpenter? I just need to confirm that they live here.”

Three of the four people in the group froze. The fourth guy faded into the shadows. Bodies shifted uncomfortably. The rest of the spectators started to distance themselves. A minute later, only the three remained standing on the neon-green plastic turf—two women and a man.

The lawyer focused on the man first. He wore suspenders. They appeared to be his best effort to keep his ample midsection from pushing off his pants. He cataloged the man’s characteristics like an itemized tax deduction—middle-aged, medium height, big belly, big nose, small nervous eyes, and small fat hands. His round head shone, polished down the center with wispy hair above the ears like a bowling ball with moss growing off the sides. A large handlebar mustache, curled and waxed at its furthermost extremities, hugged his upper lip. In his once-white T-shirt and faded denim jeans with a hole in the right knee, he looked like he should be polishing a glass behind a bar in an Old West movie. The lawyer made a couple of notes.

He switched his attention to the youngest of the three. The thin, red-lipped woman appeared to be in her twenties. Her blonde hair had been dyed cotton-candy pink. She wore high, high heels, a short, short skirt and a bright white shirt that glistened and fluttered when she moved. Her eyes, a warm, searching, hungry brown, moved between him and the hundred-

and-sixty-thousand-dollar sports car he had stepped out of. When she finished her calculations, she smiled and fixed her gaze on him with a new light in her eyes.

The final member of the trio was old as the ages, dark as desert night, and sharp as broken porcelain. Tight white curls shaded a finely shaped head and bright, wise eyes interrogated from shiny, smooth skin. She held herself proudly, her floral moo-moo of yellows, browns, and greens cascaded around her like a royal shroud.

The balding man spoke first in a deep nasal voice. "I'm Jerry. I live in apartment A. I didn't see nothin'."

The lawyer nodded. "Thank you, Mr. Everson." He smiled, made a note on his pad, and turned to the young woman. "You must be Candy Blake."

"How did you know that?" she asked with a coy smile.

"Lucky guess," the lawyer replied dryly.

"You're a reporter, aren't you? Are we going to be in the paper?"

He gave a tolerant smile. "I don't know if you will or not. What apartment do you rent?"

"I live in C." She arched her eyebrow. "That's C for Candy." The old lady chortled sarcastically at that. Candy gave her an ugly look and faced him again. "If you have any more questions, Mr. Henry, I'd be glad to answer them. You'll find me in C." She winked at him as she walked away.

"That's C for cyanide," the old lady muttered under her breath as Candy walked away.

Candy swiveled, lips pressed flat. "I heard that, Judith, you old bat." She let out a huff, and her door slammed a few seconds later.

The old lady and the lawyer stood facing each other. Jerry folded his arms across his chest. Judith didn't smile. It was a standoff. She just gave him the look of a wise old skeptic who'd seen it all. He finally smiled and held out his hand. Better to meet this one direct.

"I'm John Henry," he said warmly.

"And I'm Scarlet O'Hara," she said, ignoring his hand.

The lawyer laughed.

"Those others might believe the *s*ugar *h*oney *i*ce *t*ea you're pouring, but I'm not believing a word of it." Her dry voice crackled. "I don't know who you are, Mr. Henry, but you ain't who you say you is. That I know for sure. You look like some ambulance chaser to me. If you are still here by the time I get back to my apartment, I'll be callin' the cops on you." She shuffled toward her door. Jerry followed her until she reached her door. "Get along with you, Jerry. I don't need you watchin' out for me all the time." She waived him away.

The lawyer smiled and shook his head. No nonsense, that one. The world needed more like Judith Carpenter. When the door for D closed, he hastened to apartment B. If he was a betting man, he'd put up ten bucks that Judith was on the phone right now calling the cops. He probably had less than five minutes to accomplish his mission.

He lifted the mat and checked for a key, then dropped it without success. Instead, he fished in his pocket for a ring of keys. One at a time, he tried them in the lock. On his seventh attempt, the key unlocked the door. He stepped in and quickly shut it behind him.

First, he searched the bedroom. Next, the spare bedroom. Then the bathroom. He found what he was looking for on the kitchen table. From a plastic case in his breast pocket, he removed a thin metal object the length of a toothpick and three times as wide, sharp on one end. He inserted it into the leather seam that looped over the semi-solid core of the handle. He inspected the entry point to ensure that it was not obvious. Satisfied, he removed a camera from his jacket pocket and opened the briefcase. He photographed everything inside, careful to put it back exactly how he found it.

The lawyer closed and locked the door behind him and strode quickly to his car. As he walked, he scanned the sidewalk and street in front of him. So far, so good. His car chirped as he pushed the door lock release on the electronic key fob in his pocket.

The Audi pulled away from the curb with a whisper of its electric motor, leaving the street empty. Two seconds later, he set the cruise control at forty-five.

He pressed a button on the onboard navigation system. "Find the shortest route to Banner University Medical Center." He studied the map on the screen for a few seconds, then reached for the phone in his pocket.

With one eye on the road, he navigated toward the icon he wanted and clicked the tracking app. The map showed his current location with a small blue dot. A flashing red beacon pinpointed the GPS tracker in the briefcase. As long as he stayed within cellular range, he would be able to track its location.

He tossed the phone onto the passenger seat and gripped the steering wheel tighter. He glanced in his mirror once more. Still an empty street. He let out a tense breath. The risk had been worth it, but had he lost too much time?

Leaning forward slightly, he reached behind his head, grabbed a handful of his coarse gray hair, and pulled. He threw the wig on the floor in front of the passenger seat. With a quick tear, he yanked off the mustache and added it to the hairy pile along with his sunglasses. He settled deeper into the luxury leather seat and tried to relax.

With another glance at the navigation system map, he curled his fingers tighter around the wheel. The hospital added an unexpected challenge. Was he one step ahead or two steps behind now? If he hadn't seen this coming, neither had the others. Perhaps that gave him the edge.

Chapter 25

Frustrations

At the front desk of the hospital, a middle-aged woman greeted me with a perfunctory nod. “How may I help you, sir?”

“My sister, Cadence Plummer, was just brought in. Could you tell me where she has been taken?” I braced my hands on the counter.

The attendant looked down at her computer screen, her long fingernails clicking on the keyboard. She glanced up at me and then down again. Finally, after an impossibly long pause, she said, “No one by that name is in the system yet. Please have a seat, and as soon as I have more information, I’ll let you know.”

“I need to see—”

She raised her voice. “Sir, please sit down, and I’ll let you know when I have more information.”

My gaze cut to the double swinging doors that led to the emergency room. If I lost Cadence after all this, I’d not be able to live with myself. In helping her the last few days, I’d found a reason to live that didn’t have everything to do with me or my problems.

She cut my thoughts off before the decision to move overcame the more reasonable part of my brain. “Only authorized personnel and family are allowed in the emergency room.”

Hello? What had I just said? “She’s my sister.”

“I’m sure she is, but since she is not in the system yet, I can’t verify if you are family. So sit down and when I hear more, I’ll let you know.” She pushed a clipboard and pen through the slot in the plexiglass that separated us. "While you wait, please fill out as much information as you can." She gave me a tight smile. I knew the look. *You help me, and I'll help you ... maybe*. I took the clipboard with bad grace and found a chair in the corner.

Two hours later, a short, round, middle-aged doctor pushed through the emergency room doors. His dark, bushy eyebrows and balding head reminded me of Mr. Potato Head. He gave the room a cursory glance and settled on me. He headed my way as I stood.

"Mr. Plummer?" I stood. Maybe the battleaxe at the front desk had done her job, after all. He walked over and stopped in front of me. "I'm Dr. Anthony Hurley."

"Good to meet you, Dr. Hurley. My sister? Is she okay?"

He scrutinized me for a long beat. Sizing me up, I guessed. Probably trying to decide if he would let me into his emergency room or make me wait on the hard chairs outside another few hours as some sort of punishment for not taking better care of her.

"Come," he said. So I followed him through the swinging doors.

Once they *swooshed* behind me, he stopped, spun around, and put his hands on his hips. Oh boy. Here it came. *Just keep your cool, Timbre. Blowing up at this man is not going to help Cadence any.*

"Mr. Plummer, your sister is a very sick young woman. She is dehydrated and appears to have an eating disorder. Of more immediate concern, though, are the opiate withdrawal symptoms she is experiencing. Do you know how long she has had a drug problem?"

I shook my head. "I don't. All she told me was that she had just gotten out of rehab here in Phoenix a few months ago. I didn't even know she was in town until last week. We recently learned of our father's death. She has taken the news hard."

Dr. Hurley softened slightly. He gave a sad nod. "I'm sorry to hear that." He started off again and waved for me to follow. "Come with me."

Chapter 26

Help and Explanations

The doctor paused at my sister's door. He turned to me before opening it.

"We've given her an IV to get her hydrated. It also contains vitamins and electrolytes. I've also prescribed Buprenorphine to alleviate the opiate withdrawal. She will need to stay here for a few days. By then, the most severe symptoms will be passed. After we release her, I recommend that she return to the rehab center for at least three to six months. In cases like this, she is more likely to fall back into drug use if she doesn't have strong support from family or friends."

I met his gaze. "I'll be there for her, I promise you."

He sighed and gave me a kinder look. "I can't stress to you how important it is for your sister to receive emotional support right now. She needs someone to be there for her. She might not pull through next time."

I nodded soberly. "I get it, Doc."

He pushed open the door, and we stepped into the room. Cadence lay slightly inclined in the bed. Her clothes had been replaced with a loose blue hospital gown. A white sheet covered her from the waist down. She was as pale as the sheets. Clear tubes snaked down from IV bags that hung from a tree-like chrome cart. A monitor on the opposite side of the bed measured the slow, steady beat of her heart.

I approached and took her hand. It was cold. She didn't move. I frowned and glanced at the physician.

"She'll pull through. We gave her something to help her sleep. Right now, rest, time, and nutrition will speed her recovery."

I nodded.

She looked like a waxen doll lying there. If it hadn't been for the heart rate monitor recording the steady pumping of her heart, I'd have thought she was dead.

"I'm so sorry, Sis," I whispered. A bump at the back of my knees made me turn my head. Dr. Hurley had brought a chair for me to sit on. "Thank you," I mumbled.

He placed a warm hand on my shoulder. "She'll get better if she gets the support she needs."

As I heard the door close behind me, I sat down in the chair. I still held Cadence's hand.

***

I forced my stiff eyelids open. Where was I? Across the end of the bed, warm light from around the edges of the curtain gave the room a slight golden glow. I lay draped over my sister's bed. I still held her hand. She was still sleeping.

I released her hand and stood unsteadily. My ribs ached. I walked to the restroom next to the door in a hunched stoop. I put my hands on the wall-hung lavatory and faced the mirror. Tired, bloodshot eyes set into a blue-and-yellow-bruised face stared back at me. I was surprised they had let me in the hospital looking like this. I'd passed rooms where the patients looked better than I did.

I washed my face in the sink and gently dried it with a towel. It was still sensitive to the touch. I hung the towel and assessed my situation. I needed a shower and a change of clothes. I was trying to decide what I was going to do when I heard the door open. I looked from the bathroom as Dr. Hurley walked in cheerily.

“Good morning, Mr. Plummer.”

“Good morning, Doc. Please call me Timbre”

Dr. Hurley stepped over to the bed without saying anything. He picked up Cadence's chart at the end of the bed, looked at her vitals, and made some notes. He nodded and put the chart back where the nurses could continue to record Cadence’s progress. He turned to look at me.

“She is doing okay. Another day and she should be out of the woods.” His gaze focused on my face and then shifted to my posture.

His attention made me uncomfortable, and I tried to straighten up. I winced.

“Looks like you had a rough night.”

I nodded.

Indicating my face, he asked. “What happened?”

This guy was no fool. If I tried to lie, I undermine what little credibility I had. So, I told him a version of the truth.

“I was mugged last week. Two guys. They roughed me up a bit.” I mustered a wry smile. “They didn’t improve my looks much.”

He ignored my attempt at humor. Looking down at my chest, he asked.

“Did you get that looked at?”

I shook my head. “It’s not that big of a deal. I’ll be fine. I’ve been beaten worse by classmates when I was on the Harvard boxing team.” He looked at me skeptically but didn’t say anything.

Dr. Hurley looked at Cadence. “I’ll check on your sister when I get back on shift later this evening. I’ll see if one of the nurses can find you a cot or something to sleep on. Sleeping in a chair won't do your cracked ribs any good."

After he left, I sat back down next to the bed. Sitting made my chest ache worse, so I stood. I paced for a minute, debating my options. I needed that change of clothes and a shower. I also wanted to grab my briefcase and notes so I could continue working on my father's ciphers. At least I'd have something to do while I waited for Cadence to recover. I leaned over the hospital bed and brushed a few strands of my sister's hair out of her face.

"I'll be back in a little while, Sis," I said softly. *At least I hoped so.* Benito was sure to have a price on my head.

Chapter 27

Legal Matters

I took a shower at Cadence's apartment. As I tugged the clothes out of my backpack, my quandary became clear. I didn't have any money to buy more clothes and going back to my apartment wouldn't be all that smart. But I wasn't about to wear the same stale, smelly clothes for several more days.

I'd have to risk it. I dressed, scooped up my papers from Cadence's kitchen table, shoved them into my briefcase, and headed for the door. I stopped with my hand on the handle. I wasn't the only one who needed clothes. I returned to Cadence's room. I'd been through the entire house, so I knew she didn't have a suitcase. I grabbed a garbage bag from the kitchen and stuffed it with some of her things that I'd cleaned that first day.

On my way out, a large manila envelope crammed into Cadence's mail slot next to the door drew my eye. I pulled it out and unfolded it. It was from Layton, Barrett, and Stowe. I felt uncomfortable opening my sister's mail, so I shoved it into my briefcase and locked up behind me.

Twenty minutes later, I pulled into the parking lot of my apartment and turned off the car. I sat there searching for anything or anyone that looked out of place. After several minutes, I got out and headed to the entrance.

Once inside, I found my own manila envelope from Layton, Barrett, and Stowe shoved under the door. I stepped inside and locked myself in. My curiosity got the better of me, so I opened the envelope. Inside was a note and a check from my father's lawyer.

Dear Mr. Plummer,

Please find enclosed a check for $20,000.00. At any time previous to the will's deadline, you may cash this check instead of trying to solve your father's ciphers. I wanted to clarify this option, as I don't recall doing so at the time of our meeting.

Sincerely yours,
Eric Pincer

I reread the note, then shoved it back into the envelope and threw it on the couch along with my briefcase. I headed for the bedroom. Twenty thousand was a pittance compared to the millions my father's estate was worth. Nice try, Eric, but I was going to play my father's game to the last cipher. Yes, I wanted the money, needed the money. But it was becoming more than just about the money. I had something to prove. Whatever my father's reasoning, he wanted Cadence and me to solve his riddles. I accepted the challenge.

Seeing my sister lying there on her kitchen floor, broken, soiled, and uncared-for had changed something in me. Like a jolt of electricity to a dead heart. I'd felt something I hadn't felt in a very long time. I felt compassion. I felt duty. I felt reawakened. Like maybe my miserable life was once again worth living. I still had an agenda, but now my own plans were competing with a new desire to help someone else.

I grabbed a suitcase from my spare closet and packed a week's worth of clothes into it. I also tossed in an extra duffle bag for Cadence's clothes. Back in the living room, I slid

Pincer's envelope inside my father's briefcase and hefted it to the side opposite my suitcase.

I closed and locked the door as I left. I scanned the area as I headed back to my sister's car. Even though I had something to work toward, I still had problems to get away from. Benito Silva and Raul were still out there somewhere. I had a bill to pay, and they'd be coming to collect. I didn't intend to take another surprise beating.

I opened the Honda's trunk and placed the suitcase inside. I slammed it with a thud and checked for threats once more. I didn't see anything out of place. I watched my rearview mirror as I pulled away. No black SUV. So far, so good. As I returned my attention to the streets in front and around me, an old four-door blue sedan pulled into traffic five cars back. I couldn't see the driver clearly, but he was big. The car stood out because it looked like a well-worn version of a car that police forces all over the US had used for decades—a Crown Victoria. The one following me didn't have the forest of antennas bristling on its exterior, but it did have the big chrome dome spotlight curled on the driver's side door. The car wasn't something one of Silva's men would drive, but I couldn't be too sure. I certainly didn't want a tail back to the hospital.

I took a quick left at the next stoplight and sped up. I watched my mirror. A few seconds later, the blue Crown Vic turned the corner too.

I kept straight on, waiting for a yellow light. Two blocks later, I got my chance. The car in front of me ran the yellow light, and I kept right on his bumper. It was bright red before I got through the intersection. The Crown Vic had to stop. I took the next left and zig-zagged through a section of residential streets, and then I drove west for a mile before pulling into the four-story Phoenix Mall parking garage. I backed into the shadows and waited. Forty- five minutes later, I headed back to the hospital. No one followed me this time.

Chapter 28

Letters & Numbers

I pushed through my sister's hospital room door a half-hour later with fresh clothes and my briefcase. I stopped short. The bed was empty. The room looked like no one had ever occupied it. I stepped back out and checked the number—1123. I had the correct room. I stepped back in and knocked on the bathroom door frantically.

"Cadence?" I called. No answer.

I opened the door to the bathroom and peeked in. Also empty. I backed out and reached for the door to the hall but jumped as it opened of its own accord. I nearly collided with the nurse, who took in my wide eyes and slack expression and answered my question before I could ask it.

"Cadence has been moved to a recovery room on the second floor, 5813." She smiled reassuringly. "She's fine. The doctor upgraded her condition."

I let out an explosive sigh. "Thank you."

My heart was still beating like a trip-hammer as I headed down the hall to the bank of elevators. I pushed the up arrow and waited. A few seconds later, the doors slid open, and I stepped in. I pushed the glowing number 5 set in the stainless-steel panel.

I didn't entirely pull myself together until I was standing beside her bed. Cadence was still sleeping, but some color blushed in her cheeks now. As I watched the bedcover rise and fall with her steady breathing, I was struck by how perspective changes things. I was looking down at the ravaged, unsightly body of a drug addict, but I still saw my sister. I remembered the sparkling little girl with pigtails rubber banded out from the sides of her head. I remembered the athletic, early-teen whose face shone with excitement and determination as she drove a soccer ball down the field, her long blonde hair trailing behind in a golden flash of light. Something in those memories gave me a sense of hope. Cadence was still alive. She would pull through. I swore that I'd live to see the smile and excitement in her eyes once more.

I turned away. A rolling table used to feed patients lying in bed sat against one wall. I pulled it over and adjusted the height so I could use it with my chair and then turned the chair sideways to Cadence's bed. I got to work.

Even though I had it memorized by now, I read the first riddle again. Then I read it out loud, filtering it through my ears for another perspective.

This enciphered Old Testament passage could be described numerically as 39 is 1.

Provide the numerical reference to where it is found in the Biblical texts.

I pulled out my legal pad and read over my notes. Heavy on speculation, they were pretty meager on progress and facts.

- 25 letters in the cipher
- Six numbers of interest: 1, 11, 13, 39, 25, 67
- An equation of 1/3 possibly related to 13/39

Something about 13 and 39 bugged me. I couldn't say what, but it percolated in my subconscious like a foggy outline, a word or an idea I couldn't quite grasp.

I pushed aside my notepad and took out my laptop. The riddle used the Arabic numerals 1 and 39. This, I knew, was no accident. So I started back at square one. I ran a search for every occurrence of the numbers 39 and 1 in the Bible. A second later, only one result came back—an Old Testament reference from Ezra that talked about 139 porters who returned to Jerusalem from Babylonian captivity in the second temple era. While this passage had the numbers 1 and 39 or, more precisely, 100 and 39, I didn't see how this could be construed as 39 being 1. I read around the verse to get the larger context. I still got nothing. That line of research seemed to be a dead end.

Next, I searched for the use of the number 1 in the Old Testament. I remembered that the Hebrew word for 1 was *echad*. I groaned as I saw the results. *Echad* was used exactly five hundred times. I spent the rest of the morning and early afternoon reading every verse that contained *echad.* If my father's riddle was hidden in one of these passages, I sure didn't see it. I sat back and scratched my head in frustration.

I was missing something. I flipped back through the notes. Something still hovered in the back of my mind like a shadow. Something I knew but couldn't recall. I stopped on the page where I'd written out the numerical structure of the text. I'd circled the number 13.

My father had used two Arabic numerals in the text instead of writing them out phonetically. This gave the riddle 13 words instead of 14. 39 was used instead of thirty-nine—1 instead of one. I stared at the Hebrew cipher again.

I read the letters of the cipher out loud from right to left, starting at the top right corner since that was how Hebrew was read.

"*Bet yod zayin.*"

The fourth letter of the cipher was *mem. Mem,* I remembered, was the 13th letter in the Hebrew alphabet. Hebrew didn't have special characters to represent numbers. Instead, the twenty-two Hebrew letters each had a numerical value. Hebrew letter values made Hebrew words with unique numerical values. That must be it. My father's cipher must be a numerical play on the Hebrew word value. I just had to figure out how.

I flipped a page on my notepad and wrote out the Hebrew alphabet horizontally. There were two main ways of attributing value to Hebrew letters—the place or ordinal value, and the absolute or decimal value. Above each letter, I wrote its ordinal value from one to twenty-two. *aleph*, the first letter of the Hebrew alphabet, had an ordinal value of 1, and *tav,* the last letter, had a value of 22.

Below each letter, I recorded its absolute or decimal value. In the absolute method, the first ten letters kept their original ordinal values. Eleven through nineteen had a value related to their ordinal value but with a twist—the digits of the letters' ordinal value were added together and then multiplied by ten. *Kaf,* the eleventh letter, became 1+1(*10) or 20. *Lamed*, the twelfth letter, became 1+2(*10) or 30. The nineteenth letter, *Tsaddi*, became 1+9(*10) or 100.

From the 20th letter of the Hebrew alphabet to the 22nd , the same process was performed, only the digits of the letter's place value were multiplied by a hundred. *tav*, the 22nd letter, became 2+2(*100) or 400. I studied my table.

Again, I read my father's riddle from my notepad.

This enciphered Old Testament passage could be described numerically as 39 is 1.

1 was the crux of the riddle. It was the end result—the finished product. The Hebrew word for 1 was *echad*, spelled *Alef, chet*, *dalet*. Those letters gave a Hebrew word value of 13. Excitement tingled through me. I was onto something now. Putting this in terms of my father's riddle, I could say that 1 could be described numerically as 13. Or the reverse. 13 was 1.

I wrote the riddle out again. This time I replaced the Arabic numeral 1 with *echad.* Then I gave the riddle a fractional value.

This enciphered Old Testament passage could be described numerically as 39 is echad.

This enciphered Old Testament passage could be described numerically as (13x3) is echad.

Was I looking for three Hebrew words with a Hebrew letter value of 13? Or was there a Hebrew word that had a numerical value of 39? Even if I figured out the answer to the first two questions, I still had to grasp how 39 became *echad*, or 1, or whatever esoteric symbolism my father had in mind. Had I made progress—or not?

I sat back in the chair and scratched the sides of my head. I closed my eyes, hoping that some epiphany would strike my imagination. It didn't. All I could picture was a whirlpool of numbers and letters circling a giant drain.

When I opened my eyes again, the block of twenty-five Hebrew letters caught my attention. At the very center was the letter *tav*, the last or twenty-second letter of the alphabet. I sat up a bit straighter. In the block of twenty-five letters, *tav* would be the 13th letter of the cipher. Surely, that couldn't be an accident. Could it?

"*tav, tav, tav, tav, tav, tavtavtavtav*." I kept repeating it like some sort of mantra that would reveal the secret. It didn't, but I continued chanting the word, anyway. I stopped. A final "*tav*" sneaked out like a rebellious child.

"You're beginning to …" I didn't finish the mumbled sentence. The word *beginning* reminded me of one of my father's verse clues and a possible connection to *tav*. I slapped the page when I found it.

Ecclesiastes 7:8
Better *is* the end of a thing than the beginning thereof: *and* the patient in spirit *is* better than the proud in spirit.

Of the five verses, the third verse talked about a beginning and an end. The passage said that "better is the end of a thing than the beginning …" *tav*, this "last" letter, was the 13th from the front and back in the cipher. The fourth verse described the person speaking in the text as the "first and the last." The larger context of the verse revealed that it referred to Jesus. Was this intentional on my father's part, or had he accidentally used a verse that referred to the "first and last"? Was this a clue or a theological statement?

I put my elbows on my desk and rested my head in my hands. The pieces must fit, but how? How did 39 fit into all this? I'd made progress. I could feel it. I could almost see it. No, *see* wasn't the right word. More like, sense it. I could sense that I was close to solving the riddle but didn't quite have it yet. I sat back in my chair and sighed.

I felt eyes on me. A soft voice made me turn my head.

"Making any progress?"

Chapter 29

Revelations

Cadence stared at me with sad, tired eyes. I reached for her hand. It was cold still.

"You okay?" I asked.

"Tired," she said weakly. She looked at the table beside the bed. "Working on Dad's riddles?"

I shrugged. "Had to do something while I waited."

She nodded. "How long have I been out?"

"This time, nearly 24 hours. You had me pretty scared there for a while." I averted my gaze for a moment. "I had to call for help. I'm sorry. I know you didn't want me to bring you here, but I didn't know what else to do. You were delirious and having convulsions."

"Sorry you had to see that. I'm a real mess, aren't I?" Cadence squeezed my hand.

I returned the pressure. "We're both a mess, Sis." I cleared my throat and tried a brighter smile. "The good news is, the doctor said you can get out of here in a couple more days." Her face brightened with a weak smile. "He recommended you get some help. Said if you didn't, you might not make it. He said you really should consider rehab."

Cadence gasped. Her hand tightened around mine until it started to hurt. Her face wrinkled in a mask of terror. Her eyes moved back and forth like a trapped animal's, looking for a way to escape.

"Timbre, you can't let them send me back. I can't go back."

"You need help, Sis. You've got to kick this addiction, or it is going to kick you." I collapsed into the chair beside her bed, still holding her hand. I scooted over to face the bed. "Cadence, I found you on the floor of your apartment passed out and lying in a pool of your own vomit."

She sobbed. "I wish you'd left me there to die. I rather die than go back to rehab. They …" She didn't complete the sentence. Her thin frame convulsed with sobs. Tears ran down her cheeks and soaked her pillow. Desperation and fear glinted in her eyes. "Timbre, you've got to promise me that you won't let them send me back."

She squeezed my hand harder. Her knuckles turned snowy white, and the tendons that ran over her hand tightened like wires. Still, I struggled to form a response.

"Swear to me, Timmy! If you've ever loved me at all, swear to me that you won't let them take me back."

I shook my head. "I don't … I don't understand, Caden. Why don't you want to get help? Why don't you want to get better?"

She sobbed and tried to speak. I waited. She squeezed her eyelids tight together like she was trying to forget something or wish it away. Finally, she began to speak in a whisper. I leaned close.

"I was a horrible, uncooperative patient at rehab. I'd yell and scream and bite and scratch. They often kept me drugged up, restrained, or in a padded room. Part of it was a terrible anger at Dad for sending me away. Most of it, though, was an act. I just wanted to make everyone else as miserable as I felt."

I nodded, urging her to continue.

Her breathing started to come in short, weak pants. "This last time in rehab, after one of my particularly bad displays, I was left restrained on a bed. It was late at night." She paused, and her brow wrinkled. "It was a Sunday, the second Sunday in

January. They were short-staffed. I'd been screaming and yelling for hours, so I was left in a room unattended. One of the nurses found me there. He …" She couldn't continue. She was weeping now uncontrollably.

Horror constricted my throat. I guessed what was coming, and something inside of me broke. My eyes blurred. My face burned with her shame and my growing anger.

"No one … paid any … attention … to my screams." She finally managed to get it out in a despairing cry of anguish. The terrible shame and brokenness of her entreating expression tore the foundation out from under my broken heart.

"Oh, Caden," I groaned. "I'm so sorry. Did you report it? Did they do anything?"

She shook her head. "Who are they going to believe? A patient who was always yelling, screaming, and causing problems?" Her weeping settled into short, gasping sobs. In a nearly inaudible voice, she pleaded, "Promise me, Timmy. Promise me you won't let them take me back to that place."

She was silent then, her eyes dilated and fixed on mine, shaking and waiting for me to speak. Two things fixed inexorably in my mind. First, I didn't care what I had to do, my sister would never go back to that rehab place or any other she did not want to. Second, the man who had assaulted her would pay a terrible price. I didn't know how or when, but somehow or someday, he would be held accountable, even if I had to break him in pieces with my own hands.

"I swear to you, Cadence. I swear that you'll never have to go back to that place as long as there is one beat left in my heart." I squeezed her hand and gently brushed back her hair. "I swear."

A look of relief and gratefulness replaced the pleading in her eyes. The shadows of pain and violence remained, but they retreated deeper, into darker places. Cadence tried to curl her lips in what was probably supposed to be a brave smile but didn't get much further than tiny wrinkles at the corners of her mouth. Her lashes fluttered closed. Her hand lost some of its tension.

I reached over with my other hand and held hers in both of mine. I watched until her breathing returned to a slow, steady zephyr. Finally, I released her hand and sat back down at my makeshift desk. I couldn't fathom what I'd just heard. What a sick, twisted world we live in.

I tried to focus on my father's ciphers, if for no other reason than to take my mind off my sister's horrible revelations, but they blurred in front of me. My father, in what I could only see as some harebrained attempt to make us earn our inheritance, had locked it out of our immediate grasp. If I was going to take care of Cadence until she was better, I would need some real money. I put my hands to my head and rubbed my face.

"How are you going to make this work, Timbre?" I asked into the quiet room. "You are dead broke, and you can't even solve a 13-word riddle." I sighed. I wanted to scream with frustration and regret at my impotence. I had wasted so much of my life in pursuit of the inconsequential, and here I was when I was needed most, without any real means to do what was necessary for someone I loved.

I laid my head down on the makeshift desk. After several minutes of silence, Cadence called to me from the bed.

"Timmy," she said in a voice that held a new note of strength. I turned to look at her. She didn't open her eyes and didn't say anything else right away. I reached for her hand. She whispered, "The first cipher is at Bash."

Chapter 30

At Bash

"What do you mean, Caden? What is at Bash?"

She didn't even flutter a lash.

The first cipher is at Bash. Where was Bash, who was Bash, or what was Bash?

I waited for her to say more, to explain. I stood there for fifteen minutes in silence, trying to make sense of her words. The EKG next to the bed showed the slow, steady beat of her heart. She appeared to be sleeping, so I released her hand and sat back down.

I booted up my laptop and searched the internet for a person or place named Bash. A computer command language called Bash could execute commands from a shell script, whatever the heck that meant. There was a Department of Justice investigator named Bash, a journalist named Bash, a rapper and singer named Bash, and dozens of other people with the same name. There was even an internet page on "How to Access Your Ubuntu Bash Files in Windows."

Next, I tried an internet search on *where is Bash located in the Bible?* All this returned was the name of a place called Bashan, the ancient kingdom of Og. But maybe my sister had fallen asleep before she had completed her sentence. Maybe she had meant to say *Bashan.*

For the next two hours, I researched *Bashan* and its Biblical history. Bleary-eyed, I finally pushed back from the desk and closed my eyes. My fingers still rested on the keyboard. They tapped restlessly, waiting for my brain to send the little inspired impulse of neurons down the nerve pathways that would guide them to the correct combinations of keys and eventually the answer to my sister's enigmatic words.

"The first cipher is …" I paused, letting that hang in my mind. "The first cipher is... at Bash." Something about Bash sounded vaguely familiar, but I couldn't place it. I flexed my fingers. They were hungry to press the keys and solve this mystery, but I didn't know what direction to give them.

At a loss of what else to look for, I typed in the six words I'd heard my sister whisper.

"*The first cipher is at Bash.*"

I clicked my mouse on the search-glass next to my words. I stared at the results and slapped the table with both hands. "Son of a gun." I looked at my sister, half expecting to see her smiling at me with that sparkling grin of hers—the one she'd wear when she'd solved one of my father's riddles and had come to share her pleasure with me.

This time, there was no sparkling grin, just closed eyes sunken in the haunted, haggard visage of someone who had walked through the valley of death and not come through unscathed.

"You are brilliant, Cadence," I whispered, anyway. "Thank you."

I turned back to my computer with new enthusiasm. My sister had not whispered six words, but five. *Atbash*, not *at Bash*.

Atbash:

Atbash is a monoalphabetic substitution cipher originally used to encrypt the Hebrew alphabet.

She had probably known from the first time she'd looked over my shoulder when I had been working on the cipher at her kitchen table. I was happy to feel like an idiot for not having identified this bit of interesting Biblical history sooner.

I scanned the article, muttering a soft, "Huh." Atbash cipher was formed by mapping the Hebrew alphabet in reverse. In other words, the first letter became the last. *aleph* became *tav*.

Biblical scholars had found what appeared to be an Atbash cipher used several times in the Old Testament, mainly in the book of Jeremiah. It was one of the oldest recorded uses of a cipher in antiquity. The unaccounted use of the name *Sheshach* in Jeremiah's prophecies against Babylon had led to this discovery. Sheshach in Hebrew was spelled *shin, shin, koph*. This word, whether of a person or place, had remained a mystery until someone had realized *shin, shin, koph* was the Atbash-ciphered form of the word *Babel* or *Babylon*, spelled *beth, beth, lamed.*

I looked again at the passages of Scripture that had accompanied my father's cipher riddle. Now in hindsight, it was obvious. In the Atbash cipher, first recorded in Jeremiah, the end was the beginning.

Jeremiah 51:41
How is Sheshach taken! and how is the praise of the whole earth surprised! how is Babylon become an astonishment among the nations!

2 Samuel 24:12
Go and say unto David, Thus saith YHWH, I offer thee three *things*; choose thee one of them, that I may *do it* unto thee.

Ecclesiastes 7:8

Better *is* the end of a thing than the beginning thereof: *and* the patient in spirit *is* better than the proud in spirit.

Revelation 1:17

And when I saw him, I fell at his feet as dead. And he laid his right hand upon me, saying unto me, Fear not; I am the first and the last:

Isaiah 46:9-10

Remember the former things of old: for I *am* God, and *there is* none else; *I am* God, and *there is* none like me, Declaring the end from the beginning, and from ancient times *the things* that are not *yet* done, saying, My counsel shall stand, and I will do all my pleasure:

The passages of Scripture were clues to solve the riddle. The only passage that didn't seem to fit was the one from 2 Samuel that talked about three and one. Did that fit into the pattern? Or maybe it was just meant to be a false lead, a dead end. For now, I'd set it aside.

I opened a spreadsheet on my computer and numbered twenty-two horizontal spaces, then found the Hebrew font in the drop-down menu. After some experimentation, I figured out which keys represented the Hebrew letters on my keyboard. Above the numbers, I wrote out the Hebrew alphabet from beginning to end. Below those first two lines, I again wrote out the Hebrew alphabet, but this time in reverse.

Hebrew Alphabet	א	ב	ג	ד	ה	ו	ז	ח	ט	י	כ	ל	מ	נ	ס	ע	פ	צ	ק	ר	ש	ת
Hebrew Place Value	1	2	3	4	5	6	7	8	9	10	11	12	13	14	15	16	17	18	19	20	21	22
Atbash Cipher	ת	ש	ר	ק	צ	פ	ע	ס	נ	מ	ל	כ	י	ט	ח	ז	ו	ה	ד	ג	ב	א
Hebrew Place Value	22	21	20	19	18	17	16	15	14	13	12	11	10	9	8	7	6	5	4	3	2	1

I was now ready to solve my father's cipher. Hebrew was read right to left, so I started with the *Bet* in the top right corner of my father's cipher. Using my Atbash cipher key, *bet* became *shin*. I continued with this method until I reached the *tav* at the center of the cipher, the 13th letter. *Tav* became *aleph*. The last had become the first. The end had become the beginning. Right there at the center of the riddle, at the 13th letter, my father had encoded a symbolic motif of Jesus. I grudgingly admitted it was pretty clever. The book of Revelation, the last book of the Bible, was supposedly the testimony of Jesus given to the apostle John on the Isle of Patmos and future events. It also included the last recorded words of Christ in the Bible.

I continued solving the cipher until every Atbash letter was converted back into its original Hebrew plaintext, then I compared the ciphered text and the plaintext side by side.

ש מ ע י ש	ב י ז מ ב
ר א ל י ה	ג ת כ מ צ
ו ה א ל ה	פ צ ת כ צ
י ג ו י ה	מ ר פ מ צ
ו ה א ח ד	פ צ ת ס ק

My Hebrew was rusty, but I attempted a translation of the Hebrew passage without help from the internet. The first three letters of the text spelled the word *shama* or *hear*. The proper name of Yahweh—spelled *yod*, *he*, *vav*, and *he*—had been used twice. The final three letters of the text spelled *echad* or *one*.

I finally realized what I was reading. This was the *Sh'ma Yisrael* or better known simply as The Shema. It came from Deuteronomy 6:4. I looked up the English translation.

Hear, O Israel: YHWH our God is one YHWH:
- ***Deuteronomy 6:4***

For millenniums, this verse had been the center of Jewish worship and prayer, the focal point of both their morning and evening prayer services. More importantly, from a theological sense, this verse summarized the monotheistic essence of Judaism. Yahweh was ONE.

Then I saw it. I saw the solution to my father's riddle. His riddle had said,

You could summarize this enciphered Old Testament passage numerically as 39 is 1.

The final two words of Deuteronomy 6:4 in Hebrew were *Yahweh ONE*. These two words were the monotheistic bedrock of Judaism and of Christianity that had risen from those Judeo roots. All Hebrew words had a numerical value. One or *echad* had a value of 13. I also remembered that the personal Hebrew name of God had the numerical value of 26. Combined, these two Hebrew words equaled 39. These words combined as a theological statement unequivocally stated that YHWH was ONE. As a theological statement flavored by the numerical value of the words, you indeed could say that 39 is 1. If 39 was

1, then would 3x13 also be considered ONE? Was my father trying to make a clever statement about Christian trinitarianism?

Three in one, first and last, beginning and the end, were all clues my father had provided. These ideas were part of things I'd been taught as a child and up through high school. They were beliefs I had once held. They had brought me comfort and given direction to my life. But not anymore. An inexplicable sense of loss shook me. Loss and sadness. But wasn't that part of growing up? I didn't believe in Santa Claus or the Tooth Fairy anymore, either. In some ways, I wished I could go back to that simpler time of innocent faith.

What I didn't understand was how my father had kept his faith in the Bible. He was not an ignorant man. He was a successful man. The ciphered riddle I had just solved was super smart and clever on many different levels. So how could he still believe? Why had he not rejected his faith like I had?

I pushed the table away and stood. I turned toward Cadence. I needed someone to talk this out with. She was sleeping peacefully. Maybe it was my imagination, but as I turned away, was that a faint smile on her face?

Chapter 31

Devarim

I stared at the seven blank spaces on the computer screen in front of me. Only two hours left on the answer countdown clock until I could try again. This would be my second attempt to answer my father's first Lazarus cipher riddle.

I reread the 13 words of instructions that accompanied the riddle.

Provide the numerical reference to where it is found in the Biblical texts.

The reference to the ciphered passage was Deuteronomy 6:4. The numerical part of the reference was only 6 and 4. That only required two numbers. The numbers 6 and 4 spelled out in English were 7 letters. But SIXFOUR had not been the correct answer.

I swore silently. What good was the correct answer if I didn't know how to enter it accurately? I rubbed my hair with both hands and pushed back from the makeshift desk. I stood and stretched my arms to the ceiling, wincing as fire ran through my ribcage.

Come on, Timbre, think.

How hard could it be? The enciphered passage was six Hebrew words and twenty-five Hebrew letters.

What did my father mean by *numerical reference*? Maybe I was looking at this all wrong. I slapped my forehead with my hand. Why would the answer have been in English if the cipher had been in Hebrew?

I sat down at my computer and searched for the Hebrew word for Deuteronomy. Deuteronomy came from the Greek words *deuteros nomos,* meaning *second law*. In Hebrew, Deuteronomy was *Devarim*, which means *the words*. *Devarim* in Hebrew was spelled with the five Hebrew letters *dalet, beth, gimel, yod,* and *mem*. If I added the 6 and 4 from the reference to those five Hebrew letters, I had another seven-character answer that would fit in the provided answer blanks. But 46דברימ didn't look congruent—part Hebrew letters and part numbers. If my father's instructions were to be taken literally, I needed a numerical answer. Did that mean I should calculate the numerical value of 46דברימ using only numbers? On my notepad, I wrote *Devarim* 6:4 using the numerical value of the Hebrew letters.

4, 6, 13, 10, 20, 2, 4.

I gently rubbed my bruised chest. The countdown on my laptop rolled through the final minutes. I made my decision. I would give a straight numerical answer. When the countdown read zero, I refreshed the page. The seven blank spaces returned along with the instructions.

I entered the numbers 4 6 13 10 20 2 4 in the 7 blank spaces and pushed *enter*.

Chapter 32

New Problems

I waited. The screen turned blue and then a new page appeared.

Your answer is correct.
This page will be redirected to the next ciphered riddle in 60 seconds.

I quietly played a drum roll on my makeshift desk with the palms of my hands. I looked over at Cadence. She lay there in a death-like sleep. Her shallow breaths were barely perceptible. The smile on my face faded. I turned back to my laptop, vaguely dissatisfied. It would have been nice for her to share this small victory with me.

"One down and only six more to go," I said to myself and waited for the next ciphered riddle to appear.

A few seconds later, a new square of Hebrew characters showed on the screen. The riddle was just ten words, the instructions only eight. This time, though, instead of only twenty-five characters, there were two *hundred* and twenty-five. The square block of Hebrew text measured fifteen by fifteen. Just like in the last cipher, five verses as clues followed the ciphered text. I read the riddle several times and then skipped the ciphered text to read the verses below.

This enciphered Biblical passage describes 381 becoming 391 by 39.

Summarize using only three words from the passage.

א ב ר ע ל ם ו ט ש ב ע פ י ה מ
ג ג פ ג א ב ר ע מ ג ש ם ב ג ו
א ר ש ם מ ג ט ו פ ל א ם ב ר ע
צ מ פ א ג נ ס ש ל א מ ג ד פ ס
ש א ב ר ע ש פ ד ו א ב ר ם ע ב
ג י ע נ ס ש ם מ ג ד פ ד ש א ב
ר ע ס ג ה ב ש ל א מ ג נ ב א ם
ש א ב ם ר ע ל י ט ם ד כ פ ט מ
ג ב ש ת ל א א ב ר ע ג ו כ א ש
ם ג ק מ ש מ ג פ ו ד ש ם א ב ר
ע נ ס נ ל פ ם ל א מ ג ב ת ש ל
א ע י ב פ ם כ ע ל ג י ש ב ם ל
י ט י א ק ב י ע א כ פ ט ל כ ע
ל ט ז פ ש ח ט ל ב י ם ע א ע פ
ם ם י ה מ נ ג פ ג ש ע ם פ י ה

Isaiah 49:8
Thus saith Yahweh, In an acceptable time have I heard thee, and in a day of salvation have I helped thee: and I will preserve thee, and give thee for a covenant of the people, to establish the earth, to cause to inherit the desolate heritages;

Acts 25:11
For if I be an offender, or have committed any thing worthy of death, I refuse not to die: but if there be none of these things whereof these accuse me, no man may deliver me unto them. I appeal unto Caesar.

Genesis 22:11

And the angel of Yahweh called unto him out of heaven, and said, Abraham, Abraham: and he said, Here *am* I.

Isaiah 52:7

How beautiful upon the mountains are the feet of him that bringeth good tidings, that publisheth peace; that bringeth good tidings of good, that publisheth salvation; that saith unto Zion, Thy God reigneth!

1 John 5:7

For there are three that bear record in heaven, the Father, the Word, and the Holy Ghost: and these three are one.

I stared at the screen, not a single coherent thought forming in my mind. I waited. Maybe the answer would rise from the depths of my mind. But nothing came. I got nothing. Nothing at all. Just a ten-word, fifty-six-letter riddle that made even less sense than the first one.

I pushed away from my desk. I'd been at this for hours and I needed a break. The clock on the wall read three-thirty in the afternoon. I needed some fresh air. The nurse had told me about a quiet garden area built into a courtyard at the back of the west wing.

If only Cadence was awake and able to talk. She'd slept nearly all of the past two days since she'd told me about rehab. The doctor had stopped by several times and assured me she was going to pull through, told me that rest was her best medicine right now. He showed me how her vitals were getting stronger. He'd said she would wake up soon and want to eat. I gave a gentle squeeze to her hand and left the room.

I nodded politely to the man and woman at the nurse's station. The only sounds I heard were the beep of a monitor somewhere and the occasional squeak of my shoes on the waxed floor. I walked on by the bank of elevators. I was tired but not tired enough to get into one of them. I turned down the intersecting hall toward the stairwell. As I reached the stairs and pulled open the door, I paused to watch a hunched, gray-haired gentleman with a cane and a bouquet of roses hobble up the hall on a mission of mercy. I started down the steps with a smile on my face, making my way to the walled garden on the ground level.

A path that split around a fountain dissected the center of the small enclosure. The fountain was red, and a weak bubbling of water rose from the center of the top bowl. The water dripped and tinkled over the petaled sides and then fell in drops, threads, and splashes to the larger-petaled bowl below. A pump in its basin sent it back to the top in an endless journey. Parallel to the path, benches faced the fountain. I sat down on one. It was hot, but the fountain's moisture cooled the dry air a few degrees, and the bubbling of the fountain was soothing.

In the corner of the garden, against the outside wall, a Paloverde tree grew, its green trunk and wiry, skeletal branches and twigs supporting sparse leaves ideal to this desert climate. Dozens of multicolored butterflies fluttered and glided down to the *Buddleia Davidii* growing in various locations throughout the garden, attracted to the profuse blossoms that covered these so-called butterfly bushes. A small pale-blue butterfly glided down onto the edge of the fountain. Its translucent wings opened and closed slowly like it was cooling itself or possibly as if unwinding the complicated internal mechanisms that actuated its beautiful, living windsails.

When heated voices from the other side of the wall disturbed the garden's peaceful charm, I lifted my head. A woman's voice raised in anger. A car door opened and then slammed, then a man's deep voice asked angrily, "What's your problem, woman?"

I cocked my head sharply at the sound. I knew that deep, Spanish-flavored, guttural bass.

"Can't you read?" the woman demanded. "You are parked in a fire zone. It says *NO PARKING*."

"I'm waiting for a friend."

"Well, wait somewhere else. You are blocking access to the dumpster."

The man muttered, "Dumb …" I didn't catch the last word, but I didn't need to.

What sounded like several bags thudded on the ground, and the woman's voice rose into an outraged shriek. "What did you call me? You stupid Mexican thug. You …" She followed that up with a string of Spanish expletives that were clearly not compliments.

I stood as the confrontation devolved into more vulgar, English-laced Spanish profanity. I leaned down and crept over to the wall where one of the butterfly bushes grew a foot above the top row of bricks. I balanced on a decorative stone and peeked over the wall through the screen of leaves and flowers. Just as I feared, it was Raul Ramos. I ducked back down.

Raul's right arm was cast, but he was still the big, mean thug who had beaten me in the alley the week before. I swore silently. How had he known I was here? Did Benito Silva know about my sister? If he did, would he use her to get to me? I knew the answer to the last question even if I didn't know the first two. Benito would use anyone to get what he wanted. That included my sister.

I groaned. I had to get Cadence out of the hospital, and I had to do it without being seen or followed. A silent rage gripped me. I would not let Benito drag my sister into my mess.

I hastened back to Cadence's room. I'd only been gone a few minutes, but fear made my imagination run wild. Maybe they'd already paid a visit to her room. It was all I could do to keep myself from running.

I needed to calm down. Cadence was fine. I was fine. They wouldn't do anything in the hospital. They were waiting outside to grab me. I tried to think about it rationally. The wall of the garden where Raul was parked commanded a view of the front of the hospital as well as part of the lot where my sister's car was parked. They were waiting for me to leave the hospital, but it was unlikely they were going to assault it with guns blazing like some Hollywood movie.

By the time I got back to the room, I had calmed myself a little, but I still burst in half expecting to see her bed empty. I let out a breath when she was still there, sleeping peacefully. The yellow roses on the table next to Cadence's bed brought me up short. They were the roses the old man had been carrying.

I stepped back out and went to the nurse's station.

The nurse glanced up. "Yes, Mr. Plummer?" she asked with a weary look.

"Do you know who brought the flowers?"

"The old man said he was a family friend. He left the flowers here and said they were for Cadence Plummer."

"He didn't give his name?"

"He didn't. We usually don't interrogate old gentlemen who bring our patients flowers." Her tone carried a mild reproof. "Did you check the notecard attached to the bouquet?"

I gave her an embarrassed grimace. "I didn't."

She just raised an eyebrow.

I managed a smile. “I’ll check the card. Thank you, Miss Stachel.”

I returned to the room. I pulled the notecard from the flowers and slit the tape that sealed it with my thumbnail. As I opened the card and read the message, my hands trembled.

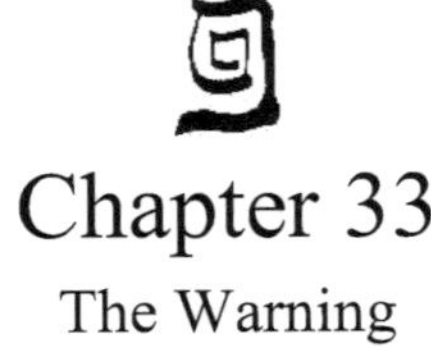

Chapter 33

The Warning

The note shook as I read the message.

You are being watched
You will be followed
You must be careful
You can trust n one

I dropped the card on my temporary desk and sat down. Again, I skimmed the list and considered each line. The final warning that *we could trust none* was perhaps most unsettling—for several reasons.

Who was giving us this warning? Was it the old man, or was he just the messenger? And how did this person know we would be followed? Benito or one of his men wouldn't have sent the warning. It could have been the man in the old Crown Vic. It certainly wasn't him who delivered the note, but he could have sent it. But why would he have sent a warning? Who was he working for? Why would he care? How had he found us? If I could trust none, then even the note was suspect. But why the warning, then? Was there something going on that created a more sinister threat than Benito?

I looked over at Cadence. Could it have something to do with her? The nurse had said the man had asked for Cadence Plummer. Did she have bigger problems than she had told me about?

I grabbed the note and crumpled it up. Maybe some sicko was just trying to mess with my mind. Sow doubt and suspicion between the two of us.

A couple of things were certain. First, I needed to do something and do it soon. Benito was a real threat. I had to deal with him first. I couldn't take the risk that Benito might drag Cadence into this. I had to protect my sister. But how? If Benito knew about the hospital, he probably also knew what car she drove and where she lived.

I was trapped. I didn't even have enough money to rent a cab, let alone flee the hospital and put us up in a safe place until I could figure out what else to do. I clenched my teeth and felt the veins in my neck throb. What if I marched out there and beat Raul half to death? We might be able to escape then.

I shook my head to rid myself of the urge. There was no guarantee that I'd be able to beat Raul. The hospital probably had cameras, and then I would be a fugitive for aggrivated assault. This option might make me feel good for a while, but it wouldn't help Cadence. She needed a safe, peaceful place to heal and regain her strength, a place where she could fight her demons and not fall back into the destructive behavior that had pulled her down in the first place. Somewhere I could protect her.

My gaze fell on the notes and laptop on the makeshift desk. Dad's ciphers didn't seem all that important right now. I turned to look at the broken, haggard shell that was my sister. I groaned. Here when I was needed most, I was again handicapped by my failures. I had no friends to turn to, no money, no credit, no special rainy-day fund, no fancy jewelry to hock. My whirling thoughts stopped short. My attention shifted to my father's briefcase. I actually did have some jewelry—my mother's wedding and engagement ring. The diamond must be worth something.

I dismissed the thought as quickly as it had formed. I'd knock over a bank or a convenience store before hocking my father's things. I'd fallen pretty far in life but not that far. The briefcase was my talisman of bad luck but also the only tangible evidence of a better life. Of a better time. Of what might have been if I'd just done things differently. The treasures inside were even more important to me than my own life. Again, I considered my sister. But were they more important than hers?

The urge to perform my yearly ritual, to relive the best and worst memories of my life, overpowered me. I pulled the briefcase toward me across the table. I started to reach for the hidden panel in the bottom but stopped. I stared at the manila envelope stuffed in the pocket. With unsteady hands, I removed it from the case and dumped its contents out on the desk. The note from Eric Pincer fell out. I smoothed it flat and read it for the second time. I looked into the envelope, then turned it upside down and shook it until the check fell out on top of the note. I stared at the check for several long minutes as a battle raged in my mind. Turning to Cadence, I studied the lines of suffering etched on her face. With clarity I wish I'd had at other turning points in my life, I knew the decision I made in the next few seconds would change my future forever.

Sweat broke out on my forehead. I clenched my teeth and flexed my fingers. I picked up the check and held it outstretched between my hands, just staring at it. Finally, I folded it, slid it into my shirt pocket, and stood. I watched Cadence for a long time. A peace I hadn't known in years soothed my troubled mind. I took a deep breath and let it out real slow. I leaned over the bed. I gently kissed her forehead and left the room.

Chapter 34

Decisions and Dead Ends

I was back at Cadence's bedside two hours later. I'd managed to sneak out the back door of the hospital without being seen. At least I hoped so. I held her boney fingers in my hand, and my forehead lay against the edge of the bed. In my pocket, I had two hundred Ben Franklins. And in my heart, for the first time in a long time, I felt all right. Not because of the money, but because I'd done something that wasn't totally selfish. Now on the blackboard of my life, there was finally a single mark on the unselfish side. I liked how it felt.

I must have fallen asleep with my head against Cadence's bed because I woke up to the movement of my hand—Cadence squeezing my fingers. I lifted my head. She made a brave attempt to smile. I returned it.

"Good to see you awake," I said.

"Good to see you too."

Cadence's mouth drooped, and shadows hung beneath her lower lashes. But it was resignation in her sunken violet eyes that made my heart skip a beat. If she was going to climb out of this valley of death she'd wandered into, she'd have to find something to live for, something to fight for.

What could I say? What could I do that would help her relight the spark of life in her beautiful eyes? I sat there silently for a long time. I'd never been a big talker. Cadence had been the effervescent one. I'd always been happy to just listen to her bubbly brook of words, ideas, and interests. Right now, I couldn't find two words to put together in my mind that didn't sound trite or stupid.

"You were right about the cipher," I finally said. Maybe it was my imagination, but did I detect a glimmer of interest deep in her eyes?

"It was Atbash, of course. But I thought you said 'at Bash.' So, like an idiot, I spent hours looking for a person, place, or thing named *Bash*."

Cadence looked down and her cheeks wrinkled at my self-deprecation. I sat up straighter in my chair. "You wouldn't believe how many famous people are named Bash. For a while there, this being a Hebrew cipher, I even looked for a place in the Bible named Bash. That turned out to be another dead end. The closest I found was Bashan, a kingdom ruled by some guy named Og."

Cadence was staring at me now. She had forgotten herself in the rehearsal of my quixotic quest to solve the Atbash cipher. Maybe I could keep that interest alive.

I leaned forward. "What do you think this Og fellow looked like?"

Her lashes fluttered at my unexpected question. She shrugged but kept her eyes locked on mine, waiting for me to continue.

"I think he was some big, ugly, one-eyed ogre holding a large wooden hammer."

Cadence's weak laugh rang out like a brittle bell. "You can be such a goofball, Timmy," she said softly. "So how did you finally figure it out?"

"Well, after I had exhausted all of my brilliant ideas with no success, I finally just searched for the six words I thought you said. 'The first cipher is at Bash.' I typed 'at' and 'Bash' as separate words, not knowing they were a single word. That didn't matter, though, because the first search engine result was about the mono-alphabetic cipher called Atbash." I shrugged. "I felt foolish. But I've gotten used to the feeling of having a kid sister as a genius."

"I wish," she said wistfully. "What kind of genius blows their future on drugs? What kind of person …" She didn't finish.

The sparkle in her eyes faded as her pupils dilated into a haunted look that pierced my enthusiasm with icy fingers of dread. Could there be something more? I couldn't imagine anything worse than what had happened to her at rehab. I scratched my head to try and hide the shudder that passed over me.

"So how did you know it was an Atbash cipher, anyway?" I forced a grin.

"I recognized the Bible reference to Shishak in Jeremiah. Dad told me about it one time. He said scholars believed that Jeremiah's use of Atbash was one of the oldest uses of a cipher ever recorded." Cadence fell silent after the admission.

Fresh sorrow filled her eyes. I was losing her. "Please tell me you didn't also have the answer to the riddle figured out as well."

Cadence shook her head.

"Well, do you want to know?" I prompted.

She just shrugged like it didn't matter.

"Come on, I've spent days working on this. Aren't you just a tiny bit curious? Even a teeny, tiny bit curious?"

Her nose wrinkled and small curves broke the slack lines of her mouth.

"Okay, I'll take that teeny, tiny smile as a *yes.*," I sat back straight in the chair like a proud student about to explain to his classmates how smart he was.

"Dad's riddle read,

'You could summarize this enciphered Old Testament passage numerically as 39 is 1.'

What little Hebrew I remembered is a bit rusty, but after converting the block of Atbash-ciphered text back into plaintext, the twenty-five Hebrew letters turned out to be a passage in Deuteronomy chapter 6, verse 4. It reads in English,

Hear, O Israel: Yahweh our God is one Yahweh,

You with me so far?"

Interest brightened her eyes again. "Go on."

"This statement in Deuteronomy 6:4 is the foundational monotheistic statement of the Old Testament. It clearly indicates the God of the Bible is 'One.' At first, I didn't understand how this verse might satisfy Dad's riddle until I remembered that each Hebrew letter also has a numerical value associated with it."

"Right."

I gave her a wry smile. "Something I'm sure you already knew. The long story short, the Hebrew statement of One Yahweh or Yahweh is One, however you want to look at it, is an important theological truth that has the numerical value of 39. *One* in Hebrew is echad, which has the numerical value of 13, and *Yahweh*, the proper name of God in the Bible, has the numerical value of 26. Therefore, if Yahweh is One, then by extension of the Hebrew value of its letters, we might also say that this two-word Hebrew phrase might also be understood as 39 is 1. Voila! We have the answer to our riddle."

Cadence made a weak clapping gesture against the bedsheet. "Impressive."

Judging by the soft, warm light in her eyes, she meant it. Before she could retreat into the shadows of her night, I continued with animation I actually felt. "Dad wasn't just content giving us a riddle to solve. I think he worked in some clever deeper meaning."

Cadence dropped her gaze and spoke quietly. "He was like that, always pushing the boundaries between fun and learning. He'd often throw in several layers of meaning or ciphers within a cipher to see if I was paying attention. I hated it when he stuck his riddle or cipher back on the refrigerator with a note that told me I'd only solved the first level, or I'd only gotten the most obvious meaning. He'd always remind me, 'Mediocrity is for those too lazy to fight for—'"

I finished with her. "Their God-given genius."

Tears welled up in Cadence's eyes. Big drops rolled down her cheeks. "I broke his heart, Timmy. It must have been devastating for him to see the mess I made of my life, to see the gift God had given me squandered."

I cringed at the truth of her words. They might as well have been taken from my own mind and off my own lips. With a violent twist of my head, I expelled the recriminations. I wasn't going to go down that road right now. I had to steer this conversation away from the failures of our past. So I plowed ahead as if her depressing self-condemnation had not interrupted my explanation.

"As I was saying, I think Dad was trying to make a deeper point with his riddle. Did you notice that the riddle and the instructions that followed are both sentences of 13 words each? In his verse clues, he included Revelation 1:17 that talks about Jesus being the first and the last. In the context of the Hebrew alphabet, this would be *aleph* and *tav*, the first and last letters. If you look closely at how Dad arranged the cipher, the center letter is *tav*—the 13th letter. In Atbash, *tav* would have been *aleph*, the first letter."

As I paused, she tilted her head to one side and pursed her lips. "I'm not sure I'm following."

"I think what I'm trying to say—" I stopped and started over. "In Dad's riddle, he said that one might summarize 39 as 1. If this is the case, then mathematically, one might postulate that 13 times 3 is also 1. Correct?"

She nodded hesitantly, but then her mouth formed a silent *O*. "So you think that Dad was trying to make his own theological statement? Some mathematical symbolism related to the trinity?"

"Not sure. I've never been able to wrap my mind around that concept completely. But yes, he did believe that the Father, Son, and Holy Spirit were all separate but a single manifestation of the One God of the Bible."

Cadence lifted herself on her elbows, struggling to sit up a bit in bed. "So you think because *echad* or 1 has the numerical value of 13, that Dad by making his riddle 13 words, and that by including verses that spoke about Jesus being the first and the last and by extension the *aleph* and the *tav*, and that by arranging the letters of the cipher so that *aleph* and *tav* were the 13th letters, he was saying in a really clever way that Jesus was God."

"Exactly!" I snapped my fingers. "You have to admit it's pretty cool. Granted, I don't necessarily agree anymore with what Dad believes, but if his use of 13 in the riddle was intentional, it was pretty darn clever."

Cadence offered that warm smile again. "I don't know if he meant to do it, Timmy," she said softly. "But that is how he thought, how he saw the world. He loved the Bible. Saw it as a limitless mine of treasure in all the literal and spiritual meaning those words might imply."

Silence lingered after her words. I don't know what Cadence was thinking, but I felt strangely happy at that moment. Content that my father believed. Unaccountably hopeful in the knowledge of his faith. How had I lost that kind of faith?

Cadence's words brought me back to the present. "So … did you start on the next riddle yet?" Her expression seemed to suggest that she didn't want me to keep her company in her haunted valley of memories.

I scratched my head and cleared my throat. "I did, but only after a couple of incorrect answers on the first one. I'm already stuck again. The new riddle makes even less sense than the first. Do you want to take a look?"

She pushed herself upright in the bed.

I stood and grabbed my computer. "Scoot over."

With some difficulty, Cadence made room for me on the bed, and I sat down beside her. My back rested on the headboard. I clicked on a webpage tab with my index finger. The page where the second cipher had been read, *This page has expired.*

I scrolled across my laptop's mouse pad with my finger until I found the refresh button at the top of the page. I clicked it and gave Cadence an apologetic grin. The grin disappeared when the page refreshed.

A new message appeared on the screen.

You are no longer eligible to participate. You have forfeited your inheritance.

Chapter 35

Forfeiture and Fortitude

Cadence jerked her head in my direction and pointed at the screen. "What does that mean, Timbre?"

I sighed and laid my head back. Finally, I said, "It means I forfeited any rights I might have had to my inheritance."

"How did you do that? You just told me that you've been working on the ciphers the last few days." Cadence grabbed my arm with icy fingers. "Did Dad make it so you'd be disqualified if you gave the incorrect answer more than once?"

"No, Sis. It was nothing like that. I cashed my check. Remember Eric told us we could solve the ciphers or cash out for twenty thousand?"

Cadence gaped at me. "Why in the world would you have done that? You get it wrong a couple of times, and you just give up?" She scooted herself up further in the bed and her eyes bore into mine. "You quit? I would have helped you. Why did you do it, Timbre? Dad wanted you to have the inheritance. Why?"

I avoided my sister's suddenly passionate gaze. I lifted my hands. "It's complicated, Caden. I don't even know where to begin."

"Try!"

I sighed again. "If you remember the last time we talked, I asked you for money to enter a poker tournament. Jenny and I had just finalized the divorce, and I was broke. Poker was a release. It helped me forget about my problems and the pathetic dead end my life had become. It wasn't cool to ask you for money. Maybe I needed someone to talk to, but in any case, I just asked for the money instead of telling you all the sad details. When you refused, I said some nasty things to you." I ventured a glance at her. "Sorry for that. What you and Dad had was special, and I shouldn't have tried to soil it with my ugly words. I can't even say that I was ever really jealous. I guess I was just bitter, lonely, and trying to make someone else feel some of my pain."

Cadence squeezed my arm. "I'm sorry, too, Timmy. I was not able to help you or even myself when you called. I was in the middle of a real bad drug binge and fighting with Dad. He wanted me to get back into rehab. He was threatening to cut off all financial support. I was a mess."

I let out a long sigh, accepting her words. After a minute of silence, I said, "Well, it got worse for me from there. I started hocking everything of value that I could find. I maxed out my credit cards, and then I finally started borrowing money from a loan shark named Benito Silva. He's a crime boss here in Phoenix. He's into gambling, money laundering, prostitution, drugs. You name it, he has a hand in it."

She shuddered and put her hand on my arm.

"I didn't know it at the time, but he was setting me up so that I would have to do his dirty work. I got into a high rollers game, and I had nearly a perfect hand. I bet big and lost. He'd played me like the fool that I am. He needed someone to bring drugs into the downtown Phoenix court system, and I was his way in."

"How much did he get you for?" Cadence asked.

"One hundred grand," I said without meeting her gaze.

Cadence tried to whistle through her cracked lips. "You bet a hundred grand on a poker game? Wow, and I thought I was the crazy one of the family."

We were silent for a while.

Cadence finally asked, "So if you were in all this debt, why did you give up on trying to earn Dad's inheritance? That surely would have covered your debts with plenty left over to start a new life."

"That's what I thought, too, when I received the call from Dad's lawyer." Since we were baring our souls, I met her gaze, not attempting to veil my pain. "You know, I literally had a gun to my head when the phone rang."

Cadence sucked in a ragged breath, and her fingers dug into my arm.

"I'm not kidding, Cadence. I had the gun cocked and pressed right here," I said as I made a gun with my fingers and pushed it against my temple. "If the phone had rung half a second later, I wouldn't be here right now. But with that phone call, I saw a way out. For the first time in years, I had hope that I might be able to straighten out my life and do it differently."

She thought about my words for a few minutes, then asked, "Do you think that the phone call was a coincidence, Timmy?"

I shrugged. "I don't know, Caden. I guess I'd like to think that it wasn't a coincidence. I'd like to think it was Dad reaching out to me from the grave. Or even that the God Dad believed in had a hand in it. But I don't believe that." I shuddered at the memory.

"Half a second. That was cutting it close."

I shuddered again. It seemed like a different person's life. Like a lifetime ago. I no longer wanted to take the coward's way out. I wanted to fight. What had changed?

I met my sister's gaze. Her violet eyes sparkled with a new intensity. I turned away. It was her. For the first time, I understood that a worthy, satisfying life came from some sort of service to others. Maybe it was just me, or perhaps all humans were built that way, but I needed to know that my life had meaning outside my own wants or desires. I'd tried it the other way and ended up with a pistol to my head and half a second between me and whatever waited on the other side of that invisible line between life and death.

Cadence gently shook my arm. "Why did you give up on the dream? After getting your reprieve, why did you cash Dad's check and forfeit the rest of the inheritance?"

"You," I said simply.

Cadence struggled to scoot over some so she could face me more directly, and her brow furrowed. "What do you mean, 'you'? You did this for me?"

I lifted a finger to my cheek. "See these bruises on my face?"

She nodded.

"I got these after I left the lawyer's office the day you and I learned about Dad's will. Benito Silva came to collect his money. He said he'd give me a beating like that again every week until I came to my senses."

Cadence gasped.

"Yesterday, I went back to your apartment to get some of our things. I also stopped at my apartment to pick up more clothes. On my way back here, I was followed by someone in a blue Crown Victoria. You know the type of car, the ones cops drive. My guess is, the guy was a *PI* hired by Silva to keep track of me. Whoever it was, I managed to lose him on the way here. Or at least that is what I thought until this afternoon when the flowers and note came."

"The flowers and note?" Cadence asked. "You didn't get them?"

My face heated. "No, Sis, I'm sorry to say, I didn't even think of it. It was a little stooped-over, gray-haired man with a cane that brought you flowers."

"You have any idea who he was?"

"No idea. But I'm getting ahead of my story about cashing the check. When I was out in the back garden this afternoon stretching my legs, I saw one of Benito's men waiting. I don't believe in coincidences. Maybe I didn't lose the man following me yesterday, and he told Silva I was here. Or maybe Silva's guy was following me, too, and I didn't know it because I was so focused on the other guy. In any case, there are at least two people, possibly three or more, interested in us."

She released my arm and scooted closer. "That's not good, Timmy."

I waved my hand dismissively. "Frankly, it doesn't matter. I promised you that I wouldn't let them send you back to rehab. I needed money to get you somewhere safe where you can get back on your feet. Back to the sparkling, happy, and healthy sister I remember. I won't let Benito drag you into the mess I've made of my life."

"Like the mess that I dragged you into?" Her wry tone hinted at sarcasm.

"That's different," I said without thinking.

The spark of fire in my sister's eye told me I was treading on dangerous ground. She moved away from me. "So, what you are saying is that I'm the damsel in distress you get to step in and rescue. You get to feel good about yourself again, and all is well?" Heat simmered in her voice. "Did you forget about the part where you came to me first, to get help solving Dad's cipher so you could get the inheritance?"

I held up my hands. "I didn't mean it like that, Caden. If you want my help, I'd like to help you. You tell me to walk, and I'll leave. But I want you to know that being here with you this past week has helped me see how much I've missed in life by being such a selfish dirtbag. You've already done more to help me than I'll likely ever be able to repay."

She pressed her lips together, studying me.

Tears blurred my vision. "I need your help right now, Caden, maybe even more than you need mine." I swept my hand in an all-encompassing gesture. "I need this right now. I don't have anything else to live for. You've given me that much. I hope you won't take that away from me."

Tears streamed down my sister's face. She scooted back against the bed and then leaned on my shoulder, grabbing my hand and holding it tight.

We sat there in the cold hospital room, tears rolling down both our faces, holding onto each other, our lives hanging in the balance. Two terrible, broken people with nothing left to lose in life but the thread of a renewed relationship. A sibling bond that had miraculously withstood time, neglect, and destructive self-interest.

After several minutes, Cadence spoke with a new note of strength. "This is how it is going to work. You help me get out of the hole I've dug myself into, and I'll help you do the same. We'll use the twenty thousand to get out of here. Someplace safe where I can recover and we can work on the ciphers. When we solve them, we split the inheritance."

I started to protest.

Cadence cut me off. Her expression was fierce and inflexible. "Nonnegotiable, Timbre." She pointed to the door. "We solve it together, and we split the inheritance, or you walk out of here right now with your twenty grand, and I never want to see you again."

I said nothing for some time. Finally, I awkwardly stuck out my right hand. "Okay, you have a deal."

Cadence shifted away enough to turn and meet my hand with hers. We shook. A new resolve burned in her eyes. The shadows that had been there were gone or hidden. She released my hand and slid down in bed.

"So … where do we go?" I asked after a few minutes of silence.

"Grandfather's cabin," she replied without opening her eyes.

Why hadn't I thought of that? Quiet and off the grid, it was the one place Benito Silva would not know about.

A moment later, she whispered, "You'd better find me some food so I can walk out of here. I'm not going to start this partnership with you pushing me out in a wheelchair."

As I stood, my hand brushed against the crumpled note lying on the table. I hadn't told Cadence what it said. Words came to my lips, but I swallowed them back. I wasn't sure why.

Chapter 36

Recuperation and Preparation

I returned from the hospital cafeteria with a bowl of chicken noodle soup and carrot slices and an apple, wrapped in a napkin. I set the food down on a clean corner of the table I'd been using. Stacking my notes and papers into a neat pile, I placed them inside the briefcase, closed the lid, and set it on the floor. I slid the table over to the bed so Cadence could reach the food.

I watched as Cadence fed herself with a shaky hand, her face fixed in firm lines.

"I think we should leave tomorrow morning, early," I said. "If you are serious about walking out of here under your own power, then you'll need time for that food to work, and another night's rest won't hurt either. Eat what you can, then I'll get you some more food later tonight. By morning, you should have enough juice to make it out to the car."

"Okay." She bent her head and, she sipped some broth.

"I need to go pick up a few things we'll need for the trip. I'll be back in an hour." As I stood, she looked up with a question in her eyes. "I'll tell you about it when I get back."

An hour later, I returned to find Cadence sleeping, and as far as I could tell, I'd made my exit and reentry without Raul's knowledge. Her bowl of soup was empty, and a couple of the carrot slices were missing. The apple lay untouched. A little pink colored her sunken cheeks, a good sign.

I took my backpack into the bathroom and closed the door. There I set out a sweater and pair of blue jeans for Cadence. They might be a little bit loose, but they'd work. Next, I removed a one-foot piece of three-inch PVC drainpipe and thirty feet of one-eighth-inch braided steel cable. Carefully, I wound the cable on the inside of the PVC pipe until only three feet stuck out of each end. With a couple of wraps of electrical tape, I secured the cable to the pipe so it wouldn't come unwound prematurely. Finally, I encircled the loose ends of the cable with tape until only six inches of the bare cable was visible at the ends. Satisfied, I tucked the taped ends of the cable into the pipe and placed it back into my pack.

Back at my sister's bedside, I watched her sleep. Was I doing the right thing by taking her out of the hospital? Every few minutes, her hand would twitch, but other than that, she appeared to have gotten over the worst part of the withdrawal.

I was a little worried about my plan to disable Raul's truck. So, every two hours, I climbed the six flights of stairs to the hospital's top floor and walked over to the big window at the end of the west wing that overlooked the parking lot. The truck was there at eleven. At one a.m., it was gone, the spot empty. My gut twisted. Had someone come to relieve Raul? If someone else was out there waiting, I didn't know where they were or what they looked like. I had no plan to deal with this contingency.

I'd check every hour until four a.m. If the truck was not there by then, I'd have to postpone our departure until I could figure another way to slip out without being followed.

Back in Cadence's room, I paced around the bed. I'd made the decision, and now I wanted to act. Patience was not one of my few virtues.

The truck was not back by three. At four—still nothing. I resigned myself to coming up with another plan. I stared blankly out the window, trying to figure one out. Then Raul's truck appeared at the far end of the parking lot. It rolled down the first two rows of cars and then parked in the shadows at the end of the third row.

Chapter 37

Disabled Detective

The luminous dial on the lawyer's Rolex Submariner read 4:08. The Crown Victoria had returned to its stake-out on the far side of the parking lot. If the man inside held true to form, he'd head to the convenience store across the street for his first cup of coffee and a couple of doughnuts. The man was probably a former detective, judging from the methodical way he kept vigil. If he was retired, he might be a *PI*. In any case, it didn't matter. Whoever he was, he had to be dealt with.

A few minutes later, the detective exited his car and started for the store. 4:15. Right on schedule.

The lawyer got up from the bus bench a hundred and fifty feet away. He picked up his cane, and in a slow, bent shuffle, he headed down the sidewalk toward the Crown Vic. From the corner of his eye, he kept the detective in view until he entered the store. When the lawyer came even with the detective's car, he stepped off the curb and tumbled into the strip of grass next to the vehicle. His cane flew from his hand and landed beside the old cop car. The lawyer made a show of staggering up, taking two steps to retrieve his cane. As he bent back down to grab it, he leaned forward to steady himself against the car with his left hand.

Concealed in the palm of his right hand, shaft pointing upward, was a sharpened ice pick. His body shielding his actions from any curious eyes across the street, the lawyer slid his arm between the tire well and the tire. A quick, hard plunge was all it took. As he straightened, he left the ice pick hilt deep in the back sidewall of the tire. Unless the driver felt up and around the backside of the tire, the pick would not be found. Best of all, the tire wouldn't leak until the wheel started to spin and dislodged it.

The lawyer fumbled with his cane, checking himself in the driver's side mirror. His gray wig remained in place, his mustache firmly attached. He brushed the grass and grit from his brown tweed slacks with his free hand.

With a limping walk, he shuffled across the lot toward Cadence Plummer's Honda Civic. From his hunched position, he glanced sideways at the convenience store. The detective was still not in sight. Even if the man had seen him stumble, it wasn't likely that he would find or even look for the ice pick hidden in the sidewall of his tire.

The problem was, the flat tire would only slow the detective down. He'd figured that out the previous night from listening to Cadence and Timbre's conversation through the wireless microphone he'd hidden in the flowers. Timbre had eluded the Crown Victoria on the way to the hospital. What the lawyer knew and Timbre did not was that the Crown Victoria had arrived at the hospital shortly after Timbre. So if Timbre had lost the tail earlier, the detective had followed him by other means.

Unless the detective was communicating with someone else, which was doubtful, he'd followed Timbre remotely. That meant a tracking device on the Cadence's Honda Civic. That also meant that the lawyer needed to find and remove the device before Cadence and Timbre left the hospital sometime later this morning. He needed to weed the playing field. Right now, there were too many variables, too many unknowns.

The lawyer glanced at his watch. It was going to be close. The detective's average time in the store was four minutes. It had been three minutes and ten seconds since he'd plunged the icepick into the man's tire.

The lawyer stepped into the early morning shadows between Cadence Plummer's Honda Civic and the faded black Chevy Blazer parked next to it. He looked over his shoulder as the detective stepped out of the store across the street. Concealed for the moment, the lawyer surveyed the rest of the parking lot. Then he crouched and ran his gloved hand under the car's rear tire well. He found nothing and moved backward, searching under the car frame. He found the tracking device on the metal frame where the bumper was attached. With a tug, he removed the matchbox-sized magnetic tracker and placed it on the ground behind the tire. No one would be the wiser until the Honda started to move.

In a hunched, stumbling shuffle, the lawyer headed away from the Civic. He kept the Blazer between himself and the Crown Victoria on the other side of the parking lot. By a circuitous route, he made his way back to his Audi and slid into the driver's seat, satisfied he'd remained unseen. Concealed behind the dark, tinted windows, he removed his disguise.

With the detective's car out of commission and the tracking device dealt with, he should not have to worry about unwanted guests at his reunion. At least, that is what he hoped.

Chapter 38

Saboteur

I stepped into the Phoenix pre-dawn a few minutes before sunrise. I had to hustle. There was no way to sneak up on Raul Ramos and his truck once the sun rose at five-thirty and dispelled the shadows I would need for my approach. I wore dark sweatpants and a black shirt, my dark-blue U of A baseball cap snug on my head. I crossed over to an alley that paralleled the rows of cars at the back of the lot. When I reached the wall that divided it from the hospital parking lot, I jogged down to the end where it met the next cross-street. The wall shielded me from any curious eyes.

At the end of the alley, I walked through the opening where pedestrians could enter the hospital lot from the adjacent sidewalk and stopped behind the white Ford pickup parked in the corner of the first row. Raul's black truck sat two rows up and directly in front of me. Thankfully, shadows lingered at this end, the glow from the parking lot lights fading near Raul's truck. My objective was the Hummer parked back-to-back with it.

Raul's driver-side door opened. I froze, crouching against the Hummer, gathering myself to make a run for it if Raul walked around his vehicle. I bent farther down and looked under the Hummer. Two cowboy-boot-clad feet emerged below the jacked-up truck and planted on the asphalt. The truck door closed. The boots only moved a step to one side and then the other, like their owner was stretching his legs.

A faint whiff of cigarette smoke tickled my nose. I waited and watched the boots. I crawled toward the front of the Hummer, Raul's legs still in sight. The cigarette smoke grew stronger. The door opened, and the boots disappeared.

I removed my backpack and rolled under the front of the Humvee. With my backpack on my belly, I slowly pulled myself forward, the rough asphalt catching my clothes. I slid out from under the Humvee and inched my way under Raul's truck. He shouldn't see me unless I did something stupid. Slowly, I inched forward until I was looking up at the U-joint that connected the driveshaft to the transmission case.

From my backpack on my chest, I removed the pipe. I pulled the loose ends of the cables from the pipe and threaded one end of the cable through the U-joint. Spanish rock blared from above, momentarily paralyzing me. I let out a long breath as Raul turned up the music. As the trumpets blared, I fished a U-shaped cable connector and a small adjustable wrench from the pocket of my backpack. I tightened down the connector and gave it a light tug to make sure it was secure.

Next, I took my electrical tape from the pocket of the pack and secured the PVC pipe to a brake line with the rest of the coiled cable. My heart beating fast now, I removed the other loose end of the cable from the pipe and carefully threaded it through the truck's wiring harness and fuel lines. I retrieved another cable connector out of my pocket and secured my loop around the truck's vitals. I slid the wrench and tape back into the pocket of my backpack and zipped it up, then briefly assessed my work.

If my plan worked, as the truck started to move, the cable would pull from the pipe and wind around the driveshaft. The driveshaft was three inches in diameter, so about ten turns, I guessed. Just about the time the truck was accelerating out of the parking lot, the other end of the cable would rip the guts out of the truck. With any luck, the violent mixture of electrical and fuel lines might cause additional damage.

All I had to do now was get away from the truck without being seen. Or at least without being apprehended. I slid back out the way I'd come. I waited for a moment. I took a deep breath and then walked in a crouch away from the back of the Humvee. When I'd gotten to about where I figured Raul would see me if he was looking in his mirrors, I straightened up and strode away with the backpack strung over my shoulder. I didn't look back.

Chapter 39

Discharged

I opened the door to Cadence's room with a satisfied smile on my face. I stopped and stared. My sister sat on the edge of the bed. She had tried to do something with her unkempt hair but had failed miserably. Still, she looked pretty good sitting there in the new blue jeans and pale blue sweater I'd bought her.

When I got over my surprise, I let the door go and stepped into the room. "Wow, didn't expect to see you up and ready to go. Figured I'd have to drag you out of bed."

Cadence gave a brave smile.

"How are you feeling?" I asked.

"Better. Really weak, though. My legs are shaky when I try to stand. I don't know how far I can walk."

I crossed the room to her. "Don't worry about it, Sis. I got your back. All we need to do is make it down to the first floor and the rear exit of the hospital."

"Let's go," she said with a determined nod of her head.

She rose unsteadily, and I waited to see if she could stand on her own. I handed her a Phoenix Cardinals baseball cap so she could conceal her unruly hair. She took it and stuffed her hair into it as best she could, then pulled the brim down low. She was wobbly, but she clenched her jaw tight, and she didn't sit back down. I could only imagine how difficult it must be for one who had always been so active and vital to feel nearly helpless and dependent.

"Okay, then," I said as she took slow, careful steps toward the door. I picked up my backpack and slung it over my shoulder. With my right hand, I grabbed my briefcase. My left hand was free to help Cadence if she needed it. I'd better let her get at least out the door before I offered. Even small victories were important.

As we stepped into the hallway, I offered my arm. She reached around my waist, and arm in arm, we strolled toward the elevators. No one tried to stop us. We didn't look to see if the nurses' station was occupied.

Cadence trembled a little bit as we stopped in front of the elevators. I pushed the down arrow. I'd have to make another exception about elevators.

"You okay?" I asked without looking at her.

"I'll make it. Just try to stop me."

I chuckled at her bravado.

We made it to the ground floor, and I led her toward the back exit of the hospital. As we pushed through the double doors, the cool Phoenix morning air hit us in a refreshing wave. I led Cadence over to one of the benches by the door, and she nearly collapsed with what sounded like a sigh of relief.

I looked down at her, lifting one eyebrow.

"I'll be fine," she snapped with a bit of heat in her voice.

I placed my briefcase and backpack down on the bench next to her. "I'll be right back. Don't catch a ride with any strangers," I said over my shoulder as I walked away.

Chapter 40

Breakout

I retraced my steps down the alley that ran behind the hospital parking lot. This time, I used a pedestrian opening halfway down the alley. As I stepped through the wall, I paused. Raul's truck had not moved. Cadence's car sat just two rows over. Once I passed the first row of cars, I'd be visible to Raul. I calculated the distance and time from where I stood to my car. I did the same for Raul in his black truck. I estimated that I'd make it to the car first if we ran at the same speed. With his delayed reaction time, his arm in a cast, and the time it would take to get out of his jacked-up truck, I should be okay.

I walked toward my sister's car, watching the big truck. I'd wait to start my sprint until he opened his door. Nothing happened. I made it to Cadence's car without any interference. As I opened the door, Raul leveled his eyes on me, but he didn't move. I got in and started the car. He started his truck.

I started to pull out and head to the back of the hospital, but instead, I turned toward the black truck. This way, I'd pass in front of it one row over. When I drew even with Raul, I rolled my window down. He revved his motor. I saluted him as vulgarly as I knew how. I shouldn't have, but that white heat had taken hold of me again. He returned the gesture and grabbed his steering wheel with his big hairy left hand.

I sped away. Raul's engine roared behind me, and I glanced in the rearview mirror. The big truck leaped from its parking space like a hunting dog released from its leash. As the truck started to turn and follow me, white smoke puffed from beneath, along with a thrashing noise that sounded like Godzilla with a ball and chain in a junkyard. I slowed down. Black smoke started to rise from the truck. As I turned the corner, I saw the flames.

When I pulled into the circular drive at the hospital's back exit, Cadence rose from the bench. By the time I slowed to a stop, she was waiting at the curb. I couldn't help the smile on my face. I jumped out of the car and ran over to where she stood. Before I could grab my briefcase and backpack, she had the passenger door open and was sliding in. I raced back to the car with my things and opened the rear driver's side door. I set my things on the seat and closed the door. We scooted out of the parking lot three smooth seconds later.

Heart soaring, I grinned at Cadence as we drove away. "So far, so good."

Cadence side-eyed me. "Did you have something to do with that screeching and thrashing sound I heard?"

I just smiled and turned onto McDowell. As we passed the front of the hospital, I swiveled for a peek at the parking lot. Flames fully engulfed the black truck, and Raul threw his arms into violent gestures at the fiery conflagration. I slapped the steering wheel and grunted.

Cadence raised an eyebrow. . "What did you do?" she asked seriously.

I winked at her. "Ask me no questions, and I'll tell you no lies."

Cadence just shook her head when I wouldn't say anything further. She closed her eyes and laid her head back on the seat. She sighed, and a smile crossed her lips. I looked over at her with fondness. I hadn't felt this good, this alive, in a really long time.

As the adrenalin and elation from our escape started to wear off, I remembered to check my mirror. No vehicles that I recognized followed us, but I mentally cataloged those behind me. After several blocks, I entered the on-ramp for the 202 and headed toward Tempe. A few of the vehicles exited as well. My heart beat faster. There were still no cars behind me that I recognized, but I couldn't be sure if I was being followed.

I turned north on 87, crossed the Salt River, then swung back northeast. None of the cars that exited with me onto the 202 had followed. I watched the mirror for the next ten miles and then finally started to relax.

An hour and a half later, we passed Mazatzal Peak on our left. A few minutes after that, I blinked and nearly missed Rye, Arizona. Payson was ten miles ahead.

Cadence hadn't said a word since leaving Phoenix. She was out cold. The smile that had been on her face had melted into a haggard mask. My mirror revealed shimmering waves of heated air rising off the miles of empty asphalt behind me. I let out a long, satisfied breath.

I checked my mirror once more. A speck of light flashed. Then I remembered the note.

You are being watched
You will be followed
You must be careful
You can trust n one

Chapter 41

Café of Memories

Hunger soon gnawed my anxiety into submission. Payson was just up ahead, and as planned, we would stop, eat, and get supplies. The highway entered the center of town on a sweeping, downhill curve. Along this main drag, private cafés, coffee shops, markets, and other local businesses competed with national chains that had invaded this quiet western town.

On the right, a familiar long low building came into view. I slowed and turned into the parking lot of a Payson landmark, the Pinon Café. In 1951, the café had opened as the Knotty Pine. I knew the place well, although I didn't recognize the new sign out front. I parked in the back between two dirty trucks. I wasn't going to take unnecessary chances.

After I shut off the ignition, I reached over and gently shook Cadence's arm. "Wake up, sleepyhead."

Cadence opened her eyes with a groggy, confused look. It took her a few seconds to get her bearings. "Where are we?"

"Payson. You hungry?"

Cadence shook her head. "Not really." She sat straighter in the seat and looked around.

"Want to watch me eat, then?"

She gave a short laugh. "Not particularly. I've seen you eat before, it ain't pretty. But I'll come with you, anyway. I should try, whether I feel like it or not."

Inside the café, rustic, knotted-pine paneling covered the walls. Stained beams and rafters held up the ceiling. A smiling waitress at the register welcomed us and told us to sit where we liked. I made my way over to a familiar table in front of the middle window. We sat across from each other and gazed out at the passing cars. Cadence turned away from the window and assessed the room with a soft snort.

"Not much has changed, has it?"

Did she shake her head in agreement or to clear her misty eyes? The memories were strong here. It had been the three of us at this table the last time.

Cadence stared out the window again with a faraway look. My stomach rumbled, and I picked up a menu. Sighing, Cadence dragged hers over and perused it. By the skeptical expression on her face, not much interested her. She tossed the menu down with a sour turn of her lips.

The waitress came after we'd had a couple of minutes. She was cordial but in a no-nonsense western kind of way. She pulled a pencil out of a mass of brown hair bunched up tight in a hair clip at the back of her head. "Coffee or something else?"

"Coffee would be great," I said.

"Regular or decaf?"

"Regular." I glanced at Cadence.

She shook her head and pointed at the menu. "No coffee, but I'd like to order the spiced oats."

"Anything to drink, darlin'?"

"A glass of orange juice, please."

The waitress made a couple of notes on her pad and turned to me. "How about you?" She smiled.

I closed the menu. "The steak and eggs."

"How would you like them cooked?"

"Medium well on both."

The waitress gave a quick nod, and the pencil disappeared again into her brown curls. She gathered the menus. "I'll be right back with your drinks," she said as she walked away.

I looked at Cadence and smiled. "Do you remember the last time we were here?"

She nodded. "It was just the three of us." She surveyed the room again before continuing. "It was summer break, my first year of high school. You had just finished your second year of college. We spent two weeks at the cabin."

Her face took on a beautiful glow as she closed her eyes. I didn't want to break the thin cord of that pleasant memory by interjecting my own recollections, so I just watched the range of emotions play across her face. Like the sun that begins its journey in the darkness before the break of day, the memories of a happier time broke through the shadows. It started with a glow that lightened the infinite shades of night. It intensified by degrees until the gray gave way to golden rays of dawn. Then, like the aborted day of an Alaskan winter, the memory hung for a moment just above the horizon and then sunk back into the shadows.

Cadence opened her eyes. The veil of sadness descended, once more obscuring the happier memories. We just stared at each other. Even though her sorrow had returned, I was strangely hopeful. She was still capable of remembering the good times. They had risen above the darkness in her mind. I had seen them. In that, I also saw hope for myself. It was something we could build upon.

"How did we fall so far?" she asked. "We were happy back then, weren't we? It wasn't all just some figment of my imagination, was it?"

"We were happy," I said. I was quiet for a minute. "Sure, we had what we thought were problems, but we were happy. We knew where we belonged. That we were loved."

"What happened, then?" Cadence asked earnestly.

I traced the woodgrain on the table with my finger as I thought about my sister's words. How *had* we ruined our lives? I glanced up at Cadence. "Poor nutrition, maybe?"

She drew her head back and frowned. "We didn't eat right?"

I tapped the table. "Each ring marks a year in the life of the tree. Some are thin and barely noticeable, and others are thick and strong. When the tree had a good year, a year with good water, nutrients, and sun, the rings grow thick and strong. Bad years are marked by thin rings of growth. A good tree, one with good roots, could last through the bad years, the years when it didn't get all the things it needed to grow healthy and strong. I guess what I'm trying to say is that we stopped feeding our trees—our lives—the things that kept us healthy and strong."

The waitress returned and slid our food in front of us. "Anything else I can get you two?"

I looked at Cadence and she shook her head.

"No, thank you."

I dug into my meal with gusto. Cadence pushed her food around the plate. Eventually, she took a spoonful and chewed and chewed like a kid who just couldn't seem to make themselves swallow. Finally, she sipped her orange juice and forced it all down. Doggedly, she took another bite. All the while, the finger of her free hand followed the tree rings on the table.

By her last bite of oatmeal, her face had turned slightly green. She pushed the bowl away and gave it a sideways glance. "That was almost as bad as the withdrawal."

She grabbed the edge of the table with both hands, closed her eyes, and steadied herself. Was she going to pass out or vomit? Finally, after a couple of minutes of slow, steady, deep breaths, she opened her eyes and said, "Well, what doesn't kill you makes you stronger. Right?"

I smiled and nodded. My sympathetic look goaded her to stand. She had always been strong and independent. I knew she hated the fact that she was so weak and sick she struggled to eat something as bland as oatmeal. The fight in her strengthened me in some way. There was a spring in my step as we left the restaurant. Just a few more miles to the cabin and more happy memories.

Chapter 42

The Homestead

Outside of Payson, Highway 87 merged with 260. The evergreens along the road became denser. Twenty minutes later, we drove through the town of Pine, and a few minutes after that, Strawberry. Fifteen minutes outside of Strawberry, 260 and 87 split again, and we turned north on 260 and the Zane Grey Highway.

A familiar excitement rose as we turned off 260 and onto the dirt forest-service road, #149. By a beeline, we were only five miles from our grandfather's hunting cabin. By the winding route we had to follow, it was closer to ten. Thirty minutes later, we arrived at the old, rusted gate with a jolt. Cadence opened her eyes and looked around.

"We're here."

The old ranch gate was a simple affair of horizontal, one-inch bars welded on top of several upright pieces of angle iron. With my finger, I reached into the open end of the second horizontal bar closest to the hinged post and pulled out a dirty key. I held it up to Cadence.

I walked over to the other side of the gate and unlocked the padlock that connected two ends of a heavy chain. It took a bit of wiggling to finally get the lock to work. As I swung the gate open, the rusted *No Trespassing* sign rattled with a haunted sound against one of the bars. A single strand of rusty baling wire held it by one corner.

I pulled through the gate and closed and locked it behind me. We drove through the heavy woods to the small clearing surrounded on three sides by a dense forest. Straight in front of us at the far side of the clearing, Grandpa's cabin stood, its pine logs gray with age, its back facing the yawning chasm of Clover Creek. A raised wooden porch of rough-sawn beams fronted the cabin. A rail of peeled pine logs intersected the porch's supporting beams, giving it a cozy, protected look. Three ribbons of black steel studded with bolts banded the heavy plank door. To the right was a large shuttered window. A barn and wooden pole corral sat on the right edge of the clearing.

We drove up to the cabin and parked. I looked at Cadence excitedly. I felt strangely young again. I saw a similar expression on her face. We got out together.

I walked past the cabin and stood at the edge of the rent in the earth that was Clover Creek. A mile away, I could just make out where it merged with West Clear Creek and wound westward for twenty-five miles like a varicose vein.

We called it Grandpa's cabin, but it was actually our great-grandfather, Henry Plummer, who had homesteaded this island in the national forest of Central Arizona wilderness. A young Henry had gone west with a group of Bostonian emigrants in 1876. They had settled near the base of the San Francisco peaks and named their new town after the stripped pine tree they used as a staff for an American flag. That landmark gave the town its name of Flagstaff.

Henry Plummer had run a sawmill for several years out of Flag then had gone into ranching. As the area became more populated, he became restless and sold out and settled on a ranch outside of Green Valley, later known as Payson. Henry never quite conquered his wandering spirit. He was also an avid hunter. These two traits kept him roaming the lonely forests of Arizona. One of his favorite places to hunt was at the intersection of Clover and West Clear creeks. By the early

1900s, there was talk of making all of it a national forest reserve. Henry had seen the writing on the wall and applied to homestead a section of land on Clover Creek later that year. He improved the property as required, and when the allotted time had passed, he received a land patent. After the entire area had been designated a national forest in 1908, Henry Plummer never again had to worry about neighbors or civilization encroaching upon his hunting grounds. The cabin had stayed in the Plummer family since then.

Cadence's shaky hand on my arm interrupted my thoughts. Together we looked out over the forested hills and gorges, the rock spires and ancient buttes. This beautiful place had been part of our heritage for over a century now. But it hadn't remained in the family without a fight. By the late 1900s, the Forest Service saw old homesteads as blisters on their domains and had done everything within their power to get rid of these blights on federal land. Grandfather Plummer had resisted these attacks and enticements with conviction. But it had been our father who had finally won the decisive legal battle that had protected the homestead and the cabin from the blind avarice of the federal bureaucracy, at least for his generation.

Now my father was gone, and I had given away my chance to maintain this legacy. Emptiness and apprehension assailed me.

I turned to Cadence. "It's up to you now, Sis. You've got to keep this in the family."

Cadence shook her head. "No, it's up to us, Timbre. We'll do this together."

Chapter 43

A Plummer's Poem

I gave Cadence a hand as she stepped up onto the wooden porch that surrounded the cabin and walked on shaky legs to one of the many dark knots on the right side of the door. She pulled out the head-high wooden knot in the fifth row of logs and stuck her finger into the cavity behind, then showed me the key with a grin. She unlocked the door, turned the handle, and pushed the door open. A bar of light played across the dark interior of the cabin. We stepped through together.

The cabin looked as I remembered it, large but not extravagantly so. The yellow logs of the bare walls, randomly spotted with dark knotholes, had been trimmed and fitted by Grandfather Henry's skilled hand. You could tell he appreciated fine work. The bottom layer of logs was so large I wouldn't have been able to encircle one of them with my arms had it been standing upright. Each layer became slightly smaller than the next as it rose to meet peeled log beams that supported the ceiling.

Two rooms divided the main living space unequally. The larger room in which we stood formed a long rectangle. A rock fireplace dominated the center of the wall on our right, the familiar bearskin rug on the floor in front. Some of the other furnishings were new. A leather couch faced the fireplace. Simple, four-legged tables separated the couch from two deep, inviting leather chairs. The chairs were the high-back kind you just wanted to curl up in with a blanket and good book. Each table held an assortment of books—the familiar, eclectic collection of western history, cowboys, mining, ghost towns, and natural history—between two cut-geode bookends. The dark-brown leather of Louis L'amour and the tan-and-red of Zane Grey mixed in for good measure.

Cadence and I walked over to the fireplace. Its tightly fitted and mortared gray stones rose from floor to ceiling. Eye-height at the point where the fireplace began to taper into a chimney, a thick slab of dark pine was secured to the stone for a mantel. Various specimens of Arizona gems and minerals the Plummer clan had collected over the years decorated the surface. I was drawn to the mantel with the same attraction I had experienced the first time my father had brought me here when I was seven.

I fingered the minerals and rocks. Some were displayed on wooden stands. Others lay scattered in between. I lifted the glittering purple amethyst geode down from the left side. As a boy, I imagined it was the most valuable thing I'd ever seen.

Cadence's voice at my shoulder said, "That's new." She tilted her head toward the framed photograph in the center of the mantel—the same one as from my father's briefcase. Dad was in the center with his arms around our shoulders. We were all smiling. Silently, we both stared at the photograph for a long time. Then, with a nostalgic shake of my head, I placed the amethyst geode back on the mantel and turned toward the main room.

"Dad has made some improvements since last time."

"He has," Cadence replied. "The couches and chairs are new. The end tables are the same."

"Yep. And …" I pointed to the kitchen at the far end of the room opposite the door we'd walk in through and gave a low whistle.

We went to inspect the granite countertop and the under-mount stainless steel sink centered on the far wall's only window. Cadence sat down at the kitchen table and watched as I investigated the cabin's upgrades. A single-lever chrome faucet decked the center of the sink. I peeked over my shoulder at Cadence. "Do you think it works?"

She laughed. "I doubt it is for show."

I lifted the handle. The water hissed out in a fully aerated stream.

"Running water?" Cadence said in reverent awe. "Remember hauling the water up from Clover Creek in five-gallon buckets?"

I nodded, still staring at the faucet. "Sixteen minutes down and twenty-eight minutes back," I mumbled. "We'd use water sparingly back then."

"These are also new." I gestured toward the shutters that covered the kitchen window, then pulled on the strap threaded through the log wall. Like a commercial garage door, the exterior metal shutter rolled up into its concealed nook above the window. Light poured into the cabin and chased away the remaining shadows.

I faced the three doors on the interior wall. I opened the first one closest to the kitchen. Once I moved inside, an ample LED light turned on. I poked my head back out of the room. "It's got lights, and he enlarged it some."

I turned and inspected the room more closely. From floor to ceiling, new pine shelves fully stocked with dry and canned goods lined the wall opposite the door. There was enough food to last us weeks. I leaned back out of the pantry.

"We won't starve. The shelves are full of food."

She drummed her fingers on the table. "Yeah, well that's more important to you than me, right now. But I'm happy you won't starve."

I chuckled and returned to my inspection. The first six shelves had been cut out of the right wall, and in an alcove halfway into the massive logs of the back wall, a refrigerator had been installed. I shook my head as I pulled open the door, half expecting to see it fully stocked as well. It was empty except for three bottles of AriZona Soda Shaq vanilla cream soda. I closed the refrigerator and stepped back to the door of the pantry.

"When did Dad do all this?"

"I have no idea." Cadence shrugged. "Last time I was here, it was as it had always been."

I closed the pantry door and returned to the main room. Against the cabin's front wall under the window sat a desk and chair. Crosscut of solid oak, densely grained and hard, and standing on four gnarled and twisted legs, the desk was a work of art. Amber epoxy had been poured into the gaps and seams and the entire piece sanded, polished, and oiled. It had been a massive tree. A new, floor-to-ceiling bookcase had been built into the wall next to the desk and filled with books. The bookcase was new. I got the impression my father had upgraded the cabin as a retreat he intended to spend more time in.

Cadence got up from the chair where she rested. With some nostalgic relief, we found the bunkroom unchanged—apart from a slight reduction in size due to the new pantry on the opposite wall. Two sets of bunkbeds still sat against each wall. Between them hung two compound bows and a pair of quivers full of competition arrows.

I walked over to one of the bows and ran my hands along the carbon-fiber curves. I looked behind me at Cadence. "Remember these?"

She nodded, and I saw a competitive flicker in her eyes. I turned away from the bows and stepped to the far bunk, the one

I'd always used. The mattress felt thicker as I sank onto it. The blankets looked new and clean, and the room had the faint smell of recent use. Cadence perched on the lower bed of the other bunk. We sat there in silence for a while. I didn't know what Cadence was thinking, but I remembered some of the great memories we'd had.

Finally, we rose to investigate the final room. Over the years, it had been used as a tack room, a woodshed, bulk storage, and primarily—because of its secondary door to the outside—a mudroom.

A window protected by another security shutter had replaced the door at the end of the room, but several well-placed LED lights gave it a bright and cheery look even without sunlight. It was no longer the dark, almost hall-like room I remembered, but rather boasted three new wonders of modern living.

Closest to us was a white porcelain sink with a single-handle chrome faucet. Next to the lavatory, a full-sized, claw foot, white enamel cast iron tub sat lengthwise to the wall. Opposite the toilet, which was centered under the window, a water heater hung on the wall. I turned on the hot water of the lavatory faucet. With a click and a quiet whoosh, the water heater lit.

I arched a brow at Cadence. "Doesn't look like we will have to bathe in the creek anymore."

"Or run to the outhouse," she replied with a rueful smile. "Only part of camping out up here I didn't care for." Her expression fell. "You know, I told Dad that one time."

I cocked my head.

"It was just after we moved back here from Virginia. I was in pretty bad shape. Dad asked if I wanted to spend some time at Grandpa's cabin. I told him I hated running to the outhouse at night and that it would be nice to have running water."

"What did he say?"

“He said that roughing it was part of the mystique of camping out.”

“Sounds about like him. So that was all?”

Cadence chuckled. “No, he winked at me and said, ‘Roughing it is getting a bit old for me, too, hon. I’ll see what I can do.’”

“Looks like he wasn’t joking about that.”

I stepped over to the tub and turned on the hot water. Cadence sat on the edge. A second later, a brief spit of air and a full stream of hot water poured out of the shower head. We watched the steamy water mesmerized. She stuck her hand into the stream and sighed. Her lips turned down. There was sadness in her eyes again. I wondered what she was thinking. Probably about Dad.

I wiped my forehead. The small room was starting to get hot and steamy. I turned off the tub and stood.

“Well, no more roughing it for you, Sis.” Cadence just sat there with her head bowed.

I leaned over the tub. On the wall, framed in wood, was a short paragraph of writing arranged like a poem. I tried to read the handwritten words behind the fogged glass. I rubbed the glass with my elbow. Cadence scoffed at my lame attempt and handed me a hand towel from the chrome ring hanging on the wall. I wiped away the fog and read the words.

Can you feel the water in your hair
A modern convenience without compare
Drop by drop it takes away
Every bit of the dusty day
Now that a Plummer has fixed the cabin
Can my Plummer now be glad in
Each day her face is clean and fair

Tears rose in Cadence's eyes. She stepped toward the tub and ran her finger slowly along the glass covering the poem. That's when I noticed it spelled CADENCE. My father had written the poem acrostically.

Cadence started weeping. The sorrow came in uncontrollable waves. Miserable, desperate, broken, mournful. I put a hand on her shoulder. She turned toward me, and I wrapped my arms around her. Her thin arms encircled me with surprising strength. Minute after minute, I held her as the pain poured out in wailing cries punctuated by gasping sobs. I'd never heard anyone cry like this, and it terrified me that one person could have such an endless well of anguish.

I don't know how long we stood there, but it seemed like a lifetime. All at once, the weeping stopped, and Cadence went limp. Her arms fell away, and she slipped through mine. I held tighter with my right arm and released my left. Leaning over, I slid my left arm under her legs and picked her up. I carried her from the bathroom.

Carefully, I laid her on the couch and then knelt beside her. I felt for a pulse. It wasn't strong, but neither was it weak. It was steady. I held my hand in front of her mouth, and her breath fanned my skin. Releasing the breath I'd held, I sat back and wrapped my arms around my knees as I stared at her. My eyes blurred. I made a brusque swipe at the tears.

I looked around the cabin. I could feel my father's personality, his presence in this room. I missed him too. He had been a good father, a good man. I had been a poor son. I hadn't lived up to his expectations, his standards, his ideals. I had rejected them, not because they were his, but because I hadn't wanted responsibility and the restrictions that went with them. And what did I have to show for it? A single, tenuous relationship I was rebuilding with my sister and a few thousand dollars in my pocket. Rejecting my father's standards and ideals hadn't brought me the freedom I'd expected. It had only brought me a different, more certain kind of slavery.

I took a deep breath and let it out slowly. Men and women with worse problems and less in their pockets had turned their lives around. They had managed to take a broken, seemingly hopeless situation and make it better. But how? I was beginning to see it had a lot to do with one's worldview. I needed a reason that wasn't about me. Cadence. I had that reason now.

With a dull ache, I realized I had had that reason all along. I'd ignored a long list of people in my headlong, self-serving rush to live life my way—my father, my sister, my wife, and friends. And those were just the people in my inner circle. I couldn't think of a single stranger I'd gone out of my way to help in my thirty-plus years of life. What a feckless life I'd led.

Could I break the destructive cycle permanently? Did I really want to?

Chapter 44

Then There Were Two

The silver Audi pulled into the parking lot of Kohl's Ranch Lodge, nestled in the ponderosa forest under the Mogollon Rim off Highway 260.

"How may I help you?" the receptionist asked as the lawyer stepped up to the front desk.

"I'd like a cabin for one night."

"How many in your party?"

"Just one."

She raised her eyebrow at that. "I do have a single room in the main lodge that is less expensive."

"No, thank you, I'd like a cabin. Cabin three if you have it." This got him another look.

"Cabin three is available."

The lawyer slid his platinum credit card across the counter and snuck a glance at his watch. He tried not to show his impatience.

A few minutes later, he was sitting at the cabin's kitchen table, using his cell phone to check on the tracking device he'd secreted in Timbre's briefcase. Yep. Still out of the service area. He'd virtually followed their journey earlier as they made their way up the Zane Grey Highway, slowed, and turned. Thirty seconds after that, the dot had disappeared.

He'd anticipated that they'd have nowhere else to go but the cabin, but he'd known for sure then. They would hunker down, and when he was ready to finish this, they would be right there waiting for him.

The lawyer walked out to his car and drove it around behind his cabin. Removing his duffel bag from the trunk, he returned to the cabin and threw it on the bed. He unzipped the bag, removed a small plastic case, and placed it on the kitchen table. Opening his wallet, he unfolded a photograph and laid it on the table next to the case.

They'd been brothers in arms, a bond some said was stronger than blood. The three of them had made a pact. They swore they'd always be there for each other, and once they finished their tours of duty, they'd study law, make a difference, and make some money.

The lawyer bowed his head. It hadn't turned out the way they planned. Life wasn't fair. There were only two of them now, and they hadn't made much of a difference in the world. They'd made the money, though.

The lawyer removed his Beretta APX 40 pistol from its shoulder holster. He ejected the clip and checked the weapon, then set it on the table and opened the plastic box of cleaning supplies. He field-stripped the weapon before wetting a cotton rag with a little Hopps 9 and cleaning the pistol one piece at a time. As he worked, he considered his next course of action.

Part of him wanted to finish this right now. The more cautious side of his brain told him to wait until he knew what was going on. He needed more information. He needed to know why. He needed to know all of those involved.

The lawyer reassembled his weapon and holstered it. He repacked his cleaning box and put it back in his duffel bag. His photograph he tucked back in his wallet. He lay on the bed with his hands behind his head. He knew where the answers could be found. But did he have time to find them before the vultures began to circle here? He had to risk it. He had to know who had set this all-in motion. Three or four days should be enough. He would leave in the morning.

Chapter 45

New Discoveries

While Cadence slept, I put away the supplies we'd bought on the way out of town. I added some of them to the full pantry shelves and a few to the refrigerator, then made roast beef sandwiches. Cadence's I wrapped in a napkin and set it aside. I ate mine in silence at the kitchen table. My sister's weeping still troubled me. She had once been so vital and alive. Could she climb out of the darkness? Would I even be able to help her? A subtle chill invaded the room. I was way out of my depth here.

A couple hours later, I found a blanket in the bunkroom closet and spread it over Cadence. Even though it was two in the afternoon, the temperature was in the low seventies. Compared to Phoenix, this was cool.

I wandered around the cabin for a while, trying to relive the pleasant memories the place conjured. My gaze fell on my briefcase I'd left by the door. I picked it up, put it on the desk, and sat down. Opening it, I pulled out my laptop and set it aside. Then I removed my notepads and placed them neatly in the center of the table.

When I switched on the rustic log lamp, its wax-paper shade gave off a warm orange glow. I slid the lamp closer so it cast its light over my pile of papers and notes. A small recess carved into one log caught my attention.

I leaned closer to inspect the hidden pocket in the wood. By tilting the lamp, I revealed a one-hundred-and-twenty-volt receptacle for power and a LAN cable for the internet. I started to turn and share my discovery with Cadence, but she was still asleep. Instead, I reached into my briefcase and pulled out the power cord for my computer. I plugged it into the receptacle. The little green light on the cord started to glow.

"Fantastic."

Curious now, I pushed away from the desk and looked under it to see if I could find how my father had managed to hide the power and internet cables, but nothing indicated how he'd worked this magic. I inspected the logs and seams of the wall behind the desk, and still nothing. Finally, I gave up.

After the computer woke up, the internet icon at the bottom of my screen showed I had internet. Well, that answered how we were going to access Dad's webpage to answer his ciphered riddles. With no cell service, it would have been rather inconvenient to drive to Payson every time we needed to enter an answer or search for some esoteric piece of information.

From the briefcase, I pulled my sister's copy of the will and flipped to the page that had her log-in credentials. I deleted my browser history, then my cookies, and then closed my browser. This should allow me to log back onto the webpage without getting the error message. I entered the address, and to my relief, a fresh login page came up.

Carefully, I typed in my sister's log-in credentials and hit *enter*. When the first ciphered riddle and its blank answer spaces appeared, I rubbed my hands together. From my notes, I entered 4, 6, 13, 10, 20, and 2, the same numbers I'd entered to solve the first cipher.

The second ciphered riddle appeared. "Okay, we are back in business," I muttered. My sister could still solve the ciphered riddles and claim her inheritance. Time to get busy. I read the second riddle and the instructions again. Then I studied the text for a while before moving on to the verse clues. Finally, I copied it all onto my legal pad.

This enciphered Biblical passage describes 381 becoming 391 by 39.

Summarize using only three words from the passage.

א ב ר ע ל ם ו ט ש ב ע פ י ה מ
ג ג פ ג א ב ר ע מ ג ש ם ב נ ו
א ר ש ם מ ג ט ו פ ל א ם ב ר ע
צ מ פ א ג נ ס ש ל א מ נ ד פ ס
ש א ב ר ע ש פ ד ו א ב ר ם ע ב
ג י ע נ ס ש ם מ ג ד פ ד ש א ב
ר ע ס ג ה ב ש ל א מ נ נ ב א ם
ש א ב ם ר ע ל י ט ם ד כ פ ט מ
ג ב ש ת ל א א ב ר ע ג ו כ א ש
ם ג ק מ ש מ ג פ ו ד ש ם א ב ר
ע נ ס נ ל פ ם ל א מ ג ב ת ש ל
א ע י ב פ ם כ ע ל ג י ש ב ם ל
י ט י א ק ב י ע א כ פ ט ל כ ע
ל ט ז פ ש ח ט ל ב י ם ע א ע פ
ם ם י ח מ ג ג פ ג ש ע ם פ י ה

Isaiah 49:8

Thus saith YHWH, In an acceptable time have I heard thee, and in a day of salvation have I helped thee: and I will preserve thee, and give thee for a covenant of the people, to establish the earth, to cause to inherit the desolate heritages;

Acts 25:11

For if I be an offender, or have committed any thing worthy of death, I refuse not to die: but if there be none of these things whereof these accuse me, no man may deliver me unto them. I appeal unto Caesar.

Genesis 22:11
And the angel of YHWH called unto him out of heaven, and said, Abraham, Abraham: and he said, Here *am* I.

Isaiah 52:7
How beautiful upon the mountains are the feet of him that bringeth good tidings, that publisheth peace; that bringeth good tidings of good, that publisheth salvation; that saith unto Zion, Thy God reigneth!

1 John 5:7
For there are three that bear record in heaven, the Father, the Word, and the Holy Ghost: and these three are one.

My first order of exploration was to see if my father used the same Atbash cipher to encipher this passage. Probably not, because it would have made the challenge too easy. After a half-hour of effort, my suspicions were confirmed. This passage was not ciphered with Atbash.

Next, I searched for the numbers 391, 381, and 39 in the Bible. None of these numbers appeared in the text as far as I could tell. I wasn't getting anywhere, but I was not discouraged. I'd gotten a glimpse of how my father's mind worked, and I could figure out the riddle and the cipher. I wasn't sure which I'd solve first, but it didn't matter. One would lead to the other.

I read through the verses one by one. I didn't try to think too hard about them, just passively absorbed the words and their meaning. I read them a second and third time. By the fourth time through, one thing stood out from the passages of Isaiah. They both spoke about salvation. The second thing I noticed—and I doubted it was even a thing—but both the Acts and Genesis references were the eleventh verses of their respective chapters. My father had used the numerical value of the Hebrew text to conceal his message in the first ciphered riddle. Would he repeat that? I read the riddle again.

This enciphered Biblical passage describes 381 becoming 391 by 39.

The last riddle centered around 39 as 1. Or, as the Hebrew text read, YHWH ONE. I scribbled *39 is 1 = YHWH ONE* on my notepad. I had a feeling that the last riddle of 39 and 1 was somehow related to the 391 of this second riddle. But what was the connection, besides the same numbers being used?

Did the numbers refer to people in a manner similar to how 39 or 26+13 referred to YHWH, the God of the Bible, in the last riddle? Was 39 a person who changed 381 unknown items into 391? I tapped the keys lightly. If 381 and 391 were not actual numbers found in the text, then maybe they were Hebrew words with those values. Maybe the verses my father had left concealed a hidden numerical message.

I flipped through my notes until I found where I'd copied the Hebrew alphabet and its letter values.

Next, I opened a web-based, interlinear version of the book of Isaiah. On my notepad next to my laptop, I started working out the numerical value of each letter of each word of Isaiah 49:8. The first word *koh*, translated *now* in many English versions of the Bible, was spelled with the two Hebrew letters, *koph* and *he.* The word value was 11+5 = 16.

The next word was *amar,* which meant *to say*. On my notepad, I spelled out the word letter by letter, with each letter's value in parentheses—*aleph* (1), mem (40), resh (200). This word's value was 241.

The next word I already knew from the last cipher. It was yod, *hey*, *vav*, *hey,* or Yahweh, the proper name of the living God of the Bible. Its value was 26. I kept going. I found the word values interesting, but nothing stood out until I got to the eighth word, *salvation*. This was the same word I'd noticed in the other passage of Isaiah my father had given as one of the clues. Salvation was spelled *yod, shin, wav, ayin, hey*. Its numerical value was 391. I sat up a little straighter in my chair. That couldn't be an accident.

Okay, so 391 was not a person but an idea, the value of the word *salvation*. I substituted the word *salvation* for 391 when I read it.

This enciphered Biblical passage describes 381 becoming Salvation (391) by 39.

Was I on the right track? The riddle didn't make any more sense when read this way. What could 381 be, or what could have the value of 381 and become 391/salvation by 39? I slouched and scratched my head, then rubbed my hands over my face.

My mind started to go down different rabbit trails, but I stopped it and sat forward again. Before I completely lost my train of thought, I wanted to confirm if the two passages of Isaiah that my father had left as clues were related by the word *salvation*. Was it the same Hebrew word? Using my interlinear text of Isaiah, I clicked on the Hebrew word *salvation*. In the sidebar of the screen, seven other passages appeared.

Psalm 119:155
Isaiah 26:1
Isaiah 49:8
Isaiah 52:7
Isaiah 59:17
Isaiah 60:18
Habakkuk 3:8.

Okay, each of these passages used the Hebrew word for salvation that had a numerical value of 391. As I suspected, Isaiah 52:7, my father's other verse clue, was on the list. I circled both references. To ensure I wasn't overlooking any additional clues, I read the other five passages, which used the 391 form of the Hebrew word *salvation*. That appeared to be a dead end, but that was all right. I was getting closer.

I spent two hours calculating the word values of each of the five passages my father had given as clues. Still, the only number that stood out was 391 for *salvation*. Was that sum just an unlucky coincidence?

I pushed away from the desk and stood, watching Cadence's slow, steady breathing for a moment. The room started to dim. The bright light streaming through the kitchen window faded into a soft glow like liquid gold, its diminishing blush entering the window at an angle where it painted a gilded rectangle on the wall.

As quietly as I could, I opened the front door and stepped out. I walked around to the back side of the cabin and continued on the faded path that led to the promontory overlooking Clover

Creek. In the distance, the 7500-foot peak of Buck Mountain and the Mogollon Rim swallowed the final sliver of sun, a glorious display.

As the rays of life-giving energy disappeared, peace enveloped me, like my father's arms had when I was a child. A long time since I'd felt that way . Was it because of being here? Or had something in me changed over the past two weeks? I shook my head. It was beyond me. Instead, I let my mind empty and stood there absorbing those final fingers of light on my face.

The fiery orange glow disappeared, and the brilliant blue sky slowly, by imperceptible degrees, faded into a gray twilight. With shadows heavy on the edge of the clearing, I returned to the cabin. Firewood was stacked neatly against the outside wall. I grabbed several pieces of dry pine and a handful of kindling from the small box next to the stack of wood.

Kneeling in front of the living room fireplace, I built a small teepee with the kindling. On the mantel, I found a box of wooden matches and struck one of the red tips against the side. With a rasp and sizzle, the yellow-and-red flame hissed to life. I put the match to the pile of pine kindling. Greedily, the flame took hold. The hungry fire slithered up the sticks in ribbons of blue and orange. I carefully added the larger wood to the flames. A few minutes later, a cheery fire crackled and snapped in the old stone fireplace.

Cadence remained on the couch, her fingers curled around the edge of the blanket she'd pulled tight against her chin. The dancing flames played across her face. Though she still looked haggard, there was also a peace about her that had not been there before.

Chapter 46

Dreams and Doorways

I spent the rest of that evening sitting in the deep leather chair staring at the fire. I must have fallen asleep because my past stretched before me like a long hallway of brick and stone. The hall had many doors, most of which had been inscribed with a date. On a few of the doors, an event was written. Some of the doors were close together, others far apart.

Good memories lined the left side of the hall, with the bad on the right. At the start of my hallway, bright light shone on many doors to the left. One after another, they stretched away, from my first memories as a child to my early teenage years and the first months of college. When I opened these doors, I saw the smiling faces of my mother, father, and sister. After the first few, my mother's face was missing. As I moved forward, some doors on the other side were locked and barred.

On the right side, up until my early twenties, the doors to the bad memories were few and far between. By the second year of college, the right side of my hallway grew crowded and dim. Broken, bent, and used items cluttered the rooms, like toys flung by a spoiled child. Most sobering of all, though, was the lonely, selfish person reflected in the shattered mirror at the far side of each of these rooms. Heart pounding, I recognized him and felt his sadness, anger, and fear as he tried to reach from the glass to escape the prison of his own making.

I rushed out of the room, slammed the door, and leaned against it, panting.

On my right, a brick wall nearly covered a single, arched door that blocked the end of the hallway. I could only see the top part of the door. Burned into the wood was a number I recognized, *391*. The number was not an event or a date—this I somehow knew. I tried to reach over the wall to touch the number but realized that I had a mason's trowel and brick in my hands. I released them, and they clattered to the floor. The tips of my fingers brushed the rough wood. Then a knocking came from the other side of the door.

Chapter 47

Cryptographs and Cryptographers

I woke with a start. My eyes darted around the dark room. My heart beat fast and hard in my chest. Where was I?

Finally, the dim coals in the fireplace drew my attention, and I remembered. I stood and shivered even though the room felt warm and cozy. I added wood to the fire and stood there waiting until the glow grew into a cheery, crackling flame. I took several deep breaths, and my thumping heart started to slow.

As the fire grew brighter, Cadence's serene face appeared among the shadows on the couch. Her eyes remained closed, and the blanket moved up and down. Seeing her calmed me still further.

I stood there with my back to the fire until I was uncomfortably warm. The cabin door reminded me of the knocking from my dream. I half expected *391* to be burned into the yellowed logs, but it wasn't.

Dreams were weird, sometimes like an angry ocean, all violent and mixed up, the ship of your consciousness riding the peaks and troughs in a confused, gut-wrenching journey that only made sense in unconsciousness. Other times, your mind sailed the sparkling blue waters of a placid lake from one flowered and wooded shore to the other. It had been a while since I'd enjoyed the lake-and-flowers version.

With a final shiver, I walked back to the desk and sat down. It was late, and I was tired, but right now, I didn't have the courage to face my dreams again. That empty, sick feeling lingered in my stomach. Better to lose myself in Dad's ciphers than wander the dark hallways of my memories.

I took a deep breath and then exhaled. I'd reached a dead end with the number *391*. Literally.

I knew *391* was the value of the Hebrew word for salvation, but that was all. I still didn't understand how it was related to the numbers *381* or *39*. I'd take another approach.

Cadence had known the first cipher was Atbash by just reading the verse from Jeremiah and its reference to Shishak. What if one of the verses from this second cipher also identified the type of cryptography used to encipher it? With this in mind, I set out to learn more about ciphers in the hopes of stumbling upon something that might be related to the verse clues.

Basics first. I typed *cipher* into my search engine, then read down through the results and clicked on the Wikipedia page for Cipher. I skimmed the page and learned that in cryptography, a cipher—or cypher—is an algorithm for performing encryption or decryption—that is, a series of defined steps that can be followed as a procedure.

Okay, I knew that. As with the etymology of many words, some uncertainty surrounded *cipher,* but you got a sense of the word by following some of the associated etymological threads. In some languages, *cipher* represented the concept of zero or nothingness. In others, *cipher* or a similar-sounding word referred to digital numbers from zero to nine, such as the German *ziffer*. The Slavs, Italians, and Spanish all referenced numerical digits as *cifra*. The Swedes had *siffra*. Farther back in time, the Greeks used tzifra to refer to a hard-to-read signature.

Ibrahim Al-Kadi, in his book *Cryptologia*, speculated that the Arabic word *sifr*, for the digit zero, evolved into the European term used for encryption. Interestingly, as cutting-edge mathematical concepts of the Arab world spread to Europe during the Middle Ages, the words *sifr* and *zephirum* became associated with calculation, privileged knowledge, and secret codes. In Paris, in the 13th century, a "worthless fellow" was called a "*cifre en algorisme*." In English, this might be translated as an "arithmetical nothing." According to some Arab historians, the European pronunciation of *cipher* derived from the Arabic *sifr* and came to be associated with a message or communication not easily understood.

By eleven, I needed a snack before I started searching for historical methods of cryptology.

I returned to the desk a few minutes later with a small box of orange juice, a peanut butter sandwich, and applesauce. I smiled to myself as I sucked on the tiny juice straw like a kid on a field trip. I took a bite of the whole wheat bread and peanut butter, then spooned up some of the applesauce. I chewed contentedly. At that very moment, I was as happy as I could remember. I had a roof over my head, I was clothed and warm, I was eating something tasty, and I had something productive to do and learn.

How had I lost sight of these simple pleasures? Why did life have to become so much more complicated? Or did it? I shook my head. Maybe in the questions lay some of the answers. Perhaps the quest for answers sowed the seeds of its own dissatisfaction. Questions that led away from the here and now to a brighter, promised future. But life couldn't always be lived in the here and now, could it? Living required food. Food required effort and money. Anything beyond that required more effort and more money. I shook off the deeper questions for now. I was going to enjoy my food and this interlude of peace and tranquility without worrying about what the future held.

I set the juice aside and took another bite of the sandwich. As I chewed, a realization warmed me. Money was no longer the driving factor in solving my father's ciphered riddles. I had started to enjoy the challenge. I felt close to Dad for the first time since college. I wanted to solve his riddles and decrypt his ciphers, to see these passages of Scripture through his eyes. Neither his will nor my avarice compelled me, but a new hunger to better understand him. These ciphers were leading somewhere—somewhere he knew. A place he wanted Cadence and me to find.

For the first time since rejecting my faith, I wondered if there was a way back.

Chapter 48

Hide and Seek

Eric Pincer hung up the phone. He placed his hand flat on the desk in front of him and leaned back in his chair. The fingers of his missing arm suffered an infuriating itch this morning—the kind you got from a dozen chigger bites or a month-old cast. The phantom limb sensations always seemed to worsen when he was under stress.

Eric pushed himself up from the table. He paced the floor between his desk and the window that overlooked the Washington Monument several miles away.

Sean O'Conner had told him the Plummers had fled the hospital. He'd checked their apartments and any other places they might have holed up but found nothing. They had disappeared. O'Conner had also relayed that Benito Silva's man had been watching the hospital. But an unknown party had disabled Silva's goon's vehicle.

This meant other players were involved, and Eric didn't like that. He'd known about Silva, thanks to O'Conner. According to O'Conner, the unknown party might have also been responsible for piercing the tire of O'Conner's Crown Vic and removing the tracking device he'd planted on the Plummers' car. From across the street in the convenience store, O'Conner had gotten a glimpse of an old man near his car, but he'd disappeared by the time O'Conner returned from his morning coffee run. He didn't even know if the elderly gent had been responsible for the hole in his tire. O'Conner said he'd gotten half a block following the Plummers before he'd heard a loud *thunk* and the hiss of air. Later, he'd found the tracking device on the ground where the Plummers' car had been parked.

Someone was protecting the Plummers. Or eliminating the competition so they could … what? Wait until Cadence and Timbre had almost solved the ciphers and claimed the inheritance themselves after the deadline ran out? Doubtful. Besides himself, people in his office, and Benito Silva, no one else knew that the ciphers would be made public in a matter of months if the Plummers didn't solve them. Possibly, Timbre Plummer had realized he was being watched and hired someone to throw them off so they could escape.

One thing was certain. The ciphers couldn't become public knowledge. That would set off a media frenzy. He could see the headlines—*Fortune to be Claimed by First to Solve 7 Ciphers.* He couldn't afford that type of attention.

But he was now blind. He didn't know where the Plummers had disappeared to, and he didn't know who was helping them or stalking them or whatever the hell was happening. Eric loosened his tie and sat back down at his desk. He was losing control. This affair could unravel all his plans. He needed to figure out how to get back on the inside. He had to find the Plummers and contain this.

Okay, what did he know? Timbre Plummer had cashed his check for twenty thousand. That meant they potentially had enough money to hide out until Cadence finished solving John's ciphers. So far, they'd solved the first one, and now they were likely working on the second. At least, they hadn't solved it earlier this morning when he had checked. Eric entered Cadence Plummer's log-in credentials on his keyboard. When the page refreshed, he nodded. They were still on the ciphered riddle about 381 becoming 391 by 39.

Eric stared at the riddle, his jaw clenching. They were beginning to infuriate him. He hadn't even been close to solving the first one. How could a drug addict and a gambling loser have managed it? Even after they had entered their first answer and he'd seen it, he still had spent hours attempting to make sense of it.

And now the second riddle was even more complicated. He'd lost another sleepless night trying to solve the new one but had come up blank. He might not be as smart as John, but he surely was more intelligent than his loser children.

Eric rubbed his eyes and massaged his temple. He didn't have time to work on the second cipher right now. But the thing had burrowed into his brain like a bacterial infection. He had a hard time concentrating on his real job, the job he got paid to do.

"Focus, Eric," he muttered to himself as he massaged his aching head.

How was he going to find the Plummers? What means could he use to track them? A cell phone? A court order was out of the question. Could he hire a hacker? Possibly. But that had its own set of complications, none of which were desirable right now. Eric stared absently at the screen. Then it came to him. He picked up the phone.

"Josh, this is Eric Pincer."

"Good afternoon, Mr. Pincer. What can I do for you?" the brusque voice of the head of the firm's IT department asked.

"I need to know if it is possible to track the IP address of someone logging into the firm's computers." He waited for the pause on the other end of the line.

"It's possible, but that's hundreds—no, probably thousands—of computers, sir. Can you narrow that down for me a bit? A particular division or person you are interested in?"

Eric cleared his throat. "Oil and gas acquisitions. Any servers related to John Plummer."

"Shouldn't be too hard as long as the IP is not masked by a VPN.. If they're masking it , it might be more difficult. Is this something I should be concerned about?" Josh asked.

Eric drummed his fingers on his desk. "Not sure at this point, Josh. Just trying to track down some loose ends in the John Plummer affair. You know, just some CYA for corporate, making sure the big wigs are protected, that's all."

"Would you like me to take a look?"

"Yes. If you can get the information, I'd really appreciate it."

"Give me a day or two, Mr. Pincer. I'll have a list of IP addresses for you and any originating information I can access. If any of these hosting companies want to play hardball, we'll have to get a court order to go further," Josh warned.

Waving his hand, Eric attempted to sound casual. "No, no, it's not that serious. Just get me what you can by normal channels. Appreciate it, Josh."

"No problem, Mr. Pincer. I'll be in touch."

After Josh disconnected, Eric placed the receiver back in its cradle. He stared at the phone. It was a little late to consider the risks he'd just taken. If this blew up in his face, there would be a paper trail and witnesses. He'd have to consider carefully how to counter that risk. Right now, though, he needed to know where John's brats had disappeared to.

Chapter 49

The Salvation Cipher

By one in the morning, I was starting to lose my focus. My eyes were heavy, and the information was just not absorbing anymore. So far, I'd learned that the oldest known use of cryptography was thought to have been hieroglyphs carved in a tomb wall during Egypt's Old Kingdom in roughly 1900 BC. These hieroglyphs were extraordinary in the sense that they were modified forms of the original inscription. It was believed the variations were meant to intrigue or amuse future generations, not necessarily to conceal the hieroglyphs' meaning

There were also clay tablets with an encrypted recipe for pottery glaze from 1500 BC Mesopotamia. From 500 BC, the Atbash ciphers from the Hebrew Bible were the next example given, then *Mlecchita vikalpa*, also known as the art of understanding writing in cipher, from the Kama Sutra of India, circa 200-400 BC.

The Scytale transposition cipher had caught my attention and imagination. This ciphering device consisted of a strip of leather or paper wound tightly around a stick or staff of a particular diameter. The message was then written vertically on this strip, letter by letter. When the leather or paper was unwound, it contained a seemingly random mix of letters. Only those recipients of the text who knew the exact diameter of the Scytale rod could rewind the strip and decipher the text.

During the Hellenistic age, Herodotus told of a hidden means of communication called *steganography*. This wasn't the concealment of a message by means of substituted symbols like cryptography, but rather a method of concealing the message itself. Examples included placing a message beneath a waxed surface on a wooden table or inking a tattoo on the head of a slave and sending him on his way after his hair had grown out enough to conceal the message from enemy eyes.

A more cryptology-based system was the Polybius Square, named after the Greek historian Polybius. This form of encryption consisted of a five-by-five square in which each of the twenty-four letters of the Greek alphabet were written. One square was left blank and was used to mark periods or spaces in the text. Along this square's horizontal and vertical axis, the numbers one through five were written. Thus, the first letter *alpha* would be represented by 1-1, Beta by 2-1, and so forth. This Polybius Square allowed the Greeks to communicate over long distances by flashing torches or other light sources the number of times corresponding to their encrypted Greek letters.

It was at this point that my eyes started to close without my bidding. Okay, just one more example. It came from the Roman era and was called the Caesar's Code, Caesar's Shift, or Caesar Cipher. In the age of the internet, the ROT-13 modern version of this cipher was used to conceal spoilers, punchlines, and puzzle solutions. The cipher got its name because the Roman alphabet consisted of twenty-six letters, and the ROT13 method shifted the alphabet by 13 letters to produce the cipher. *A* became *N*. *B* became *O*. The word *ONE* became *BAR*.

I studied the example given on the webpage.

1	2	3	4	5	6	7	8	9	10	11	12	13
A	B	C	D	E	F	G	H	I	J	K	L	M
N	O	P	Q	R	S	T	U	V	W	X	Y	Z

In Roman times, when Julius Caesar had used this inscription method, the shift hadn't always been set at 13, but at any number between one and twenty-six.

Something started to tickle my mind. Something I should remember. I was in that foggy state I hadn't felt since I tried to cram for my final exam—a fourteen-hour marathon on legal minutia—in my first year of law school. I shook my head to try and clear it. I stood and stretched. I looked down at my notes, and my gaze fell once more upon my father's clues and the second verse he'd provided a passage from Acts.

Acts 25:11
For if I be an offender, or have committed any thing worthy of death, I refuse not to die: but if there be none of these things whereof these accuse me, no man may deliver me unto them. I appeal unto Caesar.

I read the final four words of the passage out loud. "I appeal unto Caesar."

I sat back down with a surge of adrenaline. I underlined the words, *I appeal unto Caesar*. If I remembered correctly, this passage involved Paul defending himself against accusations of religious leaders of his day before Felix, the governor of Judaea. As a Roman citizen, Paul had the right to appeal to Caesar, which he did here in Acts 25:11. My father had provided a verse clue to the identity of the last cipher. I had a feeling he'd done the same thing with this one. It was too coincidental.

In front of me was a Hebrew letter cipher. The Hebrew alphabet contained twenty-two letters, not twenty-six. If this was really a passage of Hebrew Scripture, all I had to do was decrypt the first few words to determine the rest. The Caesar was a shift cipher, but I didn't know the number of shifts necessary to solve it.

I'd have to start at one and work my way through until I stumbled upon the correct number of shifts. To test each, I would work through the first six letters of my father's cipher. If the text deciphered was a recognizable Hebrew word, I'd continue with a few more letters to make sure. If the word was not recognizable, I'd move on.

The downside was that if the final shift turned out to be twenty-two, I'd be here until the break of day.

By two-thirty in the morning, I knew Dad had used a shift of eleven. I also knew why he'd chosen Genesis 22:11 as one of his clues—twenty-two Hebrew letters with a shift of eleven.

I was positive I was on the right track when the first four letters revealed the Hebrew word *matteh,* which meant staff, branch, or tribe. The next five unveiled the name *Ephraim.* The following four letters were *hey, waw, shin, and ayin*. The Hebrew word they spelled was *Howshea*' or Hosea. The name meant *salvation.*

I nearly hollered out loud. The first three words told of Hosea of the tribe of Ephraim. I wanted to wake Cadence and share this with her. If anyone would appreciate it, she would.

"Hosea meant salvation," I whispered instead. "*Salvation.*"

How odd that these two words with the same meaning were spelled differently in Hebrew. The *salvation* from Isaiah had a five-letter spelling. Here in the book of Numbers, Hosea's name, only had four. It was missing the letter *yod.*

I did a quick mental calculation, or at least, I tried to. My mind was numb. The five-letter word *salvation* from the book of Isaiah had a value of 391. *Hosea* was spelled using the same Hebrew letters, only it was missing the letter *yod.* Yod had a value of ten. This meant Hosea's name had a numerical value of ten less than 391 or 381.

Bingo!

381 was one of the numbers in the riddle. I was getting close now.

Using the words I had deciphered from the text so far, I could have just searched for the passage using my online Bible software. But it kind of felt like cheating. I wanted to figure the riddle out without the additional help of the entire deciphered passage. I wrote it out on my notepad and substituted the word *Hosea* for the number *381*. I read the riddle out loud, including my newly deciphered words which I'd included in parentheses.

This enciphered Biblical passage describes 381 (Hosea) becoming 391 (Salvation) by 39.

I scratched my head after reading the riddle several times. It still didn't make any sense. Who was or what was 39? After several minutes of fruitless effort, I entered *Hosea, tribe of Ephraim* in my online Bible search box. Shortcut time.

And … nothing. Ugh!

I turned back to Dad's cipher and decrypted the next five letters. They spelled the Hebrew word *ben,* which meant *son*, and the Hebrew name *Nun*. I typed *son* and *Nun* in my search box. I got twenty-nine results.

Nun, it turned out, was the father of Hosea. But the third search result, Numbers 13:8, really got my attention. My first search for *Hosea, tribe of Ephraim* had not returned any results because I had been using the King James Version of the Bible, and in that translation, the name *Hosea* had been spelled *Oshea* instead of *Hosea*. The verse read,

Of the tribe of Ephraim, Oshea the son of Nun. - **Numbers 13:8**

I shook my head. Why they spelled the word as *Oshea* here and *Hosea* in the rest of the Bible made no sense to me. I kept reading aloud until verse sixteen.

These are the names of the men which Moses sent to spy out the land. And Moses called Oshea the son of Nun Jehoshua. - **Numbers 13:16**

"Moses changed his name."

I scratched my head. I never knew that the Biblical Joshua who led Israel into the Promised Land was originally named Hosea. I looked at the Hebrew spelling of *Joshua.* Moses had taken Hosea's Hebrew name הושע which meant *salvation* and added the letter *yod* to give it the new Hebrew spelling of יהושע. Instead of just meaning *salvation*, the new name was imbued with the divine prefix of *Ya*, and this new compound word meant *Yahweh's Salvation.* Now, that was interesting and symbolically appropriate. So *Hosea-Salvation* became *Joshua* or *Yahweh's Salvation*, the man who led Israel into the Promised Land.

I glanced at my notes again. *Joshua* and the Hebrew spelling of the word *salvation* from both passages of Isaiah used the same Hebrew letters but in different orders. They were anagrams. I was still missing something, though.

Laboriously, I wrote out the Hebrew spelling of the words on my notepad.

יהושע

ישועה

Then I saw it. Although the spelling was different for *salvation* and *Joshua*, the letter values were the same. The same letter values meant that both words had the same value. Both words equaled 391. This was why my father had included the passages from Isaiah. *Joshua* was the Old Testament name that the New Testament rendered in Greek as *Jesus*. *Yehowshuwa'*, Joshua, and Jesus were variant English spellings of the Hebrew name that meant *Yahweh's Salvation*.

The 391 of my father's riddle wasn't just about the idea of salvation. 391 was a person whose name included the idea of salvation but went beyond that. It was about a name that projected divine salvation.

The final part of the riddle was easy. 39 had to be the value of Moses's name. I wrote out the riddle one last time, substituting the names for their numbers.

This enciphered Biblical passage describes 381 (Hosea) becoming 391 (Joshua) by 39 (Moses).

Again, I got the feeling that my father was weaving a bigger picture here with his riddles—like playing multi-dimensional chess. I tried to look at it from his point of view, dispassionately, without my skeptical prejudices, my faithlessness, clouding my thoughts. If I could figure out where he was going, it might make the other ciphers easier to solve. I might even be able to jump a few steps ahead. But I was having a hard time looking at this dispassionately. My father's riddles were getting into my head. I had only solved the second riddle, and I was already dreaming about them.

With an unaccountable sadness, I closed my eyes and laid my forehead on the desk. I saw the door with *391* written on it again. It blocked the hallway of my memories. Behind the door, I could hear knocking, but I couldn't get to the door because of the wall I'd built.

Chapter 50

Dreams and Dilemmas

A soft hand on my shoulder woke me. Sun was streaming in the window over the desk. I lifted my head to find my sister standing beside me. Cadence glowed as if she had stepped out of another world. She cast a shadow against the far wall, and around this silhouette, on three sides of the room from the middle of the wall to the ceiling, a kaleidoscope of colors glimmered. Sparks of purple of all shapes and sizes mixed with prismed circles and streaks of multicolored rainbows.

It took me some time before my mind could make sense of the dazzling display. I blinked repeatedly. I turned back to the window and saw the source of the brilliant display. Hanging in the window and piled on the sill were crystals of quartz and amethyst. Some cunning hand had arranged them to catch the early morning light. No mortal imagination could have come up with a more fantastic display of light and color.

"You okay?" Little lines wrinkled Cadence's forehead.

I nodded. "It was a long night," I said, my voice husky with sleep. I rubbed my eyes and studied her. She still looked tired and sad, but a new light shone in her eyes. Maybe a spark of strength or resolve. I wasn't sure, but it was encouraging. "You okay?"

She gave a brave smile that ended with a sad, wistful look. Then she seemed to shake off the mood and asked, "You hungry?"

My stomach rumbled in reply. She laughed as I smiled ruefully.

"I'll take that as a yes. I'll get us some breakfast going."

As Cadence removed her hand from my shoulder, she gently brushed the crystals hanging in the window and stepped aside to allow the sunlight to work its unobstructed magic. I stood and moved to the opposite side to get a better view. A frenzied whirling dervish of color and light danced around us. As the rays, sparks, and streaks of light settled into a statelier parade, I stirred the crystals once more. It was mesmerizing in a childishly satisfying way. We looked at each other and grinned like kids. For that brief moment, we recaptured a glimpse of our past innocence, pleasure, and wonder.

My stomach rumbled again and broke the spell. Cadence laughed. "You really are hungry. Aren't you?"

I nodded and pointed to my head. "I burned a lot of energy using this all night."

Cadence raised her left eyebrow. "Really? Make any progress?

"I did. I am pretty sure I solved the second cipher."

"Without my help?"

"Yeah, didn't you know your brother was a genius?"

Cadence laughed and shook her head.

I followed her to the kitchen. As Cadence cracked several eggs into the cast-iron skillet on the small stove, I mixed some pancakes. We bantered back and forth as we used to when we were still living at home.

During breakfast, I told her about the second cipher, and how both passages of Isaiah used a form of the word *salvation* with a value of 391. I told her how that line of exploration ended in a dead end, or so I thought. But then I'd recalled how she'd seen the clue to the first riddle right in the verse about Shikshak, so I'd started looking at different ciphers. She stiffened when I told her that I'd almost missed the clue about Caesar because I was so tired.

"Did you know that Moses's sidekick Joshua, who led Israel into the Promised Land, had originally been named Hosea?" I asked.

"I didn't."

"Neither did I." I lifted my fork in the air. "Did you know that *Joshua* and *Jesus* were different translations of the same name meaning, *Yahweh's Salvation*?"

Again, she shook her head. "I didn't know that, either," she said quietly.

I scratched just above my left ear like I sometimes did when nervous. I'd trained myself not to because it had been one of my tells when playing poker. I dropped my hand to the counter. I started to speak but stopped. Cadence looked at me expectantly. I met her gaze and drew a breath to tell her about my dream. But it was like my brain was telling my voice to speak, but the thoughts were too big or unsettling to pass down the neural pathways to my vocal cords. Finally, I managed to get out a single word.

"Dreams …" I cleared my throat and tried to make a complete thought. Why was this so hard? It was just a dream.

Cadence leaned forward slightly. "Was it about a door?"

I blinked at her. "How did you know?"

She reached across the table and placed her fingers on my forehead. In a voice out of the twilight zone, she said, "I can read your thoughts."

I snorted and screwed up my face.

She switched to Yoda's voice. "In you strong is the force, young Timbre."

The wonder of her laugh wiped away my confusion. Her laughter had always made me feel good inside. It was one of those natural, warm, beautiful, living sounds that flowed from a well of everything right and good about the human spirit. The Cadence I remembered was back. Or at least part of her.

I looked away from her shining face and down at the crumbs of eggs and pancakes on my plate. I couldn't ruin this rare, unconscious happiness of hers with a show of incredulous relief. My sister was going to be okay. She wasn't all magically fixed inside, but that vital part that made her so special was not dead, and that gave me hope.

In the comfortable silence that hung between us, I glanced back up at her and asked, "Seriously, Caden. How did you know about the door?"

Her smile lingered in her eyes. "You woke me up this morning muttering about a door. I thought you'd lost your mind until I got up and found you dead asleep. You kept saying something about a door, someone knocking, and something about not being able to open the door."

An awkward chuckle escaped my throat. Thank goodness she'd just witnessed me dreaming. I don't know if I could've handled it if she really had read my mind or sensed it or some other out-of-this-world mumbo-jumbo. There had been a reasonable and rational explanation, just like there had to be for my dream. Cadence waited for me to say something.

I took a deep breath. "Do you believe dreams are jumbled thoughts from our unconscious minds?"

Cadence gave a slight shrug. "I suppose," she said but then added, "At least, mostly."

"What do you mean by *mostly*?"

She shrugged again. "I'm not sure. I mean, I know many of my dreams are the jumbled subconscious thoughts and experiences that bubbled to the surface from the caldron of my existence. But I don't think that explains it all. I think there is another dimension, somehow."

I frowned as I chased crumbs around my plate with my fork. I wanted a more rational, scientific answer. She was the mathematical genius, after all. I looked up and smiled ruefully. "Not the answer I was looking for, Sis."

She spread her hands. "Well, why don't you spill it then? This beating around the bush isn't getting us anywhere. Just tell me what you are thinking, and I'll give you my opinion."

"Okay, fine." I pushed back a little from the table. "Yesterday evening, I figured out that the passages from Isaiah were linked by the use of the Hebrew word for salvation … because the Hebrew spelling of the words gave a numerical value of 391. 391, in turn, was important because it was the same number found in Dad's riddle."

Cadence nodded her encouragement.

"The number got me thinking about Dad and the effort he went to make these ciphers. That led to thoughts about you and him and the ciphers on our refrigerator. At some point, I must have fallen asleep." I went on to recount my dream, down to the moment the brick wall blocked me from the final door in my hallway of memories. "Care to guess what number was on it?"

Cadence shook her head.

"391." I picked my fork back up and started chasing the crumbs around my plate again. I stopped and looked at her, but I couldn't read her expression. "How is that possible, Sis? Did my mind put all those pieces together? I mean, come on. I didn't know yet that 391 was the numerical value of Jesus's name in Hebrew. How, then, did my brain make a door with the number of His name on it and then connect it to someone knocking behind it?" I finished with almost a pleading in my voice.

Cadence smoothed her napkin as she studied me. . Finally, she asked, "Is this really about your dreams, or are you doubting what you thought you believed about the world around you?"

I shrugged and looked away from her. Was that really why this bothered me so much? Was I having a crisis of faith? Beginning to doubt my secular worldview?

"I don't know, Caden. But I can only come up with three options. One is that this was just some cosmic coincidence. Dad's ciphers and my unconscious mind collided in an accidental way that happened to make sense in my dream. Option two is that my brain, quite spectacularly, took the accumulated knowledge of my life and produced a new and imaginative way of looking at those facts in light of Dad's ciphers."

My sister's brows raised. "And the final option?"

I hesitated. Even thinking about it made me uncomfortable. "The final option is that there is a spiritual dimension to the world that transcends the physical."

Cadence laughed outright. The look she gave me said, *Come on, bro, that was lame.* When she did respond, her tone was serious. "Your final option sounds like a skeptic wondering if there might be a God after all— a God who has taken a personal interest in you."

I said nothing. I couldn't meet her gaze. She had perceived my dilemma.

Cadence reached across the table and took my hand. She sighed. "I don't know, Timmy. I don't know if this was all just a coincidence or some act of divine intervention. But what I do know is that at the lowest point in my life, you were there when no one else was. Maybe it was chance, or maybe God sent you. Part of me wants to believe. I guess part of me does believe. I can tell you this, though—I am grateful for the first time in as long as I can remember. I'm grateful we had a father who loved us in his unique way. I'm grateful to you for being there. If this is God's doing and He sent you, I'm grateful to Him as well. I'm grateful that my life didn't end there on the dirty floor of my kitchen. I don't want to go back to the dark place that led me there. I got another chance, and I don't want to waste it."

She paused and waited silently. I could feel her watching me. I finally looked up and met her violet eyes. She squeezed my hand.

"How about we leave the question of God's existence for another day, okay? For now, let's just climb back on this wild, bucking, twisting thing we call life and hang on for dear life. Let's honor Dad and his life by solving his ciphers, by trying to understand what he saw, how he thought, what he believed. This was important to him. Let's see where it leads."

I flashed back to the gun I'd put to my head and my finger starting to pull the trigger when the phone call came. I didn't want to go back to that dark place either. Maybe it was some crazy, inexplicable coincidence, or perhaps it was some kind of divine intervention, but I was grateful for a second chance as well.

I placed my other hand on top of hers. "Okay, Caden."

"If you can do this, so can I."

That beautiful light flared in her eyes. She added her free hand on top of mine. I smiled and pulled my hand on the table out and put it on top of the stack. She yanked her hand out then and placed it on top. Then in a milling, laughing race to the top, our hands became a blur of fingers and palms that finally ended in convulsive laughter.

Chapter 51

Failed Attempts and New Findings

Later that morning, Cadence and I sat at the desk, considering three lines of instructions. Below were twelve blanks for us to enter our three-word answer. I read the instructions out loud.

Enter your answer in the spaces provided.
A correct answer will reveal the next cipher.
Only one attempt is allowed per 24 hours.

— — — —   — — — — —   — — —

I read the riddle one last time from my notes.

This enciphered Biblical passage describes 381 (Hosea) becoming 391 (Joshua) by 39 (Moses).

Summarize using only three words from the passage.

By a process of elimination, we determined that the first four blanks spelled the Hebrew word, *Hosea*. The following five blanks were for the Hebrew spelling of Joshua. The final three blanks spelled the name of Moses. Carefully, I entered the Hebrew characters using the letters and symbols I'd worked out on my keyboard by trial and error.

הושע   יהושע   משה

I raised my finger to push *enter* and paused. I looked at Cadence. “Ready?” She nodded and I clicked enter. The screen went blank for a second. Somewhere, probably thousands of miles away, a computer was comparing our answer with its programmed answer. We both groaned when a new screen appeared with the message,

Answer incorrect. Try again in 24 hours.

I leaned back in my chair, and Cadence rose from hers. She laughed at the expression on my face. “Come on, Timmy, this isn’t the end of the world. We’ll try again tomorrow.”

I gave an exaggerated sigh and stood up. “Yeah, I guess you are right. Tomorrow we’ll go with the numerical value of the letters instead.”

Cadence yawned. She looked tired but not as wasted as yesterday. She grabbed the blanket where she’d folded it on the back of the couch and lay down. “I’m going to take a little nap,” she said sleepily. She closed her eyes. “Wait for me to …”

I stepped closer and looked down at her. She’d fallen asleep in mid-sentence. I shook my head. I never understood how she could do that. I had to turn the levers, push the buttons, and toggle the switches until my mental engine stopped and the gears of my mind gradually bled off the cranial momentum of the day.

I sat back down at the desk and worked out the numerical value of each Hebrew letter of our answer. When I got to *Moses*, I stifled a groan. We had a major problem. I glanced at Cadence. I wanted to wake her up and see if she had any ideas about the discrepancy. Instead, I turned back to my notes.

The letters of Moses's name—*mem, shin, hey*—didn't equal 39. They equaled 345. Then I smiled and slapped my head with my hand.

"You dummy," I muttered.

There was more than one way to count the value of Hebrew letters. The place value of Moses's name equaled 39, but the decimal value was 345.

I stood up. There wasn't anything we could do about it now, anyway. I needed some fresh air. But first, a cup of tea.

Minutes later, I stepped out onto the porch holding a piping hot cup of Earl Grey 300. Quietly, I closed the door of the cabin. I stood there for a moment as the steamy vapor of the bergamot-flavored black tea kissed my nose. I walked over to the far side of the porch and leaned against the rail. The quiet stillness was soothing. A breeze stirred, and the pungent smell of pine carried across the clearing from the forest. Their vibrant humming reminded me of a stanza of Longfellow's poem, "A Day of Sunshine."

I hear the wind among the trees
Playing celestial symphonies;
I see the branches downward bent,
Like keys of some great instrument.

I smiled at the recollection of my youth. I could still picture the face of my middle school teacher as she read the poem aloud, and we followed along in our books. I shook my head. Funny how memories you didn't even consciously remember could be dredged up from your past. Maybe that was all my dream about the door had been—a ghost memory. I gave an involuntary shudder. I could still hear the knocking in my mind.

With a final puff, the wind stilled, and the smell and sound of the pines retreated to the green boughs of the forest sentinels. Left behind was the earthy, hot aroma of baking dirt and dry grass.

My gaze wandered toward the barn. Had my father made similar improvements there? It sure didn't look like it from the outside, but I went to investigate, nonetheless.

The barn's false front rose about three feet above the roof, which sloped toward the forest. A wooden pole corral extended from both sides of the building and encircled a fifty-by-fifty-square-foot area. The corral remained as I remembered with one difference—it was new but meant to look old. Some great care and money had gone into its reconstruction. From the backside, solar panels that covered the barn roof became visible—not the standard fixed kind but high-end panels that moved with the sun. They explained the power now available on the property. The satellite dish in one corner explained the internet.

I walked back around to the side of the barn and tried the door. It was locked. There were no windows in the barn, just this side entrance, two pairs of double swinging doors in the front and back, and two large square-shuttered openings on the side of each of the double doors in front. I didn't remember them from before. The double doors and the shuttered openings had no visible locks or handles and must have opened from the inside.

I returned to the house and got the key from its hiding place, then tried it in the side-access door. The lock was a little stiff, but I jiggled it, and it turned.

When I stepped inside, I whistled softly. The barn hadn't just been fixed up—it had been entirely rebuilt. To give it an authentic look or to disguise his work—I wasn't sure which—my father had re-sided the new barn with old wood, but inside, everything was fresh and modern. To my left were two new horse stalls. Now I understood the shuttered openings on the front of the barn. They opened from the inside to allow light in for the horse but could be locked up when the facilities were not being used.

The double doors that opened in front and back created a wide corridor through the barn. I lifted the two large tubular iron bars that secured them and swung them open on their oiled hinges. The midday sun brightened the interior. Along one side hitching posts, an assortment of hooks, combs, brushes, hoof picks, and tools hung from the walls. Some of the tools I didn't recognize, but with the manure rake and shovel, I was well acquainted.

On the other side of the hallway, two more rooms roused my curiosity. The door closest to me creaked as I opened it. I flipped the switch on the right side of the door, and the light revealed a tack room. Four empty saddle cradles sat along the back wall with hooks and bars for all sorts of tack mounted above. Several wooden bins with lids lined the left side of the room. I lifted one of the hinged wooden lids and found removable plastic tubs used to store feed—and fairly recently, judging by the sweet, molasses, grainy smell. The next bin smelled like corn, and bits of Bermuda and Alfalfa hay still sprinkled the floor across the way.

Inside the next room, a surprise awaited—a set of steep metal stairs leading down into the ground. I turned around, faced the stairs, and climbed down backward. At the bottom, a basement room extended back under the barn, roughly the same size as the building above. Large wooden timbers lined the ceiling above my head, supporting the thick wooden planking of the barn floor. The walls and floor of the basement were concrete. The damp, musty smell of the room made my nose wrinkle.

Two black polyethylene water tanks filled the backside of the room. Taller than me, they appeared to be nearly eight feet around. Piping which ran to a compact pump and pressure tank connected the tanks. Marked on the sides of both tanks at regular intervals, lines extended to numbers. The first read *250*, the next *500*, and so on, until the final line at the top read *2500*. I tapped on both tanks. Full. Two tanks at twenty-five-hundred gallons each meant that five thousand gallons of water were stored in this basement.

On the left wall, closest to the stairs, a bank of batteries ran from floor to ceiling. A heavy metal door set in a thick metal frame under the steps opened away from me with a suck of air. The room was heavy with darkness. I stooped down to enter and found the space shallow, no more than four feet deep, the width of the basement, and stinking faintly like rotten eggs. Ten fifteen-gallon, cylindrical propane tanks lined the walls. Above them, a pipe manifold connected each to a common gas line. Each manifold outlet possessed a valve. Quarter-inch copper pigtails extended from each valve and connected them to the tanks. The propane tanks explained how the cabin's hot water and a gas stove worked. The number and size of the tanks explained how my father had managed to supply the cabin with propane in such a remote location.

As I stepped back into the main room, my gaze followed the color-coded and labeled piping along the basement walls. All the piping converged on a large hole halfway up the concrete wall. I walked over and peered in. After only a few feet, the pipes disappeared into the darkness. The smaller pipes and conduit were mounted to the bottom of this conduit in a neat, professional manner. Work like this didn't come cheap.

For the rest of the day, I sat with my back against one of the swinging doors of the barn and watched the afternoon pass. Just before sundown, I walked out to the promontory overlooking Clover Creek. Slowly, the sun blazed its smoky path into the forests of the Coconino National Forest rim country. A large green spear pierced the golden ball on the horizon in a final burst of crimson light.

As the shadows crept from their wooded lairs, I returned to the cabin. Being here offered a wonderful escape from my banal life. But my past nagged me. Someday it would catch up with me. I just hoped that Cadence wasn't around when it did.

Chapter 52

Values and the Valued

I woke to the dull clunk of pots on the stove, the clinking of silverware and the sharp tap of porcelain plates and cups on a wooden table. I staggered from the bunkroom and rubbed my eyes.

A blur of color and sound, Cadence hummed a tune I didn't recognize. When she realized I was watching her, she stopped and gave me an impish grin, then pushed out her lower lip and blew a loose lock of hair out of her face. This effort was unsuccessful, so she tried to push it out of the way with the back of her hand. I laughed at the white smudge she left behind on her forehead.

"Think you're making enough racket out here?" I asked.

Cadence just shrugged and returned to the floury mixture she was attempting to roll out on the granite counter next to the sink. "Figured it was time to get your lazy bones out of bed. It's nine o'clock. We've got work to do today."

No wonder I felt so groggy. I'd slept nearly twelve hours. Lazy bones, indeed. The twenty-four hours required to enter our new answer was already up. We could try again.

Cadence turned back toward me. "After we work on Dad's ciphers, I'd like to hike down to Clover Creek later this afternoon."

Hike? I raised an eyebrow, but she refocused on the uncooperative dough. Clover Creek was a pretty ambitious goal for someone who could barely walk a few days ago. The trail might be short, but it dropped nearly a thousand feet from the promontory.

I headed for the shower without voicing my concerns. I knew better. Once her mind was made up about anything, Cadence would not be easily dissuaded. Secretly, I was thrilled she was getting her drive back. Another week and she would be running the trails again and probably dragging me along with her. I hated running.

When I stepped out of the bathroom six minutes later, the smell of biscuits made my mouth water. I joined her at the stove and laughed at the volume of eggs she was scrambling in the cast iron skillet. “You planning on feeding an army?”

“I’m starved.” She poked me in the ribs with the end of the eggy wooden spoon. I winced. “You could use a bit more protein and a bit less …” She didn’t finish her jibe.

I looked down at my belly and then my legs. The last few years, I hadn’t taken care of myself the way I used to. Much of my muscle had sloughed off or turned to fat. My legs were skinny and my waist a couple of sizes bigger. I sighed. When had I stopped caring?

The biscuits came out of the oven golden-brown and lumpy. Cadence gave them an evil eye. I had a feeling we’d be eating a lot of biscuits until she remastered the art. I’d forgotten to put butter on my list, but there was plenty of jelly and jam in the pantry. I grabbed some grape, spread it over the warm biscuit, and took a bite. Cadence watched me like a judge might her jury after three weeks of deliberations. The biscuits were delicious. I swallowed. “Not too bad,” I said with a grin. She gave me a dangerous look. I smiled.

I ate all the eggs I could manage, and Cadence had nearly turned green by the time she took her last bite. Amazing. I indulged in a mental wager as to whether she'd be able to keep it all down. By some miracle, she did.

After we finished breakfast and put the kitchen back in order, I headed for my laptop. My heart nearly stopped as I gawked at the screen. The countdown was gone, but so was the answer page. A new page displayed the third ciphered riddle. I glanced back at Cadence in the kitchen. She was looking at me, a broad smile on her face.

"I figured it out this morning," she said.

"It was the decimal value of 345, wasn't it?"

"It was. Dad used the place value of 39 for the riddle but the decimal value of 345 for the answer."

"Dirty trick," I mumbled, then scribbled on my notepad to get my pen's ink flowing. "Did Dad believe there was significance to the numerical values of the Hebrew words and letters in the Bible?"

After squeezing out the dishcloth, she came to stand behind me. "Yes. He was convinced there was significance to it. It was only the last five or ten years or so that he started exploring the subject. He didn't talk much about it at first. I think he was trying to figure out for himself if there was anything to it or just a bunch of hyped nonsense. By the time he was convinced and wanted to talk more about it …" She paused and lowered her lashes. In a soft voice, she continued. "By that time, I had started to lose interest … in just about everything but how to feed my habit."

I splayed my hands. "Hey, no judgment here." Hadn't my habit been just as debilitating?

She wiped a tear away. "I do remember him saying, though, it was the work of a guy named Casper Laubuschange that convinced him that the numerical value of Hebrew letters and words had significance to the Biblical texts. Something about certain Hebrew passages being constructed in such a way as to focus on a word or an idea. What exactly he meant by that, I never followed up to better understand."

"You always paid more attention to his theories than I did."

Cadence gave me a look of remorse and shame. "But I wish I'd showed more interest in the last few years. Dad would share for hours if I'd listened. But I was a mess, and Dad gradually stopped talking about his research."

I traced my pencil point around the numbers and letters on my notepad, then looked at Cadence. "Do you think his riddles and ciphers are his way of punishing us for rejecting his beliefs?"

Cadence shook her head and frowned "No, Timmy, I don't. I think deep down, you know better than that. Dad was never punitive and little. Strict, yes. High expectations—that too. He just wanted the best for us. I think that these riddles and ciphers are his final, desperate effort to try and reach us, to leave us something more than just money and things. His way of sharing a bit of the wonder he saw in the Bible, and his story, his faith, his values …" She paused and then said, "His hope."

"I'd like to believe that, Caden."

"I know it," she replied. "Now what about the new riddle and cipher? Any ideas?"

I turned back toward my laptop. I took a deep breath and let it out slowly, then read my father's third riddle.

In this enciphered Biblical passage, Yahweh uses 7 to confirm a covenant with 41.

Provide the four letters around which this passage pivots.

כ נ א ז ב ז י ס פ ב ד כ ק ט ס ו ו ט ס ק ר ק ס צ ת ז א ר צ ס ק ק כ
מ ג ה ס ט ע כ ב ז י ס י מ ס נ ל ק ס ת י ק ה ג ו ר ט י ט ב ש ה כ ט
מ ו ח ב מ ע מ ת מ פ ה א ע כ ק מ ש ו ת ע ו י ח ו ב ה ה ר פ צ ו מ ח
ב ס ש ח ג ת ל ז ק נ ק ז ה י ק ת ז ח כ ר ש ק ס י ל ס פ ח ט ס ח ט ס
ז ה ט ד פ ק ר ע ג ק ע פ ר פ ר ס ר פ מ פ ת ז ת ש ס מ ע ח ק ק ד ר ת
ל ס ק צ ב כ ט ג ח ע ה ז כ ח ח מ ע ד ע ו ס ד נ ז ט ש ס ע ת ז ת ד ח
ח ה ד ל ט ת ר מ נ ס ת ט כ ב ג י ר ל ט ט ש ג ת פ א נ מ ש נ ד ד מ ס
ת ק כ צ ב ב ב ר ו ע ה ת ב ב ש ג ר פ ת א פ ח ע ז ת ה י נ ח ע ו ד פ
ו ק ר ו ג כ מ כ ו ר צ ת כ נ ח י י צ כ ב ז ה ק ס ע ל ז צ ס ט ט ר ה
ק ת ת ש נ פ י ק מ ט ד צ ח ג ע ד ר נ ת א ו ד ח ג ה ר ת מ ט ל ח צ צ
ה נ מ ל ק ה ו פ ק ת ת ד ה ז נ א ל ח ג ר ב א ה ה ק ז ג כ ש פ ר ח ע
ר צ פ צ כ מ ש ז נ ב ק ר ע ד ז מ ו ק צ ש ד ו פ צ ק ו י ג כ ד ז ז כ
ח ע ר ח ק ע צ כ ש נ פ ק ו ס ר ע י מ ק פ ס ש מ נ ג ק צ ב ד צ א ג ט
ס ב ה ה ו ל ט ד ש ט צ ק ש י פ ח נ ה ק כ ז ש ש צ ט ק ט ל ג נ מ צ ט
נ ל ל צ פ ע מ ג ה א ת ת ג מ ס ב א א ק ז ג ס מ ה י ט ע ת ס פ ע ס מ
נ ד ד י ה ק נ ה מ ט ק ע ז ק ג ד צ א ו ע ד ח ט א י ז ע ט ח ר ה ת ג
ש ש ח צ ב ת ס צ י מ ת ב כ ק ה ת צ ט ג ב פ פ ת ק ו ז נ פ ע ד ט ל ח
ש ת ג ק ו ת ח ר ד צ מ ס ל מ ז ק נ ע ס כ ת ב ד י פ ו ע ה כ ב ת פ ה
ש ר ת ו ל א ו ו י ל ש א ל ש א ק ב ד י י י ח ק ג א נ ת י ז ו ו ו ק
ט ו נ ו ה י ט ט ע ג ה ע ח ע פ ע ב ו ז מ ש ד ל ש ו ז ב ח ט ב י ו פ
כ ל נ ו ת ק ש ט ב א צ ה ו ש ש ש א ק ב י כ ש ת ר א נ ס ר ש ל פ ה ה
ו ז ד ש פ פ ב ו צ ג ק ו ב כ ט ו ג ח י ס ד ו כ ג ק ט ח ב פ ע ס ק נ
ר ו ה ג ח צ צ ז ט ר ב פ ו ה ע י ר ב א י נ ו י ק ו ו ש נ מ ח ז ה ו
ר ס ד צ ז ד ס ה ב ז ו ק ע ו נ ז ע ד ק ע ז כ כ ו ד צ ט ע ב ר כ ט ה
ו ע ז ב ב מ ה ס ה ז ט ש ד ה ת כ ח א ת ג ו צ ח ש י ה ק ס ז צ ש כ ב
א ה ל ה פ צ ב ת ט ל נ ו א כ ס ר ע ק פ ע ת ק ק א צ צ ז ה ב ו ק ס צ
ז ו ש י ט מ ח כ צ פ ס פ פ ל ע צ ד ק ת ש ש מ צ ח ק ר צ ח מ ח ח א ז
א ר נ ל ב י כ ו ב א ט ב נ ע ס ר ר ט נ ג ע ג ז ב נ צ ג ה ג ח ש צ ח
א צ ל ז כ ט ל ש ח ש ק ע צ ל כ ה ת ו ז ע מ ד ד ט ק ז ו ת ח ט מ ז ע
ס ס ש ט כ ד ט מ ב ר ט י ח ל נ ש א ס ג מ א נ ו ש ג מ מ ת ס ק ט ג ל
ת ז ב ת ק מ ש א ד ל ת ר י ט כ ט ע ק ש נ ט ח י ר ק ר ר ו א ז ח ז ג
ח ז י כ ו ק ל ר ל ר צ כ ח ל צ ט מ ז ט ב כ ת צ נ ל צ ש ט ו ס צ ת צ
ר ז ש ל צ ט ק ז ל ד ע פ י ע פ פ ה ת נ ג ד ה ו ז ה א ל ח ה ג ב ר ק
מ ח ג ת ש י ל ל ט ש כ ח ס ש י י ש ל ה ק כ י ש ל ה ב ו ע ס ח ח פ ז
כ נ ד צ מ ד נ נ ח ד ז נ ד כ ל ט ק ל א ב ל ל י ע ע מ ג מ ל ז נ פ ו

Luke 1:72-73

To perform the mercy *promised* to our fathers, and to remember his holy covenant; The oath which he sware to our father Abraham,

Numbers 29:13

And ye shall offer a burnt offering, a sacrifice made by fire, of a sweet savour unto YHWH; 13 young bullocks, 2 rams, *and* 14 lambs of the first year; they shall be without blemish:

Revelation 3:7

And to the angel of the church in Philadelphia write; These things saith he that is holy, he that is true, he that hath the key of David, he that openeth, and no man shutteth; and shutteth, and no man openeth;

Romans 14:11

For it is written, *As* I live, saith the Lord, every knee shall bow to me, and every tongue shall confess to God.

Revelation 3:20

Behold, I stand at the door, and knock: if any man hear my voice, and open the door, I will come in to him, and will sup with him, and he with me.

Chapter 53

The End of the Beginning

"Nothing jumps out at me. You?" I asked.

Cadence shook her head. "No, I don't see anything … yet." Then she gave me a confident grin and a wink. "We'll figure it out. We just need to break this down." She turned back to the text.

My stare must have interrupted her pursuit of the verse clues, because she looked up.

"What?" I just shook my head. There had been a slight change in her appearance but she was different somehow. Her cheeks were a bit fuller. But the real difference was in her eyes—they sparkled with enthusiasm. At this moment, she had beat back the demons of her past and was living in the here and now.

"What?" she asked again. "What are you shaking your head about?"

"Just glad to be here with you, Sis. I'm—" I started to tell her that I was happy to escape my own lonely, screwed-up past, but I caught myself. Why spoil her enthusiasm with my recriminations? "So where do we begin?"

"How about you work on the riddle, and I'll tackle the cipher?"

"Okay, but I think I have the easier part of the bargain." I tapped the cipher on the screen.

"We'll see," she said with that twinkle in her eyes again. Her expression firmed, and she indicated the laptop by a tilt of her head. "We're starting to get an idea of how Dad thinks and

maybe a glimpse of where he might be headed with this. Read through his riddle and the passage of Scripture he gave us and tell me anything that comes to mind. Anything at all that you think as you read it. Don't try to think too hard."

I gave her a skeptical look but played along. I started with the riddle.

In this enciphered Biblical passage, Yahweh uses 7 to confirm a covenant with 41.

I pointed at the text. "This is the first time Dad has used the proper name of God in one of his riddles."

Cadence nodded. "Anything else?"

"The focus of the passage is Yahweh confirming a covenant with an individual or group of people represented by the number 41."

"Right. Okay. Now the instructions."

Provide the four letters around which this passage pivots.

I paused a moment, but I was drawing a blank. I shrugged. "I don't know what to make of that, other than the obvious. Our answer needs to be four letters, probably a word, and somehow, this word is the pivot of the passage." Next, I read the passages of Scripture aloud to Cadence.

Luke 1:72-73

To perform the mercy *promised* to our fathers, and to remember his holy covenant; The oath which he sware to our father Abraham,

Numbers 29:13
And ye shall **offer** a burnt offering, a sacrifice made by fire, of a sweet savour unto YHWH; 13 young bullocks, 2 rams, *and* 14 lambs of the first year; they shall be without blemish:

Revelation 3:7
And to the angel of the church in Philadelphia write; These things saith he that is holy, he that is true, he that hath the key of David, he that openeth, and no man shutteth; and shutteth, and no man openeth;

Romans 14:11
For it is written, *As* I live, saith the Lord, every knee shall bow to me, and every tongue shall confess to God.

Revelation 3:20
Behold, I stand at the door, and knock: if any man hear my voice, and open the door, I will come in to him, and will sup with him, and he with me.

Cadence's gaze was intent on me as I read the last passage, I let out a long breath, and my neck prickled. There it was, the door of my dreams and the knocking. I shivered.

"Don't overthink," she said. "Just tell me the thoughts or words that came to mind."

I closed my eyes and pictured the images the words had conjured. "A covenant, sacrifices, a key, a knee, a door, knocking, and Jesus."

"Okay." She met my eyes as they opened and grabbed my shoulder. "Now you have subjects upon which to focus. There is a pattern. We just have to figure it out. In the first two

ciphered riddles, Dad provided at least one verse that told us the type of cipher he used. There is no reason to believe this one is different. And given that, at least two of the other verses relate to the riddle itself."

"And the final verse?" I couldn't get past my father's unsettling use of this passage about Jesus knocking at the door.

It had to be a coincidence, didn't it? I'd dreamed about the door with 391 on it and the knocking behind it before I knew the number represented Jesus's name. Was my father messing with me from the grave? Or was this more evidence of how screwed up my mind really was?

I wasn't ready to accept the only other option. I mean, if there was a God, why would He care about someone as messed up as me? Surely, He had better things to do than stir the dreams of a broke gambler who'd gone out of his way to reject Him. That didn't make any logical sense. And it darn sure wasn't deserved.

I shook myself to get rid of the uncomfortable, inexplicable thoughts. The look I gave Cadence must have spoken volumes.

She shrugged and made an *I don't have an answer for you* expression with her hands. "Forget your dream for a minute. What about the verse itself? In what way does it relate to the other ciphers?" Cadence waited, then, when my mouth slackened, she beamed.

"The final verse tells us something about the previous cipher, doesn't it?"

Cadence held up her hand for a high five. "Exactly!"

I hesitantly slapped her hand with my own. The insight wasn't truly any great victory on my part. She'd practically had to walk the idea right up to me and hit me in the face with it. I had to admit it was pretty neat, though.

Cadence continued, "Dad's final verse is his way of telling us more about his thoughts on the deeper meaning of the previous cipher."

I laughed good-naturedly at Cadence's enthusiasm. Her undisguised joy at figuring out this piece of the puzzle extinguished the beginnings of a peevish thought of mine that she seemed always to be one step ahead of me. After all, this was about her. Not me. This was her inheritance we were trying to earn. I beat the self-centered monster back into its cage and barred it with the light of my sister's happiness. The visual brought a genuine smile to my face.

"It's cool, Cadence," I said with unfeigned enthusiasm this time. "Pretty freaking cool. So, if you are correct, then Revelation 3:20 is Dad's way of telling us that Joshua, Yeshua, or literally 'Yahweh's Salvation' is the person behind the door. The hidden theme of his ciphers?"

"Sure, something like that," she replied with her wide smile. "And the final verse of the second cipher? Do you remember it?"

I recited the verse. "'For there are three that bear record in heaven, the Father, the Word, and the Holy Ghost: and these three are one.'"

"And how is it part of Dad's theme?"

Rubbing my chin, I shifted in my chair. "John 5:7 confirms for us that the 39 and 1 or the 3x13 of Dad's first cipher was the numerical way of showing that the Old Testament's Yahweh was one god with three manifestations—or something along those lines."

Cadence nodded in agreement. "And the fifth verse of the first cipher?"

I frowned. "Aren't we getting off track here?"

She held up her hand. “Hold on. If the fifth verse of each cipher is important, then don’t you think we should at least consider the fifth verse of the first cipher? Who knows, it might be a missing piece of the puzzle later on.”

“Okay, I see your point. Maybe we should check it out.”

Cadence flipped back in my notes. When she got to the first cipher, she read it out loud.

Isaiah 46:9-10

Remember the former things of old: for I *am* God, and *there is* none else; *I am* God, and *there is* none like me, Declaring the end from the beginning, and from ancient times *the things* that are not *yet* done, saying, My counsel shall stand, and I will do all my pleasure:

This time it was my turn to ask, “Any thoughts?”

Cadence was silent for some time. “Well, if the fifth verse is part of the theme of Dad’s ciphers, then I’d say they’re meant to show us that God has a purpose that He determined from the beginning. A purpose that will not be thwarted. An end He’s already declared and cannot be altered.”

All I could think of were the words my grandmother had written in my father’s Bible. Words of similar certainty about the future. A certainty born out of her faith in this unfathomable God of the Bible. I looked away from Cadence’s intent gaze.

“I think Grandmother believed that, too,” I said softly.

“What do you mean?”

“In Dad’s Bible, she wrote something that this verse reminds me of.”

The color in Cadence’s face drained away like she’d been mortally wounded. Her happiness and enthusiasm vanished in a look of nervous dread. “What did she write?” she asked in a husky whisper.

“What’s wrong?”

“What did she write?” Cadence insisted.

I stared at her in dumb confusion.

“Tell me,” she pleaded.

“It was nothing to get excited about, Cadence,” I tried to reassure her.

“Just tell me, please.”

I closed my eyes and recited the words I saw as clearly as if I held the Bible in my hand.

I know in whom I have believed, and am persuaded that he is able to keep that which I have committed unto him against that day.

My eyes opened when Cadence gasped. Before I could say anything more, she fled from the desk and disappeared into the bunk room.

Chapter 54

Pushing Through

I listened to Cadence's muffled cries for as long as I could stand. I had no idea why the words from my father's Bible had caused such emotion. Was it because they reminded her of him? Or was there something else I didn't know?

Rising from the table, I walked to the bunkroom door and knocked softly. "You okay, Caden?" Several stifled sobs were my reply. "Can I come in? You want to talk about it?" I clutched the door handle.

"Please leave me alone for a while, Timmy."

"You sure?"

"I'm sure," she said softly. "I just need some time alone right now."

"Okay, Sis." I turned away from the door, not a little confused and worried.

I sighed as I opened the front door and stepped out onto the porch. My sister's sorrow or pain or whatever it was unsettled me. The past few days, she'd seemed so alive and hopeful.

I sat down on one of the rough porch benches my father had built. I must have dozed because, the next thing I knew, a soft hand on my shoulder made me jump. Cadence stood there, her eyes puffy and red. In place of the day's earlier smiles and enthusiasm was a deep etching of regret and sadness. She sat down beside me and leaned her head on my shoulder.

After some time, I cleared my throat. "You want to talk about it now?"

Her slight frame shook beside me. After a moment, she said, "Not now, Timmy. Maybe not ever."

We left it like that. For hours, we just sat there as the day slid slowly by in strength-giving peace and quiet. Finally, Cadence stirred, and the pressure on my shoulder eased.

"I'm ready to tackle Dad's cipher again if you are," she said.

Tranquility had replaced some of her sadness, but her aura of regret remained palpable. Most noticeable of all, she had a hard time meeting my eyes. She was holding something back, and whatever it was had left a terrible mark. I wanted to say something but pestering her wasn't going to help. She'd have to bleed the bitter poison when she was ready.

Instead, I stood. "I'm ready, Sis," I said with enthusiasm neither of us felt. Sometimes life is like that. You go through the motions whether you feel like it or not. You suck it up and move forward.

We sat back down at the table, and after a few false starts, I asked, "What comes to your mind when you read the riddle and the verse clues?"

"Numbers," Cadence said mechanically.

"Any particular numbers?"

"7, first of all. 41, 13, and 29, but 7, I believe, is the key."

"Explain."

Cadence gave a hesitant smile. Then a little miracle happened. Whatever troubling thoughts had been stalking her faded, and some of her enthusiasm returned. I breathed a silent sigh of relief.

"I was hoping you'd ask," she said. "First of all, Dad had a thing for 7. He used the number a lot in the riddles and ciphers he made for me. He believed it was the most important number in the Bible. The next thing that stands out to me is that in the riddle, 7 seems to be the activating agent. Call it a catalyst if you want. In the riddle, it is the symbol that Yahweh uses to confirm a covenant with 41. My guess is that 41 is a person. 7, I'm not sure about. It could be a person, a group of people, or a number of things. I'd be willing to bet, though, that 7 is the key to this thing. We figure out 7, solving the riddle and cipher will not be far behind."

"Okay, 7 is important - I get that," I raised my hands, "but what about 13, 29, and 41? What's important about them?"

Cadence shrugged. "I'm not sure how they fit in here, but they stand out."

"Stand out, how?"

Cadence tapped the eraser of the pencil she was holding against her tooth, as though she was trying to put into words something she couldn't explain. Or that she sensed. "Well, 7, 13, 29, and 41 all have one thing in common, for sure. They're prime numbers, only divisible by one and themselves. The 4th, 6th, 10th, and 13th, to be exact."

"Why is that important?" Once again, she'd lost me. But then, I didn't have my sister's passion or her keen mind.

"I don't know what it is, but it seems more than coincidental. Did you notice the passage from Numbers 29:13? The sacrifices offered in the passage are 13, 2, and 14, the sum of which is 29. There is something here I can't put my finger on."

Cadence seemed to drift off into a world all her own. Fine by me. It was certainly better than the one she'd just emerged from. I tried to follow along as she mumbled something about thirty percent of the time, 7 or one of its factors were used, but I soon lost interest. I stood up and stretched. Cadence looked up briefly.

"I'm going to get some fresh air. My brain is jumbled."

Cadence nodded and smiled absently.

I headed for the door. Right now, the pieces of my father's riddle jangled and clanged in my head like the wrought iron art hung in a little old lady's garden. The clarity of the outdoors called.

As I turned the door handle, I heard, "seven numbers. thirty percent of the time seven or one of its factors are used. Dad would have…." The click of the door latch behind me cut off the rest of her words.

Chapter 55

New Thoughts and Ancient Keys

From the ledge that overlooked Clover Creek, an intermittent stirring of the wind brought a wet, pine-infused scent from below. What a beautiful and untamed land, this wild rim country! Below me, a ribbon of silver water flashed and sparkled in the sun. The yellow rays were just now reaching into the depths of the canyon. I took a deep breath of the heady, pine-laced air.

My sister had a special connection with my father, no doubt about it. Solving Dad's riddles and ciphers seemed to provide her a way to reconnect to him. Yet, at the same time, what a field of landmines. Just the mention of words written in his Bible had taken her someplace terrible. How did one navigate such a razor-edged path?

The truth was, the worries I held for Cadence were but reflections of similar fears about my future, about myself. Could I walk away from my past? Outrun my mistakes? How would I keep myself from falling back into that self-serving, listless existence I'd led for the past eight years? Looking back at it from where I stood now allowed me to see the ugliness of it all, the futility of it, the unworthiness. As much as I might want to, how could I avoid a relapse? Could the ciphers help?

I kicked puffs of dirt up with my shoes. Invisible currents twirled and twisted the little clouds of dust. They were pulled and pushed, lifted and dropped, separated and drawn back together, but always mixing and fading until they seemed but a figment of my imagination.

Although I couldn't see the wind, I knew it was there by the effect it had. Such an elementary principle, yet so applicable. But I lived in a secular world. Wasn't one of its unspoken rules that we only believed in what we could experience through our senses?

I kicked another cloud of dust into the invisible energy of the wind and gave a frustrated laugh. Was that what my dream about the door had been—my mental mix of dusty memories injected into an unseen force?

Following the tortured path of my thoughts made solving my father's riddles seem like first-grade math homework. "Better stick with your addition tables," I muttered.

I laughed then at the irony. My father had infused his riddles with the basics of arithmetic. He believed God was One. Granted, his 39 is One or 13x3 is One, if that was indeed what he was trying to infer, was a bit more of a complicated mathematical or theological proposition. But at least I could understand what he seemed to be saying. My dream, not so much. Or maybe I just didn't want to see?

I wandered over to the slab of rock perched on the edge of the expanse below, sat down, and wrapped my arms around my legs. The vastness in front of me made me feel small and insignificant. Who was I in all this? What was my purpose? Were those even valid questions?

Growing up, I'd been told by my father that I was special, unique, intentional. My professors and the secular world told me I was insignificant, unintentional, an accident—just a freaking, cosmic, biological accident. What I believed about the world around me and my place in that world had influenced decisions I made, the paths I'd chosen, and ultimately, would influence my destination. What was my destination?

These thoughts tore at my mind like the tempered steel fingers of a harrow breaking the tough soil of a neglected field. Crushed between two opposing world views, I leaned forward and put my chin on my knees. I didn't have the answers, the certainty that my mind searched for. I would have to accept that for now. What I did have was an opportunity to glimpse my father's mind. To get to know him better by solving the puzzles he'd left for us. This game of his clearly had purpose and meaning. It also had a destination. Considering the vapid, wasted life I'd led, even living vicariously through my father's thoughts was better than where I'd been and what I'd done the last few years. Maybe at the end of this journey, I'd understand his faith. Perhaps I'd better appreciate my lack of it.

So where was he taking us with his riddles? What picture was he drawing with his creative math? Cadence's instincts were probably right—7 might be the key, the activating agent, the medium of exchange, in the most recent riddle. But why 7? Maybe the *why* was not the most important question right now. What about the other interrogatives—where, what, when, and how? To begin with, I needed to know *what* this number 7 represented and then *how* it was used by Yahweh to confirm a covenant.

When I got back to the house, I found Cadence asleep on the couch again. She had tucked herself in with a blanket and looked as snug as a bug in a rug. Her lips gave the barest evidence of a smile. Her face had a reassuring peace about it.

After I sat down, I reviewed Cadence's latest notes. As I thumbed back through the pad, I discovered three more pages tucked beneath.

The second page looked to be our father's Hebrew cipher text that Cadence had neatly copied into a grid. The last page was some sort of ciphering device, a smaller grid of the Hebrew alphabet labeled at the top, *Vigenère Tableau*. Each letter of the Hebrew alphabet was written in the first line of twenty-two boxes, from *aleph* to *tav*. In the second line of the grid, the Hebrew alphabet was written again, but this time, shifted by one character. This process was repeated with each line of the grid until the final line began with the Hebrew letter *tav*.

Vigenere Tableau

ת	ש	ר	ק	צ	פ	ע	ס	נ	מ	ל	כ	י	ט	ח	ז	ו	ה	ד	ג	ב	א
א	ת	ש	ר	ק	צ	פ	ע	ס	נ	מ	ל	כ	י	ט	ח	ז	ו	ה	ד	ג	ב
ב	א	ת	ש	ר	ק	צ	פ	ע	ס	נ	מ	ל	כ	י	ט	ח	ז	ו	ה	ד	ג
ג	ב	א	ת	ש	ר	ק	צ	פ	ע	ס	נ	מ	ל	כ	י	ט	ח	ז	ו	ה	ד
ד	ג	ב	א	ת	ש	ר	ק	צ	פ	ע	ס	נ	מ	ל	כ	י	ט	ח	ז	ו	ה
ה	ד	ג	ב	א	ת	ש	ר	ק	צ	פ	ע	ס	נ	מ	ל	כ	י	ט	ח	ז	ו
ו	ה	ד	ג	ב	א	ת	ש	ר	ק	צ	פ	ע	ס	נ	מ	ל	כ	י	ט	ח	ז
ז	ו	ה	ד	ג	ב	א	ת	ש	ר	ק	צ	פ	ע	ס	נ	מ	ל	כ	י	ט	ח
ח	ז	ו	ה	ד	ג	ב	א	ת	ש	ר	ק	צ	פ	ע	ס	נ	מ	ל	כ	י	ט
ט	ח	ז	ו	ה	ד	ג	ב	א	ת	ש	ר	ק	צ	פ	ע	ס	נ	מ	ל	כ	י
י	ט	ח	ז	ו	ה	ד	ג	ב	א	ת	ש	ר	ק	צ	פ	ע	ס	נ	מ	ל	כ
כ	י	ט	ח	ז	ו	ה	ד	ג	ב	א	ת	ש	ר	ק	צ	פ	ע	ס	נ	מ	ל
ל	כ	י	ט	ח	ז	ו	ה	ד	ג	ב	א	ת	ש	ר	ק	צ	פ	ע	ס	נ	מ
מ	ל	כ	י	ט	ח	ז	ו	ה	ד	ג	ב	א	ת	ש	ר	ק	צ	פ	ע	ס	נ
נ	מ	ל	כ	י	ט	ח	ז	ו	ה	ד	ג	ב	א	ת	ש	ר	ק	צ	פ	ע	ס
ס	נ	מ	ל	כ	י	ט	ח	ז	ו	ה	ד	ג	ב	א	ת	ש	ר	ק	צ	פ	ע
ע	ס	נ	מ	ל	כ	י	ט	ח	ז	ו	ה	ד	ג	ב	א	ת	ש	ר	ק	צ	פ
פ	ע	ס	נ	מ	ל	כ	י	ט	ח	ז	ו	ה	ד	ג	ב	א	ת	ש	ר	ק	צ
צ	פ	ע	ס	נ	מ	ל	כ	י	ט	ח	ז	ו	ה	ד	ג	ב	א	ת	ש	ר	ק
ק	צ	פ	ע	ס	נ	מ	ל	כ	י	ט	ח	ז	ו	ה	ד	ג	ב	א	ת	ש	ר
ר	ק	צ	פ	ע	ס	נ	מ	ל	כ	י	ט	ח	ז	ו	ה	ד	ג	ב	א	ת	ש
ש	ר	ק	צ	פ	ע	ס	נ	מ	ל	כ	י	ט	ח	ז	ו	ה	ד	ג	ב	א	ת

I flipped back to my father's cipher Cadence had written out. How might this 'tableau' be used to untangle my father's cipher text?

After several minutes of futile effort, I returned to my sister's first page of notes. The only thing that made much sense was that she had circled a word and a number—the word *key* from the passage of Revelation that our father had given as one of his clues and the number *7*. She'd drawn a line across the page connecting the two circles. Clearly, she also believed 7 was the key. But it was one thing to have a key and quite another to know how or where to use it.

Chapter 56

Covenants and Cream Soda

After another half hour of torturing my brain trying to make sense of my sister's notes, I pushed them aside and focused on my line of research. I pulled my laptop close and typed in *confirmed a covenant*. Doubtful my father would make it that easy, but who knew. At the very least, I'd have a better idea of how many and what kind of covenants there were in the Bible.

I hit *enter*. A second later, one result was returned. "That looks promising."

Maybe I had hit pay dirt, after all. The passage was from the book of Daniel, chapter 9, verse 27. I wrote the first portion of the verse in my notes.

And he shall confirm the covenant with many for one week: …

Could it be that easy? A week was 7 days. My excitement tempered as I read further. A couple of hours later, I decided that Daniel 9:27 was not the answer to the riddle.

Apparently, Jewish and Christian scholars passionately debated the 'he' of Daniel 9:27. Some claimed the 'he' referred to Christ, and others just as certain that the 'he' referenced a future, apocalyptic anti-Christ. Still others suggested 'he' was some Jewish pseudo-messianic figure. In any case, I could pretty confidently say the 'he' was not Yahweh, the living God of the Bible. This then disqualified the passage as a solution to my father's riddle, which clearly stated that Yahweh used 7 to confirm a covenant with 41.

My stomach growled. The clock on my laptop proclaimed that it was nearly one p.m.

A few minutes later, I made a couple of turkey sandwiches. I left one on the kitchen table for Cadence. I sat back down at the desk with mine. As I munched, I broadened my search. Instead of inputting the exact words *confirmed a covenant*, I searched for the words separately and added an asterisk after each. This new search string should snag variations like *confirmed, confirming, confirms*, and others.

Five hits this time. The Daniel 9 reference was still there, but now I had four more. The first two looked promising. One was from the book of Chronicles and the other from Psalms. Both referenced a covenant Yahweh confirmed with Jacob and Israel. This covenant, it seemed, was initially made with Abraham.

I wrote *Abraham, Jacob*, and *Israel* on my notepad. Above these names, I added in parentheses, *confirmed covenant*. Below, I made myself a note to check out the values of their names. If one of these men's names had a numerical value of 41, then it might help me narrow my search for this covenant.

Before diving into a deep exploration of those two passages, I read the last two search results to see if they might not be more promising. They were both from the New Testament book of Galatians, the third chapter. There was one reference to a *confirmed covenant* in verse 15 and another in verse 17. Hmm, very intriguing—not because the verses were better choices but because it looked like they referred to the same or similar covenant mentioned in the first two results of my search. Excitement tingled through me.

Altogether, five passages in the Biblical text referred to a confirmed covenant. From my cursory exploration, four talked about the same covenant. Or, at least, they pointed to a covenant made with the same person. That person was Abraham. I wrote all four verses down in my notepad along with any related context. I underlined the word *covenant* and confirmed in each passage.

1 Chronicles 16:14-17

He is YHWH our God; his judgments are in all the earth. [15]
Be ye mindful always of his covenant; the word which he
commanded to a thousand generations; [16] Even of the
covenant which he made with Abraham, and of his oath unto
Isaac; [17] And hath confirmed the same to Jacob for a law,
and to Israel for an everlasting covenant,

Psalm 105:6-10

O ye seed of Abraham his servant, ye children of Jacob his
chosen. [7] He is YHWH our God: his judgments are in all the
earth. [8] He hath remembered his covenant for ever, the word
which he commanded to a thousand generations. [9] Which
covenant he made with Abraham, and his oath unto Isaac; [10]
And confirmed the same unto Jacob for a law, and to Israel
for an everlasting covenant:

Galatians 3:15-16

Brethren, I speak after the manner of men; Though it be but a
man's covenant, yet if it be confirmed, no man disannulleth,
or addeth thereto. [16] Now to Abraham and his seed were the
promises made. He saith not, And to seeds, as of many; but
as of one, And to thy seed, which is Christ.

Galatians 3:17

And this I say, that the covenant, that was confirmed before of God in Christ, the law, which was four hundred and thirty years after, cannot disannul, that it should make the promise of none effect.

From what I could make of the passages, those from Chronicles and Psalms referenced a covenant God had made with Abraham and his descendants. The New Testament author of Galatians picked up on this theme and explained how that Abrahamic covenant was about one of his descendants or *seed*. This *seed,* the author explained, was Jesus. I sat back in my chair and tried to wrap my mind around how these Scriptures fit into the bigger picture my father must be trying to paint.

I could be on the right track. The first riddle dealt with the nature of God as ONE, or in a more symbolic sense, 39 or 3x13 as ONE. The second riddle showed that 391 was the number of Yahweh's Salvation and the proper name of the Old Testament hero Joshua and the New Testament's Jesus. The third riddle now referenced a covenant and 7 as Yahweh's means to confirm said covenant with someone or something described as 41. If 41 was a reference to Abraham and the covenant that Yahweh confirmed with him, then that covenant could potentially be the promised *seed,* Jesus, that Galatians was talking about.

I read through my notes a second time. A lot of *if*s, but so far, my suppositions seemed to be a harmonious continuation of the underlying thread of my father's riddles, his telling of the end from the beginning.

I was taking speculative leaps here, but if I was correct, I might've found a shortcut to solving the riddles. 7 might be the key to solving this riddle, but Jesus 391 might be the master key to unlock them all. In my notes, I circled the word *David*, which I knew from the larger context referred to Christ as the offspring of King David.

Okay. The best way to test my theory was to see if Abraham's name was equal to 41. If it did, it was pretty likely that I was on the right track.

I got that feeling of excitement in my stomach as I started to work out the Hebrew letter values for Abraham's name, *אברהמ*. I wrote each letter on my notepad, followed by its positional or place value.

א= *1*

ב = *2*

ר = *20*

ה = *5*

מ = *13*

41

I tossed my pencil in celebration. The place value of Abraham's name did equal 41. My father's riddle was indeed about a covenant Yahweh confirmed with Abraham. What's more, the first and last letters equaled 1 and 13. Those two numbers kept popping up.

I turned back to my notepad and wrote out the riddle with *Abraham* in place of *41*.

In this enciphered Biblical passage, Yahweh uses 7
to confirm a covenant with 41 (Abraham).

Bit by bit, I was cracking this puzzle. Now all I had to do was figure out how 7 fit into the riddle. Who or what was 7? I didn't know much about the number and its use and symbolism in the Bible. That I needed to remedy because it was becoming increasingly clear that the solution to the riddle hung on the number 7. Maybe 7 was the key to the cipher, like my sister indicated in her notes.

A groan from the couch made me turn my head. Arms extended, fists clenched, eyes closed, Cadence was thrashing her head and moving her arms as if she was fighting someone. I jumped up and hurried to her side. I called her name, and when she paused, I put my hand on her sweaty forehead.

"Caden? Cadence, it's Timbre. It's okay, Sis. I'm here," I said gently.

Cadence's arms and head went rigid, and she gave another heart-rending groan. Her unfocused eyes opened. Finally, after what seemed like minutes but was probably no more than seconds, they fixed on my face. Her arms fell to her side, and she turned her head toward me. Gradually, the fear in her eyes receded into relief.

She swung her legs off the couch and sat there collecting herself. Her jaw squared and then she gave me a brave smile.

"You okay?"

She nodded, lips firm. "I'm okay, just a bad dream, is all."

I wanted to ask what it was all about. But by the thrashing and groaning sounds she had made, did I really? Cadence rubbed her hands across her face like she was trying to rub out the bad memory.

I asked anyway. "You want to talk about it?"

Her expression drooped, and she shook her head. "These are my demons to fight. You don't need to get them into your head too." She stood. The look she gave me said, *case closed.*

"Okay, Sis. But if you ever need to talk about it, I'm here for you."

"Thank you, Timmy," she said with another sad shake of her head.

"You hungry?" I asked, changing the subject.

"Starved."

I took that as a good sign. "I made you a sandwich." I indicated the kitchen table with my head.

She put her hand on my shoulder to steady herself and then walked over and inspected the sandwich's contents. She raised a speculative eyebrow. "Looks yummy," she said with a particular expression I wasn't sure how to take.

I shrugged. "The best I could do with what we brought. We should probably head into Payson tomorrow to pick up some more supplies. Now that we know there is a fridge here, we can get a lot more fresh fruits and vegetables. If we are going to get you back in shape, we are going to need some healthy food."

Cadence took a bite of her sandwich and nodded. "Sounds good. I have a hankering for bananas and mangos."

I laughed. "Strange combination. But if that is what you want, mangos and bananas, it is."

Cadence wandered to the front door and stepped out with her sandwich. She moved to the porch rail and stared toward the edge of the forest. I came out and sat down on the steps. A minute later, she sat beside me. She finished the sandwich and brushed the crumbs off her pants. We lingered in comfortable silence for some time.

"Thirsty?" I asked. When she nodded, I returned to the house and grabbed two of the bottles of vanilla cream soda I'd seen in the fridge. I lowered myself beside her again and twisted off a lid. It gave a hissing gasp. I handed her the chilly bottle.

"Thanks," she said quietly. She waited until I twisted off my lid. We clicked the bottles together in a wordless toast. Raising them, we both took a long pull. The soda was ice cold, and the carbonation gave that pleasant burning sensation all the way down.

After that first taste, Cadence gave me a look, and I knew what she was thinking. Her lips curled into a smile behind the mouth of her bottle. She was thinking of our father. Each evening on our camping trip up here, he'd pull three ice-cold vanilla cream sodas out of a cooler. We'd sit on the steps of the porch and take a long draught together. After that first pull, my father would let out an exaggerated sigh of contentment and would say, "This is really living." We'd all laugh and then finish our drinks in silence. It became a tradition every evening.

Cadence and I took another long, thirsty drink. We looked at each other again, and then both of us uttered a long "Aaaaaahhhhhh," followed a second later by, "Now this is living." We clicked our bottles together again and finished them in silence.

After half an hour, I shifted my position and fidgeted with my bottle. Finally, I asked Cadence, "You want to hike down to the creek?"

She didn't turn to answer until after she had wiped her sleeve across her eyes. When she did look, they were still misty. "I'd like that."

Chapter 57

Conspiracies and Complications

Eric Pincer opened the file folder. Inside, Josh Harland had provided the last year's web traffic accessing the company servers from the oil and gas division. Most of the activity originated from computers within the firm's network. Harland had further limited the search to server access from the John Plummer office, then grouped the access by IP address and chronologically.

Eric thumbed through his notes until he found May tenth, the day the Plummers had entered the first Lazarus Cipher. He turned to the file from Harland and searched down the list of IP addresses until he came to the date. A unique IP address had accessed the servers that day and the day before.

"This must be it," Eric muttered. Next to the IP address for that date, Harland had noted, *Hughes Satellite internet, unknown location.*

Eric reached to scratch his missing arm. He placed his hand back on the table, unsatisfied. Satellite internet probably meant a remote location. Somewhere typically off the grid. That eliminated residential dwellings, hotels, motels, and other commercial establishments. And left, what? Ships, RVs, and buildings in remote locations. Hmm …

Eric dialed his secretary's extension.

"What can I do for you, boss?"

"Alex, would you pull up the Plummer estate file? I'm looking for any satellite internet service fees for John's estate."

"Yes, sir." A pause gave way to the clicking of a keyboard. " Last month I paid the yearly contract for Hughes Satellite internet for one of Mr. Plummer's properties. "

"Any idea which one?"

"I'm sorry. It doesn't provide a physical address, sir. Mr. Plummer's P.O. box in Phoenix is listed. The billing account notes simply list the location as *PC*, whatever that means."

Eric smiled. He'd found them. "Thank you, Alex. That will be all."

He placed the phone back in its cradle and pushed back from his desk. *PC*, that had to be the Plummer cabin. He'd been to the old homestead once before on a hunting trip with John. It was a wild, beautiful, lonely place. But … internet? His visit must have been eight years ago now, and back then, there hadn't been running water or electricity, let alone internet service. A couple of solar panels and a satellite dish could have fixed that.

Maybe he'd underestimated John's children. It was an excellent place to hide—a bad place to be found, though.

Eric stood and paced in front of the window that looked out over the capital. He stopped and stared at the stone obelisk in the distance—a giant middle finger to the rest of the world, all six hundred and sixty-six feet of it. That's how he thought about it, anyway. The ultimate symbol of male machismo. He'd believed the lie it represented at one time. He tried not to look down at his nonexistent arm as the burning crawled its way up from his missing fingers to the livid stump. He'd believed it was about God and country until the day he'd lost his arm and his—Eric shuddered, and his face grew hot with shame.

They'd been told the war was about weapons of mass destruction and securing the world against an Iraqi dictator, but that was a lie too. In the abstract world, it had been about the projection of power and influence. In the real world, it had been about oil and the money it generated.

He squared himself and lifted his good hand toward the shining white phallus in the distance. Eric muttered a vulgar curse as he curled back all but his middle finger and saluted. He laughed at the bitter irony of the gesture. Only one thing brought Eric pleasure now—he lived to pay the debts he owed himself.

He walked back behind his desk and turned to face the wall. On the bookshelf sat a single framed photograph, a picture of John, Rory, and himself standing in front of their Humvee. They had been the only real family he'd ever had. But that had changed too. Eric saluted the photograph. Now he was a family of one.

Chapter 58

Remembrance and Disclosure

We left the bottles on the steps and headed for the trail at the edge of the promontory. It was steep and overgrown with weeds. Halfway down, the pitch grew steeper, and rocks and dirt rolled under our feet. In places, the trail was faded because of disuse, and we were forced to make our way from memory.

As we wound our way, the dry, warm scent of pine gave way to an earthy, green, wet scent of plants that lusted for water. Except for a lone sentinel here and there, the pine trees retreated, yielding the canyon to gnarled oaks with serrated trunks and thick grayish-brown bark. The small waxy green leaves of the oaks greedily harvested the sunlight in this deep rent in the earth.

I pointed at a distinctive bush growing on the opposite bank, part way up the side of the canyon. "Remember what those are called?"

"Manzanita. It means *little apple* in Spanish," Cadence answered.

I puckered my lips and nodded. The twisted red bark of its trunk supported oval leaves from which usually hung clumps of small round berries. I still remember the first time I'd tried them. Sour green little things, and you had to imagine the hint of apple.

We kept moving downward. A heavy silence hung in the warm canyon air like a blanket of snow on a cold winter day. Near the bottom of the trail, we rested. A faint sound replaced the silence so subtly that it took me a minute to identify the low, hollow roar of the rushing waters of Clover Creek. Cadence acknowledged the familiar sound by looking back. We were almost there. Our pace quickened as our feet touched the level ground at the bottom of the trail. Flashes of yellow and green leaves told me the water-hungry cottonwoods and majestic sycamores were near.

I could see the creek bottom now, its tangled bushes and hedges growing out of the fresh deposits of rocks and dirt left behind from the last flood. Head-height in this green ambuscade, debris from the previous hard rain warned of the danger of being caught down in the confines of this narrow chasm. Grasses and thick-leaved water plants waved for several feet on both sides of the bank. The formless, hollow sounds of water, muffled and dispersed by the trees and distance, grew into a rushing, splashing, and tinkling cascade.

We stopped abruptly as we emerged from the dense screen of trees at the edge of the creek. Here, the trail doubled back on itself to avoid an outcropping of rock. As kids, we called it "horseshoe crossing." On the other side of the creek at the open end of the shoe, a castle-like boulder rose twenty feet in the air. Like a sentinel, it watched over the secluded little bowl of sand enclosed by the water.

Cadence and I stood side by side, absorbing the sounds, like a dusty street the first drops of rain.

She looked at me. "The sounds of God's …."

"Symphony," I finished in quiet reverence.

Our father, hands wide, had exclaimed those words each time we'd stood here together. As kids and young adults, we grew to expect his reverent outburst at this place. Our father had been a serious man, which made his infrequent expressions more unusual and memorable.

For the first time in my life, I caught a sense of what he might have felt. If God did exist, as my father believed, I could think of few sounds more satisfying, more invigorating, more calming than this watery symphony as it played its way through the rocky canyon floor.

Unconsciously, I took my sister's hand as we'd done so many times as children. Loath to interrupt my father's divine composition, we stood side by side and let it play its restorative harmonies to our starving souls. Time seemed to stand still. A minute, an hour … I don't know how long we listened in rapt silence.

Cadence stepped closer to the creek bank, and I let go of her hand. Three slipping, sliding steps down the bank, she reached the edge of the water. Jumping from rock to rock, she crossed to a large lichen-covered boulder on the other side and sat down. With a tilt of her head, she called me to join her.

I laughed. "No way, Sis."

She untied her shoes. The socks went next. With a laughing gasp, she slid her feet into the ice-cold mountain water.

"Oooh," she sighed as the water ran over her feet.

"Come on, Timmy," she called. I shook my head and sat down. "You wimp." She laughed. "You never put your feet in."

I shrugged as I watched her. First thing, she always had to put her feet in. I never did unless I was going swimming. It was as if she needed to get as close to the source of that life-giving sound as she could get. She closed her eyes, placed her hands behind her head, and leaned into them, elbows locked, head back facing the sun. It was a picture I would take to my grave. This place was restoring her. Seeing her here with her feet in the sparkling water, the sun shining on her pale face, and its rays glistening through her hair made me want to believe in God.

The sense of an unseen conductor playing a terrestrial symphony to his human audience intensified in my mind. Behind me, a woodwind section resonated. The pine section high up in the canyon hummed, the oaks in the lower flats whispered, and the sycamores and cottonwoods that lined the creek rustled and rattled. The gurgle and roar, the rush and hiss, and the tinkle and splash of the water, in an infinitely complex and endless melody, played upon the rocks, pebbles, and sand of the creek bottom, like fingers upon a living string of liquid that stretched from the mountains to the sea. The buzz of bees and chirp and warble of a bird completed the orchestration.

I rubbed my face. This place was making even my skepticism falter.

"Do you remember what our mother was like?" Cadence asked unexpectedly from the other side of the creek. I jumped a bit and opened my eyes, and she watched me earnestly.

"What made you ask that?"

She sat up and spread her arms wide. "This place." She made a panoramic gesture. "Anyone who would give their children names like ours would have loved a place like this. Don't you think?"

The *flash, flash, flash* of our mother's face as she spun the two of us on the merry-go-round of my memory delayed my reply.

"She was beautiful," I said. "I remember that she was beautiful."

Cadence nodded as if that confirmed her memory as well. I knew what her next question was going to be. I waited for it. It was part of a ritual we'd performed countless times as children—a ritual that had gradually faded sometime in our early teens.

"What did she look like, Timmy?"

"Her hair was the color of golden coffee. Her eyes were a sparkling violet, and her face was like a pale moon." I waited again.

"You forgot a part, Timmy," Cadence said quietly, her head down and eyes closed like she was concentrating. I'd never asked what she was thinking when she bowed her head like that. I just assumed Cadence was trying to find a glimmer from her own memory of our mother, a glimmer that maybe my memories help stimulate. Finally, she stared at me expectantly.

"She had a firm chin, high cheek bones, and a pretty nose like yours."

"Thanks, Timmy." Her tone sounded as wistful as it had so many other times.

Growing up, it had been a game. A way to keep our mother's memory alive. How might our lives have been different if she had stayed?

"She would have loved this place, Cadence," I said.

Cadence's chin jerked up. My words were not part of our tradition. She must've heard the certainty in them. "How do you know that?"

I hesitated. Should I tell her about the letters in Dad's briefcase? So many years of keeping this to myself, but … would they do more harm than good?

Our father had refused to answer our questions about our mother over the years. The only thing he would say was that she was no longer with us. Growing up, we'd assumed this meant she had died. I'd only learned the truth after reading those letters. But still, how could she have walked out of our lives? We were only little children. What kind of person could do a thing like that to her family? I couldn't bring myself to hate my mother, but her betrayal ran deep, and my ever-present anger simmered to the surface when I thought about it.

“Mom was a musician,” I said finally. “She and Dad met in a jazz bar in Ansbach while he was stationed in Germany after Desert Storm.”

Cadence stood and tiptoed across the creek toward me, her face full of questions. When she was standing below me at the bank, she asked, “Did Dad tell you that?”

“No,” I said quietly.

“How do you know, then?”

“I read their letters.”

Chapter 59

Truth and Transformation

Only the crackling of the fire and the rustling of paper broke the silence as the dancing shadows of my sister played upon the wall. She sat in the center of the bearskin rug facing the hearth with one of the letters from my father's briefcase in her hand. Around her in a disordered half circle were strewn the rest of our parents' correspondence. At the center of this rainbow lay a photograph of our mother that our father had tucked into one of their letters.

For the past several hours, Cadences had devoured and reread the letters. Now and again, she would turn to look at me where I sat on the couch, and then, without a word, she would continue to read. I'd expected tears and anger. Instead, her expression reflected sadness mixed with a hungry relief, as though some emptiness had been filled or some needed connection made.

Finally, I had to ask, "What do you think?"

Cadence pressed the letter she was holding to her chest. "I'm happy you shared them with me."

"Aren't you a little angry or resentful she left us?"

Cadence placed the paper on the floor in front of her. She picked up the photograph and cupped it in her left hand. She pivoted to face me, then studied the picture. "No, I'm not angry or resentful, Timbre," she said quietly.

"Why not?"

"The letters don't say why she left. She might have had a reason we don't know about."

Was she in some sort of denial? I leaned my arm over a pillow. "You'd forgive her if you had the chance?"

"I already have," she muttered. Cadence studied the photo for a long time before looking up again, her eyes wet. "I'd like to meet her someday, given a chance. I've missed her every day of my life."

I shook my head. "I don't think I could forgive her. I don't understand how you could either."

Cadence gave me another sad, knowing look. "You and I were raised to believe in God, right?"

"What?" My posture stiffened, and my tone quickly became combative. "What are you talking about? We were talking about our mother, not God."

"Just answer the question. Growing up, we believed in God, yes or no?"

Where was she going with this? I was probably three moves away from checkmate. Reluctantly, I said, "Yes. We believed in God growing up … until we were old enough to know better."

"All right. For the sake of argument, let's say God does exist."

"Okay, I'll play."

She arched a brow. "If God does exist and somehow you discover this to be true, wouldn't you want God to forgive you for abandoning him?"

Check mate.

Her words hit me like a punch to the gut, and I turned away from her frank gaze. I saw the door of my dreams again with the number *391*. I heard the knocking. Cadence had walked me right into that one. I hated to admit it, but yes, if the God of my youth did exist, I would indeed want Him to forgive me for walking away. And in the grand scheme of things, my reasons for walking away, just like my mother's, would probably not be all that important to Him.

"Yeah, I guess I would," I said begrudgingly.

Cadence glanced down at the picture once more. "Me, too," she said. "Me too."

"But God doesn't exist," I protested after a couple of minutes of silence. "And our mother does."

"And you know God doesn't exist, how?"

My tongue tangled—because right then, my memory or my conscience or whatever it was reminded me of the old Proverb, *only a fool says in his heart there is no god.*

Cadence shook her head like she was dealing with a child now. She chided me gently, "You had a gun to your head, and the phone rang? You had Jesus knocking on door 391 of your dreams before you even knew what that meant. You found me half-dead on the floor of my kitchen and gave me a reason to want to live again."

I grabbed the edge of the pillow and pulled it in front of me. All true. The more she spoke, the more my anger and resentment melted away.

There were tears in her eyes now. "I prayed every day of my life until I was too stoned to care. I prayed that someday, I'd get to know more about our mother. And today, those prayers came true." Her gaze bored into me, demanding my acknowledgment. "I learned today that our mother does exist and that she still might be alive. Maybe God does have a plan for my life, and for yours, too. I'm finding the strength to believe that again, Timmy."

I drew a deep breath, but no words came. The sparkling intensity of my sister's eyes made me avert my gaze.

It would take more than a bunch of coincidences and raw emotion for me to believe in God again. I would have to be blind, though, not to see the transformation happening to

Cadence. That tragically broken girl I'd found on the kitchen floor was healing. Her inner strength was being restored. If she wanted to believe that God was behind it, who was I to argue? Who was I to rob her of her renewed faith?

Chapter 60

The Key to Revelation

After breakfast the next morning, Cadence and I made the 45-minute drive into Payson for groceries. Cadence wanted to drive, so I opened my notepad on my lap and chatted about my progress on the Abraham riddle. She didn't say much. Just an occasional *yes* or *uh-huh*.

"I think you are right about 7 being the key." I cut a glance sideways, but her eyes remained fixed on the road, her hands at two and ten on the wheel. I pointed to the bank. "Hey, look, a moose!" Still nothing. "Earth to Cadence. Anyone home?" I touched her arm.

She jerked, then her shoulders relaxed. "Sorry, Timmy."

"What's on your mind this morning, Sis?"

"Just thinking about Mom and Dad." Her voice sounded dreamy.

Maybe I shouldn't have told her about our mother, at least until after we'd finished working on the ciphered riddles. She was lost in another world. I could see where this was going. Now that she knew our mother might be alive, she wanted to find her.

Come on, Cadence, the twenty grand isn't going to last us forever. It certainly isn't enough for us to go looking for our mother, was what I wanted to say. But I couldn't help asking, "You want to find her, don't you?"

All it took was one look.

I gave a long sigh. "I tell you what. Let's solve these ciphered riddles and get your inheritance. Once you are all set up, if you still want my company, I'll look for our mother with you."

Cadence gave a firm nod.

I stuck out my hand. "Deal?"

"Deal!" she said and shook my hand. Cadence's head jerked to the front, and she swerved back onto the road as the car thumped and bumped in the ruts on the side.

"The deal is off if you kill us before we get to Payson."

Cadence laughed as she straightened back out.

"So, if you can talk and drive at the same time, tell me about your notes on the cipher. I couldn't make heads nor tails of them other than that you circled *key* and *7*."

Cadence nodded slowly as if she was ordering her thoughts along different tangents and vectors. This time, she didn't take her eyes off the road as she explained. "I believe Dad's cipher is what cryptologists call a keyword cipher. So far, he used a different type of cipher for each of his riddled passages. The first two ciphers were just teasers to get us used to solving his puzzles and maybe let us become a little complacent. "

"Hold on. How do you know it is a keyword cipher?"

Her eyes twinkled as she glanced at me. "In each of the ciphers Dad has given us so far, there has been at least one passage of Scripture that's told us the type of cipher we are dealing with."

I thumbed back through our notes to the five verse clues and read them again. Cadence waited patiently while I processed.

"This one?" I held my finger at Revelation 3:7. "You think it's a keyword cipher because this passage talks about *the key of David*?"

"Yes, it is the only passage I can connect to a particular type of cipher." She drew another breath but paused.

"But …?"

"But as I said, I think Dad has eased us into his Lazarus ciphers. Now he has jumped several levels of complexity."

That's fantastic. As if the first two were not hard enough.

Cadence waved her hand. "A keyword cipher is a whole different animal. Without special software and a high-end computer, it could take us months to solve … if it's even possible."

She let the gravity of her words hang in the car for a moment, then the corners of her lips twitched.

I gently slapped her shoulder. "You yanking my chain again?"

She snickered. "Maybe a little. If we can figure out the word Dad used to prime the cipher, we should be able to solve it without too much difficulty. Since the cipher uses Hebrew words, the keyword will be in Hebrew." She shot me a questioning look, no doubt checking to see if I tracked with her, but I pointed out the windshield. She'd wandered over the white line again.

"Keep your eyes on the road, Sis."

She looked straight ahead but could no longer hide the smile on her face. I hated when she did that. It was one of the reasons I'd never been part of her and my father's battle of wits. I didn't think of myself as stupid, but compared to Cadence, it seemed my mind functioned with a paper and pencil while a quantum computing device pulsed between her ears.

The worst part of it—once my sister got that competitive twinkle in her eyes, using my gray matter to solve the problem became ten times harder. And she knew it. Next would come the laughter. I clenched my teeth, just waiting.

To her credit, she held it in longer than ever before. Her lips grew pursed in a tightly curved line. But something in her glowing look of uncontaminated happiness evaporated all my frustration in an instant.

I released a gusty breath. "I swear, you get more enjoyment out of turning my thoughts into scrambled eggs than solving your darn ciphers."

Cadence's mirth exploded then, and laughter filled the car. I couldn't resist. Both of us laughed until our eyes watered. Cadence pulled off to the side of the road, and we convulsed until our bellies ached and our throats were sore. The laughter would die out for a minute, and one of us would try to say something, and it would start right back up again. Finally, after we were all dried out and the only sound was the quiet idle of the car's engine, Cadence grasped my hand.

"Thank you, Timmy. I needed that." She grabbed the wheel, checked her mirror, and pulled back onto the highway, a new sense of peace on her face.

I needed it, too—humor. I'd always taken myself way too seriously. I watched the asphalt markings as they stretched away until the next curve a mile ahead, then laid my head back against the headrest and sighed. I closed my eyes and relaxed.

Then it came to me.

Cadence had said that since the cipher was written in Hebrew, the keyword would also be in Hebrew. All of my father's verse clues were from the New Testament—except one. Numbers 29:13 was the only passage from the Old Testament and thus, it was originally written in Hebrew. If the keyword to the cipher was to be found in my father's clues, it would be in the passage from Numbers.

Cadence and I exchanged a glance. She must have seen the realization on my face. She nodded as if she knew.

"Numbers 29:13."

Her eyes were back on the road, and she just nodded again.

"Do you know what word in the verse?" I asked.

She shook her head. "It shouldn't be that hard to figure out, though. Knowing how Dad thinks, the word has a numerical value or several letters symbolic to the riddle. 13, 41, 29, or 7, I figure. If I had to guess right now, I'd say 7, both as the pivot of the riddle and the key to the cipher."

"Yes. I'd agree."

I didn't have the experience solving my father's riddles and ciphers that Cadence had, but I was beginning to understand how his mind worked. I had an idea of the Hebrew words behind the English translation of Numbers 29:13, but I had no way to be sure of their form or spelling. I laid back and relaxed, resigning myself to the wait until we got back to the cabin.

After a few miles of silence, I turned to Cadence again. "What about the keyword cipher? Can you explain it in terms your mentally challenged brother can understand?"

Cadence got a big smile on her face. "I thought you'd never ask."

Chapter 61

Keywords and Casanova

"First, we need some definitions." Cadence winked at me.

I rolled my eyes at her and cringed. "I don't want dry definitions. I want the Cliff Notes or the Keywords Ciphers for Dummies version."

"Okay." She let out a long breath. "This is actually pretty tricky if you don't have something to write it out on."

I waved my notepad dutifully, and she nodded.

"Good. Since Dad's ciphers have been given in Hebrew and the Hebrew alphabet is twenty-two letters, picture a grid of 22x22 squares. That gives us 484 little individual squares."

No way was I about to draw out that many boxes in the car, but I made a few notes.

"Picture a Hebrew letter in each square. Because Hebrew is read from right to left, we start with the top right corner of our grid and place *aleph*, the first letter of the Hebrew alphabet, in the first square. Then, continuing from right to left, we write out the rest of the alphabet until we fill each of the twenty-two squares of the top row. In the second row, we again write out the twenty-two letters, only this time we start with the second letter, *bet*. This moves the first letter, *aleph*, to the last position. The third row begins with the third letter and so on until all twenty-two rows of the grid are filled with Hebrew letters."

"I'm following." I tapped my pencil against my leg. "The top row should start with *aleph* and end with *tav*. The farthest right column should start with the same *aleph* and end at the bottom right square with *tav*."

“Yes.” Cadence grinned over at me. “If you constructed the tableau correctly each letter at the top of the grid will run diagonally through the grid..”

“Hold on.” I raised my hand. “I remember seeing the Vigenère tableau in your notes. Okay, I found it.” I frowned at the chart a moment. “I see what you’re saying.”

Vigenere Tableau

ת	ש	ר	ק	צ	פ	ע	ס	נ	מ	ל	כ	י	ט	ח	ז	ו	ה	ד	ג	ב	א
א	ת	ש	ר	ק	צ	פ	ע	ס	נ	מ	ל	כ	י	ט	ח	ז	ו	ה	ד	ג	ב
ב	א	ת	ש	ר	ק	צ	פ	ע	ס	נ	מ	ל	כ	י	ט	ח	ז	ו	ה	ד	ג
ג	ב	א	ת	ש	ר	ק	צ	פ	ע	ס	נ	מ	ל	כ	י	ט	ח	ז	ו	ה	ד
ד	ג	ב	א	ת	ש	ר	ק	צ	פ	ע	ס	נ	מ	ל	כ	י	ט	ח	ז	ו	ה
ה	ד	ג	ב	א	ת	ש	ר	ק	צ	פ	ע	ס	נ	מ	ל	כ	י	ט	ח	ז	ו
ו	ה	ד	ג	ב	א	ת	ש	ר	ק	צ	פ	ע	ס	נ	מ	ל	כ	י	ט	ח	ז
ז	ו	ה	ד	ג	ב	א	ת	ש	ר	ק	צ	פ	ע	ס	נ	מ	ל	כ	י	ט	ח
ח	ז	ו	ה	ד	ג	ב	א	ת	ש	ר	ק	צ	פ	ע	ס	נ	מ	ל	כ	י	ט
ט	ח	ז	ו	ה	ד	ג	ב	א	ת	ש	ר	ק	צ	פ	ע	ס	נ	מ	ל	כ	י
י	ט	ח	ז	ו	ה	ד	ג	ב	א	ת	ש	ר	ק	צ	פ	ע	ס	נ	מ	ל	כ
כ	י	ט	ח	ז	ו	ה	ד	ג	ב	א	ת	ש	ר	ק	צ	פ	ע	ס	נ	מ	ל
ל	כ	י	ט	ח	ז	ו	ה	ד	ג	ב	א	ת	ש	ר	ק	צ	פ	ע	ס	נ	מ
מ	ל	כ	י	ט	ח	ז	ו	ה	ד	ג	ב	א	ת	ש	ר	ק	צ	פ	ע	ס	נ
נ	מ	ל	כ	י	ט	ח	ז	ו	ה	ד	ג	ב	א	ת	ש	ר	ק	צ	פ	ע	ס
ס	נ	מ	ל	כ	י	ט	ח	ז	ו	ה	ד	ג	ב	א	ת	ש	ר	ק	צ	פ	ע
ע	ס	נ	מ	ל	כ	י	ט	ח	ז	ו	ה	ד	ג	ב	א	ת	ש	ר	ק	צ	פ
פ	ע	ס	נ	מ	ל	כ	י	ט	ח	ז	ו	ה	ד	ג	ב	א	ת	ש	ר	ק	צ
צ	פ	ע	ס	נ	מ	ל	כ	י	ט	ח	ז	ו	ה	ד	ג	ב	א	ת	ש	ר	ק
ק	צ	פ	ע	ס	נ	מ	ל	כ	י	ט	ח	ז	ו	ה	ד	ג	ב	א	ת	ש	ר
ר	ק	צ	פ	ע	ס	נ	מ	ל	כ	י	ט	ח	ז	ו	ה	ד	ג	ב	א	ת	ש
ש	ר	ק	צ	פ	ע	ס	נ	מ	ל	כ	י	ט	ח	ז	ו	ה	ד	ג	ב	א	ת

Cadence reached over to point at the table, and the car crossed the middle lane. I pulled the notepad away and grabbed the steering wheel.

“Watch the road.”

“Sorry,” she said and put both hands on the wheel. She cleared her throat and continued, nonplussed. “See how *aleph* is in the top right corner of the table extends away from that point on a horizontal and vertical axis?”

“I see that.”

"Do you remember playing Battleship as kids?"

I nodded.

"It's similar. Remember Battleship had a grid with A-B-C-D-E-F-G-H-I-J down the side and 1-2-3-4-5-6-7-8-9-10 across the top? I'd call out A4, and you'd place a pin on the grid where the *A* column and the *4* row intersected?" She paused and glanced at me to make sure I was with her.

"Keep going, I'm tracking you."

"Okay. Here's the tricky part. In order to cipher your plaintext, you take the first letter of your keyword and find it on the right column. Next, you take the first letter of your plaintext, and you find it in the top row of the table. Where these two letters intersect, you'll find the first letter of your ciphered text."

"Gotcha."

"For example, if the first letter of your keyword is bet and the first letter of your plaintext is *tav*, you will find your first encrypted letter on the grid where that column and line intersect."

I stared at her.

"So find it."

I ran my finger along the table until I found where the two letters intersected. "It's *aleph*."

"Okay, now you repeat this process for each letter of your keyword and ciphered text."

I scratched my head. "What happens when you get to the end of your keyword? How do you keep encrypting your plaintext?"

"In one of two ways. You can repeat the keyword and use it over and over again. This is a less secure method and can be solved rather easily. If you want to make it extremely difficult, you use an auto-key. That means that once you've reached the end of your keyword, the ciphered text itself becomes the key."

"Huh?"

Cadence's hands tightened on the wheel. "Stick with me here, Timmy. In our case, our key was a single letter, *bet*. Using the vectors of *bet* and *tav,* we got our ciphered text of *aleph*. Since our key is *bet* and it gave us the ciphered text of *aleph*, we now use *aleph* as our next auto-key letter. Once that auto-generated key gives us a new Hebrew letter, that becomes our next key. The longer your keyword, the more secure your cipher becomes."

My finger followed her explanation on the Vigenère tableau. It made sense. She continued.

"You can look at it this way. Your keyword primes the cipher. Every new letter your cipher generates then becomes a new letter in a self-generating auto-key. The auto-key cipher was nearly impossible to crack in antiquity. Despite its nearly unbreakable security, it had a couple of drawbacks which kept it from being used."

"How is that?" I asked, intrigued now that I understood how the cipher was generated.

Cadence let go of the wheel with one hand and waved it around.

"First of all, it is slow and tedious. For long correspondence, it was too time-consuming to cipher the plaintext and just as time-consuming to decipher. The second drawback was the auto-key itself. Because the auto-key was generated from the original keyword, if a single character error was ever made in the transposition of the cipher, the rest of the text from that point onward would become indecipherable. The message would be lost."

"Right." I grasped the concept, but it would take working it out on paper for me to really understand. I glanced at Cadence. "So no more Mr. Nice Guy. Our father is going to make us work for it this time."

She chuckled. “You could say that.”

“What if he made a mistake, and it’s all gibberish?”

She gave a doubtful laugh this time. “It’s unlikely Dad made a mistake. It’s even more unlikely that the mistake was made in the first few lines. All we need to solve the cipher are a dozen or so characters. Once we have the Hebrew letters, we can figure out the Hebrew words. Then we can simply search for that string of Hebrew words in the Bible, and we’ll find the passage.”

“And once we know where the passage is from, we can just count the remaining Hebrew characters in the cipher to determine its total length.”

“Exactly. So, if we can decipher one line of the cipher Dad left, we should be good to go.”

I held up my notepad. “Why is it called a Vigenère tableau?”

Cadence cleared her throat theatrically and quoted aloud.

All things in the world are a cipher… All nature is a cipher, a secret writing. The name and essence of God and his wonders, the very deeds, accomplishments, words, actions, and character of mankind – what are they, but a cipher?

She ended with a stab of her finger into the air. The car swerved slightly.

“Ah, Sis, I’d prefer if you’d keep both hands on the wheel. You’ve had a hard enough time today keeping it between the lines.”

She gave me one of her funky grins and grabbed the wheel with both hands. I waited for her to explain, and she waited for me to ask.

I sighed. “So what gives with the quote?”

"I was quoting our friend, Blaise de Vigenère. He was the sixteenth-century Frenchman credited with the invention of the polyalphabetic or keyword substitution cipher—although Girolamo Cardan, a Milanese mathematician and physician, might deserve the credit. It's a bit muddled, actually. To make matters worse, historians attributed the more simplistic version of the repeating keyword cipher to Vigenère, ignoring his contribution to the much more secure auto-key system. As late as the early twentieth century, *Scientific American* was attributing the weaker repeating keyword cipher to Vigenère and touting it as 'impossible of translation' even though it had been solved several times in antiquity."

I rubbed my hair, probably leaving it as frazzled as my brain. I stared out the window as the highway disappeared over the Mogollon Rim. We were getting close to Payson now. I laid my head back and listened as Cadence's history lesson ran on.

"In any case, today, Vigenère is the most famous name associated with the polyalphabetic substitution cipher, even though his work and contributions were misattributed and forgotten for nearly four hundred years." Cadence shook her head. "Funny, the world of cryptology."

Yes, hilarious, but I loved this side of my sister. Thus, I fueled her fire. "So this Vigenère fellow is the one who came up with the auto-key method you believe Dad used for this cipher."

Cadence nodded. "Yep."

"What happens if we don't figure out the keyword? Can we still solve the cipher?"

"It's possible, but it would be extremely difficult. Especially in the time we have left. If we had to do it without the aid of computers, it could take weeks, months, or maybe even years."

My mouth turned down. "We don't have months."

"I know, Timmy, and we won't need months. We will find Dad's key. Unless I miss my guess, the keyword will also be an important part of the message. You know, layers within layers."

"I hope you are right."

"I know I'm right. Dad wanted us to solve these ciphers because each one solved gives us another piece of a larger puzzle."

Individually, the ciphers appeared to be simply interesting or unusual Biblical trivia. Taken together, they were beginning to assume a new and intriguing life of their own. I'd started this quest with the single purpose of solving the riddles and collecting my inheritance. I'd forfeited my rights to most of that inheritance by taking the payout. Now, I found myself wanting to solve them not just for my sister's sake, but because I had become engrossed by the challenge and interested in the story my father had woven.

"You want to hear another cipher story?" Cadence interrupted my thoughts. I looked at her, and she smiled appealingly.

"Sure, just as long as I don't have to do any ciphers in my head again and you stay on the road."

"Promise. You'll like this one … maybe …"

I groaned.

"Once upon a time …"

I groaned again, louder.

Cadence laughed beautifully, the kind of laugh brimming with life, happiness, and mischief. She turned to me with a grin on her face.

I pointed at the road. "Seriously, Sis, watch the road."

Her knuckles tightened on the fake leather. "Sometime in the mid-eighteenth century, a wealthy aristocrat named Madam d'Urfé was discussing chemistry, magic, and alchemy with a friend. During the course of their conversation, the subject of the transmutation of baser metals into gold was discussed. Madam d'Urfé showed her friend a ciphered manuscript and told him it contained highly prized instructions for such transmutation. She told him the cipher was unbreakable. Madam d'Urfé was so confident, she gave the man a copy of the manuscript. Weeks later, d'Urfé asked him if he'd been able to interpret it, and he said that he had."

Cadence paused in her story as she parked in front of the grocery store. She removed the keys from the ignition. She turned to face me and continued.

"She replied to him that she did not believe it was possible. He asked her, 'Do you wish me to name your key, Madam?' He then told her the keyword was NABUCODONOSOR, the Italian spelling of the word *Nebuchadnezzar*. She was astounded and asked him how he had discovered the word. Instead of telling her the truth, he told her that a genie had revealed it to him."

I laughed.

Cadence paused in her story. "I hope I can remember this next part correctly. In his diary, he wrote something to this effect …

"I might have informed her that the calculation which enabled me to decipher the manuscript furnished me also with the key, but the whim took me to tell her that a spirit had revealed it to me. This foolish tale completed my mastery over this truly learned and sensible woman on everything but her hobby. This false confidence gave me an immense ascendancy over Madame d'Urfe, and I often abused my power over her. Now that I am no longer the victim of those illusions which pursued me throughout my life, I blush at the remembrance of my conduct, and the penance I impose on myself is to tell the whole truth, and to extenuate nothing in these Memoirs."

Cadence shot me a glance. "Care to guess who this rascal was?"

"No clue, Sis. But he sounds like a sick, manipulative jerk."

"He was one of the most infamous womanizers of all time …" She looked over again at me to see if the hint was enough.

"Casanova?" I asked incredulously.

"Yep, none other than Giacomo Girolamo Casanova, the cryptanalyst. The story's point is that polyalphabetic ciphers were known to have been solved, even given their aura of invincibility. In fact, in 1863, a major in the German infantry published a general solution to polyalphabetic ciphers. It still would take a great deal of work, but they can be solved."

I raised my brows as I reached for my door handle. "So you are giving me a little hope even if we can't figure out the key?"

"Yep. One way or another. Sooner or later, we will solve the cipher."

It better be sooner rather than later.

Chapter 62

Ciphers and Sacrifices

We bought our groceries at the Payson Safeway, ate an early lunch at the Pinon Café, and were back at the cabin by midafternoon. After putting the supplies away, I sat down at my father's desk by the window, opened my laptop, and pulled up an interlinear version of Numbers 29:13.

Cadence hung over my shoulder, leaning close as the verses came up. A grinding and crunching in my ear made me turn. She was munching on an apple, unconscious of the disturbing noise.

I frowned at the apple. "Really, Caden, do you have to chew that in my ear?"

She straightened and mouthed a silent, *Sorry*. The smile that accompanied the look belayed the apology. She shrugged. "I'm hungry."

My irritation faded. Her face was fuller. The black rings around her eyes were still there, but even they had shrunk. Just a few days ago, she was barely alive, and now she was hungry. I shook my head. What a razor-thin path we walked. I turned back to my laptop.

"Just don't chew in my ear, okay?" I said gruffly, trying to hide my deeper feelings.

We read the verses together. We started with the English version and then the Hebrew.

Numbers 29:13

And ye shall offer a burnt offering, a sacrifice made by fire, of a sweet savour unto YHWH; 13 young bullocks, 2 rams, *and* 14 lambs of the first year; they shall be without blemish:

Numbers 29:13

והקרבתמ עלה אשה ריח ניחח ליהוה פרים בני־בקר שלשה עשר
אילם שנים כבשים בני־שנה ארבעה עשר תמימם יהיו

Cadence was back at my ear. We saw it simultaneously, but Cadence extended her finger first. She pointed at the initial word of the passage. “7 letters,” she said in a voice garbled by a mouthful of apple.

I craned my neck around and shook my head. She offered another sheepish grin and swallowed the mouthful, apple chunks and all.

Cadence was pointing at ‘*qarab’,* meaning *to come near, approach, enter into*, the only 7-letter word of the passage.

We spent several more minutes looking at the other nineteen words. None of them stood out. We were convinced that 7 was the key to the riddle, and now there was a good possibility that a 7-letter word was the key to the auto cipher as well. I did a quick search for the word in the Old Testament.

Cadence chuckled after counting the results. “The word is only used 13 times in the Bible.” Our eyes met. She arched her eye at me. “Another coincidence?”

I shrugged. “I don’t know. But let’s stay focused on solving the riddle. The only way to know if *qarab* is the keyword is to try it.”

“Let’s do it, then,” Cadence replied as she dug the notepad and Vigenère tableau from the briefcase.

I opened the webpage that presented our father’s third cipher and peered at Cadence expectantly. “Okay, walk me through this again.”

כ נ א ז ב ז י ס פ ב ד כ ק ט ס ו ו ט ס ק ר ק ס צ ת ז א ר צ ס ק ק כ
מ ג ה ס ט ע כ ב ז י ס י מ ס נ ל ק ס ת י ק ה נ ו ר ט י ט ב ש ה כ ט
מ ו ח ב מ ע מ ת מ פ ה א ע כ ק מ ש ו ת ע י ו ח ו ב ה ה ר פ צ ו מ ח
ב ס ש ח נ ת ל ז ק נ ק ז ה י ק ח ז ח כ ר ש ק ס י ל ס פ ח ט ס ח ט ס
ז ה ט ד פ ק ר ע ג ק ע פ ר פ ר ס ר פ מ פ ת ז ת ש ס מ ע ח ק ק ד ר ת
ל ס ק צ ב כ ט ג ח ע ה ז כ ח ח מ ע ד ע ו ס ד נ ז ט ש ס ע ת ז ת ד ח
ח ה ד ל ט ת ר מ נ ס ת ט כ ב ג י ר ל ט ט ש ג ת פ א נ מ ש נ ד ד מ ס
ת ק כ צ ב ב ב ר ו ע ה ת ב ב ש ג ר פ ת א פ ח ע ז ת ה י נ ח ע ו ד פ
י ק ר ו ג כ מ כ ו ר צ ת כ נ ח י י צ כ ב ז ה ק ס ע ל ז צ ס ט ט ר ה
ק ת ת ש נ פ י ק מ ט ד צ ת ג ע ד ר נ ת א ו ד ח ג ה ר ת מ ט ל ח צ צ
ה נ מ ל ק ה ו פ ק ת ח ד ה ז נ א ל ח נ ר ב א ה ה ק ז ג כ ש פ ר ח ע
ר צ פ צ כ מ ש ז נ ב ק ר ע ד ז מ ו ק צ ש ד ו פ צ ק ו י ג כ ד ז ז כ
ה ע ר ח ק ע צ כ ש ג פ ק ו ס ר ע י מ ק פ ס ש מ נ ג ק צ ב ד צ א ג ט
ס ב ה ה ו ל ט ד ש ט צ ק ש י פ ח נ ה ק כ ז ש ש צ ט ק ט ל ג נ מ צ ט
נ ל ל צ פ ע מ ג נ ה א ת ת ג מ ס ב א א ק ז נ ס מ ה י ט ע ת ס פ ע ס מ
נ ד ר י ה ק נ ה מ ט ק ע ז ק ג ד צ א ו ע ד ח ט א י ז ע ט ח ר ה ת ג
ש ש ח צ ב ת ס צ י מ ת ב כ ק ה ת צ ט ג ב פ פ ת ק ו ז נ פ ע ד ט ל ח
ש ת נ ק ו ת ח ר ד צ מ ס ל מ ז ק נ ע ס כ ת ב ד י פ ו ע ה כ ב ת פ ה
ש ר ת ו ל א ו ו י ל ש א ל ש א ק ב ד י י י ח ק ג א נ ת י ז ו ו ו ק
ט ו נ ו ה י ט ט ע נ ה ע ח ע פ ע ב ו ז מ ש ד ל ש ו ז ב ח ט ב י ו פ
כ ל נ ו ת ק ש ט ב א צ ה ו ש ש ש א ק ב י כ ש ת ר א נ ס ר ש ל פ ה ה
ו ז ר ש פ פ ב ו צ נ ק ו ב כ ט ו ג ח י ס ד ו כ ג ק ט ח ב פ ע ס ק נ
ר ו ה ג ח צ צ י ז ט ר ב ב פ ו ה ע י ר ב א י נ ד י ק ו ו ש נ מ ח ז ה ו
ר ס ד צ ז ד ס ה ב ז ו ק ע ו נ ז ע ד ק ע ז כ כ ו ד צ ט ע ב ר כ ט ה
ו ע ז ב ב מ ה ס ה ז ט ש ד ה ת כ ח א ת נ ו צ ח ש י ה ק ס ז צ ש כ ב
א ה ל ה פ צ ב ת ט ל נ ו א כ ס ר ע ק פ ע ת ק ק א צ צ ז ה ב ו ק ס צ
ז ו ש י ט מ ח כ צ פ ס פ פ ל ע צ ד ק ת ש ש מ צ ח ק ר צ ח מ ח ה א ז
א ר נ ל ב י כ ו ב א ט ב נ ע ס ר ר ט ג נ ע ג ז ב נ צ ג ה ג ח ש צ ח
א צ ל ז כ ט ל ש ח ש ק ע צ ל כ ה ת ו ז ע מ ד ט ק ז ו ת ח ט מ ז ע
ס ש ט כ ד ט מ מ ב ר ט י ח ל נ ש א ס נ מ א נ ו ש ג מ מ ת ס ק ט ג ל
ת ז ב ת ק מ ש א ד ל ח ר י ט כ ט ע ק ש נ ט ח י ר ק ר ר ו ז א ח ז ג
ח ז י כ ו ק ל ר ל ר צ כ ח ל צ ט ט מ ז ט ב כ ח צ ג נ ל צ ש ט ו ס צ ת צ
ר ז ש ל צ ט ק ז ל ד ע פ י ע פ פ ה ת נ נ ד ה ו י ז ה א ל ח ה ג נ ב ר ק
מ ח ג ת ש י ל ל ט ש כ ח ס ש י י ש ל ה ק כ י ש ל ה ב ו ע ס ח פ ז
כ נ ד צ מ ד נ נ ח ד ז נ ד כ ל ט ק ל א ב ל ל י ע מ ג מ ל ז נ פ ו

Cadence wrote the Hebrew keyword, והקרבתמ, from Numbers 29:13 at the top right side of her Vigenère tableau. She pointed at the first letter of the keyword.

Vigenere Tableau והקרבתמ

ת	ש	ר	ק	צ	פ	ע	ס	נ	מ	ל	כ	י	ט	ח	ז	ו	ה	ד	ג	ב	א
א	ת	ש	ר	ק	צ	פ	ע	ס	נ	מ	ל	כ	י	ט	ח	ז	ו	ה	ד	ג	ב
ב	א	ת	ש	ר	ק	צ	פ	ע	ס	נ	מ	ל	כ	י	ט	ח	ז	ו	ה	ד	ג
ג	ב	א	ת	ש	ר	ק	צ	פ	ע	ס	נ	מ	ל	כ	י	ט	ח	ז	ו	ה	ד
ד	ג	ב	א	ת	ש	ר	ק	צ	פ	ע	ס	נ	מ	ל	כ	י	ט	ח	ז	ו	ה
ה	ד	ג	ב	א	ת	ש	ר	ק	צ	פ	ע	ס	נ	מ	ל	כ	י	ט	ח	ז	ו
ו	ה	ד	ג	ב	א	ת	ש	ר	ק	צ	פ	ע	ס	נ	מ	ל	כ	י	ט	ח	ז
ז	ו	ה	ד	ג	ב	א	ת	ש	ר	ק	צ	פ	ע	ס	נ	מ	ל	כ	י	ט	ח
ח	ז	ו	ה	ד	ג	ב	א	ת	ש	ר	ק	צ	פ	ע	ס	נ	מ	ל	כ	י	ט
ט	ח	ז	ו	ה	ד	ג	ב	א	ת	ש	ר	ק	צ	פ	ע	ס	נ	מ	ל	כ	י
י	ט	ח	ז	ו	ה	ד	ג	ב	א	ת	ש	ר	ק	צ	פ	ע	ס	נ	מ	ל	כ
כ	י	ט	ח	ז	ו	ה	ד	ג	ב	א	ת	ש	ר	ק	צ	פ	ע	ס	נ	מ	ל
ל	כ	י	ט	ח	ז	ו	ה	ד	ג	ב	א	ת	ש	ר	ק	צ	פ	ע	ס	נ	מ
מ	ל	כ	י	ט	ח	ז	ו	ה	ד	ג	ב	א	ת	ש	ר	ק	צ	פ	ע	ס	נ
נ	מ	ל	כ	י	ט	ח	ז	ו	ה	ד	ג	ב	א	ת	ש	ר	ק	צ	פ	ע	ס
ס	נ	מ	ל	כ	י	ט	ח	ז	ו	ה	ד	ג	ב	א	ת	ש	ר	ק	צ	פ	ע
ע	ס	נ	מ	ל	כ	י	ט	ח	ז	ו	ה	ד	ג	ב	א	ת	ש	ר	ק	צ	פ
פ	ע	ס	נ	מ	ל	כ	י	ט	ח	ז	ו	ה	ד	ג	ב	א	ת	ש	ר	ק	צ
צ	פ	ע	ס	נ	מ	ל	כ	י	ט	ח	ז	ו	ה	ד	ג	ב	א	ת	ש	ר	ק
ק	צ	פ	ע	ס	נ	מ	ל	כ	י	ט	ח	ז	ו	ה	ד	ג	ב	א	ת	ש	ר
ר	ק	צ	פ	ע	ס	נ	מ	ל	כ	י	ט	ח	ז	ו	ה	ד	ג	ב	א	ת	ש
ש	ר	ק	צ	פ	ע	ס	נ	מ	ל	כ	י	ט	ח	ז	ו	ה	ד	ג	ב	א	ת

"Take this *waw* and find it in the vertical column at the right of the tableau."

I did as she instructed and slid my finger down the tableau until I found the sixth letter, *waw*.

"Keep your finger on that row marked by the *waw*." Cadence now pointed at the first letter of our father's cipher in the top uppermost right corner of the thirty-three by thirty-five cipher grid. It was the letter *koph*. "Now, using your finger where you've marked the tableau, slide it to the left until you find *koph*."

Again, I followed her directions. "Okay."

"Now slide your finger from koph straight up that column until you reach the top."

"Done. And … it is *waw.*"

"Congratulations," she said, "you've solved the first letter of a polyalphabetic keyword cipher."

I wrote the letter *waw* on the notepad. "What's the next letter?"

"It's the letter *hey.*"

I repeated the process and decrypted the letter *yod.* It took five more minutes and a couple of missteps on my part, but we finally had the first seven letters of the cipher solved. I recognized two words. The first four letters spelled the Hebrew word *haya,* which meant to be, become, or come to pass. The next three letters spelled *ahar*, meaning to tarry, delay, or come after.

I read the two words out loud as they might be translated in an English sentence. "And it came to pass after …"

I looked at Cadence. I couldn't hide my excitement. We both knew that it was very unlikely that the first seven letters would spell two identifiable Hebrew words if we had used the wrong keyword. I switched screens on my laptop.

Cadence protested. "What are you doing?"

"I'm going to search for that two-word phrase in the Hebrew text. If we have the correct keyword, that two-word Hebrew phrase will show up someplace in the Old Testament." I typed in the two words into the search box of the Hebrew Bible online text, then gave Cadence a glance with my finger over the *enter* key.

"Come on, Timbre. Do it already."

"You know, if we find these two words in the Hebrew Bible, they should be in some context related to Abraham."

"They should," Cadence agreed. She pushed my finger down against the key. "Now, let's find out."

Chapter 63

Progress and Promises

A second later, nine results appeared—three from Genesis, one from 1 Samuel, three from 1 Kings, one from Nehemiah, and one from Job. I wrote the references in my notepad with bullet points.

- Gen 22:1; 39:7; 40:1
- 1 Sam 10:5
- 1 Kgs 13:33; 17:17; 21:1
- Neh 13:19
- Job 42:7

We gave ourselves high fives. After reading the first verse, we shared another excited glance. The first reference in Genesis 22 was about Abraham. As quickly as we could, we read through the other eight results. Only the first mentioned Abraham.

I sat back in my chair and looked at Cadence. "It has to be Genesis 22," I said, barely able to contain myself.

Cadence indicated the computer screen with a tilt of her head. "Only one way to find out." She pointed at the Hebrew text of Genesis 22:1. "There are fifty-seven Hebrew letters in this verse. Let's decipher the first fifty-seven letters of Dad's cipher, and then we will know for sure if we have the correct passage."

"Okay. Only fifty more letters to be absolutely certain." As I worked on the cipher for the next hour, Cadence piled a stack of books on the edge of the desk next to Dad's bookcase. Every time I glanced up, Cadence was absorbed in whatever she was reading—fascinating material, judging by her expression. Forty-five minutes into my efforts, Cadence asked for my notepad and furiously started taking notes.

An hour and a half later, I was certain that the first fifty-seven letters of my father's cipher were from Genesis 22. I looked at Cadence and waited until she finished writing. She lifted a radiant face and held up a finger. "Just give me fifteen more minutes. I think I've almost figured out why 7 is important to the riddle."

I raised an eyebrow at her but said nothing. I knew better. She could tune me out like old analog radio. I turned back and stared at the thirty-three-by-thirty-five grid of ciphered text, a little cross-eyed. With that many squares, there were a total of eleven hundred and fifty-five letters to decipher. Minus the fifty-seven I'd already solved, I had another one thousand and ninety-eight characters to decrypt. My father's instructions said that to solve this riddle, we needed to find the four letters around which this passage pivoted. If the instructions were to be taken literally, I needed to know the extent of the Biblical passage he had enciphered.

There were two ways to do this. I could spend the next two days deciphering the ciphered text one letter at a time, or I could count the total number of letters in the cipher text, minus the 7-letter keyword, and compare that to the text from Genesis. If the number of letters in the ciphered text matched the number of letters in a certain number of verses from Genesis 22, it would be a pretty good bet that I had the entire passage figured out.

No brainer—I'd go with the second method. I already knew there were eleven hundred and fifty-five characters in my father's cipher. So all I had to do was count eleven hundred and fifty-five characters starting in Genesis 22 and see where it ended up.

The eleven hundred and fifty-fifth letter turned out to be the final letter of Genesis 22:19. My father had used a polyalphabetic cipher to encrypt the first nineteen verses of Genesis 22. What an amazing amount of effort. I shook my head. Just deciphering the first fifty-seven letters had taken me over an hour.

While I waited for Cadence to finish whatever she was doing, I read through the entire passage of Genesis 22:1-19. Notes in the text said that this passage was called the *Akedah* or *Binding*. It was the story of Abraham's test of faith.

I remembered the story from Sunday school. God had told Abraham to take his only son, Isaac, up on a certain mountain and sacrifice him. Abraham obeyed. But there was more to it than that. Abraham didn't just accept this mission as the death of his son, but in faith, he believed that he and Isaac, no matter what transpired on that mountain, would return.

I sat back in the chair and laced my fingers behind my head. As I stared at the passage on my computer screen, I wondered how you got that kind of faith. It sounded fanatical. Was it something missing in your mind? Or was it something added—given? I certainly didn't have that kind of faith. I didn't even believe God existed anymore. I darn sure didn't have enough faith to bind my son to an altar with the intent of murdering him, and then to believe he would somehow be returning off the mountain with me.

But Isaac did return with Abraham that day. Or so the story went. Seeing Abraham's faith, God provided a substitution. Taken literally, Isaac was living proof of Abraham's faith in God's promise. Earlier in Genesis, God had promised Abraham that He would raise up a great nation through Isaac's descendants.

Faith. Was it something everyone had or could have? Was it real or imagined? Was it like a seed you planted and nurtured, or did it come full-grown with deep roots and wide branches? As a child, I had believed. Even as a teenager, I'd believed. After leaving home and entering college, that faith had crumbled. Only doubt and skepticism remained. I was too knowledgeable for faith now, wasn't I?

Cadence tossed the pencil in her hand onto the sheet of notepaper she'd been writing on. Her faraway look of a mind trying to sort and organize the pieces changed into one of laser-like focus. "Wow," she said, looking at me. "This is amazing stuff. Incredible!"

I couldn't help but smile at how stoked she was. She looked like I might if I had turned over an ancient gold coin while digging in my garden.

"Okay, so Dad's riddle said that Yahweh used 7 to confirm a covenant with 41. We already know that 41 likely represents Abraham. Confirmation of that came when we figured out that the ciphered text was from Genesis 22. What we didn't know was what 7 represented. How could Yahweh use 7 to confirm a covenant with Abraham?" She paused, lowered her chin and widened her eyes. "You following?"

"Yes, and our search for this 'confirmed covenant' only turned up five references, four of which talked about a covenant originally confirmed with Abraham, but nothing about 7 as the expedient or means by which that covenant was made between God and Abraham."

She bobbed her head. "Yes, but …" She clasped her hands. "Oh, you are going to love this, Timmy."

"Well, spill it then," I said, laughing at her excitement.

"Okay, while you were working on the cipher, I read through Genesis 22 looking for the 7 who Yahweh might have used to confirm a covenant with Abraham. All I found that could remotely be seen as expedient or agent between Yahweh and Abraham was the oath Yahweh swore with Abraham after he demonstrated his faith in his willingness to sacrifice Isaac. Then I remembered that one of Dad's clues was the passage from Luke that talked about a covenant which the passage referred to as an oath Yahweh swore with Abraham." She paused. "You still with me?"

"Go on," I said, starting to catch her excitement.

Cadence searched through my notes until she found the Luke 1:72-73 passage that our father had given as one of the clues. She underlined two words as she read it out loud.

To perform the mercy promised to our fathers, and to remember his holy covenant; The oath which he sware to our father Abraham,

"How do you spell *7* or *sheba'* in Hebrew?"

I pondered that unexpected question for a second. "*Shin, bet, ayin.*" I picked up the pencil on the desk and wrote the Hebrew spelling in the notebook.

שבע

Cadence smiled broadly. "Good. Now tell me what the Hebrew root for *sware* is."

"I don't know," I said after a bit of thought.

Cadence gave me a look. It was a look I hadn't seen since she was eleven years old when she'd come to me with the discovery of the numerical value of her name. "The Hebrew root for *sware* is *shaba*. Care to guess how it is spelled?"

I shook my head.

"Shaba is spelled *shin, bet, ayin*." Cadence pointed to the Hebrew spelling of *7* I'd just written in my notebook. She underlined each letter and tapped them with her pen. שבע

"You serious?"

"Yes." She slapped the desk. "*Sheba* and *Shaba*—*seven* and *swear*—are spelled precisely the same. They are the same word with two meanings."

"Dad's riddle was a play on words. Wow."

"Because of Abraham's faith, Yahweh swore with him. He literally *seven*ed with him."

"I see it!" I stood up, "That swearing, that oath of sevens with Abraham, is what the passage of Luke was talking about in the verse clue Dad gave us."

"And that oath promised, what?"

I leaned over and rested my hands on the desk as my mind returned to my father's verse clues. Finally, I said, "Ultimately, the oath or swearing of sevens promised that Abraham's seed would be as numerous as the stars in the heavens and that through Abraham's descendants, his seed, all nations of the earth would be blessed."

The hair on my arms prickled. My father had elegantly connected his ciphered riddles.

When I had originally searched for *confirmed a covenant*, one of those passages from the New Testament had explained what the promise to Abraham had been all about. I flipped a few pages in my notes and read the passage out loud.

Galatians 3:15-16

Brethren, I speak after the manner of men; Though it be but a man's covenant, yet if it be confirmed, no man disannulleth, or addeth thereto. [16] Now to Abraham and his seed were the promises made. He saith not, And to seeds, as of many; but as of one, And to thy seed, which is Christ.

I glanced at Cadence. “According to Paul here in his letter to the Galatians, Yahweh’s oath of sevens with Abraham was about Abraham’s seed, Jesus, becoming a blessing to all nations of the world.”

Cadence’s expression sobered. “Dad’s riddles are about Jesus—Yeshua, Yahweh’s Salvation!”

They were indeed. They were my father’s way of telling us one last time about Jesus and Yahweh’s doorway to salvation. I shivered as I pictured that heavy wooden door in my dreams and heard the echoes of knocking

I sat back down. I wasn’t ready to deal with those thoughts now. Maybe never.

Cadence was watching me with questions in her eyes. I couldn’t meet her gaze.

“How about we finish this?” Swiveling around, I opened my father’s webpage with the third ciphered riddle.

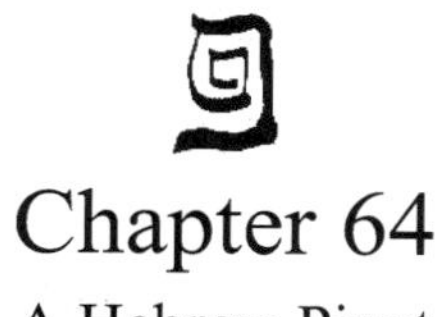

Chapter 64

A Hebrew Pivot

I read the riddle and instructions out loud. Then, turning a fresh page in my notepad, I rewrote my father's riddle with the solutions in parentheses. Below this, I wrote the answer instructions, underlining *four letters* and pi*vots*.

In this enciphered Biblical passage, Yahweh uses 7 (a swearing of sevens) to confirm a covenant with 41 (Abraham).

Provide the <u>four letters</u> around which this passage <u>pivots</u>.

"Any idea what he means?" I asked.

Cadence studied the pad for a minute. "Okay. If we can take this at face value, then Dad is saying Genesis 22:1-19 pivots around four letters. What it doesn't say is if this pivot is literal or figurative."

"By figurative, you mean a person or idea?"

"Yes. Maybe we need to figure out who or what is the central focus or theme of the passage."

"Do you think this is meant to be a figurative pivot like Abraham, Yahweh, or Isaac? The names *Yahweh* and *Isaac* are both spelled with four Hebrew letters," I added hopefully.

Cadence cocked her head to the side like she was trying to fish something out of her mind.

"And if it is not a person or idea we are looking for?" I asked trying to bring her back from wherever she had gone to.

Her lips parted slightly, and she was back again with that knowing look of hers. I started to speak, but Cadence held up her hand. "Hold on. Remember I told you about the guy Casper Laubuschange and Dad's interest in how the Hebrew authors of the Bible constructed certain passages numerically?"

"Yeah, the guy whose writings convinced Dad there was a numerical structure to some passages of the Hebrew text?"

Cadence nodded.

"Okay, so?"

"Well, what if Dad's pi*vot* is actually a numerical pivot?"

"You mean, what if those four letters are literally the numerical center of the passage?"

"Yes, exactly. It shouldn't be too hard to figure out."

"It shouldn't. I already know that there are 1155 letters in Genesis 22:1-19." I pointed at my scribbled notes.

Cadence followed my finger, then rolled her eyes up and whispered under her breath for a second. "Half of 1155 is 577.5. That means our four letters might start at the 576th letter of the passage."

Silently, we counted the Hebrew letters of Genesis 22:1-19. When I got to the word *aqad,* I looked at Cadence. "What did you get?"

She pointed at the same word. "What does it mean?"

"It means *to bind*. It's the word used to describe the entire passage. Genesis 22:1-19 in Jewish tradition is called the *Akedah* or *Binding*."

"It's right at the center of the passage," Cadence rose optimistically.

I shook my head. "Yeah, but it is spelled with five letters, not four. The riddle asks us for the four letters around which the passage pivots."

"You don't think we should try just four letters of the word?"

I leaned my head and shook. "Dad's riddles so far have been …"

"Precise," she offered.

"Yes, precise is part of it, but it's more than that. They've been perfect, intentional, purposeful. If his answer is a Hebrew word, I don't see him using just four letters of it. It doesn't fit his MO."

After staring at me a moment, Cadence snapped her fingers. "Words!"

"What do you mean?"

"You said if Dad's answer is a Hebrew word, he wouldn't just use four letters of it. We've been counting the letters of the passage, but letters make words. What if he meant for us to count the words?"

We started counting again. This time it went faster.

"I got 307 words in the passage," Cadence said.

A second later, I got the same number. "Okay, then. That is an odd number, so it doesn't divide evenly."

"That means it pivots around a single word!" we both said.

I did the math on my notepad. If my father's pivot was based upon the Hebrew words of Genesis 22:1-19, then we were looking for the one hundred and fifty-fourth word. That meant there were one hundred and fifty three words before the pivot and one hundred and fifty-three words after the pivot.

"Hey, look at this." I pointed at the notepad.

153 + 1 + 153.

I scratched my head. "Why does 153 look familiar?"

Cadence grinned. "Probably because it was the number of fish Jesus's disciples drew up in their net after he told them were to cast it. Many Biblical scholars believe it has some symbolic significance, although they are not in agreement about what that is. In Genesis 6:4 it is the value of the Hebrew Beni HaElohim – Sons of God. Mathematically, it's a pretty neat number too. 153 is the sum of all numbers from one to 17. It's also a triangular number. Even the cubed sum of its digits are equal to 153."

Okay, then. I returned to counting the words in the *Akedah*. When we both paused on the same one hundred and fifty-fourth word, we shared an understanding look. *Isaac*. Isaac was the pivot and the answer to our father's third riddle.

"Wow," I said, writing out the numerical structure of Genesis 22:1-19 with Isaac at its center.

153 + Isaac + 153.

Sons of God, indeed! I tapped Isaac's name with my pencil. "If placing Isaac here at the exact center of the Hebrew word count was purposeful, it was pretty impressive. Doubly so, when you take into account that the numerical center of the letter count highlighted the word *aqad*."

"Isaac's binding," Cadence murmured.

"What?"

Cadence pointed at my numerical word formula. "I know we are trying to solve Dad's riddles, but try and take a step back to appreciate how exquisite this passage might have been from Dad's perspective."

"Go on."

She pointed at the number *41*. "We have Abraham, a man of faith whom God promises that through his son Isaac, he'll have a multitude of descendants. Then, years later, in a test of Abraham's faith in that promise, God asks him to sacrifice that heir. Abraham obeys, and just before his very own hand plunges the knife into his son, God provides a sacrificial substitute. A sacrifice and substitute that many claim is symbolic of a similar divine sacrifice of God's own son. To show his appreciation for Abraham's faith, Yahweh swears an oath of sevens with Abraham." Cadence paused and cocked her head at me. "Did you know this was the first recorded oath Yahweh swore with anyone in the Bible?"

I shook my head and waited for her to continue.

"Anyway, this oath of sevens promised in part that, through Isaac's seed, all nations of the earth would be blessed. That blessing, the New Testament Jewish authors believed, referred to Jesus. And all this, we just learned, is packaged with numerical precision, a passage of 307 words, and at its center, the word *Isaac*—Abraham's promised seed, a generational grandfather of Jesus. Further, that single word is preceded and followed by 153 other words. This unusual number is only explicitly stated one place in the entire Bible. That occurrence is found in a story about Jesus and his disciples after the resurrection."

Cadence's earnest smile beamed down on me. "Wouldn't you have loved to have been there when Dad first stumbled upon this? Can you imagine how this must have encouraged his faith in the congruency of the Bible's message?"

Her words were said with such sincerity and warmth I couldn't help but feel their glow. Yes, my father's riddles were having the effect he'd intended on my sister—unfolding her faith like the petals of a flower. That strength, that power—whatever you wanted to call it—was transforming her. I could not deny it.

What could I say? I certainly didn't want to impede her transformation. I'd rather die than see my sister back in the condition I'd found her. If this renewing of faith gave her hope, then so be it. I reached for her hand and squeezed it.

"Yes. I would have liked to have listened to Dad sharing this with us," I said as I let go of her hand. I indicated the cabin, the fireplace, the room. "Right here, in front of a crackling fire."

I meant it too. I regretted not making things right with my father. Looking back with hindsight, I could see that he was a good man. Imperfect but decent. Most of all, he'd loved us. He'd also loved God—his Lazarus Ciphers were evidence of that.

I met her penetrating gaze. "I miss him, Caden. I wish he was here with us."

She gave a jerky nod, and a couple of tears rolled down her face. Cadence wiped them away with an embarrassed laugh. "I've turned into a crybaby. How about we solve this riddle?" She indicated the open screen on my laptop.

I nodded and faced my computer. I typed in the four Hebrew letters of Isaac's name in the blank spaces given. Then, I pressed *enter*, and we waited.

Chapter 65

Directives

A rumble filled the air as the Escalade drove down the yellow bar of late-afternoon sunlight that poured through the open warehouse door. The black SUV stopped in the center of the empty depot, a blight on a sheet of sunshine. Then, as if infected, the luminance retreated as the warehouse door slid down behind the vehicle in a rattling roar of chains and corrugated metal.

Benito Silva sat in the back seat looking through the windshield at the heads of his organization. They stood in a half-circle in the flicker of fluorescent lighting at the back of the warehouse. Each person in the room represented an important part of his criminal enterprise, but a white heat boiled in his gut as he surveyed them. They had hardly looked up when he drove in. There had been a time when they'd stood at attention, some out of respect, others out of fear. But today, they talked, smoked, and lounged in various stages of impertinence.

A little apart, Raul waited in the center of this group. He stood straight and tall, proud and aloof, but broken. The sight of him, right arm in a cast, nose black and blue, was pathetic. Benito's lieutenant had been bested, and the rest of them knew it. It showed in their attitude.

Benito clenched his teeth as the blood started throbbing in his ears. His vision narrowed like he was looking through the spyglass of a door. No wonder the rest of them stood around like they were waiting to meet a washed-up principal. Benito stubbed out his cigarette, the crumpled, stub a fitting symbol. He made his decision.

He nodded at his driver, who was watching him in the mirror. The driver jumped out of the car and hustled to open his door. Well, that was something. He was new and scared. He'd heard what happened to the last driver. He was showing the proper type of attitude.

Benito stepped from the Escalade. For the occasion, he wore a white Giorgio Armani wool suit and a vermilion silk tie. He gave his old friend a tight smile and extended his left hand to accommodate Raul's handicap. Their hands clasped.

"I'm sorry, my friend," Benito said as he lifted the German Luger P08 he'd concealed in the fold of his suit. As understanding dawned in Raul's eyes, Benito pulled the trigger.

Raul nearly crushed Benito's hand as the bullet entered his chest. Benito kept pulling the trigger until his pistol emptied. As the bullets punched their nine-millimeter holes, his friend's eyes revealed no surprise or fear—only disdain and maybe a touch of pity. Then the eyes went blank. Raul released Benito's hand as he fell to the floor. Benito gave his friend one last look, then he stepped up on the body.

Benito held the pistol at his side, still smoking. A current tingled up his arm. The weapon felt alive, a living thing with energy of its own. It gave him a new sense of awe. Had his grandfather experienced the same rush of power when he'd used the weapon back in their homeland? He would never forget the day he first set eyes on the weapon.

The hinges of that rusty little door he'd found behind the armoire had given a mournful groan, eliciting a hair-raising thrill as he had pushed it open. He'd taken a step forward and stared down into the blackness. The damp, musty smell of stagnant decay had slithered up the stone steps and tingled his nose. His torch had clicked as he turned it on and shone its feeble light down the stone steps. The beam of his light diminished into shades of black and gray where the outlines of the landing showed. With his left hand curled tightly around his flashlight and the fingers of his right brushing lightly against the wall, he'd made his descent. At the landing, a short passage opened into an unknown, dark expanse. He played his light along the walls as they disappeared into the blackness. The stones beneath his feet were cool. He stepped toward the darkness, his heart beating wildly.

The passage ended in an open room. As his light traversed the space, his hair stood on end. He froze, mouth agape. A red banner covered the entire far wall, at its center a white circle with a broken black cross. Below the banner on a rotting wooden table sat a picture and the pistol. He'd moved closer to this unusual altar. The picture was of his grandfather shaking hands with one of the most infamous men the world had ever known. Both men were smiling.

Benito couldn't help the smile now as his legs strengthened and his heels clicked together. He almost saluted at the memory, but he stopped himself and his eyes refocused.

Slowly, his burning gaze shifted to the men in front of him in the flickering fluorescent lights of the warehouse. The throbbing in his ears had stopped. In its place, a god-like aura enveloped him. Everybody in the room came to attention. Every eye focused on him. Every ear waited for his words. He said nothing for a long time. He just stood on the body of his lieutenant as the glistening puddle of crimson spread around him.

"This is the price of failure," he said.

More silence followed. When the aura began to fade, Benito pointed his empty Luger at a hulking, leather-clad figure and motioned him forward. Henry Mortman moved instantly. He approached with fear written on him like the graffiti on the bricks of a dark alley. Henry stopped at the edge of the scarlet pool. Benito gestured him into the growing lake with another jerk of his pistol. A metallic smell enveloped them. Benito reached into his pocket with his free hand and handed the man a piece of paper.

"Henry, at this location are a brother and sister. I want them brought to me alive. Succeed, and you'll get his job," he said and looked at his feet. "Don't fail me." Benito stomped his hand-made white leather *Himer und Himer Maßschuhe* dress shoes. "Or you'll take his place." Benito turned and stepped off his pedestal. Crimson footprints followed him to the open door of his Escalade.

Two dozen pairs of eyes squinted as the light of day once more penetrated the warehouse with a rattling roar. Two dozen pairs of eyes followed the retreating darkness.

Chapter 66

Faith and Fallacies

Cadence and I celebrated with high fives as we read the message.

Congratulations, your answer is correct.
This page will be redirected to the next ciphered riddle in 60 seconds.

A new page appeared. Together we read our father's fourth challenge and the verse clues he'd left to help us solve it.

In this enciphered Biblical passage, there are 45 that belong, 42 that are described, and only 41 found.

Provide the two words that encapsulate this passage and the two numbers that provide the primary continuity.

Daniel 9:4
And I prayed unto YHWH my God, and made my confession, and said, O Lord, the great and dreadful God, keeping the covenant and mercy to them that love him, and to them that keep his commandments;

Revelation 9:11
And they had a king over them, *which is* the angel of the

bottomless pit, whose name in the Hebrew tongue *is* Abaddon, but in the Greek tongue hath *his* name Apollyon.

Matthew 16:26
For what is a man profited, if he shall gain the whole world, and lose his own soul? or what shall a man give in exchange for his soul?

Deuteronomy 7:12
Wherefore it shall come to pass, if ye hearken to these judgments, and keep, and do them, that YHWH thy God shall keep unto thee the covenant and the mercy which he sware unto thy fathers:

Galatians 3:14-16
That the blessing of Abraham might come on the Gentiles through Jesus Christ; that we might receive the promise of the Spirit through faith. Brethren, I speak after the manner of men; Though *it be* but a man's covenant, yet *if it be* confirmed, no man disannulleth, or addeth thereto. Now to Abraham and his seed were the promises made. He saith not, And to seeds, as of many; but as of one, And to thy seed, which is Christ.

Fifteen minutes later, Cadence was the first to speak. “Thoughts? First impressions?”

I shook my head. It was not because I didn’t have any thoughts rolling around up there, but because none of them made any sense—as if I could feel the edges of a paper but not quite read what was written on it.

I squinted at her. "I got nothing. You? Anything stand out?"

Cadence bit her lower lip. "Nothing comes to mind. But look here." She pointed at the verse clues. "So far, Dad has used one or two of the passages as clues to the type of cipher while one of the verses provides continuity to the other ciphers and the overreaching theme of the message."

"Yes, we've established that."

Cadence pointed at Daniel 9:4 and Deuteronomy 7:12. "Do you know what this *covenant and mercy* refers to?"

I shook my head. "I don't."

"Could it be related to the covenant of Galatians 3:14-16?"

I slid the Bible over, turned to Daniel 9, and assessed the passage's immediate context. Cadence read over my shoulder. Daniel's *covenant and mercy* appeared to be the first words he pled to Yahweh on behalf of his captive people and their desolate city.

Flipping to Deuteronomy 7, I read through the chapter. Cadence turned the page, frowning, her lip pinched between her teeth, and I kept reading chapters 8 and 9 with her. By the time we were done, we were nodding and smiling. The *covenant and mercy* mentioned by Daniel was a quote from Moses in Deuteronomy. This *covenant and mercy* was the very same ancient *oath of seven*, that redemptive promise God made with Abraham.

Cadence thumped the desk with a rhythm that did her name proud. "Now we are getting somewhere. The *covenant and mercy* of Daniel and Deuteronomy is the same covenant talked about in Galatians."

"Yep." I pointed at Revelation 9:11 and Matthew 16:26. "What about these two? Do you think they have something to do with the cipher?"

Cadence nodded. "Dad has tried this on me before. I think this might be a simple substitution cipher."

"A what?"

"A substitution cipher. When he tried this, he'd substitute the letters of one language for those of another. That's all a cipher is, anyway—taking one set of symbols—for example, the letters of the English alphabet—and exchanging it for another set of symbols. Those symbols can be invented, they could be numbers, or they can be the letters of another language. Often, the process by which one is exchanged for the other is done by some mathematical means."

I murmured agreement. "Like exchanging Hebrew for Greek letters" I said, tapping the passage of Revelation 9:11.

"Exactly."

I read the two passages aloud as I carefully copied them onto a new page of my legal pad. I underlined the words that we believed were clues. The first verse clue gave us two different languages, and the second talked about an exchange. Flimsy evidence, really, but we had what others didn't. Experience—we had solved three ciphers already. Familiarity—we were becoming accustomed to the way our father did this. And knowledge—particularly, my sister's.

Revelation 9:11

And they had a king over them, *which is* the angel of the bottomless pit, whose name in the <u>Hebrew</u> tongue *is* Abaddon, but in the <u>Greek</u> tongue hath *his* name Apollyon.

Matthew 16:26

For what is a man profited, if he shall gain the whole world, and lose his own soul? or what shall a man give in exchange for his soul?

The ciphertext was in Hebrew, so if our intuition was correct, the original passage came from Greek. Greek meant it came from the New Testament. That connection was all I needed to remember why the riddle seemed so familiar. I swiveled my chair to face my sister and spoke quietly.

"I know the passage."

She raised an eyebrow. "Okay, genius, what is the passage?"

"It's from Matthew 1. The passage is about Jesus's lineage," I said soberly.

Cadence's brow remained furrowed, and she bit her lip. "There is a story here, isn't there?"

I fiddled with my pencil, turning it in circles on the desk. My first year at Harvard, I'd been fresh and naïve. Religious Literacy: Myths and Traditions had opened the first crack in my reservoir of faith. As the year wore on, that crack had widened, and I'd let my faith slowly drain out.

There was no better way to sow doubt in a person's faith than to start to unravel one of its most basic claims. My professor had done just that. Looking back, I don't think he had done it maliciously. At least, I didn't want to believe that. But he'd opened a crack of doubt in my dam of faith, nonetheless.

He'd begun with the first chapter of the first book of the New Testament. I mean, if you couldn't count on a simple list of names to be true, then what could you count on?

I raised my gaze. "Do you remember when you had your first doubts about your faith?"

Cadence got a faraway look in her eyes. Her expression changed to one of remorse and guilt. “It wasn’t that way with me.” Head down, she remained silent for a long time.

“How so?” I finally asked.

She sighed and rotated the palms of her hands. “When I got to college, I was excited and way too naïve. You know the peer pressure and the partying. It seemed like one endless party with breaks in-between for study. At first, I resisted the invites. But I had more time on my hands than most of my friends.” She didn’t want to say it, but I guessed the reason.

“Because you are a genius.”

She glanced up at me. Checking to see if I was serious? Cadence shrugged, “I admit it. My mind works differently than most. Or it did.”

Cadence shook her head like she was ridding herself of something. “Most of what they were teaching me I already knew from my own studies at home. But there was an endless selection of books and ideas to explore, and I was eager to learn. I guess I must have gotten a bit bored, or maybe I just felt guilty for not being more sociable. So, I said yes. I went to one of their parties.” Cadence let out a sob, and a big tear plopped onto the desk. There was another long silence

“I did something so terrible, Timmy.” She looked up, willing me to understand. She searched my face.

“What?” I asked finally when she didn’t continue.

Cadence turned looked away and shook her head. Maybe I hadn’t passed some test she had been giving me, or maybe she wasn’t ready to tell, but Cadence just continued with her story. “Then everything changed for me. From that point on, I tried to hide from my faith, or it hid from me. But every day I was reminded of what I had forfeited. When I realized it wasn’t temporary, I dove headlong into the party life to try to forget.

Beer became hard liquor, then weed, and harder and harder drugs in ever-increasing quantities. Then the overdose, and I couldn't hide it from Dad anymore." Cadence gave a long sigh like she was breathing out some of the poison she held bottled up inside.

"I'm so sorry, Sis." I squeezed her hand.

"I guess I couldn't outrun my faith," Cadence finished with a sad, remorseful, but strangely hopeful expression. She searched my face earnestly. "I don't know how to explain it, Timmy. Working on these ciphers, taking Dad's hand as he walks us through the Biblical promise of redemption, it's restoring me somehow."

"I see it," I said simply. "I can't deny my eyes. I must admit I don't understand it, but I see it." The pain, doubt, and desperate fear that had haunted her eyes, if not totally gone, were fading as hope and faith edged out the shadows.

Cadence placed her hands over her heart. "I know it probably sounds corny from your rational point of view, but my heart is hungry for what we are learning. I realize that my faith never really died. I just failed to nurture it. With its renewal, I am beginning to have hope again, to feel like there is a purpose to living." She tilted her head as if she needed me to understand what she was trying to say.

I let out a sigh. "I get it, but I wish I could say the same for myself. Your hope and enthusiasm are rubbing off, but my faith still seems like a dead tree in an empty wasteland."

" Really?"

I gestured to Dad's riddle. "The wasteland started here for me." My face relaxed as I absorbed my sister's concern. "I don't have to tell you about it, you know. The last thing I want to do is somehow throw something out there that might undermine your …" I searched for the word. "What's changing you," I finished lamely.

Cadence reached for my arm. "If I couldn't kill my faith with what I've done, I don't believe anything you say could either."

I tried to read any doubts or false bravado in her face, but all I sensed was a firm resolve and genuine interest. I don't know why, but I wanted to share my doubts with her. So far as I could tell, I had no hidden desire to convince her of my point of view. Maybe part of me wanted to believe. Perhaps I just wanted to talk it out.

Cadence gave me an encouraging nod.

I stood. "How about a cup of tea first?" A few minutes later we settled into the big leather chairs in front of the fireplace and I began my story.

"My first semester of college, my professor gave Matthew 1 as an example of why the Biblical texts are no more than important historical documents. He argued that the lineage of Jesus in Matthew 1 was not accurately recorded."

"Oh dear." Cadence cringed.

"Although he did not come right out and say it, he implied—and rightfully so, I might add—that if the first chapter of the first book of the New Testament couldn't be counted on to relay correct information about its most important hero, then how could it possibly be considered a reliable text? Much less, inspired?" I put words to my private thoughts, no longer relying on my professor's arguments but my own hopeless tangle of uncertainty. "What kind of divine guidance would give an erroneous rendering of the Son of God's own lineage?"

"What was his evidence?" Cadence asked.

"The best possible kind," I replied as I relived that first pang of doubt. "He started by putting the text of Matthew 1:1-16 on a projector and reading it out loud. Then he asked us all to tell him how many names the text indicated were in the lineage of Jesus. Next, he read Matthew 1:17 which told us there were fourteen generations between Abraham and David, fourteen generations between David and the captivity, and fourteen generations between the captivity and Jesus. We could see the text for ourselves. I mean, 14 plus, 14 plus, 14 isn't really hard math, so nearly the entire class came up with 42 names."

"I agree … basic math."

A scoff escaped me. "Yeah, well, I can still remember the indulgent look he gave us when we said, '42 names.' Then he put up the actual names contained in the lineage of Jesus in Matthew 1. Care to guess how many were on the list?"

She pointed at Dad's riddle on the computer screen.

In this enciphered Biblical passage, there are 45 that belong, 42 that are described, and only 41 found.

"41?" she asked.

"Yes, there were only 41 names, not the 42 that were described. His next slide was the real kicker. He showed a list of Jesus's ancestors as given in the Old Testament."

Cadence raised her finger. "There were more names in that record, weren't there?"

I nodded. "So, not only was the description of fourteen-plus-fourteen-plus-fourteen generations misleading, because there were actually only 41 names, but that mistake was compounded further by the fact that the Old Testament had four names that were missing from Matthew's list!"

I finished with an exasperated gesture of my arms. It still rankled me—the letdown, the disappointment, the foothold for that insidious root of doubt that had grown into disillusionment and anger.

Cadence didn't say anything for a minute. She probably wanted to let me simmer down before she gave her opinion. When she did speak, she asked me something I didn't expect.

"What if it wasn't a mistake?"

Chapter 67

Names and Numbers

I rolled my eyes at Cadence. "How could it not be a mistake?" I asked incredulously. "The Matthew lineage was missing four kings."

Cadence ignored my attitude. "What if the author of Matthew left out the four kings for a reason?"

"To what purpose?"

She shrugged. "I don't know. But if you are correct that Dad's riddle is about Matthew 1, then he certainly believed there was something more to it than just a mistake."

I rolled my eyes and cocked my head. "How do you figure that?"

"Well, he didn't avoid the conundrum of missing names, did he?"

"No, I guess he didn't."

"What did he do?" she asked, pushing me.

I thought about that for a while. Then I got a glimmer of light through the forest of my doubt. I looked at her. "He made the incongruity of the list the heart of this riddle."

Cadence beamed at me with that beautiful light of hers. "What are the chances, Timmy, that Dad figured out something your wise professor might have missed?"

She had my attention. "Like what?"

Cadence still wore that smile, and she shrugged again. "I don't know, but that is probably what Dad wants us to figure out."

"You really believe that, don't you?"

"I do," she said with a swift nod. There wasn't the tiniest bit of doubt in her look or tone. "Think about it, Timmy. What has Dad already shown us with the other ciphers?"

"Well …" I tapped my lips with my finger in an exaggerated thinking posture. "The last cipher showed us how God swore an oath of sevens with Abraham." I cut my gaze to her, questioning.

"What else?"

"That oath promised, in part, that Abraham's seed would bless all nations."

"How?"

Now *I* could swear. Sometimes, Cadence sounded like my third-grade teacher, but also like Mrs. Grimes, she usually led me to an *aha* moment. "Through Jesus."

Cadence spread her hands open. "And now we have what your professor tells us is an erroneous lineage from Abraham to Jesus that just happens to be 41 names, a number that also just happens to equal the numerical value of the name of the man with whom Yahweh swore that oath of sevens."

I nodded my head slowly and widened my eyes. "Oh wow …"

Cadence's smile broadened. "Don't scholars believe that the Gospel of Matthew was written to a Jewish audience?"

"Yes."

"An audience," she continued, "that would appreciate symbolic nuances that might escape us today?"

"Possibly."

"What if there is a structure, symbolic or literal, that scholars have missed? Something that Dad believes is important. Something related to his belief that Jesus was the *seed* promised in Genesis 22."

I began to grasp the picture Cadence was painting, as yet blurry. "Okay. So where do we start?"

"Let's start by confirming that Matthew 1 is the actual passage Dad ciphered. No reason to jump ahead of ourselves unless we are certain."

"Fair enough." Even if not, this had been an enlightening discussion.

We returned to the desk. It turned out that our supposition was rather easy to confirm. My father had substituted the letters of the Greek alphabet for the letters of Hebrew. To make the number of letters match in both Greek and Hebrew, he had included three Greek consonants with the former and the five final forms of the Hebrew alphabet with the latter. This made for 27 letters in both alphabets. In less than thirty minutes, we knew that my father's cipher was indeed the first 17 verses of Matthew 1.

Cadence reached over and closed the laptop. "Let's take a break. We've been at this all afternoon. How about we make some dinner, get some rest, and tackle this again in the morning?"

I stood up from the desk, stretched, and yawned. "Sounds good."

An hour later, tummies full, we were sitting side by side on the porch steps. I twisted the tops off two cream sodas and handed one to Cadence. We clinked the bottles together. Cadence took a sip. I took a long pull. The ice-cold soda burned all the way down, just as I liked it. The chorus of the night raised to bid farewell to the day. We sat in silence and admired the vast, starry sky.

Cadence whispered the famous words we'd been taught as children.

“The heavens declare the glory of God, the firmament showeth his handywork, day unto day uttereth speech …”

I joined in and we finished together.

“… and night unto night showeth knowledge. There is no speech or language where their voice is not heard.”

We touched the mouths of our bottles together once more. The soft sound of clinking glass brought a momentary silence to the chorus of the night. Then one by one, two and three, and finally, all at once, the orchestration continued.

I stared up into the unfathomable, glittering expanse as the melodies of the night played in my ear. The voices spoke to me. The voices mocked me. They challenged my lack of faith. A few more bricks fell from my wall of doubt.

Chapter 68

The Messiah Paradox

My eyes opened as the front door thumped closed. Moments later, the bathroom door clicked, and the shower started running. I sat up in bed. I felt like a kid at camp. Cadence had already come and gone from somewhere, and I was missing something. I rubbed my eyes and stood. I was a little unsteady and had to grab the post of the bunk bed.

I made it to the kitchen and put a coffeepot on the stove. With no electric pot, I had to cowboy the brew. I added several scoops of grounds and a few crushed eggshells to the pot. Good thing my father hadn't completely done away with the old ways. I scrambled up some eggs and fried a little sausage as I waited for the coffee. After rummaging in the pantry, I found some strawberry jelly for the whole wheat bread I was toasting on a flat cast iron camping skillet on the back burner of the stove.

Cadence came out of the bathroom a minute later. She wore the new pair of blue jeans we'd picked up in Payson and a loose, short-sleeved white cotton shirt. It was the smile on her face and the rosy color in her checks that I noticed most. The dark rings were fading now. I shook my head at the mystery of life, the tenacity of the human spirit, the wonder of renewal and restoration.

"Morning," I said, my voice still a little husky from sleep.

"Morning yourself, sleepyhead," she said brightly.

I started to pour myself a cup of coffee. "Heard you come back in this morning. You must have been up early."

She spoke over her shoulder as she washed her hands. “I ran down to the creek.”

I looked up sharply. “You ran down to the creek?”

Her smile brightened. “I couldn’t make it back up at a run, but it felt so good.”

I stared at her for a long moment. I wanted to protest, to scold. She might have fallen or run into a wild animal. Or worse. My expression must’ve betrayed my concern, for hers dimmed slightly. I don’t know how I did it, but instead of acting like an overprotective brother—or worse yet, a scolding parent—I simply said in a quiet voice, “Just be careful, okay? I’d hate for something to happen to you. I’d be stuck up here all alone.”

Laughter and the light shone from her violet eyes again. “Okay, Timmy, I’ll be careful. But you could always come with me.” She surveyed my waist. “Looks like you could use a little exercise yourself.”

I rolled my eyes and groaned. What could I say? Not like I could stop her from running. I took a sip of the coffee. “I’ll think about it.”

Yet I’d be running with her tomorrow morning. I was too concerned about something happening to her.

Cadence had taken over the scrambled eggs, and she cast me a glance. “You okay?”

I nodded and took another sip of the strong coffee, then forced a smile. “I’m fine. I just don’t want you to get hurt, that’s all.”

Cadence knocked the wooden spoon on the pan to remove the loose eggs. Then she turned off the burner and placed the lid on them to keep them warm. “Don’t worry, Timbre. A few more days, and I’ll be able to outrun the bears or anything else out to get me.”

She'd always been that way—headlong into life, afraid to miss any of it. Too busy living. No time for worries or fears.

We sat across from each other at the wooden table. Cadence seemed to sense my reserved mood. To try and cheer me up, she chatted about what she'd seen on her run—the squirrel that had scolded her from the oak, the scrub jays that had squawked at her from the brush, and the whitetail deer that had been drinking at the edge of the creek.

"So what's on the agenda for today?" she asked after we finished breakfast. "I'd like to work on the Matthew ciphers for a few hours. After lunch, we could go down to the creek again if you are up to it. This afternoon, maybe a few more hours on the cipher?"

"Sounds good to me," I said.

At that moment, I saw the note of warning in my mind, and it made my hair prickle.

You are being watched
You will be followed
You must be careful
You can trust n one

I couldn't shake the shoots of fear the note had germinated in my mind. Being found up here defenseless and alone by someone who meant us harm would be my worst nightmare. It would be nice if we had something to defend ourselves with. I looked at Cadence with an idea.

"What do you think about restarting our archery competition? If I remember correctly, I beat you real bad last time we were up here."

She turned red in the face and spluttered for a moment. I laughed. She was the most competitive person I'd ever known.

"Timbre Plummer, there wasn't a day since I was born that I couldn't whip your butt in archery. Why, the last time we were up here, I beat you so bad it wasn't even fun anymore."

I rolled my head back and forth like she'd lost her mind. "Not how I remember it, Sis. Not at all."

She gaped at me, seemingly unable to speak. I laughed harder. I couldn't help myself. If over-competitiveness was a weakness, then that was one of hers. After a minute of her sullen silence, during which I couldn't stop chortling, she finally realized I was yanking her chain.

She grinned a little. "I'll refresh your memory later," she said with a laser look.

We spent all morning exploring the lineage of Jesus in Matthew 1. It was like opening a Pandora's box of intriguing possibilities. By eleven, we had figured out the answer to Dad's fourth encryption. Or so we thought.

The lineage of Jesus in Matthew 1 began with Abraham and ended 41 names later with Jesus or *Yeshua*, as I was starting to think of His name in Hebrew. The Hebrew reminded me that *Jesus* meant *Yahweh's Salvation.* So, the two names that *encapsulate this passage* must be Abraham and Yeshua.

My father's use of Matthew 1 also confirmed and continued the theme from the previous riddles. Pretty cool. Genesis 22 connected Abraham to a promised *seed* by means of an oath Yahweh swore with him. The New Testament verses my father provided showed how the writers believed that this oath with Abraham, the *covenant and mercy*, as Moses and Daniel called it, was a promise of Yahweh's Salvation. It was only fitting, then, that the first chapter of the first book of the New Testament began with the lineage of Yeshua that traced his line back to Abraham and that ancient oath of sevens. This enigmatic list of names further enhanced the symbolism by sealing it with the number 41, the place or list value of Abraham's name in Hebrew.

The two numbers that provided the *primary continuity* were a little more difficult. My father's use of the word *primary* convinced Cadence that both numbers were prime numbers because he had a "thing" for primes. If this assumption was correct, 41 was one of the two numbers. Not only was it the value of Abraham's name, it was also the 13th prime. It wasn't until we laid out the lineage of Yeshua as described by Matthew that we filled in the other blank—13, a prime number we'd seen repeatedly in my father's riddles.

We studied the names I'd written out on my notepad, arranged into three groups of fourteen names, as Matthew described. To the left of each column of names, I numbered them. I drew a double line between *Joram* and *Ozias* in the second column, where three of Yeshua's ancestors had been left out. Below the column in parathesis, I wrote their names—Ahaziah, Joash, and Amaziah. Between *Josias* and *Jechonias*, I drew another double line where a single name had been left out. I wrote the missing name, Jehoiakim, below as well. In the final column, I wrote Jesus in as the 13th generation. In the 14th generation, I placed a question mark.

Lineage of Jesus (Yeshua)

As Described in Matthew 1

14 Generations From Abraham to David	14 Generations From David to the captivity	14 Generations From the captivity to Jesus

As Given in Matthew 1

Abraham	1	Solomon	1	Salathiel	1
Isaac	2	Reaboam	2	Zorobabel	2
Jacob	3	Abia	3	Abiud	3
Judas	4	Asa	4	Eliakim	4
Phares	5	Josaphat	5	Azor	5
Esrom	6	Joram	6	Sadoc	6
Aram	7	Ozias	7	Achim	7
Aminadab	8	Joatham	8	Eliud	8
Naasson	9	Achaz	9	Eleazar	9
Salmon	10	Ezekias	10	Matthan	10
Booz	11	Manasses	11	Jacob	11
Obed	12	Amon	12	Joseph	12
Jesse	13	Josias	13	Jesus	13
David	14	Jechonias	14	Jesus ?	14

(Ahaziah
Joash
Amaziah)

[Jechonias]

Cadence gave me a cheeky grin. She scooted her chair closer and leaned toward the desk. "With 41 names given but 42 described or intended, Matthew might have been making a symbolic statement about Yeshua's death and resurrection. In that final column, only 13 names are given, but 14 were intended. He came as the 13th generation, that so-called 'suffering servant,' so many Old Testament texts described."

"Like Isaiah 53?" I quoted part of the verse, "'He was wounded for our transgressions, he was bruised for our iniquities: the chastisement of our peace was upon him; and with his stripes we are healed.'"

"Exactly."

Cadence turned back to the list. "What if Matthew was trying to represent the resurrection by making Yeshua the 14th generation as well?"

"I guess it's possible." I scratched my head. "So, you are saying, as given, Yeshua was the 13th generation, but as intended, he was the 14th?"

"Sure. Why not?" She pointed at King David as the 14th generation in the first column. "Aren't there verses in the Old Testament that speak of Christ in terms of ruling from the throne of David?"

"You think, then, that Matthew is symbolically showing Yeshua came as the suffering servant of the 13th generation and, as indicated in prophetic symbolism, will someday rule as king from the throne of David as the intended 14th generation?"

"It's congruent, isn't it?"

I typed in a search about *throne David* into the online Bible software. Then I read the result.

> Isaiah 9:6-7
>
> For unto us a child is born, unto us a son is given: and the government shall be upon his shoulder: and his name shall be called Wonderful, Counsellor, The mighty God, The everlasting Father, The Prince of Peace.

> Of the increase of his government and peace there shall be no end, upon the throne of David, and upon his kingdom, to order it, and to establish it with judgment and with justice from henceforth even for ever. The zeal of YHWH of hosts will perform this.

Cadence tapped the screen. "See what I mean? It looks to me as though the lineage of Yeshua in Matthew 1 was more about the author trying to draw his Jewish reader's attention to how Yeshua fulfilled Old Testament promises than proving his precise lineage from Abraham."

"In other words, it was purposely contrived to develop a deeper truth."

"That would make more sense than the argument that Matthew couldn't read the Old Testament, wouldn't it?" She drummed her fingers on the desk.

I stared at the question mark I'd written on the notepad and muttered, "Yeshua … Yahweh's Salvation."

His Hebrew name got me thinking about Jehoiakim, the missing name between the 13th and 14th generations in the second column. If the list was really symbolic or some sort of literary device, what were the chances that the missing names were also part of the symbolic puzzle?

Cadence glanced over at me as I typed Jehoiakim's name into the search box. When I read the result, I looked up at her with a raised eyebrow. She didn't see it at first, but her mouth came open when she finally did.

"No way …"

I nodded. "It looks like *yes way*. Pretty cool, actually. Jehoiakim's name means *Yahweh raises up*."

"And Matthew just happened to leave that name out between the 13th and 14th generations—right where the knowledgeable Jewish reader would go looking for the missing name." Cadence arched her eyebrow. "Didn't I tell you those names might be missing on purpose?"

"That's not exactly what you said. If I remember correctly, you asked, 'What if it wasn't a mistake?'"

"Same thing," she said dismissively. She knew I was teasing her again. Cadence pointed at the 13th and 14th names in the second column. "What do Josias and Jechonias mean?"

I typed *Josias* in first. Cadence slapped me on the shoulder when the result came up. *Josias* meant *whom Yahweh heals*. She crossed her arms, and I couldn't help laughing at her smug, confident expression.

She raised her chin to indicate the computer screen. "Go on. Let's see what kind of mistake the 14th name is."

Jechonias meant *whom Yahweh establishes*. Even my skepticism couldn't overcome what was now obvious. My skin prickled just a little. I wasn't willing to call it inspired, but it was certainly clever, if not genius.

I wrote out the wordplay of the 13th and 14th names found in the final two columns.

13 Josias (whom Yahweh heals)
Missing Name Jehoiakim (Yahweh raises up)
14 Jechonias (Yahweh establishes)
13 Yeshua *14 Yeshua*
(Yahweh's Salvation)

We both laughed softly. Cadence read the name meanings in a sentence. “Whom Yahweh heals, He raises up, and He establishes, Yeshua—His Salvation.”

I turned to Cadence and said soberly, “You were right. It doesn’t look like a mistake. Even if it wasn’t inspired, it is an impressive literary device. This wordplay and the missing names parallel to Old Testament’s silence on how this transformation from Suffering Servant to Ruling King takes place.”

“Yeah,” Cadence answered, “and Matthew hid the key by omitting it from the text. By removing the other three kings between the 6th and 7th generations in the second column, he aligned the wordplay so that the 13th and 14th generations of the second column were parallel to Yeshua as the 13th and 14th generations in the third column.”

I shook my head. “He immortalized a ‘mistake’ that would always be there, waiting to be used as the key to one of the Old Testament’s greatest mysteries.”

I clicked on the tab on my laptop where I’d looked up Isaiah 53. In my notepad below the Matthew equation, I copied the entire Isaiah passage about the suffering servant. I had a feeling I might be revisiting it in the future. After that, I copied the passage from Isaiah 9.

Isaiah 53:3-11

He is despised and rejected of men; a man of sorrows, and acquainted with grief: and we hid as it were our faces from him; he was despised, and we esteemed him not. [4] Surely he hath borne our griefs, and carried our sorrows: yet we did esteem him stricken, smitten of God, and afflicted.

But he was wounded for our transgressions, he was bruised for
our iniquities: the chastisement of our peace was upon him; and
with his stripes we are healed. 6 All we like sheep have gone
astray; we have turned every one to his own way; and YHWH
hath laid on him the iniquity of us all. 7 He was oppressed, and
he was afflicted, yet he opened not his mouth: he is brought as a
lamb to the slaughter, and as a sheep before her shearers is
dumb, so he openeth not his mouth.

He was taken from prison and from judgment: and who shall
declare his generation? for he was cut off out of the land of the
living: for the transgression of my people was he stricken. 9
And he made his grave with the wicked, and with the rich in his
death; because he had done no violence, neither was any deceit
in his mouth. 10 Yet it pleased YHWH to bruise him; he hath
put him to grief: when thou shalt make his soul an offering for
sin, he shall see his seed, he shall prolong his days, and the
pleasure of YHWH shall prosper in his hand. 11 He shall see of
the travail of his soul, and shall be satisfied: by his knowledge
shall my righteous servant justify many; for he shall bear their
iniquities.

Isaiah 9:6-7

“For unto us a child is born, unto us a son is given: and the government shall be upon his shoulder: and his name shall be called Wonderful, Counsellor, The mighty God, The everlasting Father, The Prince of Peace.

Of the increase of his government and peace there shall be no end, upon the throne of David, and upon his kingdom, to order it, and to establish it with judgment and with justice from henceforth even for ever. The zeal of YHWH of hosts will perform this.

I closed my eyes, and the brick wall appeared. A pile of broken bricks that hadn't been there before sat on the floor in front of it. More of the door behind the wall was visible now too.

Was I losing my mind or my skepticism? I expelled a soft breath and pulled up the webpage for my father's fourth cipher, the familiar instructions greeting us. Cadence just squeezed my shoulder and waited for me to enter the answers.

Enter your answer in the spaces provided.
A correct answer will reveal the next cipher.
Only one attempt allowed per 24 hours.

___ ___ ___ ___ ___   ___

___ ___ ___ ___ ___   ___

Because there were five blanks followed by a space and a single blank, the answers would not be in English. While the English name *Jesus* was five letters, *Abraham* was not. In English, it was 7 letters. In Greek, Abraham was six letters. Only in Hebrew were both names spelled with five letters.

Due to a similar process of elimination, one might deduce that the single blank following the names was meant for an Arabic numeral. If our assumptions about the Matthew riddle were correct, the numbers we needed to supply were the prime numbers 41 and 13. I typed in the Hebrew letters and the two Arabic numerals, then pushed *enter*.

א ב ר ה מ	41
י ה ו ש ע	13

Chapter 69

Seeking

Once again, we waited for our answer to travel the thousands of miles at near-light speed to a computer where the correct responses were stored. The churning excitement in my stomach returned. When the new page loaded, we both gave an audible sigh of relief. I raised my hand, and Cadence gave me a high five.

I read the new riddle out loud several times. It sounded tough.

In this enciphered Biblical passage, the seeds of dedication were sown with a word and watered in a blessing that promised salvation.

Provide the 13 letters of this passage that connect it to the previous four ciphered texts.

The only thing that stood out to me in the instructions was that my father finally admitted the other four ciphered texts were related in some way. Cadence and I had already figured this out. Each additional ciphered text had confirmed it. This knowledge allowed us to further narrow our focus. But now that the admission was out in the open, was it some sort of diversion? Was he going to change direction to throw us off?

I copied the riddle and the cipher onto a fresh page of my notepad.

כ ד א ל ז א ה ד ע ל צ צ י י ס ג נ ב א ת ח ל
כ מ ה ג ד א ח נ ח ז ט א י ע ס צ ז ד ר ת ר ל
ל ע ר צ ז ז ע פ ב ד ח ש ו ת ה ג ג נ א ה ס ה
ל ש ז ק ב מ כ ק ק ט ק ס ש ר ת י ז ר כ ל ק ת
ע ר א ח י ו ק מ ת ל י ע ת ח נ ז ז מ י כ ז צ
ר צ ח ב י ט ב ת נ ה כ ש ל ס ג ע ע ע צ ס ר ג
ט ט כ כ ע ש ו ב כ ד י ד ת פ ע ט ל ט ר ס ג ז
ה מ ס ה ה ע ש ה נ ה ה צ ח פ י ק ג ט ר ח ח א
ע פ ב מ ע ז ד ש ר ד י ז כ ל ז ח ר י ל ו ש ל
צ כ ל ל א ע ט י ר ת כ ה כ ש ז ר צ ה ס ס ד ל
י ו ז ל ב ל ג ד ק ע מ א כ ת ג ד פ ו ת ח ש ט
א ט ר כ נ ה ע מ ה ע ה ו כ נ ה ג ו י ה ז ה ל
ש מ ט ל ב א ט מ ת ס י א ד פ ש ת נ ש ל ס י פ
ע י ח ש ט צ א ת ר ט נ ח מ י ג ה פ ג ט ר י ל
ב ס ל ל ב ש ז כ ו א ח צ כ ק ל פ פ ג ש ו ו צ
ג ש נ ח ו א מ ת ד ד ח ס פ נ ז י ג ה ט ז ש ל
ל ח נ פ ט ד ח ס פ א ו פ ר ח ע מ ו נ ל נ ר א
ב כ ס ט ר א ק ו נ ש ח ל ל מ ו פ מ ג ת ס ח ס
מ כ ב ב ט ר ק ו ו ב ב ת נ ל ח ו ז צ ח ו ח ל
ת מ פ מ כ ב ח ק ל ק ו ה י ר ת ז פ ד ק ר ר ר
פ כ ש ק פ ל ש א ז ר ח י ד ס מ ח ז ר פ ה ר ה
כ ר ש ט י ד ק ז ס י ב ע ת ש ג ה ר מ ר פ ע ח
ק צ ח י ס ו צ צ פ ב ק ר ל א ט ת ח ק מ פ כ ג
ס ש ו ת ק ע ב כ ס צ כ פ א ז מ ש ו ב י כ ח ח
י פ פ כ ו ו ב נ ע ד ט ח ז ל ע ט ס צ ל ח ג מ
ד ט ע ב ע ב ה נ ש ג ש ה ע ס א א ד ה א ס ק נ
ע ש ט ל ע פ כ ת מ ט ל נ ח י פ י ז א כ ו ד צ
ו ח ח ג ר נ ה י צ ד ע פ נ מ ב פ כ צ ש פ צ ח

The only information I could gather from the ciphered text itself was that it described a grid of twenty-two by twenty-eight, with six hundred and sixteen Hebrew letters this time. Since the Hebrew alphabet possessed twenty-two letters, the prime factors were eleven and two. Not sure if that meant anything, but I filed it away in the *may be useful* category for future retrieval.

Next, I copied the five verse clues. Of those, Genesis 22:17 stood out. This passage was part of the Akedah from the third ciphered text.

John 20:25
The other disciples therefore said unto him, We have seen the Lord. But he said unto them, Except I shall see in his hands the print of the nails, and put my finger into the print of the nails, and thrust my hand into his side, I will not believe.

Acts 2:22
Ye men of Israel, hear these words; Jesus of Nazareth, a man approved of God among you by miracles and wonders and signs, which God did by him in the midst of you, as ye yourselves also know:

Genesis 22:17
That in blessing I will bless thee, and in multiplying I will multiply thy seed as the stars of the heaven, and as the sand which *is* upon the sea shore; and thy seed shall possess the gate of his enemies;

John 8:12
Then spake Jesus again unto them, saying, I am the light of the world: he that followeth me shall not walk in darkness, but shall have the light of life.

Acts 3:26
Unto you first God, having raised up his Son Jesus, sent him to bless you, in turning away every one of you from his iniquities

I looked over at Cadence. "You get anything?"

She didn't respond right away, but judging by the movement of her head, she was reading the riddle and the verse clues again. So intense. The neural sparks and flashes of her brilliant mind practically blinded me.

When she finally turned my way, her expression resembled that of a chocolate connoisseur after taking the first bite—that magical moment when the silky-smooth chocolate begins to melt between the tongue and palate. Riddles, ciphers, and puzzles were my sister's chocolate. By the look on her face, this riddle and cipher made up some pretty fine chocolate.

"You really love this, don't you?" I asked.

She nodded, almost reverently. But something besides the joy of discovery tinged her look, like ghost peppers marring her mind candy. Frustration? Sadness? Disappointment? Something that didn't quite fit.

I had the feeling she was going to tell me about the shadows, but she didn't.

She put the tips of her fingers on her blonde head. "I … It's … I can't really describe it accurately. It's like my mind is starving and this is a type of food. No, that's not exactly right either. It's like—"

"Chocolate for the mind," I interjected.

She shook her head. "No, it's not like an addiction. More like a necessity. Deep thinking and solving problems are for my mind what air is for my lungs or blood for my heart." She searched my face.

It didn't fully explain that fleeting mystery expression of a moment ago, but it added a nuance. "Yeah, I think I understand. So … what did you make out of that oxygen for your brain?"

Once again, the shadows flickered over her brightness. "The oxygen is not flowing as well as it used to, but there are a couple of things worth mentioning."

"Shoot." Even working with a hand tied behind her back, so to speak, she'd have noticed things I missed.

Cadence pointed at the riddle. "I'm going to read these passages out loud, like you did with the Abraham and Isaac riddle. Tell me what jumps out at you, the theme or idea. Okay?"

"Got it." I liked it when the answers weren't wrong or right.

In this enciphered Biblical passage, the seeds of dedication were sown with a word and watered in a blessing that promised salvation.

Provide the 13 letters of this passage that connect it to the previous four ciphered texts.

I repeated the key phrases aloud as I wrote them below the ciphertext.

Seeds of dedication
Blessing that promised salvation

Cadence underlined the instructions. "Did you notice that Dad made an important admission in his riddle that confirms something you and I have begun to suspect?"

"He admits that all of the challenges are related."

"Exactly!" The excitement of a treasure hunter glittered in her eyes. "That means there are a few letters, a word, or a phrase in the ciphered passage that links all five of the riddles and ciphers."

"Sounds easy when you say it like that," I stated with a crooked grin.

Cadence ignored my sarcasm and pointed at the verse clues I'd copied onto my notepad. She tapped the page like a schoolteacher trying to refocus the attention of one of her unruly students. "Underline the words, thoughts, or ideas that stand out when you read each of them."

"Okay."

John 20:24-25
But Thomas, one of the twelve, called Didymus, was not with them when Jesus came. The other disciples therefore said unto him, We have seen the Lord. But he said unto them, <u>Except</u> I shall see in his hands the print of the nails, and put my finger into the print of the nails, and thrust my hand into his side, <u>I will not believe</u>.

Acts 2:22
Ye men of Israel, hear these words; Jesus of Nazareth, a man approved of God among you by <u>miracles</u> and wonders and signs, which God did by him in the midst of you, as ye yourselves also know:

Genesis 22:17
That in <u>blessing I will bless</u> thee, and in multiplying I will multiply thy seed as the stars of the heaven, and as the sand which is upon the sea shore; and thy seed shall possess the gate of his enemies;

John 8:12
Then spake Jesus again unto them, saying, I am the <u>light</u>

of the world: he that followeth me shall not walk in darkness, but shall have the light of life.

Acts 3:26
Unto you first God, having raised up his Son Jesus, sent him to bless you, in turning away every one of you from his iniquities

When she'd finished reading, I wrote the ideas that I had underlined into a column on my notepad.

Except I see (doubt)
I will not believe
Miracles
Blessing
Light of the World
Sent Him to bless

Cadence gave me a thoughtful nod. "So which of these clues seem most relevant to the overall messianic theme of Dad's Lazarus Ciphers?"

After rubbing my jaw, I squinted at the notes. "Genesis 22:17 and Acts 3:26 both talk about a blessing that Dad has demonstrated is part of one continuous Messianic thread." With my finger, I underlined the number *13* in the riddle. "The themes of blessing and salvation are similar to how Dad is using the number *13*. We can probably assume it is not a coincidence that it keeps coming up."

"I agree. No way it's a coincidence."

I let out a long breath. "Now that we know that Jesus was the 13th generation in Matthew 1, I think it's a safe bet that Dad is using the number *13* as a representation of Jesus, or Yeshua."

Cadence angled her head and quirked a brow. "You really think this is all Dad's imagination at work here? I mean, he's not making anything up. He's just connecting dots that already exist in the Biblical texts—dots that have existed for millenniums."

"True, but just because the dots seem to be related does not mean that they were intentionally designed to be."

"So … coincidence?" she challenged.

"Possibly, but it also could just be one Biblical author picking up on the *13* theme or symbolism and trying to build upon it. I mean, you have to admit that's exactly what the author of Matthew 1 did. Didn't he? He modified the listing of Jesus's generations to make Jesus the 13th. If there is a Messianic or redemptive theme related to *13* in the Old Testament, it's possible Matthew figured out a clever way to capitalize on the symbolism."

"And the story of the 13th and 14th generations? How do you explain that it tells a pretty nuanced redemptive story about Jesus? The very same redemptive story the New Testament claims."

I scratched my head with a lopsided grin. I probably needed to back off my devil's advocate role here. To be fair, I was pressing the skeptical angle a little harder than I believed. My doubt was having its own crisis of faith.

"I don't know, Sis," I said sincerely. "I'm still skeptical that these ciphers are anything more than Dad's ploy to get us to think about the Bible's redemptive story in a new way. Maybe just his way of trying to make us reconsider our skepticism and our faith or lack thereof."

The words of John 20:24-25 that I'd copied drew my gaze.

The other disciples therefore said unto him, We have seen the Lord. But he said unto them, Except I shall see in his hands the print of the nails, and put my finger into the print of the nails, and thrust my hand into his side, I will not believe.

I directed my sister's attention to the passage about Thomas. "I guess I have too many doubts. I'd like to grasp onto something more tangible. Something concrete that isn't just fascinating Bible verses or facts tied together with numbers and a great deal of imagination. I sympathize with Thomas. As macabre as it might sound, I'd like to touch the nail scars and see the gash in his side. Then maybe I could believe."

"And if you never get that chance?"

I shrugged. "I guess I'll just go on being an appreciative skeptic. I mean, after all we've been through, I see the value in believing. The importance of faith in one's life cannot be discounted. I know what it is like to try and live without faith and an associated set of moral values. I can tell you it's self-destructive. But as to faith in a personal, living God, I'm just not there."

Cadence gave me a warm smile and placed her hand on mine. "Fair enough, Timmy. But promise me you'll try to keep an open mind? Let's finish this together. This is going somewhere. I can feel it! The purpose and intensity of these riddles are growing. I believe that by the time we've solved the 7th cipher, you'll have something more tangible than the threads of Dad's imagination connecting a bunch of dots. There is more than just a beautiful human mind at work here. Dad might have caught a glimpse of God's creative genius."

"I'm in, Cadence … for the duration." I managed to lift the corners of my mouth. "I want to believe like you. I want to know the truth. If Yahweh, the God of the Bible, exists, I want to know him. I just …"

When I failed to complete my thought, Cadence grasped my hand. "That's good enough, Timbre. If God does exist, He'll be found by someone who is diligently seeking Him."

"You believe that?" I lifted my brows.

"I do," she said with a firmness that indicated absolute certainty.

"All right, then." With a sigh, I closed my eyes, and the image of the door in the dark hallway of my dreams appeared once more. But light now shone around the edges. I didn't remember it being there before. Funny, the games your mind plays.

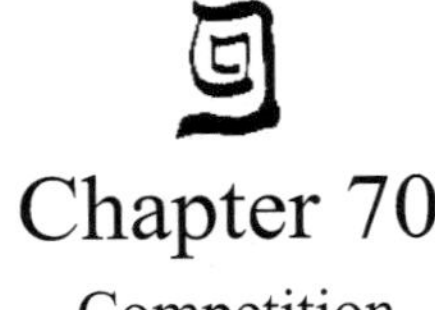

Chapter 70

Competition

With a whisper of feathers and the twang of a taut string, the carbon-fiber arrow catapulted toward the target a hundred feet away. The old gunny sack stuffed with pine needles shuddered with a rustling thud as the arrow plunged into the paper target ring just outside the black center. Although the silence next to me kept me from turning to gloat, I couldn't help the smile. Cadence shook her head.

For the last two days, we'd still worked on our father's latest word puzzles, but we'd made little progress. We were at a dead end on both riddle and cipher. So we'd thrown ourselves into our archery tournament.

The first day, my sister's shaking arms as she tried to pull back the bow she had once handled with aplomb, almost broke my heart. When we'd last competed here, Cadence could hit the black center of the target six out of seven times. Yesterday, she had not hit the bullseye once. Some of her arrows had even missed the paper. She'd done better today, but I was still besting her. Even though I probably shouldn't have, I felt good—really good.

We retraced the path we'd worn in the dry grass to the hoary old pine tree where we'd hung the gunny sack. Cadence was seething because she marched on her heels like a general leading her army. We stopped in front of the target. I paused to appreciate my handiwork and savor another victory. Cadence yanked out her arrows and held them in a clenched fist. I secured the paper target as I gently pulled my arrows from the two inner rings.

I could feel her eyes on me, but if I looked at her, I might not be able to contain myself. I finally turned. "Was this how you felt all the time?" I said with a grin.

She raised her fistful of arrows, and I ducked, but she just let out a frustrated growl that ended in a scream. She marched away. My laughter followed her all the way back to the shooting line. It really wasn't fair. She could barely pull back the bow even now. Oh, but she had tortured me for years with that laugh of hers every time she beat me. The only thing that kept guilt from swamping me was that this competition had lit a competitive fire in her.

For the past two days, she'd been doing pushups, chin-ups, and any other exercise she could think of to strengthen her arms. Her appetite had doubled, and she was constantly eating something, as if her body was making up for lost time. Rebuilding itself from all the abuse she had given it. She was still lean, but a healthy glow now freshened her skin. In only a matter of time, I'd be on the losing end of this competition, so I was going to enjoy it while it lasted.

"Are you going to come back here or just stand there gloating?" she asked imperiously.

Arrows in hand, I wandered back to the shooting line. It was my turn to shoot. "Watch and learn, Sis," I said in a pompous tone.

Showing off now, I let three arrows fly in quick succession. By unholy luck, two of them hit the bullseye, and the third landed right at the edge of the black. I kept my face forward again—but this time to hide my surprise. I was goofing off, and I'd shot my best set yet.

"Why don't we take a break, Cadence?" I asked as casually as possible.

"I'm not going to take a break until I knock the smirk off your face." She lifted her chin. "If I have to wear my fingers down to the bone, I'm going to beat you at least once today."

I laughed. She didn't.

She notched an arrow and drew the bowstring back against her cheek.

Maybe she needed a little "encouragement." "I doubt that, Sis. Your glory days are over. There is a new boss in town." I beat my chest with my fists and raised my hands.

A hint of a smirk curled her lips. "Doubting Thomas," she said as she released the string. In some act of divine justice, Cadence's arrow nailed the very center of the bullseye.

I dropped my arms with a *smack* against my jeans. "Crud," I muttered under my breath.

Cadence notched another arrow.

"I bet you can't make it in the bullseye again." A little extra pressure might help me out.

I heard her mutter "Doubting Thomas" under her breath again. But she didn't release the arrow. She just stood there with a faraway look on her face, like she was frozen in time.

My heart skipped a beat. "What's wrong?"

"Doubting Thomas," she whispered. She released the tension in the bow without letting the arrow fly.

Then she started running toward the cabin.

Chapter 71

A Doubting Thomas

I stood there dumbfounded as she disappeared into the cabin, bow and arrows in hand. Had she lost her mind? I walked towards the cabin with trepidation. What would I find when I stepped through that open door?

What I didn't find was my sister rocking herself back and forth on the floor in some sudden mental breakdown.

Instead, Cadence stood next to the desk, holding one of the books from my father's bookshelf—*The Code Breakers: The Comprehensive History of Secret Communication from Ancient Times to the Internet*, by David Kahn. She looked up when I entered.

"Listen to this." Her voice was strong and rich.

Well, at least she hadn't lost it. "This better be good." I flopped down into the desk chair and gave her an expectant look. "You nearly took two years off my life with your crazy talk and mad dash."

Cadence laughed and started reading.

One cipher system invented before the telegraph was so far ahead of its time, and so much in the spirit of the later inventions, that it deserves to be classed with them. Indeed, it deserves the front rank among them, for this system was beyond doubt the most remarkable of all. So well-conceived was it that today, more than a century and a half of rapid technological progress after its invention, it remains in active use. ...

Cadence looked up. “Care to guess who this inventor and statesman was?”

Hm. A hundred and fifty years ago. Before the telegraph. I didn’t know when the book Cadence was reading from was written, but the two clues provided by the text dated the inventor to the early nineteenth century or late eighteenth century.

“Doubting Thomas—Thomas Jefferson,” I exclaimed.

“Correct.” She grinned. “Did you know that Thomas Jefferson was an original American Doubting Thomas? Dad’s first two verse clues talked about Doubting Thomas and Jesus’s miracles. Thomas Jefferson didn’t believe in the divinity of Jesus, nor His miracles. In fact, he was such a skeptic, he made his own Bible in which he sacrilegiously cut out every mention of the miracles that Jesus performed.”

“Jefferson invented a cipher system?”

Cadence nodded. “Some time in the late 1700’s as Secretary of State, he invented what he called a wheel cipher. Unfortunately, he filed away his idea and forgot about it. In 1922 his designs were rediscovered in his papers in the Library of Congress. Here is the kicker. That same year the U.S Army started using a similar device.

Cadence flipped a couple of pages. “David Kahn finishes with this tribute to Jefferson:

So important is his system that it confers upon Jefferson the title of Father of American Cryptography. And so original is it that it sets Jefferson upon a pedestal far more prominent than those accorded to men like Vigenere and Cardano, whose names are usually thought to be household words in the history of secret writing.”

Cadence set the open book down on the desk. "Dad used a Jefferson cipher wheel to encrypt the text." She spoke matter-of-factly and pointed to the picture in the book. "That is what it looks like."

The object in the picture resembled a miniature bread roller. Instead of a single wooden cylinder, the cylinder had been divided into 26 disks. The edge of each disk was equally divided 26 times, with 26 letters of the English alphabet randomly inscribed in each space. Each disk was divided the same way, but the alphabet had been distributed so that no two disks possessed the same order of letters. A horizontal bar across the cipher wheel connected the handles on each end. That bar, I supposed, allowed the cryptanalyst to line up a row of letters and its user to read a line of text across the front of the cipher wheel.

"So, exactly how does this cipher wheel work?"

"It's simple," Cadence began.

I chuckled. "Of course it is."

She rolled her eyes and continued. "First of all, you need two cipher wheels that are exactly alike—one for the person encrypting the plaintext and one for the person deciphering the ciphertext. You take the text you want to encrypt and, using the letters on each disk, you write up to twenty-six letters of your message on the wheel. You use the bar across the front to line up the letters of your message. This also keeps the letters in the wheel aligned. This is important for the next part."

I closed my eyes to envision it. "Go on."

"Once you've spelled out the first twenty-six letters of your message on the wheel, you lock the wheel so none of the disks can move. You then take the bar underlying your message and turn it around to another part of the wheel." Cadence made a twisting gesture. "Any of the other twenty-five lines of random text will work. You simply choose one of the other random lines of text and write them down. You repeat this process with the entire message you want to encrypt."

"And to decipher the text?"

"To decipher the text, the person simply takes the ciphered text and spells it on his copy of the cipher wheel. He locks the wheels so they can't turn. Then he spins the alignment bar around the wheel until he sees the original message. If both wheels are identical, once the encrypted message is spelled out on the cipher wheel, one of the other twenty-five lines of the disk will automatically spell out the plaintext message."

I stared at the cipher wheel for a while, working out its function in my mind.

"Ingenious," I muttered under my breath. Finally, I looked up and cleared my throat. "We have one minor problem, Sis. Forgive me for stating the obvious, but we don't have a cipher disk, let alone the one Dad used to write this Hebrew cipher if, in fact, it is a Jefferson cipher wheel he used."

Cadence beamed. "No, we don't have one. But … I believe I know where we might find one." There was an air of mystery in her voice.

"Where?"

"In Dad's library at home in Phoenix."

I frowned. "Why would Dad have a cipher disk?"

"He collects them. *Collected*," she corrected herself. A shadow crossed her face as she paused. "Dad has a large collection of antique ciphering devices from around the world. When he couldn't find one he wanted, he'd make his own or have one made. If this is a Hebrew version of a Jefferson cipher, we'll find the cipher wheel in his library."

I considered that. We'd have to leave the safety of the cabin, and it would take at least four or five hours to get there and back. There was some risk, but what choice did we have?

When Eric Pincer first told us that there was a time limit to solving the ciphers before they would open to the public, I'd thought it a dirty trick to play on us. But now, the more I learned about the ciphers my father had created, the more I realized that he had designed them so that only Cadence or I could solve them. Probably both of us. He was using the ciphers to draw us back together. Even if he didn't succeed in restoring our faith, he had accomplished one of his goals. Cadence and I had renewed that special relationship we had growing up.

Chapter 72

The Siege

An hour later, we were nearly finished putting the cabin back in order. We only planned on staying in Phoenix long enough to find the Jefferson cipher wheel.

Cadence sat on the cabin steps as I lowered the protective shutters over the windows. Even though we'd return the same day, I didn't want to invite any unwelcome guests to break into the cabin in our absence. As I lowered the final security shutter over the window in the kitchen, the cabin grew increasingly gloomy. After the last ray of light had squeezed between the shutter and the frame, it took my eyes a moment to adjust.

Cadence called me, alarm in her voice. I dashed to the front door as three pickup trucks stopped in a row, facing the house. For a moment, nothing happened. They just sat there, fifty feet back. Cadence and I froze. I took my eyes off the dark, tinted windows of the vehicles and glanced at Cadence's little Honda, parked halfway between the cabin and the other vehicles. My father's briefcase was already in the car.

As if choreographed, six doors opened at once. From those six doors, five men and one woman emerged. Each held an assault rifle. They wore a variety of clothing, but mostly black and a lot of leather. Two of the men wore tank tops, allowing the MS-13 tattoos on their arms to be prominently displayed.

I'd left the gate locked the last trip to town, so either they had cut the lock or the fence. In either case, this visit was not an accident. Benito Silva had found me. I cursed under my breath and started down the steps for Cadence's car. As I passed her, I whispered, "Get in the cabin and be ready to lock the door."

Like most common criminals, they seemed surprised that I was not cowed by their armed presence. Oh, I was scared, all right, but I would rather die than lose my father's briefcase to these gang bangers. That briefcase meant more to me than my life. That briefcase had saved my life. That briefcase held the keys to the rest of my life. No way was I going to let them desecrate its precious memories.

I made it three-quarters of the way to the car before the six of them turned their rifles on me. I kept walking. Gambling with my life again. Betting that Benito Silva wanted more than my dead body returned to Phoenix. Benito was the type of sicko who would need to hurt me or Cadence to regain his self-respect, not to mention the respect of his organization. He had to prove he was better than me. He needed to dominate me. Whatever he had in mind, it would be painful and humiliating.

As my fingers curled around the passenger door handle, the gang bangers' attention turned toward the cabin. Probably Cadence going inside. Ignoring them, I opened the car door. I wrapped my hand around the handle of the briefcase. A harsh voice spoke.

"Get away from the car, *Cabrón.*" I leaned back out of the car, briefcase in hand. As I turned toward the house, one of the big guys in a tank top spoke again.

"Stay right where you are. You take another step, and I shoot you down like a dog."

I ignored him and started walking. He would have already shot me if they intended to kill us. A glance at the cabin told me what had distracted them. Cadence stood in the doorway. Her compound bow was drawn back, and an arrow was in place. The fierce look on her face scared me more than the thugs behind me did. The hair on my head stood up.

The zipping hiss of a bullet just over my head was followed a split second later by the cracking roar of a gunshot.

"I said stop!" yelled the same voice behind me. Another zipping hiss like tearing silk passed over my head. This time it was closer. Air fanned out by the supersonic projectile brushed my skin.

At nearly the same instant, the arrow from Cadence's bow streaked over my left shoulder. I started to run as a cursing scream rose from the same man giving the commands. A roar erupted behind me as five rifles opened fire. As I reached the porch steps, a burning sting in my leg caused me to trip and fall headlong onto the porch. Behind, the leader screamed at his men and the woman to stop shooting.

Cadence stepped out from behind the doorway and let loose another arrow. Bow in her left hand, she leaned down and grabbed my hand with her right. In a dragging crawl, she pulled me over the threshold. I looked over my shoulder as the big man, an arrow sticking out of his thigh, shot one of his men who wasn't listening to his command to stop firing.

As Cadence slammed an barred the door, the shooting faded and finally stopped. The yelling did not. It was dark with the security shutters down and the door closed. Cadence let go of my arm. I heard her fumbling around by the desk. I felt for the wall and scrunched myself upright against it.

The light came on a few seconds later. Cadence bent to examine my leg, which was bleeding enough to leave a crimson trail across the floor. Was her expression one of fear or anger? She jumped up and ran for the kitchen. After a moment, she was back with a kitchen knife and a couple of towels.

I recoiled. "What are you gonna do with that?"

"Just be still." She carefully cut open my pant leg. When the wound was fully exposed, her shoulders straightened, and she let out a long sigh. She placed the towel against the wound. There was no bullet hole. More of a long groove from which blood welled up.

She looked up at me, then at the briefcase still grasped tightly in my hand. "You bloody fool."

Teeth still clamped tight, I managed a halfhearted grin. "It's important to me."

"More important than your life?"

"Maybe."

Cadence took my free hand and placed it on the towel covering the wound. She stood up and walked to the pantry. The light flicked on. She returned carrying a first-aid kit.

Cadence proceeded to clean the wound with hydrogen peroxide and rubbing alcohol. Her administrations proved more painful than the gunshot itself.

"What are you, a horse doctor, or something?" I complained.

She gave me a look that told me I'd better shut up, or I'd have more serious injuries to worry about.

When she had finished patching me up, I let out my breath. "Thank you."

She just shook her head at me. Then she put away the first-aid kit and started to clean the blood off the floor.

What were we going to do next? That they hadn't killed us was a plus. But now we were trapped in the cabin, a jail cell of our own making, with our jailers outside waiting. It was a stalemate for now. Eventually, they would have to try and break in or burn us out. They couldn't be sure we didn't have any guns, but with Cadence's weapon of choice being a bow and arrow, they probably guessed we were not well-armed. As time wore on, they would become more desperate and bolder.

We needed to get out of here before they could figure a way in.

Chapter 73

A Bad Idea

I lay against the rough logs of the cabin wall and worked my way mentally through our predicament. Eventually, I relaxed my hand around the handle of the briefcase. That gave me an idea. Maybe getting the briefcase was not as dumb as Cadence had thought.

I dragged the briefcase close and set it upright, then grabbed the edge of the desk and tested my weight on my injured leg. Other than the stinging burn, it felt okay. I placed the briefcase on the desk and sprung the lid. Pulling out the laptop, I opened it and turned it on.

"Cadence," I called. She stopped her efforts to remove the bloodstain on the floor and walked over. "Would you email the sheriff's department, the forest service, and anyone else you can think of? Tell them who and where we are and that we are surrounded by armed men who are shooting at our cabin. Tell them we need help ASAP."

She looked at me with a question in her eyes. "What are you going to do?"

"I'm going to get us out of here," I replied.

"How?"

I smiled. "You aren't going to like it."

She sat down and started typing as I headed for the pantry. Once inside, I grabbed a flashlight left conveniently by the door. I'd wondered why the light was there, and now I had an inkling of why.

I clicked on the flashlight and inspected the floor of the pantry. I started closest to the door and worked my way to the back wall. There I found what I was looking for—an innocent-looking knothole that my father had not filled. That knothole was in a section of the floorboards that did not overlap like the rest. I stuck my finger in the hole and tugged. A twenty-inch section of the floor lifted away. I aimed my flashing into the dark hole, then lay on my belly, stuck my arms and head in, and shone the flashlight around. The cabin floor sat about two feet off the dirt, and there in the far corner on the side facing the barn was what I expected to see.

The laptop had given me the idea. Dad had upgraded the cabin with plumbing, electrical, and gas. When I'd inspected the basement in the barn, I'd seen the utility chase and all the pipes and wires running into it. I knew the chase must run from the barn to the house but hadn't thought much more about it until now. Necessity was the mother of invention. I smiled wryly and went to check on Cadence.

"Find what you were looking for?" she asked, looking up.

I nodded. "Come with me."

After hitting *enter* to send an e-mail, Cadence stood and followed.

In the pantry, I handed her the flashlight. "Far corner closest to the barn."

She got on all fours, then stuck her head and arms in the hole, and took a look. She came back out a second later, pale and wide-eyed. "If that is what I think it is, you are nuts. No way you are getting me in there.

"It's the only way, Cadence. We can crawl to the barn through the utility chase. We will sneak out the back door of the barn. It's about ten miles as the crow flies to the Happy Jack

RV Park. We'll catch or rent a ride from there and be back in Phoenix by morning."

"Crawl? That hole is barely wide enough for me to worm through." She bounced a glance off my shoulders and belly. "What if one of us gets stuck halfway between here and the barn?"

"I'll make it, even if I have to strip to my underwear."

Cadence was still shaking her head, an almost pleading look in her eyes now. "You know I hate tight spaces, Timbre. We could wait until the sheriff gets here."

"And if he doesn't show up?" I pointed to the door. "How long do you think they're going to wait? They can't be sure we haven't already called the cops."

As if to emphasize my point, boots thudded on the porch steps. Then came a voice. "You can't hide in there all day. You've got ten minutes to come out unarmed with your hands in the air. If you don't, we are coming in to get you."

It wouldn't be as easy as the man tried to make it sound. Dad had upgraded the cabin to keep vandals out when he wasn't up here. It was built like a fort. But a determined assault would eventually succeed. I needed to buy us some time. I neared the front door, Cadence close behind me.

"Will we be harmed?" I hollered.

The voice called back. "I have orders to bring you in alive."

I looked at Cadence. He didn't answer my question. We could be severely harmed and still be brought back to Benito Silva alive.

I closed the lid on my laptop and put it back in the briefcase.

We turned back toward the pantry. Cadence's body language told me she feared what was under the floor more than what was outside. Not me. I hated tight spaces, too but we were up here in the middle of nowhere. They could do what they wanted to us, and no one would hear or care. No, we were going through the utility chase, even if I had to push her every inch of the way.

Chapter 74

Bad Choices

I reached up through the floor and pulled the knot-holed panel back in place above us. Awkwardly navigating the tight space with the briefcase gripped in one hand, I crawled over to where Cadence shone her flashlight into the utility chase. Close up, it looked smaller than I remembered.

"You first, Sis."

"Are you kidding me?" Cadence's voice bordered on shrill. "Fine, chivalrous brother you are. Send the girl down the dark, creepy hole to check it out first. What if there is some animal in there? What if there are thousands of rats? Or a snake or something?"

"You have to go first because you are smaller and have a better chance of getting through. If I get stuck, you can still escape and go get help. Plus, if I go first, I can't be sure you'll follow, now, can I?" If I made it through, I sure as heck didn't want to have to come back to get her.

"What if I get stuck in there, Timbre?" she asked, almost pleading now. Genuine fear glittered in her eyes.

"I'll come push you through, Sis."

"How are you going to come rescue me from being stuck in a pipe when you are even bigger than me?"

Good point. If Cadence got stuck down this pipe, it was unlikely I'd be able to rescue her. A painful shiver slid down my spine. This was beginning to look like a really bad idea.

Pounding on the cabin door pushed me over the edge. I looked into the pipe one last time. Then the braided nylon tape in the conduit sparked an idea. Not the best idea, but better than nothing. I started pulling the tape free as fast as I could. Cadence watched until the end finally came free and landed on top of the large pile of nylon cable.

"Extend your foot," I said gruffly.

She only hesitated a moment before complying. "What are you doing?"

As I tied the nylon strap to her right ankle, I explained. "This is a utility fish tape. It's high-strength nylon that electricians use to pull wires and cables through pipe conduits. If you get stuck or freak out, I'll pull you back. Okay? Once you get to the other side, you can help pull me through if I get stuck." I took hold of both her shoulders and stared into her eyes. "Okay?"

She swallowed hard and nodded.

"Cadence, we need to do this, and we need to go now. If they find us down here, we are in real trouble. I'm not going to let them get their hands on you."

My words appeared to take hold as a look of resolve replaced her fear.

Without another word, Cadence stuck her arms into the hole and wiggled in after them. That nylon fish tape played out through my hands as though it had a life of its own. What seemed like forever but was probably only a few minutes later, the fish tape stopped moving. I clutched the last two feet.

I cupped my hands and called down the pipe. "You okay?"

A disembodied voice came back. "Don't ever ask me to do something like that again, or you are no brother of mine."

I smiled in relief and tied the flat nylon cord to my left wrist. I grabbed my father's briefcase, turned off the flashlight, and put it in the briefcase. I tried to shove the briefcase into the pipe edgewise. It wouldn't fit. Panic flashed through me. I turned the briefcase lengthwise and tried again. It fit this time. I looked down at my belly. I swore right then and there that if I got out of this alive, I would never touch another doughnut as long as I lived.

Grabbing the drain line lying in the bottom of the conduit, I pulled and wiggled in after the briefcase. Once I wedged my chest inside and my legs dangled outside, the fear hit me. My shoulders rubbed on both sides of the pipe. Only by keeping my arms extended like some subterranean diver would they pass through. I almost chickened out right there. I'd never had a claustrophobia problem, but terror crept up from my gut. I tried to force the thoughts out of my mind.

The utility pipes touched my belly. I grabbed a couple of them and tried to drag myself forward. I could only pull a few inches before my elbows hit the sides of my tubular tomb, and then my shoulders would wedge tight. I started to sweat.

"Pull," I yelled down the pipe. The nylon tape jerked tight and bit into my wrist. "Stop! You're going to yank my hand off." On the plus side, the pain got me mad. Maybe mad enough to make this work.

Cadence's petulant words floated my way. "You said pull."

"Pull gently, just enough to take the slack out. Okay?"

With the gentle pressure, I started to move. I used my toes and forearms to lift my weight off the pipes beneath. Then, like a centipede, in exasperatingly small movements, I inched my way down the pipe. The farther I got, the madder I became. The more chafed and blistered my hands and arms became, the faster I moved.

I don't know how long I kept going in this manner, but I finally had to rest. My back muscles were so fried I couldn't keep my body in the plank position, and my belly fat dragged on the pipes below, making forward progress nearly impossible. I swore again. When had I stopped caring?

As I rested, my mind began to work again. And not in the right kind of way. The sharp talons of fear grabbed my vitals. This galvanized me into a sort of frenzied, mindless effort. What seemed like a lifetime later, I burst out of the pipe into the barn's basement and fell to the floor in a heap of hurting, tangled relief. I must have had a wild look on my face because Cadence looked frightened.

"You okay?"

I lay panting where I'd fallen. "I'm going to have nightmares about that for as long as I live."

Cadence shone her flashlight on her arm. Goosebumps stood out prominently. She turned the beam back on my face. "If you ever try to make me do something like that again, you won't have that long to live, Timbre."

With that, she leaned close and untied the nylon cord around my wrist. Grabbing my arm, she tried to lift me off the floor. I couldn't move my arms or legs. They felt like they didn't belong to my body—except for the pain from my blistered elbows. Finally, some strength returned, and with some help from Cadence, I managed to sit upright against the basement wall.

"We've got to get moving," she said, taking my arm again.

I nodded and rose on wobbly legs, then swayed back and forth. At last, I took a step. Cadence reached for my briefcase, and we made our way to the basement steps. I managed the stairs by myself and peeked out the door of the basement. The barn was quiet and empty.

As we approached the big double, swinging doors, banging came from the direction of the house. I found a crack wide enough to look through and peeked out. Five of the assailants stood on the porch, taking turns attacking the front door with a tire iron. Judging by the arguing and swearing, they were having more trouble than expected. A chuckle escaped, and I shuffled aside for Cadence to look.

On her tiptoes, she peeked out before stepping back with a soft snort. “Let’s get out of here before they discover there’s a solid steel core beneath that log veneer.”

Chapter 75

The Phoenician

We stepped out of the Uber and into another world. The warm smiles of the concierges greeted us as they stood respectfully behind our open car doors. The hot Phoenix air had lost its burn in the early evening sun. In front of me, like a causeway to a temple of the ancient Aztecs, the white marble entry invited us into the luxuries displayed behind the beckoning glass and lights. The Uber's doors closed simultaneously, and the concierges returned to their positions.

The driver accelerated out from under the *porte cochere* and faded into the shadows of the palms, then disappeared with a flash of the setting sun reflecting off his window. The final long rays of golden light streamed across the emerald green lawns and crimson geraniums that lined the serpentine road.

My right hand gripped the familiar leather handle. Cadence stepped beside me and tucked her hand into the crook of my left arm. She giggled and squeezed. A warm, affectionate smile lit her eyes. "Shall we?" she asked quietly, like some famous movie actress to whom this sort of thing was a common occurrence.

I gulped and nodded. This was quite a cultural shock from the serene, natural tones of pine logs and blanch grass of the Mogollon Rim. When I didn't move right away, Cadence leaned in and whispered in my ear.

"Your mouth is hanging open, Timmy." She giggled again at the audible click of my teeth.

I might as well be a Beverly hillbilly at the entrance to the Taj Mahal. Despite all my complaints, I was thankful now that Cadence had coaxed me into a stop at the mall to get a change of clothes. She looked the part perfectly. She wore a flowing white cotton skirt that swayed and rippled gracefully as she walked. Pale arms just beginning to show the signs of a healthy tan and new muscle tone contrasted with her matching white cotton short-sleeved shirt. Embroidered around the sleeves and collar were small ivory butterflies. An airy aqua-and-sky-blue silk scarf provided a splash of vibrancy and contrast to her ensemble.

Cadence lifted her dark glasses. “Come on, Timbre. We can’t stand out here all day. You promised me dinner.”

I nodded and startred to move.

Our escape from the barn had proven rather anti-climactic. The building had shielded us from sight as we ran into the trees at the edge of the corral. A few seconds later, the majestic ponderosa pines offered sanctuary. We ran northeast for ten minutes and then slowed to a walk.

Just after we’d crossed Clover Creek, I’d gotten myself into my current predicament. If Benito had found us in the wilderness, he likely had someone watching other places we might turn up. That included my father’s house. Cadence had told me that if I’d buy her dinner, she’d get us into our father’s house without anyone the wiser. I went along with it since all I knew about my father’s house in Phoenix was the address—5813 Wonderview Hill Road—I had seen listed in the will.

Tired and thirsty but in overall good spirits, we’d arrived at the RV park five hours later. We caught a ride with an older couple returning to Phoenix from a trip to the Grand Canyon. They’d dropped us off at the Phoenix mall.

And now we were entering a luxury resort that Cadence happily informed me Forbes awarded a five-star rating. Two giant four-level white curves of concrete and glass, like stepped pyramids or monumental stairways to the heavens, snuggled into the bosom of Camelback Mountain. Seventy feet below, nestled in the final curves of the resort, half a dozen multi-level swimming pools sparkled and glowed in the late-afternoon desert sun.

Cadence gently led me into the astral-themed lobby of the Phoenician resort. We passed over a large tile eight-pointed star made of long white narrow obtuse scalene triangles mated with brown tile of equal size and shape. Tiles of brown and tan hues surrounded the design. Above us, a recessed circle nearly twenty feet in diameter glowed with the hue and texture of the moon, light pouring forth from the edges as it would during an eclipse.

Crimson, emerald, orange, and azure glowed from the terraces overlooking the resort pools and golf course. At the entrance to the Mowry & Cotton restaurant, a maîtr' d' greeted us. At our request, he seated us on the covered patio.

We sat side by side in teakwood chairs with ivory cushions. I faced the swimming pools to the south. To my left, Cadence's face glowed with the majestic colors of an Arizona desert sunset. I opened my menu, and after a quick scan, lowered it.

"Did you see the prices?"

Cadence didn't look up. If anything, as she slid her sunglasses onto her head, the smile on her face grew a little bigger. By now, I was getting a little irritated with her. Why such a cavalier attitude? She'd dragged me to one of the most affluent parts of Phoenix with no more explanation than she wanted me to take her to dinner. We were living it up as if we'd already inherited our father's fortune when we should be trying to find that cipher wheel and save our necks.

"At this rate, we'll run out of money before we solve the ciphers," I muttered under my breath as I looked back at my menu.

"It takes money to make money, brother," she said enigmatically.

I gave her another scowl.

"Just trust me, okay? Enjoy your dinner. Enjoy the moment. Pretend that this is the last hour we will ever spend together. Savor it."

"But Cad—"

She placed her hand on mine. "A month ago, I never in my wildest dream would have believed I'd be sitting here with you. I'm happy, Timbre. Don't spoil it, okay?"

It was more of a request than a command. I sighed, and with a major effort, I pushed aside my worries and aggravations. She was right, of course. I was sitting here in a spectacular setting with a special person. I slid my hand out from under hers and placed it on top. I squeezed her hand gently and then picked up my menu again.

A minute later, our waiter came. "I'm Ray. What can I get you to drink this evening?"

I glanced at Cadence. "I'm ready to order if you are, Sis."

Cadence put down her menu and smiled at the waiter. "I'm ready," she replied brightly.

"What will you have, ma'am?"

"I'd like a Coke, the Bucatini Pasta, and an avocado Caesar salad."

The waiter scribbled his notes and looked at me. "Sir?"

I really wanted the filet mignon, but the forty-eight-dollar price tag was a bit hard to swallow. The twenty-two-dollar burger was much more feasible. I didn't respond right away, and I could feel Cadence watching. She started laughing again, and my ears got hot.

"I can come back in a few more minutes," the waiter suggested.

For whatever reason, this was important to Cadence, and the truth be told, I didn't know what tomorrow would bring, so I wasn't going to spoil the night for both of us by being a stick in the mud. "I'll take the filet mignon, medium well, the *burrata panzanella* salad, and water."

On impulse, when Ray asked if that would be all, I added wild mushroom flatbread. Cadence beamed as he whisked away to fetch our drinks.

Two hours later, we'd finished dinner and dessert. I left two hundred dollars on the table to cover our meal, tax, and gratuity. I was a high roller now.

"I enjoyed dinner, Sis," I said—and meant it.

Cadence smiled and hung on my arm as we walked back through the lobby. I headed for the reservation desk to see if I could order a taxi or Uber. Cadence saw where I was going and held me back.

Cadence tugged on my arm. "Indulge me just a little longer, Timmy. Take a walk with me?"

At least she wasn't asking to stay here at three hundred dollars a night. I shrugged and escorted her through the front doors into the cooling night. Passing under the *porte cochere,* we crossed the circular drive and over to the second curved wing of the resort. Cadence led me through its lobby, up the stairs, and out the back door toward Camelback Mountain.

"Where are we going, Cadence? "

She turned along the lighted path of the golf course. The city traffic was muted here, and Phoenix glowed and twinkled as the last vestiges of light faded in the west. We walked along the golf course until we reached the 13th fairway. Halfway down the outside edge of the green, Cadence let go of my arm and took a narrow trail that led away from the course.

I stopped for a moment, gaping. “What are you doing, Cadence?”

She didn’t look back or attempt to explain. I could barely make out the narrow trail in the gloom. Here I’d indulged her all evening, and she wanted me to take a nature walk up Camelback Mountain in the dark. I hustled to catch up to her and give her a piece of my mind, but she was a white wraith weaving in and out of the cactus and thorn hedges. Several times, I nearly lost sight of her in the shadows. Then she disappeared around a screen of desert brush.

I couldn’t see the trail anymore. I clenched my teeth. When I reached the brushy hedge, the mournful squeal of unoiled metal turned my head. There, nestled between two ancient mesquite trees a hundred feet away, was a wooden gate set in an adobe brick wall. If it hadn’t been for the sound, I’d have walked right on by. On the pillars on each side of the gate, a dim, orange glow illuminated the immediate area. A bronze plaque glinted as the gate opened for a moment to reveal Cadence’s ghostly form. The gate squeaked again as it swung closed. This time, there was a click. Cadence’s melodious laughter filled the night air, the sound so pleasant, so pleasing, it left no room for the rasping chirp and hissing buzz of insects—or my aggravation. As the warm Phoenix night bore her mirth away, the chirp and buzz returned.

I headed for the gate. My hand only got halfway to the handle before the seven letters written on the bronze plaque stopped me.

Plummer.

Chapter 76

A Doubter's Paradox

"I'll be darned," I murmured. She *had* said that if I'd buy her dinner, she'd get me in Dad's house with no one the wiser. I turned the handle on the gate and pushed it open. Cadence waited inside.

"You took long enough," she said, her rich laugh filling the night again.

"You got me good. I didn't see that coming at all."

"Hope you are not too mad. I wanted to surprise you."

Before I could say anything, she handed me a key.

"Lock it, would you? We don't want any more bad guys sneaking up on us."

I did as requested and handed the key back to her.

"Come on. I'll show you the way." She started down a dirt path lined every few feet with solar-powered lights that gave off a warm, orange glow. Cadence led the way through a desert-landscaped garden, past the pool, and around the side of a house to a garage entrance. Using the same key, she unlocked the door and hastened to a security panel on the wall. She entered a code I didn't catch. When the panel beeped twice, she turned back toward me.

"The password is our birth dates. If you don't enter it within thirty seconds, a private security company will show up within five minutes. Then the police."

"You seem to speak from experience." I raised my eyebrow at her.

"Yeah, I forgot one time when Dad was out of town."

While I closed and locked the side door of the three-car garage, Cadence turned on the lights. One space was empty. A new four-wheel-drive Dodge Ram 2500, a subdued off-white, sat farthest from us. Next to the truck was a gray Jeep Wrangler.

"Want to see the place?" she asked, reaching for the door.

"Sure, but let's not turn on any lights in case someone is watching." I set down my briefcase and opened the lid to retrieve one of the flashlights we'd used to escape the cabin, then handed it to Cadence. "Keep it shaded with your hand."

She gave me one of those looks only a sister can give. "I'm not an idiot, Timmy."

We stepped into the house. Cadence led passed granite countertops and down a tiled breezeway between the dining room and the living room to the back of the house. Opening a door on our right, she entered and waited until I joined her in what appeared to be our father's office, then closed the door. There were no windows. After Cadence turned on the lights, I could see why. Antique books covered two of the walls. Glass shelves upon which were displayed all sorts of plaques, papers, and gadgets such as one might envision in Leonardo DaVinci's office lined the third.

My father's desk, apparently handmade, sat opposite the door. I stepped closer and ran my hand along the silky-smooth surface of the wood, the deep reddish-brown of mesquite. I whistled under my breath. "Beautiful."

We both turned to the mesquite wood pedestal that stood in front of my father's collection of cipher artifacts. Atop the pedestal was a glass case with a blueish tint. On the lid of the case, writing had been laser-cut into the glass. Some unseen means of luminescence radiated the glass case and its contents. This clever means of illumination also caused the words to stand out in glowing relief.

Inside the glass was what we had come for—a stainless steel or aluminum version of a Jefferson cipher wheel. We stepped closer to the case and leaned down for a look. Beautifully engraved along the edge of each of the wheel's twenty-two shining metal disks were the random letters of the Hebrew alphabet.

"It's beautiful," Cadence whispered, almost in reverence.

I straightened and read the words on the glass cover aloud.

Now to him that is of power to stablish you according to my gospel, and the preaching of Jesus Christ, according to the revelation of the mystery, which was kept secret since the world began,

But now is made manifest, and by the Scriptures of the prophets, according to the commandment of the everlasting God, made known to all nations for the obedience of faith:

To God only wise, be glory through Jesus Christ for ever. Amen.

- Romans 16:25-27

Cadence locked eyes with me. "He did this for us, you know," she said quietly.

The import of her words settled on me as if tangible. "I know."

Cadence touched the words on the glass. "He made this Jefferson wheel in the hope that we'd someday find it. But more than that, he wanted us to see this cipher wheel through the lens of this passage of Scripture. This is his manifesto. His mission."

I reached up to place my hand on the glass next to Cadence's and ran my finger along some of the foggy, glowing letters.

Nodding slowly, I considered the words, their meaning, and the incredible lengths our father had gone to ensure we'd hear the message of Jesus, of Yeshua—Yahweh's Salvation—one last time.

"He must have really loved us."

These ciphers and riddles, this cipher wheel and its illuminating display, were not a whim. They were not the result of a last-minute effort by a desperate man. This elaborate mission represented a lifetime of study, years of planning, and a comprehensive understanding that allowed for a cunning execution. This was my father's magnum opus, his last, desperate attempt to reach Cadence and me from the grave. His quest was to tell us about the mystery of Jesus so that we, too, might have faith.

A chuckle escaped my lips as I placed both hands on the glass and bowed my head. If my father was watching us from somewhere up there right now, he was probably laughing at the absurd, ironic delight of this lighted display. This was an encryption device invented by Thomas Jefferson, a man so hostile to the idea of the divinity of Christ that he was willing to desecrate the very words that spoke of it. His invention was the tool my father chose to encrypt the information he believed would convince us of that divinity. Then, with exquisite taste, he enclosed the cipher wheel in a case of shining light and covered it with a passage of Scripture that talked about Jesus and the revelation of a mystery kept secret since the world began.

As I looked down through the glass at the Hebrews letters so precisely cut into the burnished metal of cipher wheel, I wondered what new information, what secrets they would reveal. Would those words allow me to reach back into the past and put my fingers into the nail holes and my hand into the spearman's gash in his side?

Chapter 77

From This Day Forward

The next morning, we sat side by side at my father's handcrafted desk. The shining cipher wheel lay in front of us on the hard, sangria-colored wood. Everything we'd found so far told us that this cipher wheel was the solution to our father's fifth cipher. Now we needed to test our theory.

We'd decided the previous evening that we would stay here for a couple of days or at least until we'd solved the fifth cipher. The refrigerator had been emptied of any food that could spoil, and the house was so spotless, there must be some sort of cleaning service hired by the trustee of my father's estate. We didn't want to be surprised by any unwelcome visitors, so I'd filled all the deadbolt keyholes with caulking I'd found in my father's toolbox in the garage. I also unplugged the automatic garage door openers. Hopefully, this would buy us enough time to sneak back out the way we'd come.

We stayed away from the windows that were not shaded, and we did not turn on any lights that might be seen. I'd slept fitfully in the guest room of the house. Cadence slept in a bedroom our father had kept for her.

I'd let my guard down at the cabin, assuming we were safe, that no one would find us there. But someone *had* found us. Whoever had sent us the note of warning had been correct. Somehow, we had been followed. But how? As far as I knew, no public records existed on my grandfather's homestead. It was listed in the will, but no address had been given. If Benito

Silva had found the cabin, he shouldn't have any trouble finding my father's mansion built into the side of Camelback Mountain.

On the plus side, my father's house was one of several expensive homes in a very affluent neighborhood. Anyone loitering or staking out the place would be noticed and likely reported to the police. Certainly, anyone of the caliber of Silva's men would be as obvious as a beached whale and as welcome as a desert sidewinder. These facts still didn't allay my fears.

Cadence shook my arm. "Earth to Timbre. Hello, is anyone home?"

My eyes focused back on the cipher wheel. I shook off the unpleasant feeling and offered a sheepish grimace. "I didn't sleep well last night. I guess I was daydreaming a bit." I cleared my throat theatrically. "So … you want to go first?"

Cadence nodded, and I slid the cipher wheel toward her. Gently, she turned the disk wheels to get a feel for the device.

I opened my laptop and accessed the webpage for the cipher. I enlarged the image of the cipher and angled the computer so Cadence could read the first line of encrypted Hebrew.

We quickly learned there was a trick to the cipher wheel—several, in fact. The most difficult part turned out to be keeping the individual cipher wheel disks aligned as you looked for the correct letter on the next disk. After fifteen minutes of concentrated effort, Cadence completed the first line of ciphertext. She turned the nuts at the end of the cipher wheel to lock all of the wheels. Then, she handed me the cipher wheel, and I slowly turned it around in search of a legible line of Hebrew text.

The 13th row revealed the Hebrew plaintext.

בעשרימוארבעהלתשיעיבשנת

I gave a rough translation for Cadence. "Twenty-four ninth year."

My fears were forgotten. Not only was there a purpose to our efforts, but the quest itself had gotten into my blood. I decrypted the second line of twenty-two letters of ciphered text and read it out loud.

"Two Darius to be done word YHWH to …"

Shooting Cadence a quick smile, I typed the Hebrew text into my web browser and tapped the search box. Only one result was returned, Haggai 2:10. Cadence and I both read the passage out loud.

Haggai 2:10

In the four and twentieth *day* of the ninth *month*, in the second year of Darius, came the word of YHWH by Haggai the prophet, saying,

"Now we are getting somewhere," Cadence said as she pointed at the ciphered text. "Should we count the number of Hebrew letters in the cipher so we can tell the extent of the passage Dad is quoting?"

"We could just decipher the last twenty-two letters. That should give us the boundaries of his passage, shouldn't it?"

Cadence nodded. "That would probably be faster."

A few minutes later, I had the final line deciphered. The first two letters didn't mean anything to me. They were probably from the preceding line of ciphered text. There were four words that I could make out, though. I read them out loud for Cadence's benefit.

"From this day bless Haggai."

The final three letters—bet, yod, koph—didn't spell a word I recognized. But what we had was enough. The entire passage quoted was Haggai 2:10-19. According to my online Bible, verse 19 ended with the words, *From this day bless.*

The word *Haggai* and the final three Hebrew letters had been tacked onto the end of the passage for some reason. I pointed at the unaccountable additions.

"Any idea why he added this to the passage?"

Cadence gave me a benevolent smile. "What are the values of the final three letters?"

I looked at the letters again and then slapped my head. Of course! Two, ten, nineteen. It was the reference to Haggai 2:10-19.

Cadence tapped the letters with her index finger. "Dad didn't need the reference, but my guess is, he added it to fill in the remaining blocks of text. Without those 7 letters of the reference, the ciphered text would not make a box of exactly 22x28 Hebrew characters."

"That makes sense, but how do we find the 13 letters of this passage that make it relevant to the other four ciphers?"

Cadence tucked an errant bit of hair behind her ear and then straightened. "Can you pull up an English version of Haggai chapter 2 for me? I'd like to get the context of the entire passage. Maybe that will provide the clues we need to solve the riddle."

Chapter 78

A Word, A Date, and a Blessing

I held up my legal notepad and read the words of my father's riddle out loud for the 3rd time that morning.

In this enciphered Biblical passage, the seeds of dedication were sown with a word and watered in a blessing that promised salvation.

Provide the 13 letters of this passage that connect it to the previous four ciphered texts.

Eyes closed, Cadence listened attentively, as she had each time. I could almost see her mental wheels turning. We'd both read the entire chapter of Haggai 2, and just to be thorough, we'd gone back and read the entire book of Haggai. What we knew from the text and a quick search of an online Bible dictionary was that Haggai was one of the so-called "minor" prophets. He lived during the reign of the Persian king Darius Hystaspes, otherwise known as Darius the Great. He prophesied to the repatriated Jewish subjects of Babylon, whom Nebuchadnezzar had taken captive nearly seventy years earlier.

I set my notepad down and looked up at Cadence. "Any ideas?"

Cadence took a pencil from the desk and circled three words in my father's riddle—dedication, word, and blessing. She tapped the words with the end of her pencil and then flipped the page of the notepad to where I'd written the verse clues.

John 20:25

The other disciples therefore said unto him, We have seen the Lord. But he said unto them, Except I shall see in his hands the print of the nails, and put my finger into the print of the nails, and thrust my hand into his side, I will not believe.

Acts 2:22 Ye men of Israel, hear these words; Jesus of Nazareth, a man approved of God among you by miracles and wonders and signs, which God did by him in the midst of you, as ye yourselves also know:

Genesis 22:17

That in blessing I will bless thee, and in multiplying I will multiply thy seed as the stars of the heaven, and as the sand which *is* upon the sea shore; and thy seed shall possess the gate of his enemies;

John 8:12

Then spake Jesus again unto them, saying, I am the light of the world: he that followeth me shall not walk in darkness, but shall have the light of life.

Acts 3:26

Unto you first God, having raised up his Son Jesus, sent him to bless you, in turning away every one of you from his iniquities

Cadence pointed at the first two verses, John 20:25 and Acts 2:22. "We know these two clues were given to tell us the type of cipher Dad used." She crossed them both off. "That leaves the final three as possible clues. Both Genesis 22:17 and Acts 3:26 talk about a blessing. Our working thesis so far has been that Dad's riddles are meant to tell us about Yahweh's Salvation to mankind. About Yeshua, Jesus."

The way she held a breath after that last sentence, she wasn't finished. I encouraged her to continue with a tilt of my head.

"Acts 3:26 shows that the New Testament believers saw Jesus as the fulfillment of Genesis 22:17 and the blessing promised to Abraham's seed, a blessing that the New Testament clearly describes as redemptive in nature." Cadence waved across the desk toward the empty glass case. "The verses on that case confirm that Dad saw the message of Yahweh's Salvation—his Yeshua, if you will—as the mystery that was preached by the prophets of the Old Testament."

She stood up and walked around the desk to the case, then read the verses out loud.

Now to him that is of power to stablish you according to my gospel, and the preaching of Jesus Christ, according to the revelation of the mystery, which was kept secret since the world began,

But now is made manifest, and by the Scriptures of the prophets, according to the commandment of the everlasting God, made known to all nations for the obedience of faith:

To God only wise, be glory through Jesus Christ for ever. Amen. - Romans 16:25-27

After reading the verse, she returned to her seat and flipped back to the page where I had written our father's riddle. She handed me the pencil. “What part of Dad’s riddle might we say was in keeping with the overall redemptive theme of the ciphers?”

As the pieces started to fit, a smile crept over my face, and I circled the words *blessing that promised salvation.* I handed the pencil back to Cadence. It was my turn to ask a question. “What four words from the Haggai passage might be in keeping with this theme?”

Cadence didn’t even hesitate. On the notepad below the riddle, she wrote the final words of the English translation of Haggai 2:19.

from this day will I bless you

“What day?” she asked, returning the pencil.

I pointed at Haggai 2:18 and then Haggai 2:1 and added the dates below the words she had just written.

24th day, 9th month, 2nd year of Darius king of Persia.

Who knew where this would take us, but I liked this back and forth. I handed the pencil back to Cadence. “What took place on this date?”

Her eyes moved back and forth as she read the verses backward from verse 19. Then she wrote on my pad.

The day the foundation of Yahweh’s temple was laid.

She scrunched her eyebrows together and gnawed on the pencil eraser.

"Summarizing," I said, "we have a verse that talks about a promised blessing. We even have a date from which that blessing would begin. We also have an event on that date."

Cadence lowered the pencil. "The laying of the temple foundation."

"I don't see how that blessing and the temple foundation connect to Dad's overall theme of Yeshua."

The gnawing stopped again. She turned to me with a spark of something in her eyes and a smile. "We know that Dad found a connection between Haggai 2 and his other riddles. Right?"

I nodded. "Yes. His riddle tells us that."

"But we can't see any connection between the completion of the second temple's foundation, Yahweh's blessing, and the overall redemptive theme."

"I don't."

"I don't, either," Cadence said matter-of-factly. "But … we have one verse clue left that seems out of place. Why did Dad include the passage from John 8?" She turned the page back and read the verse from my notes.

> **John 8:12**
> Then spake Jesus again unto them, saying, I am the light of the world: he that followeth me shall not walk in darkness, but shall have the light of life.

A few goosebumps rose on my arms. "It wasn't an accident, was it?" We both looked at the glowing glass case that had held the Jefferson cipher wheel. "The light of the world."

I slid the laptop in front of me and pulled up John chapter 8. Excitement practically hummed between us. Our glances tangled and we laughed. He had us now. This wasn't just fun. I wasn't even sure how to describe it. It was fun, fulfilling, and fantastic. It was a treasure hunt in every sense of the word. Only, somehow, along the way, we'd stopped thinking in terms of the monetary value of the treasure. At least I had. By the glowing smile and light in Cadence's eyes, I was pretty sure her treasure would also be found in the words and numbers we were reading now and the meaning our father had conveyed in them.

We started with John chapter 8 and learned that Jesus's statement, "I am the light of the world," was made in the temple. We finished John 8 without drawing any real connections between this statement and my father's riddle. I sat back in the chair, but Cadence kept reading, scrolling through chapter 9 and then into chapter 10. She stopped with her finger on a verse and turned to me, the look on her face priceless.

I sat up with a squeak of my chair and read the verse she was pointing at, John 10:22.

John 10:22-23

And it was at Jerusalem the feast of the dedication, and it was winter. And Jesus walked in the temple in Solomon's porch.

It was my turn to read back through the context of John 8-10. Jesus made His statement in John 8 that He was the light of the world during the Jewish Feast of Dedication. The events of John 8-10 all took place during that same time frame. That meant there was a connection between the two. Clearly, it wasn't a coincidence that my father's riddle talked about the *seeds of dedication* and his verse clues mentioned Jesus standing in the temple on the Feast of Dedication proclaiming that He was the "light of the world."

I nudged my sister's arm. "What do you know about the Feast of Dedication?"

"Not much," she replied. "Other than it is another name for the Jewish celebration of Hanukkah."

I turned back to my computer and typed in *the feast of dedication*. I read the top result to Cadence.

The Feast of Dedication, also more commonly known as Hanukkah, is a Jewish festival commemorating the recovery of Jerusalem and subsequent rededication of the Second Temple at the beginning of the Maccabean Revolt against the Seleucid Empire in the 2nd century BCE. It is also known as the Festival of Lights because a candle is lit successively during each day of its celebration.

Hanukkah is observed for eight nights and days, starting on the 25th day of Kislev according to the Hebrew calendar. The events commemorated by this festival are believed to have taken place in the year 164 BCE.

Cadence tapped her eraser against her upper teeth in a distracting staccato.

I frowned at her. "Ever wondered where that eraser might have been?"

She just gave me a blank stare. The tapping stopped. The lights were out, but someone was definitely home—kind of like the two of us in my father's house. Things were happening behind the scenes.

I attempted to concentrate, but my mind felt like what Cadence looked like. Only, she was still firing on all cylinders, and I was stalled out.

"Timbre, can you look up Kislev's month number?"

My satisfaction at being potentially useful disintegrated into my own blank stare. "What?"

"The month number. You know, January is month 1 in our calendar. What month is Kislev in the Biblical calendar?"

A light went on in my head. A few strokes of my keyboard later, I had the answer. "Ninth month." To my credit, I saw the connection to the riddle just a few seconds after her eyes sparked.

"The Feast of Dedication or Hanukkah begins on the twenty-fifth day of the ninth month."

When Cadence offered a pregnant pause, I kept her thoughts going. "The ciphered passage from Haggai talks about a word of Yahweh that went out on the twenty-fourth day of the ninth month."

Cadence ran her finger over our notes from the book of Haggai. "That means that the temple's foundation was completed in the second year of Darius on the eve of what, two hundred and fifty-six years later, would become a very important day in Jewish history related to this very same temple."

"The celebration is memorialized by the lighting of candles." I gaped at Cadence. "It was no coincidence, then, that Jesus stood up in the temple during the Feast of Dedication and proclaimed that he was 'the light of the world,' was it?"

"No, it probably wasn't. He was using the context of the time and place to make a pretty big theological statement. It was probably considered blasphemous to many of the people there. Certainly to the Scribes and Pharisees." Cadence tugged a hairband from the pocket of her jeans and wrapped it around her hair.

"I'm sure it didn't make him any friends. But how does all this relate to the riddle? What are the *seeds of dedication*?"

"I think that the *seeds of dedication* is a metaphor Dad used to describe the day which precedes Hanukkah. This twenty-fourth day of the ninth month was the day from which the word of Yahweh went forth in a promised blessing, that '*from this day will I bless you.*'"

"Okay, I'm following you. But how does this information connect this riddle and the Haggai passage to the other four riddles and ciphered texts?" Tilting back, I crossed one leg over the other.

"I don't know, exactly." Cadence's lips pressed into a wavy line that momentarily reminded me of a cartoon character. "But we do know that if Dad is congruent in his other riddled and ciphered texts, he will use this riddle to make a connection to Jesus, whom he has been describing for us as Yahweh's Salvation. Maybe if we can figure out the 13-letter answer, it might shed some light on the connection."

"The 13-letters are not an accident," I spoke with certainty.

"No, they aren't. The number has played some part in nearly every cipher so far." Cadence paused and tapped the notepad where I'd written my father's riddle out. "What would you say is the most important statement of Dad's riddle?"

I scratched my temple as if it might stir some of my gray matter. "I'd have to say, his statement of *a blessing that promised salvation*."

"What salvation?"

"Yahweh's Salvation," I replied without thinking.

"Okay, so how many letters?" When I frowned, she rephrased. "How many letters is Yahweh's promise?"

When my expression didn't change Cadence nudged me. "From this day I will bless you …"

"Oh, okay, I got you." I switched screens on my computer and looked up the Hebrew version of Haggai 2:19. I could have gone back to my father's cipher and checked, but I wanted to make sure I was reading it right and not depending on my translation.

When the passage came up, Cadence tapped the screen with the end of her pencil and counted the letters out loud. When she'd finished, her grody little eraser had left 13 smudge marks on my screen—the 13 letters of Yahweh's word of blessing to the Jewish people, a promise that stated, *from this day I will bless you.*

Neither of us was as excited as we might have anticipated. Even if these 13 letters were the correct answer, a blessing on the eve of a day that two hundred and fifty-six years later would become known as Hanukkah was hardly a direct connection to Jesus, even if He did stand up on that day and claim He was "the light of the world." Okay, the riddle was pretty cool, but its connection to the other riddles was weak at best. I'd been hoping for something more. Something more tangible, stronger, more compelling than my doubts. Something dazzling and exciting.

Cadence seemed to sense my mood. "Shall we try the answer?" she asked with dampened enthusiasm.

I nodded. Maybe it would be wrong, and we'd have to look in a new direction.

A few seconds later, we had our answer. The 13 Hebrew letters of blessing had been correct. We now looked at our new riddle and ciphered text.

I shoved away from the desk and stood. I was fried. I rubbed my eyes and checked my watch. Early afternoon. We'd been at this all day. I couldn't concentrate on the new riddle because I was still thinking about the last one. We had to be missing something.

Chapter 79

The Door to Salvation

I ran down the hallway, my heart pounding in terror. The darkness was thick and living. My hands, torn and bleeding from a frantic search for escape, only found doors to my worst nightmares. Shadows chased me and phantoms swirled around me. I stumbled over rough shapes on the floor and fell. I grabbed one and pushed myself up to my knees. I knew what it was. I hurled it at the darkness from which I'd come. The ghouls lurking there howled and moaned. I grasped another brick and threw it. Then another, and another. By the time I grabbed the last missile, sweat dripped from me. After I hurled it, a brooding silence followed.

Palpable sorrow consumed me as I sat upright against the rough wall. —the wall I'd constructed across the hallway of my dreams. It blocked my way to the future. Worst of all, it trapped me in the past. This time, I couldn't even open the doors to the good memories. The doors to their rooms had all been locked.

On shaky legs, I rose and peered over the half-constructed wall. The door was there as expected. Around its edges, a warm and comforting light glowed, beckoning me. The number *391* glowed faintly. I strained to reach over my wall to touch it, but my fingers were still inches away. That's when the knocking started again.

I tore at the bricks, but not a single one moved. I lay my forehead on the wall between my bloody hands and fingers as grief swept over me like a mighty wave. I began to weep. The torrent of salty tears stung my torn fingers. The restless shadows started to move again.

A soft, warm hand brushed my wet cheek. A voice called to me. The darkness vanished, and my sister's face appeared. I sat up and looked around. Judging by the concern on Cadence's face, I must have been a sight. I swung my feet off the bed and sat on its edge. Rubbing my face, my hands came away wet.

"I heard you from Dad's office," Cadence said. "You okay?" She straightened and frowned as I rubbed my hands through my hair.

"You make any progress?" I asked finally.

She gave me a raised eyebrow. "You sure you're okay?" She sat down on the bed beside me. "Want to talk about it?"

When I remained silent, Cadence sighed and headed for the door. "I made us some lunch if you are hungry."

My mumbled thanks got lost in the closing of the door. I sat there for a few minutes, trying to pull myself together. The dream had been so real. I examined my fingers that just moments before had been bloody and burning. There was no evidence of my struggles. I shivered. I could still feel the hot breath of the shadows on my neck.

Wakefulness brought relief. My racing heart gradually steadied. Just a dream. How could it seem so real? What greater hell could there be than the hopelessness I'd felt just moments ago? Quite literally, a hell of my own making.

I crossed the room, and as I reached for the handle on the door, the knocking in my mind resumed. My heart skipped a beat, and I turned the handle. Thank God, it opened. As I crossed the threshold, I pictured stepping through the door in my dreams. What if Yahweh's Salvation really waited behind door 391? Was that the way to escape the darkness of my past? Now, that would be a real blessing. I paused with those thoughts rolling around in my head like a marble in a funnel. Around and around, they traveled. Around and around, each pass a little bit closer to their intended destination. A blessing … salvation …13 letters …

Son of a gun, that was it!

I raced into my father's office like the apparitions of my dreams were chasing me. That's what the look on Cadence's face said, anyway. I plopped down in the chair beside her. She resumed chewing on the cracker that had been motionless between her lips when I rushed into the room. I reached for my notepad and flipped the pages. When I found what I was looking for, I gave Cadence an excited glance. A trace of worry lingered in her eyes, but that had mostly been replaced with curiosity.

"I had an idea about Dad's fifth riddle. What was the meaning of the final four words and 13 letters of Haggai 2:19?" I asked.

Cadence thought for a moment. "From this day will I bless you."

In a column down the edge of the pad, I began to write out the 13 Hebrew letters of the final four words of Haggai 2:19. I divided each word with a line.

"These 13 letters are the answer to Dad's riddle, which he described as a *blessing that promised salvation.*"

Next to each Hebrew letter, I wrote its numerical value.

Cadence saw what I was doing and started giving a running total of the letter value as I went. "Forty, ninety, ninety-five, one hundred and five …" She added the 13th letter to her running total. "Three hundred and ninety-one," she said almost reverently as I wrote the total below my column.

I threw my pencil on the desk and flopped back in the chair. We both stared at the result for a long time.

מ = 40

נ = 50

ה = 5

י = 10

ו = 6

מ = 40

ה = 5

ז = 7

ה = 5

א = 1

ב = 2

ר = 200

כ = 20

391

I couldn't hold back my excitement, and I jumped up from the chair. "That is so freaking awesome," I said as I paced back and forth in front of my father's desk.

Cadence refrained from an outburst, but her eyes glowed. I faced her, throwing my hands apart.

"The blessing that promised salvation! The word of Yahweh to Haggai was a command or reminder to consider that *from this day forward*, from the day the second temple's foundation was laid on the eve of Hanukkah, Yahweh promised the Jewish people a four-word, 13-letter blessing. That blessing equaled 391. That is what Dad is trying to tell us with this riddle. Dad saw this as a promise of salvation, Cadence, of Yahweh's Salvation. Wow. Awesome, so awesome."

Cadence didn't say anything for a while. Finally, she asked, "So do you believe?"

"Believe? Believe what?" I stopped pacing and looked at her.

"Do you believe that God left a coded message in the text? Or do you think that Dad just stumbled upon a cool numerical coincidence in this passage of Haggai? A coincidence he used to link this Old Testament passage with Hanukkah and Jesus's statement that he was 'the light of the world'?"

I was so stoked to find that my father's riddle was a congruent continuation of his theme that I hadn't really considered whether its original author might have intentionally made it so. But amazingly, whether this was coincidence or hidden, inspired symbolism wasn't that important to me. At this moment, I was just happy to know that my father's riddles were still going somewhere. They still had the congruency and cleverness of intent. They were still building to something.

I took a stab at expressing this to my sister. "I don't know, Cadence. Right now, I guess I don't care. Each one of these riddles has added a piece to a larger picture. Each one is a work of art in its own right. I can't imagine how these pieces fit into the masterpiece Dad is trying to share with us, but I want to see the big picture. If the sum of its pieces is any indication, it should be something breathtaking to behold. And that is good enough for me right now."

Cadence smiled and nodded her head. "That's good enough for me, too."

Chapter 80

Pay to Play

We woke late the next morning. After a meager breakfast on the back patio, we headed back to our father's office and started on the sixth cipher. For a while, I just watched Cadence work on the ciphertext. I was supposed to be tackling the riddle, but my mind was stuck in neutral. The truth was, I lingered halfway between the land of the living and my nightmares. My dreams about the door and knocking created a sense of urgency, of unfinished business.

I turned back to my notepad and the sixth riddle I'd copied.

This enciphered Biblical passage of 100 words
can be written numerically as 49 – 49 - 49.

Provide the 13th & 14th keywords of this passage.

How could a passage of 100 words be written numerically as 49-49-49? That didn't make any sense. It certainly wasn't mathematical, which meant it was probably a play on words. I thought about that for a while and got nothing, then considered the box of ciphertext again. I shook my head. More Hebrew ciphered characters that were coded gibberish.

With no better ideas, I started counting the letters in the ciphertext—a block of 22x19 characters. That meant there were 418 Hebrew letters in the passage my father had encrypted. Unless … he'd included the reference in the cipher like he had last time. Then the Hebrew passage would be a few characters shorter. So we were looking at a passage of Scripture that was 100 words and 418 or fewer Hebrew letters. Not much to go on, but it was a start.

ב ע ה נ ש צ ז ה נ ל ג ט ד צ ג ב ד כ ג א ל נ

ז ה ס ב י ב ב ו נ ג ט ב י ו ד ו מ ב צ ד א ב

ט ח ב נ ב ק ג ד ב י ג ה נ ב ד ע ב מ י כ מ ד

ס ב כ ה א צ ו כ ז ט מ ה א ל ג ח ז ל נ ד ע ז

ג ז ז ז ג ל מ י נ י ב מ ד ג ג ח ו מ ד ה ט ע

ר ט ג ז א ל ד א י א ט א נ מ י ל ט ז א ט ד צ

ד ח ז ד נ ד ז ג ה ה ו ל כ צ ב ס ד ש מ ב ע ו

ד ג ש נ ז ב נ ר נ ט ט ז ד כ ו א א ס ו א צ ד

ז ב ל ה י ד ע ה ע ד ע י ו ח ב כ ע ה ז ו ב ב

ד ר ה כ ג ט ס ה נ ג ג ש ז ט ג ו נ ק ג ד ג מ

נ י מ נ ר ו ב א נ ד נ ת ד נ ז ב ג ד ד כ ה ט

ד א כ נ פ ד ט ר ט ט א ו ו פ ה ה ר ב ס ו ט ר

ל ג י א ס ו ה ט ב י נ ש י ס ט ז א ו ז ט י א

א ג ס ז פ ב ב נ ג פ ט מ ד א צ י ה י ג ב א ג

א ב ד ע ט ו ה צ ט מ ה ל א ע ס ט ז ד ו ב ח ו

ע פ ע מ ז כ א ש ב ד ה א ה נ ז ע ב פ ז נ ב י

ד ל ב ה ז א ו ב ה ח נ ח ב ק ג א ע ח ע ב ח פ

א ב ח א ז ז ז ב נ ע ח ב י כ ש צ ו מ ז ט ז ס

ה מ ב ז ד ג ו נ א ל ה צ כ ד ש ס ג י ל מ ח ו

After pursuing the ciphertext, I looked over the verse clues. Instead of the usual five, there were seven. This was probably important. He'd never left more than five verse clues before.

None of the verses gave me any ideas about the riddle or the cipher. The only thing I noticed was that all of them were short. Was that important or just a coincidence? I copied the verses onto my notepad.

Psalm 34:15

The eyes of YHWH *are* upon the righteous, and his ears *are open* unto their cry.

Psalm 37:6

And he shall bring forth thy righteousness as the light, and thy judgment as the noonday.

1 Chronicles 6:28

And the sons of Samuel; the firstborn Vashni, and Abiah.

Psalms 2:4

He that sitteth in the heavens shall laugh: the Lord shall have them in derision.

Proverbs 21:3

To do justice and judgment *is* more acceptable to YHWH than sacrifice.

Psalm 139:23

Search me, O God, and know my heart: try me, and know my thoughts:

Psalm 92:14

They shall still bring forth fruit in old age; they shall be fat and flourishing;

As I read the verses, I grew a little queasy. If God really existed, and He searched my heart and thoughts, what would He see? Would He laugh or cry?

That line of thinking wouldn't help me solve the riddle—that was for sure. I brushed the cracker crumbs from my fingers and looked at Cadence. "Anything yet?"

She glanced up but gazed beyond me. If I could read her thoughts, could my brain handle it? Or would my gray matter melt? Maybe I would simply pass out. Maybe it would be like sticking my mouth over a gushing firehose to get a drink. I'd probably drown if I tried to take a sip of her mental synapsis. I laughed at the image.

Cadence came back from wherever geniuses go in their brains. "What's so funny?"

I gave her a funky grin. "Nothing really, just trying to picture what it would be like to get into your head."

Cadence smiled at me like a teacher in the first grade might at her particularly funny student. "You can be such a goofball, Timmy." She pointed at the ciphered text. "On the twelfth line here, what is this Hebrew character?"

I leaned closer. "Do you mind?" I asked as I reached for the laptop to slide it over in front of me. She sat back from the desk and watched as I enlarged the screen to zoom in on the character she indicated. "It looks like the letter *pay* but with an additional squiggle or something in the center. I've never seen one before."

I enlarged the image until it started to pixelate. "Almost looks like another tiny little letter *pay* is inscribed inside the first one. Let's see how many we can find."

"I got 7."

"Me too." I changed screens, typed in *pay* in the search box, and read the entry from Wikipedia.

Pay, also Pe, is the seventeenth letter of the Semitic abjads, including Phoenician, Hebrew, Aramaic, Syriac, and Arabic. The Phoenician letter gave rise to the Greek Pi.

I glanced at Cadence. "Did you know that?"

"I didn't," she said, shaking her head, but a tiny smile lit her face now.

Under *variant forms*, I found the answer we were looking for. I read it out loud to Cadence.

פ *A notable variation on the letter Pe is the Pe Kefulah, "Double Pe". The Pe Kefulah is written as a small Pe scribed within a larger Pe. This atypical letter appears in the Torah scrolls (most often Yemenite Torahs but is also present in Sephardic and Ashkenazi Torahs), manuscripts, and some modern printed Hebrew Bibles. When the Pe is written in the form of a Double Pe, this adds a layer of deeper meaning to the Biblical text.*

"A deeper meaning to the text?" I rubbed my bristly chin, but Cadence's smile had widened. "What? You're smiling like you know something I don't."

"I do. How bad do you want to know?"

"Not bad enough to beg, but bad."

Cadence grabbed a pencil from the gold-lettered coffee mug on my father's desk. She started writing numbers on a fresh page of my notepad—the transcendental number *pi*. She stopped after she'd documented the sequence up to the first occurrence of the number *7*. If her recollection was correct, it showed up in the 13th decimal digit of *pi*. All nine numbers excluding zero appeared by the 13th decimal digit.

3.1415926535897

She underlined the number sequence. "Once in a while, Dad would use the digits of *pi* to encipher one of the messages he left for me on the refrigerator."

"How did he do that?"

"It was rather simple, actually—the enciphering part, that is. He took a string of the digits of *pi* equal to the letters of the message he was encrypting and placed that section of *pi* under the numerical value of the letters in the message. If the value of the digits of *pi* was smaller than the letter value of plaintext, he would subtract the *pi* value from each letter value. If the individual values of *pi* were greater than the letter value of the plaintext, then he would add the *pi* value."

I did my very best to appear unfazed, but I didn't fool my sister.

"Here, let me show you." She started writing her name in her neat, cursive hand.

"Sis, could you write in block text? It would be easier to read."

Cadence raised an eyebrow at me but erased her name and wrote it again using block text. Her fingertips turned white as she pressed the pencil into the paper. Next, she recorded the place value of each letter of her name underneath its respective letter. Below this, she wrote out the first 7 numbers of *pi*. She pointed at her simple cipher.

"As you can see, my name has the numerical value of 3,1,4,5,14,3,5. Once the first 7 letters of *pi* have been either added or subtracted from it, the result is 0,0,0,4,9,12,3. Those letters spell CADDGFC."

I tilted my head. "The zeroes?"

She pursed her lips. With exaggerated slowness, she said, "Resulting values of zero keep their original letter character."

C A D E N C E
3 1 4 5 14 3 5 (value of my name)
3 1 4 1 5 9 2 (value of *pi*)
0 0 0 4 9 12 3 (result)
C A D D I L C (letter value of result)

I made a scoffing sound. "Well, that's not very hard."

Like a puffed-up desert horny toad when no longer threatened, Cadence deflated when I laughed to cover up my hurt feelings. "As I said, the ciphering is the easy part. The hard part is finding what snippet of *pi* Dad used to encrypt the text."

And *pi* was a theoretically endless string of random numbers.

Cadence grimaced in response to my doomed expression. "Exactly. No easy task. If we had a really powerful computer and lots of time, we could set it to compare each of the four hundred and eighteen letters of Dad's cipher against a four-hundred-and-eighteen-number section of *pi* to see if we could find recognizable words. But … we don't have an unlimited amount of time *or* a super computer."

"So … what, then?"

Cadence gnawed on the eraser a moment before she spoke. "We have to figure out the 7 verses clues. They hold the key to the string of *pi* he used."

"Where do we begin?"

"I've no idea." She tossed her hands up. "I'm about finished for today, anyway. I didn't get a nap like someone else I know."

Some nap.

Cadence stood up and stretched her arms. "You want something to eat?"

"Not right now, Sis. I'm going to work some more on this. I don't feel like sleeping."

What I didn't say was that I didn't want to face my nightmares again right now. Cadence gave me a knowing look and closed the office door behind her.

Chapter 81

Crime Scene

Eric Pincer pulled up to the sheriff deputy's SUV parked in the front of the entrance to the Plummer homestead. He extended his ID through the window. The deputy checked it and then spoke into his radio mic clipped to the right side of his tactical vest.

"They are expecting you, sir," the deputy said, handing Eric his ID. He pointed to an unmarked car along the side of the road. "Please, park there. No vehicles are allowed past this point. You'll have to hoof it in."

The previous evening, the Gila County Sheriff's Department had reached out about a shooting at the Plummer cabin. Somehow, they had figured out he was the executor of the Plummer estate, and they had contacted his office to gain access to the cabin. He'd taken an early morning flight out of DC and driven straight here from the airport.

Eric set his briefcase on the gravel road and loosened his tie. The scent of pine was oppressive in the late-afternoon sun. He set off down the rough road. It ended where a dozen sheriff vehicles, one FBI blazer, and a couple of BATF Suburbans were parked on the sides of the road in a clearing crisscrossed with caution tape. Little flags and paint marked forensic evidence. By the looks of the two black SUVs and the Honda Civic parked in front of the house, a small war had been fought.

Eric approached the band of yellow police tape. A tall, wide-shouldered sheriff in a cowboy hat and boots stood on the other side. Eric set his briefcase down again and fished out his identification. The officer waved it away and lifted the tape.

"Thank you for coming, Mr. Pincer." He started to extended his right hand and stopped. Smoothly he switched hands, "I'm Sheriff Lehi Smith."

Eric set down his briefcase and proffered his hand, "Good to meet you, Sheriff." To hide his embarrassment he looked around. "What happened here?"

"From our preliminary investigation, some M13 gang bangers from Phoenix assaulted the cabin. We believe there may be victims inside. We've tried to gain access to the cabin, but so far, it has resisted our best efforts. Come, I'll show you."

Eric followed the sheriff up the porch stairs and stopped at the front door. White paint marked the outlines of bodies in various forms of deadly repose on the floor. The sheriff knocked on the scratched and abraded steel showing behind the door's missing log veneer.

"The door is some kind of high-tech steel Kevlar sandwich. When the first deputy arrived on the scene, he said that the gang members were assaulting the door with tire irons. As you can see, their efforts were unsuccessful. "

"Were you able to arrest any of them?" Eric held his breath a moment, awaiting the response.

The sheriff shook his head. "Nope. They opened fire on my deputy as soon as he stepped out of his vehicle. He returned fire and retreated to safety until backup arrived."

"Glad he's all right."

"Right." The sheriff waved his hand at all the paint markings on the porch and those in the yard. "Whoever was in that cabin, they must have wanted pretty bad. The occupants wouldn't surrender, and the gang wouldn't back down. We picked them off one by one. Funny thing, all during the firefight, one of them, a big guy with an arrow sticking out of his leg, kept trying to gain access to the cabin. My guys said it made no sense. Maybe they were high on drugs or something, but whatever was in that cabin was more important to them than their own lives."

"Why didn't you just chainsaw a hole in the log wall to gain access?"

Smith nodded laconically and pointed at a pile of sawdust next to the door. "Tried that, but your Mr. Plummer must have been a mighty paranoid man. Every foot, he drilled high tensile steel rods through the logs vertically and horizontally. Tore up our chainsaw. Figured if we tried to cut the rods out with a torch or cutting wheel, we might burn the cabin down. Ruin any evidence that might still be in there. And the heirs might not be too happy with that." The sheriff spit a black wad of chew off the edge of the porch, then looked around with an appreciative eye. "Place like this is one of a kind. Couldn't bring myself to risk it."

"You said you thought there was someone inside?"

"Still do." He indicated a streak of blood disappearing under the door. "The perps were still trying to gain access to the door when we arrived. That means whoever they were after must have been inside. Also, we did not find any bows outside the home."

Eric nodded and replied, "And you have a guy with an arrow in his leg."

Smith spit another wad of chew into the yard and again gestured toward the door. "We made a hell of a noise trying to raise someone. No response. Probably dead by now."

Eric set his briefcase down on the log bench against the cabin wall. He opened it and retrieved a small manila envelope that tinkled with the sound of keys. He poured the contents of the envelope into the open briefcase and picked out a single key with a green tag.

As he stepped toward the door to insert the key, he asked, “Any idea what this was all about?”

“We figure it was some drug dispute. This is a remote place. It would make a good hangout for drug dealers bringing product into Phoenix.”

Eric rotated the key until the lock clicked, then took a step away from the door and to the side. The sheriff unholstered his weapon. Standing on the other side of the door, he turned the door handle and pushed it open. Nothing happened.

Eric waited on the porch as Smith and two of his deputies entered the cabin. Eric heard doors opening and the word “clear” repeated several times. A couple of minutes later, the sheriff returned with a befuddled look on his face.

“The place is empty.”

Eric’s head jerked around. “Empty?”

“Shore enough. The bloodstain ends just inside the door against the wall. No bodies, though.”

Eric peered in. “May I look around?”

“Sorry,” the sheriff said. “Not until our forensic team has had a chance to go through the place.”

“I understand.” Eric swiveled to face outward. “How about the barn?”

“Forensics is going through it now, but it seems pretty clean.”

“How’d you get in?”

“The back double doors were unbarred.”

As they spoke, a deputy approached from the barn. “You got to see this, boss.” He waved behind him. “They found something in the basement.”

Eric followed Smith to the barn and stopped when he held up his hand at the door. "Wait here, please."

Five minutes later, the sheriff returned with the forensic team. "They are done in there. We found out why there were no bodies in the cabin."

"They're down there?" Eric asked.

Smith shook his head. "Nope. Craziest thing you ever saw. Come on, I'll show you."

Eric followed the sheriff inside as the forensic team headed to the house. The scent of hay lingered in the air despite the lack of animals in the neat barn. Smith led him to the back, opened a door, and indicated some descending stairs with a nod.

"This Mr. Plummer was an interesting man."

Eric didn't know whether to chuckle or growl. "You have no idea."

Smith ducked his head as he started down the steep stairs. The sheriff preceded Eric over to the utility pipe that yawned black into the basement side wall facing the cabin. A pile of flat nylon utility rope for pulling wires, cables, and piping through lay below, and the sheriff pointed at a smear of blood just inside the pipe.

"We'll test the blood to be sure, but by the looks of it, whoever was inside that cabin escaped through here."

Eric gazed down the dark hole and shivered. "No way in hell," he muttered.

The sheriff chuckled. "Whoever they were, they must have been desperate or crazier than my old horse with a belly full of locoweed."

Eric stepped back from the opening and admired the room as Smith headed for the stairs. John hadn't told him about the upgrades to the cabin and barn. Impressive. His old buddy had gone first class all the way. He'd created a self-sufficient refuge with all the modern conveniences in the middle of nowhere. With enough food, one could disappear up here for months, maybe even years. Jealousy stabbed him in the gut. Those two brats of John's didn't deserve a place like this.

Well, he'd have to see about that. They didn't have much time left to solve the riddles, and this latest incident with Benito's men wouldn't endear them to the little gangster.

Eric jerked with the tap on his shoulder. Turning to face Smith, he concealed his anger behind an emotionless mask.

"Mr. Pincer, it's time to go."

Eric followed the sheriff up the stairs and out of the barn.

"Anything else I can do for you, Sheriff?" Eric asked when they were standing back at the foot of the porch steps.

Smith removed his hat and scratched his head. "I understand that the late Mr. Plummer has two children?"

"He does."

The sheriff replaced the Stetson on his head. "Are they aware of what has taken place up here?"

"They are." Eric felt the tingling itch start to worm its way up his missing arm. He steeled himself. His demons were headed for a banquet today.

"Please inform them that this is a crime scene until the investigation is over. I will notify you when we are finished with our investigation. Until then, let them know the place is off-limits."

"I doubt they have any plans to come up here in the near future, Sheriff." A crooked smile broke his face. Eric tried to restrain it. "But I'll make sure they don't. Right now, they have more pressing matters to attend to." Eric left the sheriff standing there with a puzzled look on his face.

He was halfway back to Payson when his phone beeped with an incoming text. It was from Josh Harland.

A new IP address has accessed the servers. It's from John Plummer's house.

Eric pressed down on the accelerator. As he sped toward Phoenix, he punched out a terse email on his phone and sent it off. He threw his phone onto the seat next to him. It would be dark, but if he hurried, he might make it back in time.

Chapter 82

Doubts and Nightmares

I stared blankly at my notepad where I'd written out the seven verses my father had given us with his sixth ciphered riddle. For half an hour, I mustered enough focus to imagine how my father might have concealed within them the location of his *pi* cipher key. I got nothing.

I stood up and paced in front of my father's desk. What did I know? To find the *pi* cipher key, I needed to learn where in the endless digits of *pi* my father began his key. That would require a number. He'd left 7 doubled *pi* in the ciphered text, and 7 verse clues. My ciphered text ran four hundred and eighteen characters, so my *pi* cipher key, wherever it began, would also be four hundred and eighteen numbers.

I'd already tried the obvious possibilities. Initially, I used the first four hundred and eighteen digits of *pi*, starting right at the beginning. Then I tried *pi*'s decimal digits. Then I started my string using the 7th, 13th, and 418th digits of *pi*. My last idea was counting out where the double *pay* were located in the ciphered text and using those numberes as the *pi* key starting points. This produced no intelligible results.

It would be something symbolic—of this I was nearly certain. So far, he had woven together what taken separately might be considered interesting but random pieces of Biblical information. As each additional thread of his cryptic tapestry was added, a bigger picture emerged. Even for a Doubting Thomas like me, the picture was fascinating if not thrilling.

What was different about those seven verses? Well, there were seven instead of five. The final theme verse also seemed to be missing. But there was something more—all seven were roughly the same length.

I reached for the notepad on the desk and counted the letters of the first verse. Sixty-one. Then the idea struck me. He wouldn't have counted the verse letters in English. All the verses were from the Old Testament. He would have used Hebrew. I walked back behind the desk and sat down. For the next thirty minutes, I carefully copied out the English and Hebrew version of each verse on my notepad. When I finished, I stood back up, pad in hand.

As I walked around my father's office, I started counting the verse letters again. Psalm 34 had twenty-nine Hebrew letters. Psalm 37 had 27. Except for the last verse, which had 30 letters, all the other verses landed in the twenties range. A relatively tight range, but not tight enough to draw any conclusions from. I stared at my pad. It still seemed random.

Psalm 34:15 = 29 Hebrew letters

עיני יהוה אל־צדיקים ואזניו אל־שועתם

The eyes of YHWH *are* upon the righteous, and his ears *are open* unto their cry.

Psalm 37:6 = 26 Hebrew letters

והוציא כאור צדקך ומשפטך כצהרים

And he shall bring forth thy righteousness as the light, and thy judgment as the noonday.

1 Chronicles 6:28 = 22 Hebrew letters

ובני שמואל הבכר ושני ואביה

And the sons of Samuel; the firstborn Vashni, and Abiah.

Psalms 2:4 = 24 Hebrew letters

יושב בשמים ישחק אדני ילעג־למו

He that sitteth in the heavens shall laugh: the Lord shall have them in derision.

Proverbs 21:3 = 25 Hebrew letters

עשה צדקה ומשפט נבחר ליהוה מזבח

To do justice and judgment *is* more acceptable to YHWH than sacrifice.

Psalm 139:23 = 27 Hebrew letters

חקרני אל ודע לבבי בחנני ודע שרעפי

Search me, O God, and know my heart: try me, and know my thoughts:

Psalm 92:14 = 30 Hebrew letters

עוד ינובון בשיבה דשנים ורעננים יהיו

They shall still bring forth fruit in old age; they shall be fat and flourishing;

I stopped walking and stared at the double *pay* I'd crudely drawn at the top of the page. My father had used 7 of them in his cipher. The double *pay* indicated that there was a deeper meaning to the text. Deeper meaning meant more information that was not obvious. I slapped the notepad against my leg.

"Of course," I muttered. Hebrew letters had deeper meaning built into them. I already knew this. It wasn't the letter count I should be looking at. It was the letter value. That was probably why the verses were similar lengths—because the numerical value was a similar length.

Before working out the numerical value of the verse, I headed to the kitchen to get a glass of water. For a minute, I scrounged around in my father's pantry for something to snack on. The only thing I found that appealed to me were some unshelled peanuts. I balanced the peanuts, my glass of water, and an extra bowl for the shells and headed back to the office with my pad under my arm. I got as far as the dining room.

It was dusk outside, and I didn't feel like secluding myself back in the office. The orange, crimson, and gold that painted Camelback Mountain was starting to fade into shades of purple and gray. I slid open the glass door. The heavy hand of the sun had lifted, and the desert had taken a cooling breath. A voice from the security system said "dining-room door open" as I stepped out onto the sandstone patio. The solar, battery-powered lights at the edge flickered on.

I sat down on one of the chairs near a light and placed my snacks on the nearby table. I edged my chair closer to the light and grabbed a handful of peanuts.

By the second verse, my pulse picked up. Psalm 34:15 had a numerical Hebrew letter value of 1378. Psalm 37:6 had a numerical value of 1379. The third verse had a value of 1380. If the numerical progression was consistent, then the final verse would have a value of 1384. I tested my theory by jumping to the last verse and found that, indeed, Psalm 92:14 had a numerical value of 1384. To be sure, I checked the value of the remaining verses. When I finished, I surveyed the column of numbers at the edge of my notepad.

1378
1379
1380
1381

1382
1383
1384

Seven verses with specific numerical values. Certainly not an accident. How he had managed to find the exact value of these verses out of the thousands in the Bible boggled my mind. This sequence had to be the key to my father's *pi* cipher. I set the pad down and grabbed another handful of peanuts.

If Cadence's description of how my father's cipher normally worked was correct, then I'd find the key to his cipher starting at the 1378th digit of *pi*. Or possibly one of the other following six digits. Why had he used seven numbers? To provide the starting point of the key, all he really needed was one. I scratched my head.

There was only one way to find out. returned to the office to grab my laptop. I needed to find somewhere I could download a spreadsheet with the first two thousand digits of *pi*. I lifted the laptop, and my gaze fell on the cable. That's when I remembered my father didn't have Wi-Fi. Cadence said he was rather obsessive about security and didn't trust Wi-Fi networks. Plus, she said, he often complained about the potential dangers of electronic pollution. That seemed a bit quirky, but who knew. Maybe a hundred years from now, our children would have three hands because of some unforeseen consequence of electronic pollution. With a grim chuckle, I sat down at my father's desk, plugged the LAN cable in, and started my search for a table of *pi* values.

A few minutes later, I had formatted a spreadsheet and downloaded *pi* to the millionth digit. The 1378th digit of *pi* turned out to be a 2. The 1379th digit of *pi* was a 6. It wasn't until I wrote out all seven numbers of *pi* from the 1378th to the 1384th digit that I realized what I was looking at.

26 391 41

The key my father had chosen for his *pi* cipher began with the numerical value of YHWH's name, followed by the value of Yeshua's name, and then the value of Abraham's name. How rare must these values be?

After a few minutes of searching, I sat back in my chair and blew out a breath. The central value of my father's *pi* key was the first occurrence of 391, the Hebrew value of Yeshua's name, in the digits of *pi*. Moreover, this first occurrence of 391just happened to be flanked by the Hebrew numerical value of the names Yahweh and Abraham.

What were the odds? Finding *391* in *pi* by itself might not be all that special, but finding the first occurrence of that number surrounded by two numbers that arguably possessed related Biblical significance to that number was … was difficult to comprehend.

If the God of the Bible did exist, did He leave a clue in *pi* for skeptics like me to twist our brains in knots about? Was YHWH, the living God of the Bible, up there in heaven laughing at me right now? The Doubting Thomas who had just had his mind blown.

The words I'd memorized as a kid in Sunday school came to my mind again.

The fool hath said in his heart, there is no God.

Was I that fool? I sighed and put my hands behind my head.

Intrigued, I started tinkering with the digits of *pi*. A few more coincidences left me even more confused. The sum of the digits 2639141 equaled twenty-six, the Hebrew value of YHWH's name. 1381, the center value of those 7 digits of *pi*, was the 221st prime number. 221, in turn, possessed the factors 13 and 17. These were the prime numbers found in Yeshua's and YHWH's name, respectively

"Front gate," an electronic voice said.

I stood up from the desk and walked out into the now-dark living room. From the darker shadows of the wall, I peeked out the front window. Anger and fear left me shaking.

Chapter 83

Playing Cadence

A black Escalade made its way up my father's long, winding driveway. Not again. How had Benito Silva found us?

I ran to Cadence's room. She was asleep like an angel resting between earthly missions. Gently, I shook her.

Her eyes opened and focused on my face. She sat up in bed. "What's wrong, Timmy?"

"Benito Silva is here. We've got to go."

She came wide awake at that. Without another sound, she slid out of bed. As she gathered a few belongings, I headed for my father's office. With quick, violent actions, I shoved my things into the briefcase. I took one quick look around. Maybe I'd get to come back here sometime. This place felt like my father. It reflected his personality and his passions.

On the way out, I paused at the Jefferson cipher and ran my hand across the words etched on the glass case.

... Now to him that is of power to stablish you according to my gospel, and the preaching of Jesus Christ, according to the revelation of the mystery, which was kept secret since the world began,

I left the office and closed the door behind me, then peeked out the front window once more. The black Escalade was parked beside the large fountain in front of the house. Benito, the little runt, walked up to the front door flanked by two men with buzz cuts and sunglasses. Their dark, tailored suits failed to hide rippling muscles. The bodyguards, hired muscle, or whatever they were, walked with the lithe, effortless movements of men whose bulk was not just for show. These were not undisciplined gangbangers like he'd sent up to my grandfather's cabin.

As the doorbell chimed, Cadence came out of her bedroom with a backpack over her shoulder. We exited out the back sliding door to the patio. Closing it behind us, we padded as quietly as possible over the gravel and sand on our way to the rear gate we'd entered two days before.

Cadence used her key to unlock the deadbolt. "Ready?"

I nodded and gripped my briefcase tighter. She started to open the gate when I grabbed her arm. "I forgot the notepad. It's on a table on the patio."

"Forget it. We can come back for it later," she whispered.

I shook my head. "It has our answers and notes for the ciphers. We can't finish this without them." I handed Cadence my briefcase. "Take this. I'll be right behind you. We'll meet in the lobby outside the restaurant where we ate. If I don't show up in five minutes, call the police. Whatever you do, make sure you stay in a very public place."

"Be careful," she called to me as I headed back down the trail.

I ran as quietly as I could. When I reached the bushes that encircled the patio, I stopped and cursed under my breath. Somehow, Benito and his men had gotten into the house. In the shadows, I skirted the patio until I was directly behind the table where my pad lay. I dropped to my hands and knees and wormed my way through the light screen of desert growth that lay between me and the table with the notepad until I could grab for it. The silhouettes of men searching the house passed back and forth in front of the windows as I slowly backed out the way I'd come.

When night again concealed me, I straightened and ran for the gate. As I reached it, I looked back. No one was following me. I smiled as the latch clicked into place.

"You lose again, Benito," I muttered as I jogged down the dim trail that led to the golf course.

The greens were in sight when I tripped. Hands outstretched, I measured the path with my full body length, and my nose plowed a furrow in the dirt. I lay there stunned for a few seconds before I managed to push myself back up onto my hands and knees. Shakily, I stood. It took another few seconds to spit the dirt and sand out of my mouth, along with that familiar, metallic taste of blood. From my cut lips or my bloody nose? I leaned over to pick the pad up and nearly passed out.

Grunting, I slowly straightened. I listened. Only the faint sounds of the desert night answered. I started for the beckoning glow that illuminated the emerald lawn marking the edge of the golf course.

By the time I reached the lobby of the Phoenician, I had regained my equilibrium, but by the glances I got, I must have been a sight. I stood under the moon pool in the center of the lobby and turned a complete circle searching for Cadence. She was not there. Panic clouded my vision as I turned in a circle once more.

I approached the front desk and asked the receptionist, "Did a young woman with a briefcase and a backpack come in here a couple of minutes ago?"

"No, sir. Do you need medical attention, sir?"

I followed her startled gaze. Dirt, sand, and desert leaves mixed in a crimson collage on my white t-shirt. I looked back at the young lady as she reached for the phone. Calling for security? If I were her, I probably would too. A wild, bloody man comes into my hotel asking for a young woman? For all she knew, I was a crazy murderer.

"I tripped and fell on the golf course trail," I mumbled as I turned toward the lobby entrance. I hurried out before security showed up.

Cadence was not here. I could not come up with a single good reason why that would be so. I left the hotel and headed back toward my father's house. Maybe Cadence had lost the trail on the way here. Maybe she'd fallen and I, in my headlong rush to escape, had passed right by her. Maybe … No, I wasn't going to go there. That possibility gave me an instant, nauseous, nervous feeling in my stomach.

Peering into the shadows, I retraced my steps down the narrow trail to my father's back gate. I stepped off the trail more than once to inspect a rock formation that my imagination told me looked like a body. When I reached the back gate, I froze in the dim glow of the light. My heart started pounding in my chest. The gate I'd closed behind me now stood wide open. I listened for a moment. The blood roaring through my ears made the only sound.

Cautiously, I moved through the gate. No one was hiding behind it, so I continued down the trail to the house. I reached the shadows around the patio and waited. For five minutes, I watched the dark windows for movement. Nothing. I stepped into the circle of light that illuminated the opening to the patio. Slowly, I walked up to the back entrance and then stopped—rooted to the spot by the words written in red spray paint across the sliding glass door.

Call me.

I'll play a Cadence for you at my place.

B. S.

Chapter 84

Countermeasures

I dropped my notepad, placed a hand on each side of the message, and leaned my head against the glass. Silva had my sister. My worst nightmare had come true. I balled my fist and pounded the window. If he hurt her in any way, I would kill him.

I pushed off the window and jerked the door open, then searched the entire house. All the rooms were empty, and the house had been left undisturbed. I returned to my father's office and sat down behind his desk. I felt small, diminished, sitting there now. I reached for the phone and started to dial Benito's number from memory. I got the area code punched in and then slowly hung up.

Benito would hurt Cadence. Of this, I had no doubt. But as a sadistic narcissist, he'd want me there when he did. He needed to prove he was in control. He'd want to see the relief and hope in my eyes when I saw that she was okay. Then he would destroy that hope one painful scream at a time. I shuddered in violent rage. If I wanted to get Cadence out of the mess I'd dragged her into, I had to think this through very carefully.

Half an hour later, once more in control of my fury, I made a call. It wasn't to Benito Silva. It was to one of my less reputable former clients. For several minutes, I explained to him what I wanted. Yes, I would be paying cash. And a bonus for getting it done in three hours. He hesitated at this but finally agreed.

I hung up and stood. Calmly, I walked back to the patio door and retrieved my notepad. In the garage along with other camping equipment I'd noticed when I'd searched the house earlier, I located a backpack. I used it to gather the supplies I would need and placed everything in my father's Jeep Grand Cherokee. I went to his room, removed my bloody clothes, and shoved them in a grocery bag from the pantry. Then I changed into a pair of my father's blue jeans and a heavy denim shirt. My dress shoes I exchanged for a pair of his hiking boots. After a glance in the bedroom mirror, I entered the bathroom and removed the rest of the evidence of my fall.

I plugged in the garage door and got into my father's Jeep. I pushed the button on the automatic door opener on the visor and watched as the door slid smoothly up, then drove away without a backward glance. I didn't head directly to Silva's place. I had several stops to make first. I let my anger build slowly. I was past the point of being scared but not to the point of reckless abandon. The words of my boxing coach echoed in my mind. If I lost control, Silva would win, and my sister would be dead. I took several deep breaths as I drove down the foothills of Camelback Mountain. Benito Silva must not win this round. I gripped the wheel harder. He would not win.

Chapter 85

Searching for Answers

The lawyer inserted his identification card into the reader, and the door to the service elevator slid open with a quiet whirr. He stepped onto the elevator and pushed *6*.

A few seconds later, the doors opened again, and he exited into the corridor, his tool bag in hand. With the tip of his baseball cap pulled low, he approached familiar faces. He let out a soft breath when those faces passed without any recognition. At a door marked *SERVERS*, he slid his key card over the electronic lock, and the door buzzed. He turned the handle and entered.

The warmth of electronics and the shrill humming of servers made him think of a hornet's nest. He hastened to a workstation at the side of the room, then took an external hard drive out of his tool bag and inserted its cord into the slot on the workstation. He moved the mouse. The dark monitor came to life with an ID and password request. He entered the numbers and symbols and then placed his hand on the flat plate next to the workstation. A green glow emanated from the plate as the machine read his hand biometrics. The monitor flashed again.

Identification Authenticated.

The lawyer navigated to the server menu of the Oil and Gas Division. He selected the files he wanted and clicked the icon to begin the download. After a few seconds, the status bar read, *1% of 3.21 Terabytes. Estimated download time, 27 minutes*. He turned slightly so he could keep the door in view while he watched the green status bar slowly extend across the monitor. As he waited, his phone gave a familiar beep.

He pulled the cell out and tapped on the status icon that popped up. He'd programmed the tracking app to notify him any time the device in the briefcase moved more than a hundred feet in any five-minute period. Now the little tracking icon left John Plummer's house on Camelback Mountain and headed toward downtown Phoenix. He hadn't expected them to leave the cabin, but he hadn't been too concerned when they had ended up at the house in Scottsdale.

Twenty-five minutes later, the lawyer's mild interest turned to concern when the icon stopped near The White Wolf. He stared at the status bar with growing unease, as though he could see through the screen like a lens. The White Wolf meant Benito Silva, and that could only mean trouble. And here he was thousands of miles away, tracking down corporate fraud when he needed to be in Phoenix.

He pounded the workstation, then steadied the tremor in his hands by gripping the edge as he awaited the final minutes of the download. After today, he wouldn't be able to come back to this place. When they read the access and download logs, they would know.

When the download completed, the lawyer jammed the hard drive into the pocket of his cargo pants. He burst out of the server room door and right into the shocked face and wiry body of Josh Harland. They went down in a tangle of arms and legs. The lawyer was first to his feet and ran towards the service elevator. Behind him, Harland shouted as running steps followed.

"Security, we have unauthorized personnel in the building. Gray hair, beard, mustache, a blue Cardinals baseball cap and blue pants, and a brown shirt. He's carrying a tool bag. He just entered the—" The doors to the service elevator slid closed, cutting off the rest of Harland's words.

Heart hammering, the lawyer pushed *2* on the screen and watched as the numbers descended. The elevator stopped with a slight jerk. The doors slid open, and he set his tool bag between them. The rubber of his tennis shoes squeaked on the waxed floor as he hustled to the back of the building and the emergency stairwell. He kept his head down and ignored any curious looks.

A minute later, he exited through a fire escape. A wailing alarm followed him down the alley. Two minutes later, he was in his rental car and headed to the airport. He had gotten what he'd come for … but at what cost?

Chapter 86

The White Wolf

In an alley one block from The White Wolf, I parked next to the pearl-gold 1970 Cadillac Sedan Deville—a two-and-quarter-ton beast of a car that had seen much better days. A single streetlight at the end of the alley dimly illuminated the once-iconic American luxury car. There wasn't a panel on the car that wasn't dented or without rusted metal showing. Two of its four headlights were broken, and its bumper hung down on its left side. A spider web of cracks raced out in all directions from a bullet hole in the driver's-side windshield. No hub caps, two missing door handles, and a driver's side mirror with a broken reflector all indicated its severe state of disrepair.

A long-haired hippy of a man sat cross-legged on its hood. He wasn't smiling.

I got out of the Jeep and raised an eyebrow at the vehicle. "Does it run? Or did you tow it here?"

"Beggars can't be choosers," Johnny Lancaster replied sourly.

I looked up and frowned. "Based on what you are charging for this thing, I'm certainly not begging."

Johnny shrugged. "Best I could do on short notice. My uncle has a junkyard. This thing was slated for the crusher next week."

"So it runs?" I asked again.

Johnny slid off the hood and walked around to the door. He sat down in the driver's seat and turned the ignition key. After several growling turnovers, the old Caddy caught. With a slight backfire and a belch of black smoke, the 472 cubic-inch V8 engine came begrudgingly to life. Johnny revved it a few times, and valves knocked along with some other unknown and unnatural metallic sounds.

I waved for him to shut it off. “That will do.”

Johnny exited the car and walked over to where I stood. I handed him a white paper envelope. He split it open and ran his thumb over the green bills inside, then glanced up apologetically. “No offense, Mr. T, but everyone makes mistakes.” He returned to counting the bills. When he was satisfied, the envelope disappeared into his baggy shorts.

I leveled a stare at him. “Everything else I asked for?”

“It’s in the back.”

“Thanks, Johnny. We’re square now.”

Johnny raised an eyebrow. “Really?”

“Yes, really.”

“Again, no offense, Mr. T, but in that case, I hope I don’t ever see you again.”

“Feeling is mutual, Johnny.”

Johnny strutted from the alley, his hand in the pocket with the envelope and his long hair swaying back and forth across his tattooed shoulders.

I pulled the key from the Cadillac’s ignition, opened the hatch of my father’s Jeep, and transferred the needed supplies onto the gashed leather seats in the back of the Cadillac. Sliding into the Jeep, I retrieved a baseball cap from the passenger’s seat and pulled it down tight to cover my face. I slipped a baggy sweatshirt on and zipped it up. Then I started up the Jeep and pulled slowly out of the alley. I turned left and parked on the curb half a block from The White Wolf.

I walked back to the Cadillac. With the things Johnny had purchased for me, I made my final preparations. When I finished, I started the old Cadillac, drove around the corner, and parked diagonally across from the club.

Neon lights advertising the establishment's nightlife gave a Vegas glow to the front of the building. Several security lights high on its sides illuminated the back, where thankfully, the black Escalade sat in the reserved space. The 1WOLFE personalized plate—more of a warning than a vanity—confirmed it belonged to Benito. I'd heard stories about the few who had tried to mess with The White Wolf or its owner. If I didn't succeed tonight, I'd be one of those stories.

I clenched my teeth, and my face flushed. I was doing my best to keep it in check, but I was close to losing it. The little white runt had taken my sister. He'd drawn first blood, and now I was bringing the war to him. I looked at my watch. 2 a.m. The last of the nightclub's patrons would be gone, but I needed to make sure its owner was indeed inside.

Chapter 87

Running Man

Cadence's hands were tied behind her back as she sat on a chair in the middle of a dim room carpeted with thick, luxuriant white shag. A desk lamp that illuminated her captor and the regular, pulsing glow of his cigarette offered the only light. For the last hour, he'd been sitting behind his desk, smoking one cigarette after the next like a machine. Between draws, he stared at her through the smoky haze with an expressionless gaze. He was waiting for something. Cadence couldn't help the shiver that passed over her. What a frightening, repulsive man.

Silent as a mummy, a big man with a close-shaven head stood blocking the steel door through which they had entered earlier. He'd only spoken once since he'd placed his big, hard hand over her mouth as she had stepped through her father's back gate. In a thick Eastern-European accent, he had hissed in her ear, "Keep silent, or I hurt you."

After that, a gag had been placed in her mouth. She'd been thrown into the back of a large black car. Now she sat waiting, as Silva did. Probably for her brother. Her face flushed, and she almost laughed. Timbre was coming—of this, she had no doubt. He might be an imperfect mess, but he was a man, and he would be coming loud, angry, and violent. The thought muted her fear, and her Plummer blood thrilled.

The phone on Silva's desk rang four times before he picked it up.

"Good morning, Mr. Plummer. So nice of you to call." Silva tapped a cigarette on a golden ashtray.

Cadence caught her breath.

Silva fell silent as he listened, then Cadence cringed at the mocking laugh that erupted from him. The clouds of yellow smoke that swirled around the desk gave him a ghoulish look.

"She's in good hands, Timbre," Silva said, taking a more serious tone. After a short silence, he spoke again. "We need to talk about your debt. It has increased substantially in terms of monetary value and … how shall I say this … and in terms of blood, sweat, and tears."

More silence.

"Are you there, Timbre?" Silva asked conversationally. And arrogantly. Then, "She is indisposed at the moment."

Silva held the phone away as her brother's voice grew from garbled anger to a raging clarity. The gangster stood from behind his desk, his hand a white claw as he placed the phone back to his ear. He started pacing, his back hunched, every moment stiff with fury.

"I will make her pay for your insults. I will make you watch," Benito said into the phone, his burning gaze turned toward Cadence. She shivered under the raking fury. Silva stopped moving and hissed, "My place." He listened, then added, "Half an hour."

Silva faced Cadence again, his expression hesitant now. Slowly, he made his way over. He slipped the phone into his pocket while he untied the gag in her mouth. Pulling the phone back out, he pushed the speaker button and held it to her face. "Your brother."

Cadence mustered her composure, but her voice was brittle. "Timmy?"

"Are you okay, Cadence?"

"I'm okay."

"Has he hurt you?"

"No," Cadence said quietly.

After hair's breadth of a pause, Timbre asked, "Are you in a room with white carpet?"

Why had he asked that?

Silva pulled the phone away from her face with a scowl. "Enough questions." He held the cell up to his mouth and spoke succinctly. "Half an hour, Timbre, or I'll start playing Cadences without you."

As Silva started to walk away, Cadence screamed.

"Yes!"

Silva whirled around and gave her a vicious, back-handed slap. This time, she screamed in outrage. Silva disconnected the call and raised his hand to hit her again. He held it there, ready to strike, but she lifted her chin high as the unsettling thrill of the Plummer rage built inside of her. Silva stared into her eyes, seemingly fascinated by her response.

"Go ahead, hit me again," she goaded him. "You hit like a child, you pathetic little monster." Her captor's expression darkened, but she didn't stop. "You better start running. My brother is coming for you, Silva. You'd better run, little man. Run, you hear me?"

Silva hit her again. She turned her head back slowly this time. She was laughing now. "That's all you got? My girlfriends hit harder than you."

Silva's face contorted into a twisted, ghoulish fury. He reached into his jacket and pulled out his pistol, then placed it to Cadence's head. "What did you say?" he hissed.

Before Cadence could goad him further, gunfire sounded from the front of the building. Silva straightened and lowered the gun, cocking his ear. The blasts grew louder and more frequent. He spoke to the man at the door.

"Go see what's going on."

“He’s coming for you, little man,” Cadence mocked him.

Silva ignored her and walked back around his desk. Moments later, a crashing roar shook the building. Silva jumped as the room plunged into darkness. Cadence heard him fumbling about his desk. An emergency light came on over a door at the back of the room. She stood and got a few steps toward the exit when something hard poked her in the back.

“Keep moving. Try to run, and I’ll shoot you.”

Chapter 88

Run, Caden, Run

I picked up the prepaid phone on the seat beside me and dialed Benito Silva's number. After four rings, Benito's smug, arrogant voice burned my ear.

"Good morning, Mr. Plummer. So nice of you to call."

"Where's my sister?"

His mocking laugh rang out. "She's in good hands, Timbre." I was seething now. I wanted to march into the White Wolfe with an ax in hand. "We need to talk about your debt." His voice had taken on a more serious tone. "It has increased substantially in terms of monetary value and … how shall I say this … and in terms of blood, sweat, and tears."

I bit my lip.

"Are you there, Timbre?" Benito asked conversationally. The arrogance was back.

"I want to talk to my sister."

"She is indisposed at the moment," he said softly.

"If you've hurt her, I will kill you and burn your place down around you. Do you understand?" I half shouted into the phone. "I will hunt you down and destroy you, you little albino reptile. One hair on her head is missing, and your life is over. Do you understand me, Benito?"

The silence on the other end of the phone stretched on for some time. I was panting with anger now. I had to hold it together for just a little while longer. Tonight, one way or another, I was going to end this. If I didn't, I was unlikely to get another chance. If I waited for the cops, Cadence would just disappear. She would be killed or worse, sold to some third-world hell-hole as a sex worker.

Benito finally spoke, clipped and cold. Angry. "I will make her pay for your insults. I will make you watch."

"Where?"

"My place.

"When?"

"Half an hour."

"Okay, but only after I've talked to Cadence. If she's been hurt or you've taken her to some other place, then you hang up right now and start running. Because I'll be coming for you. I'm going to be your worst nightmare, Benito."

Another silence. I pictured Benito Silva trying to decide what to do. Few men had probably ever talked to him the way I just had, and those who had were likely no longer living. I was betting my sister's life on the fact that Benito Silva wanted to hurt me more than her. I took a deep breath and tried to slow my throbbing heart.

My sister's voice came over the phone. "Timmy?" She didn't sound as terrified as I'd expected. A long sigh escaped my lips. Cadence was there, just a few hundred feet away from where I was sitting. I had to make sure, though.

"Are you okay, Cadence?"

"I'm okay."

"Has he hurt you?"

"No," she said firmly but quietly.

"Are you in a room with white carpet?"

"Enough questions." Benito again, brusque. "Half an hour, Timbre, or I'll start playing Cadences without you."

"Yes!" Cadence screamed in the background. I smiled grimly. Cadence was on the second floor of the nightclub. A second later, I heard the smack of flesh and she screamed. The smile on my face disappeared. I started shaking with rage.

"You shouldn't have done that, Benito," I shouted into the phone and hung up. With unsteady legs, I stepped out of the old Cadillac. I leaned against the warm metal of the car's back door and tried to tame my shaking rage.

When I got my emotions partially under control, I opened the door of the car, grabbed four arrows from the back seat, and laid them on the roof. Around the tip of each arrow, I had wrapped several large M-80 firecrackers. I'd already combined the fuses and added an additional short length of fuse to each bunch. Next, I removed three road flares and set two of them on the driver's seat and one on the roof of the Cadillac. I reached back into the vehicle for my father's compound bow that I'd found hanging in the storage room off the garage.

I rolled the window of the Cadillac down an inch. I inserted the flare and rolled it back up, pinching it in the window. I struck the flare with its cap, and it lit the old Cadillac in a hellish glow. Notching an arrow, I held the end of the fuse against the brilliant orange flame. When it started to hiss, I raised the bow and drew it back to its full length. I released and watched the missile arch over Benito's building following the trajectory by the faint glow of the fuse. It bounced off the building across the street from the White Wolfe. Too far.

I notched another arrow and adjusted my aim. As I released the arrow, explosives echoed from the other side of the building. I aimed higher this time. I wanted the explosions to come down in front of Benito's place. If possible, I wanted all of Benito's men in front of the building.

In quick succession, I fired the remaining arrows into the growing din. I left the bow on the sidewalk and started the Cadillac, then dialed 911 on my burner phone.

“911. What is your emergency?” the calm voice asked.

“There is a gunfight at The White Wolf nightclub on Tenth Street. Sounds like there are explosions. People may be hurt,” I panted into the phone in a terrified voice.

Without waiting for the operator to respond, I ended the call, threw the phone onto the back seat, and started the Cadillac. I shoved the remaining unlit flares into my waistband. With a metallic snap, I buckled the seat belt. I put the old sedan in gear and gunned the engine, aiming for the side of the building where the electric meter box was located.

I was hunched down in the seat and doing forty-five when I hit the bricks with my two-and-a-half tons of American luxury. Like a fist through a house of cards, the vehicle punched a hole in the side of the building with a tearing roar. The good side of my bumper severed the electric pedestal with a shower of sparks. Everything went dark except what my remaining headlight illuminated. The car came to rest with the bumper inches away from the double doors at the front of the building. My single functioning headlight gave an eerie glow to the empty room and the remains of the stairs clinging to the far wall.

I jumped out of the Cadillac, reached behind the driver’s seat, and grabbed a five-gallon can of gasoline. After I’d emptied the contents over the car, I removed the cap on the second can and flung it across the dance floor, where it left a spiraling, glossy trail of liquid in its wake. I tossed my cell phone into the car.

Pounding on the front door where Silva’s goons were trying to get back in told me I was running out of time. They would eventually think to come around the side. As I ran for the jagged opening I’d punched into the building, I struck a flare and tossed it into the Cadillac. With a concussive roar, the gas fumes lit. I stumbled outside and left the growing inferno to do its work. Sirens soon wailed in the distance.

Hugging the shadows against the wall, I made my way to the back of the building. As I turned the corner, men ran around the opposite side. The flaming hole needed to distract them long enough for me to finish this. I crouched in the shadows under the emergency stairwell, which was faintly illuminated by a single light across the street.

Above me, the emergency exit door crashed open. My sister cried out in pain as a brutal voice hissed.

"Get moving, or I'll put a bullet in your head right here."

Feet clattered on the landing above. I straightened until my head touched the stair above me. Uncertain steps descended the concrete-and-steel emergency staircase. I slid two feet of black nylon rope out of my pocket and wrapped it double around both hands.

As the steps approached, I slid the loop between the stairs at my eye level. The step above my head vibrated with a light tread, and my sister's foot lowered into the loop of rope I held ready. She stepped out, and a small, polished shoe followed. With a flick of my wrist, I jerked the loop tight, trapping the heel under the back edge of the stair.

My timing was perfect. About the time Benito Silva felt the pressure of my rope on his ankle, his other foot was stepping downward. Momentum and the weight of my father's briefcase in his hand did the rest. With a crack like the stem of a crystal vase, his ankle broke, and he fell headlong down the stairs. His scream of pain was cut short by the impact of his face on the concrete and steel of the second-to-last step. He didn't move. But I did.

I bolted from under the stairs and grabbed my sister's arm with my left hand. Benito lay stretched out full length, my father's briefcase on the asphalt at the bottom of the stairs. Scooping it up with my right hand, I tugged Cadence away from the building.

Judging by the resistance in my sister's body, she had no idea who held her arm. Once the Escalade was between us and any potential pursuers, I leaned close and spoke in her ear.

"Run, Caden, run."

Chapter 89

Escape

As we raced across the street, my sister's arm relaxed. Once we were in the shadows on the other side, I let go and set down my father's briefcase. I reached into my pocket for a folding knife. Cadence turned to face me, and I carefully cut the plastic zip ties. She threw her arms around me, and we held each other tight for a few seconds.

I released her as flashing lights came around the corner two blocks away. "We need to get out of here, Sis," I said as I bent to pick up the briefcase.

I scooped up my father's compound bow as we passed. We made it to the Jeep without further problems. It wasn't until we were a couple of miles away that I finally blew out a breath and pulled off my baseball cap.

Cadence studied me as we drove in silence. My rage had evaporated, and in its place, an uncomfortable, sour emptiness had taken its place. I looked over at my sister, and our eyes met in the faint glow of the car's console lights.

"You really okay?" I asked.

"I'm good now." Her gaze lingered another moment. "Are *you* okay?"

I let out a long sigh. "I am now. I'm so sorry that you got dragged into this, Caden."

She placed her hand on my arm. "Do you think you killed him?"

"I hope so."

"I hope you didn't," she said quietly.

I glanced over at her, eyes widening. She'd been kidnapped and assaulted by the man, and she still hoped I hadn't killed him? My blood surged at the very thought of Benito Silva and what he had intended to do with her.

"Why?" I finally asked.

"You'd have blood on your hands, Timbre. Taking another person's life changes you, even if it is in self-defense or a just cause."

"How would you know?" Surely, my sister had not killed someone. That thought made me go cold inside. But her expression relayed deep sadness.

"I was in one of my uncontrollable, drug-induced rages …"

I glanced at her out of the corner of my eyes as I turned at a stoplight.

She gave me a sad, knowing smile. "You are not the only one who has a hard time controlling the Plummer fire. Anyway, I was out of my mind on drugs. Dad was there, and I was raving at him. He told me I had to go back to rehab, that he didn't know how else to help me. I told him if he put me back in that place, it would kill me or I'd kill him." A sob escaped, and she continued so softly I could barely hear. "I didn't really mean it. I was just saying whatever I could to try and hurt him. I wanted him to hurt as bad as I did, I guess. Words can be a terrible thing, Timmy."

My tight shoulders relaxed a notch. "Yes, but you didn't kill him.

Cadence was silent for some time. "No, but my words that night hurt him more than a knife or bullets ever could.

I still remember the tears my words brought to his eyes. Those were the first and only I ever saw him shed. Then he told me how wrong I was. He told me how he was haunted by the men he had killed, how he could see their faces in his dreams. Even though he knew they were his enemies, he said he left part of his soul on the battlefield along with the men he had killed."

Cadence's words troubled me. Not because I might have killed a man tonight. They troubled me because I felt nothing. If I'd had time, I would have stomped Benito Silva's guts out there on the stairs. Part of me still wanted to. Was I some kind of monster because I didn't see Benito Silva as a human being?

No. I shook my head. He'd come for my family, and he'd gotten what he deserved, dead or just broken.

After a couple more miles, I looked over at Cadence. "Any ideas where we might go from here? My plan only got me this far."

"Have you thought about the timing of Silva finding us?" Cadence asked, ignoring my question.

"What are you talking about?" I hadn't gotten enough sleep to keep up with my sister right now. "I have no idea how he found us the last two times, if that is what you mean."

"I'm not asking you how he found us, but about the timing. Both times he's found us have something in common."

I'd gotten rid of my cell phone before we'd left for our grandfather's cabin the first time. The only thing each occurrence had in common was Cadence and I and—

The tires skidded over the dirt on the side of the freeway just outside Phoenix as I jerked my head around to look at the briefcase in the back seat. Cadence yelped. I pulled back onto the highway in a cloud of dust.

My fingers tightened on the wheel, and my neck prickled. "We've got to pull over at the next exit."

She frowned at me. "How long has it been since you slept?"

"That's not why. The briefcase, Caden. There must be some sort of tracking device in it."

Her mouth opened, then closed. "You really think so? I was thinking how Benito has shown up each time shortly after we've entered our cipher answers in the web portal."

"Crap." How had I missed that? It made sense. "You think Benito has somehow managed to access the server that Dad is using to run his Lazarus Ciphers?"

Cadence gave a decisive nod. "They could be tracing our IP address."

I slapped the wheel. "Either way, I want to check out the briefcase, so you can drive."

I flipped my blinker on, took the next exit ramp, and immediately pulled to the shoulder. When we changed places, I grabbed Dad's briefcase and settled it on my lap. As Cadence buckled up, I asked, "So how do we prevent them from finding us again next time we enter our answer?"

"We could start by using what we know against them."

"How do we do that?"

Instead of answering, Cadence accelerated up the ramp, but rather than continuing in the direction we'd been going, she made a hard turn and crossed the bridge. I reached for the overhead handle as she whistled under a yellow light and back onto the freeway the way we'd just come.

"What the heck, Cadence? Who taught you to drive?"

"Dad," she said with a crooked smile.

"You're a maniac."

"Says the person who drove a car through the side of a building and lit it on fire."

Couldn't dispute that. "Care to let me in on the reason for your dramatic course change?"

"Let's head south to Tucson. We'll check into a hotel. Pull up Dad's server and enter an answer for the sixth cipher. If someone is still tracing our movements, we'll let them chase their tails for a while." Cadence looked over to see what I thought about her idea.

"Yeah. About time we started making them jump through our hoops. If you're right, this diversion could buy us some time." I rotated the briefcase to face me. "But if I'm right …" I sprung the latches.

Her lips pressed firmly. "We could be setting ourselves up for another ambush."

"Exactly."

She blew out a breath. "Okay then. Let's see if you are right."

As Cadence focused on the road for once, one by one, I took my father's treasures from the secret compartment and set them on the dash. When I'd removed every pen, pencil, and piece of paper, I searched the case inch by inch. Maybe I was paranoid, but I'd let my guard down too many times.

Starting with the inside of the bottom of the case, I looked for anything out of place, any broken stitch, anything unaccounted for. I finished with the inside. Nothing. Then I started on the outside. Nothing there either. After carefully inspecting each of my father's treasures one more time, I placed them back in their secret home. Next, I checked each pen and pencil and in between each paper. Finally satisfied, I closed the case and stood it upright on my legs.

Cadence gave me an *I-told-you-so* smile. I couldn't even argue. Some spy I would make.

As I started to lift the briefcase to place it back on the seat behind me, my fingers brushed the broken stitches under the handle.

As I leaned in close, metal glinted inside the broken stitch. I opened the briefcase again and retrieved a pen. With the tip, I picked on the stitch until the leather seam spread open under my assault. Alarm quivered through me.

"Uh, Cadence …"

Chapter 90

Detours

The sliver of metal I slid out of the handle's seam was shorter than a toothpick but flat, silver with a tiny circuit board attached to one end. Was it tracking us? Did it record or transmit our conversations? I looked to Cadence and held my finger up to my lips. Her eyes widened.

I jerked my head around. Was anyone following us? No headlights were close, but that didn't mean anything. We were on an interstate, and there were cars everywhere. Whoever had planted this device could be trailing us right now from miles away. If they had been listening to our conversations, they knew everything—where we were going and where we had been. They knew all the answers to our father's ciphers. Who was responsible? Was it Benito or someone else?

The familiar burn of anger rekindled. I rolled down my window. We needed to get this thing as far away from us as possible.

"Are you hungry," she asked, tilting her head toward the device.

What? I raised my eyebrows.

"I'd like a bite to eat," she continued. "And a bathroom break. How about we grab some food and stretch our legs?"

I raised an eyebrow at her. "Okay. I'm not really hungry, but you're driving."

We stopped at the next gas station. Cadence pulled up to the only available pump. I left the device on the seat, and we both got out.

"What are you doing?" I asked after closing the door behind us and we'd stepped away from the car.

"I don't think we should toss the device until we think this through. If we toss it now, whoever is following us will know we are aware of the device. If they are listening, then they already know we are planning to go to Tucson."

"Okay." I shifted my weight. "But what do you suggest we do with it once we get to Tucson?"

Cadence shrugged. "We could leave it in the hotel room."

I shook my head. "If we stop moving for a long period, they will probably get suspicious."

"Or they'll just try to grab us again. Let's not make any rash decisions. Right now, keeping it a little longer is not going to change anything."

"I guess you are right."

She glanced at the brightly lit storefront. "You want anything from inside?"

"No, thanks." I reached for my billfold and handed it to her. "Put thirty dollars on pump five, will you?"

While I pumped gas, my mind crunched our current problem. How could we buy ourselves more time before they realized we had found the device?

The exhaust brake of a big rig rolling down the off-ramp rattled with muffled rage, drawing my attention as it tried to slow its huge diesel engine and load. In the glow of the street lights, I read the bright orange lettering across the side of the trailer. *Horizons Moving - We move so you don't have to.*

"We move so you don't have to," I muttered. I turned to look at the electronic device on the seat of the Jeep, then jerked my head back around as a hand touched my shoulder.

"A bit jumpy?" Cadence grinned as she returned to the driver's side.

"Not funny." I laughed nervously. "But I think I know what we can do with our little electronic friend." I pointed at the eighteen-wheeler turning into the truck stop.

Cadence looked at the truck and then back at me. Understanding lit her face.

***

Two hours later, we'd checked into a local hotel, and entered a fake answer for the sixth cipher. Afterward, we drove to the Triple-T Truck Stop off I-10 and parked. Now we waited. Our best chance was to find a trucker headed south. If we got lucky, we might find one which would take our electronic device to New Mexico and then on to Texas.

An Allstate Moving rig pulled off the exit and headed our way. I eyeballed Cadence. She shrugged. We watched as the truck pulled into the parking lot and headed for the gas pumps. That wouldn't work. The gas pumps were too well-lit and impossible to approach without being seen.

Car haulers, flatbeds with rolls of wire, and freight liners with logos painted in bright colors across their enclosed trailers packed the lot. But we had not seen which direction any of these trucks had come from.

I retrieved my notepad from the briefcase and wrote a message.

We need to do this before it gets light.

Cadence took the pad from me.

Unless the truck is headed for Grandpa's cabin, it doesn't really matter, does it?

I guess not.

Cadence held out her hand for the device. I shook my head and started to open the door. She grabbed my arm and spoke aloud. "Wait."

She took the pad.

I have a better chance of getting away with this than you.

Why? I asked and shoved the pad back at her.

She wrote, *Duh, I'm a girl!!!* and held out her hand again. When I didn't surrender the device, she grabbed the pad back.

Don't be a stubborn dork, Timbre, she scribbled furiously. *"You know that these truckers won't be nearly as suspicious of me as they will some dude!*

She tossed the pad back to me and shoved her palm my way. This time, her look told me I would lose this argument one way or another. I handed her the device. She was right. Cadence opened the door.

"I'll be right back with some hot coffee. Give me a couple of minutes and come pick me up at the convenience store," she said and winked at me. Then she disappeared into the rows of trucks.

I cursed under my breath. I didn't like this at all. For all we knew, our pursuers could be right here in the parking lot with us. I put the car in drive and headed after Cadence. My heart started to beat faster as I passed row after row of trucks, craning my neck left and right, and found no sign of her. How had she disappeared so quickly? After five minutes, I was as frantic as a parent who'd lost their four-year-old at a carnival

I turned a corner at the far end of the lot and headed back to the center of the truck stop where the convenience store was located. There she stood on the sidewalk, eyes narrowed and lips pursed, two coffee cups in hand.

I pulled even with her and leaned over to open the passenger-side door.

Cadence handed me a coffee. "Where were you?" she asked as she sat down and closed the door.

"I was looking for you."

"I've been standing here for a couple of minutes."

"Well, I was worried one of those truckers or the people who are following us might have taken you. So you got the device planted?"

Cadence eyeballed me. "No, I got it right here in my pocket still." She took a sip of coffee, the steam curling around her nose while I waited for details. She raised her eyebrow. "Well, are you going to sit here all day, or are you going to drive?"

"Where to?" I asked, even though I obediently put the car in drive.

"I want to go back to Grandfather's cabin."

My mouth fell open, but her gaze met mine, dead serious.

"I want to go back, Timmy. There is peace there. The place restored my soul. I want to get away from all this." Cadence swept her hand at the cars, buildings, and headlights flashing outside her window.

"But it's not safe."

"Why not? A crime scene is the last place Benito or his goons will think to look. Anyway, they will be chasing their tails for a while. Our little electronic friend is on its way to Kentucky."

"How do you know that?"

"I asked." A smug smile curled her lips above the rim of her cup.

"You what?"

"I asked," she repeated. "I met a nice trucker from Kentucky. Big, hairy guy with a sexy Southern drawl and a smile as wide as Texas. He was just stepping down out of a brand-new Kenworth. I made a big deal about his truck, and he asked me if I wanted to take a look inside."

My heart went cold. "You didn't."

"Sure, I did. Why not? He seemed like a decent enough sort, kinda cute. Anyway, I left our little friend behind in his sleeping cab."

"You are killing me, Cadence," I said as I pulled out of the truck stop. "Just so you know, if they do find us back at the cabin, I'm not crawling through that pipe again. I'll run unarmed into a firing squad, but I'm not getting back in that hole."

Cadence's warm, rich laugh was like pouring oil on troubled waters. My hands relaxed on the steering wheel. Her mirth embodied the peace, companionship, and stimulating thought we'd shared while working on the ciphers up there on the Mogollon Rim.

I wanted to go back too. And she was probably right. The cabin would be the last place they would look for us. At least I hoped so.

Chapter 91

Return

The double spires of Picacho Peak swept by on our left as the first crimson rays of dawn melted the night's gloom. The shadows along the interstate lengthened as the sun burned its way free of the rocky hills that had hidden its flaming glory. It felt good to be alive.

I looked over at my sister. She hadn't taken more than a few sips of her coffee before falling asleep. The unruly strands of her blonde hair were just starting to glimmer with the kiss of early morning radiance seeping through the passenger-side window.

She smiled as she slept, a dreamy smile. None of our recent troubles were evidenced there. I didn't understand the peace that had transformed the broken person I'd picked up off the floor just a few weeks ago. Her pleasant somnolence warmed the cold, dark furrows of my heart.

I had no such peace. It wasn't like I was unhappy. I was grateful to be alive. Grateful that I hadn't pulled the trigger that lonely, bitter afternoon. But deep inside, that same fire still smoldered—a restless burning thing that I couldn't always control, that in some ways I didn't want to control. I pictured the burning inferno I'd left behind just a few hours earlier, and the hair on my arms prickled. I'd come so close to losing control. I'd been a breath away from jeopardizing my sister's life. I gripped the wheel tighter. If I'd bounded up those broken stairs with an ax like I'd wanted to, both Cadence and I would have died. I shivered at the thought.

On the outskirts of Phoenix, we swept by the fields of white cotton, golden and green with the grace of dawn. I yawned and took another sip of now-cold coffee to help clear the fog.

Three hours and a couple of stops for supplies later, I turned off Highway 260 onto the dirt forest service road that led to the cabin. The gravel crunched under the tires as I wound my way through the peaceful ponderosa forest. I rolled down the window and took a deep breath of the pine-scented air.

Cadence stirred. When I hit a particularly bad rut in the road, she lifted her head and sat up. She inhaled deeply also, sampling the sweet evergreen aroma. "What a glorious smell! I'm glad we're back."

I smiled and avoided the next rut in the road. Cadence rolled down her window, and the cool mountain air poured in. Her hair danced in the wind. Her enthusiasm proved contagious. This was a special place. So many good memories, the bad ones didn't seem to matter as much.

I pulled up to the gate of the homestead five minutes later. Yellow police tape stretched across the opening.

"Looks like your SOS must have gotten someone to respond." I pointed at the many tire tracks both here and beyond the gate. "Whatever happened, there was quite a response."

I got out of my father's Jeep and lifted the caution tape, then motioned for Cadence to pull through. Once she was on the other side, I closed the gate and retrieved a new chain and lock I'd purchased in Phoenix. After securing the entrance, we drove up to the cabin. Besides the damage to the wood veneer of the door and the bullet holes in some security shutters and logs, there was no significant destruction. I had envisioned coming back to a charred pile of logs.

Cadence got out first. I was right behind her.

"Looks like a battlefield," she observed.

We walked up onto the porch, and Cadence retrieved the key from its hiding spot. We stepped inside the dark cabin. Light passing through the bullet holes in the safety shutters illuminated the shattered glass of the front window.

While Cadence cleaned up, I went back outside to attend to security. For the next hour, I ringed the forest around the clearing with solar-powered motion sensors purchased in Phoenix. The sensors were networked and controlled by a Wi-Fi-enabled app on my computer. My father would roll over in his grave if he knew I was polluting this place with Wi-Fi.

When I finished, I moved the Jeep into the barn and locked up. My sister's car still sat in the driveway in front of the cabin—only now, it was riddled with bullet holes. Tiny pieces of shattered glass lay scattered around it like ice confetti.

Cadence looked up from the kitchen stove when I closed the cabin door behind me. She was up to her elbows in flour, and she gave me a look that said, *Don't even*. It was lighter inside the cabin now. She had opened the security shutter over the kitchen window. She pooched out her lower lip and blew an errant strand of hair from her face and then returned to kneading bread. I refrained from teasing her about how domesticated she was becoming.

I sat down at my father's desk, turned on my laptop, and logged into the security system's control app. I had downloaded the app at the store because I didn't want to use the internet at the cabin just in case someone was monitoring that as well.

As the system booted up, one by one, it identified the motion sensors. Later, I would test the network by having Cadence try to enter the property from various points of her choosing. I looked up at my sister beating on the dough. Now would probably not be a good time to ask.

I removed the notepad from my father's briefcase. If we were going to save this place, we needed to get back to work on his Lazarus Ciphers. We only had another nine days to solve the remaining ciphers before they would be made public. And someone might already know the first five answers because of the electronic device. I looked around the cabin. To think of losing this place to a stranger was unacceptable to me.

As I turned the pages of the notepad to the *pi* cipher, it hit me that I hadn't told Cadence about my discovery. I went into the kitchen where she was working, laid the notepad on the counter, and pointed at the seven Hebrew verses and their numerical values.

Psalm 34:15	29 Hebrew letters	Hebrew letter value = 1378
Psalm 37:6	27 Hebrew letters	Hebrew letter value = 1379
1 Chronicles 6:28	22 Hebrew letters	Hebrew letter value = 1380
Psalms 2:4	24 Hebrew letters	Hebrew letter value = 1381
Proverbs 21:3	25 Hebrew letters	Hebrew letter value = 1382
Psalm 139:23	26 Hebrew letters	Hebrew letter value = 1383
Psalm 92:14	30 Hebrew letters	Hebrew letter value = 1384

"I figured out the *pi* cipher key."

Chapter 92

The *Pi* Cipher

Cadence tried to blow the unruly hair out of her face again. When that didn't work, she brushed at it with the back of her flour-coated hand. All that accomplished was leaving a streak of white across her cheek. I laughed. She didn't. I took the strands of errant hair and tucked them behind her ear.

"Thank you," she said gratefully. She stared at the list for a full minute. "So how do you know you are correct?" she asked as she started kneading the dough again.

I knew she'd ask that. My face stretched into a wide grin. "There are 7 double pey hidden in Dad's cipher, right?"

Cadence nodded.

"There are 7 verse clues."

She gave me another curt nod that said I needed to make my point.

I turned the page with a flourish. "If we take the 1378th through the 1384th digits of *pi*, we get this number."

26 391 41

I pointed at the number, which I'd separated to emphasize the familiar components. "26-391-41 is only found twice in the first one million digits of *pi*."

Cadence widened her eyes. "You checked?"

"No, I just made that up. Of course, I checked. This first occurrence of these 7 numbers, which Dad highlighted by these

Hebrew verse values, also happens to contain the first occurrence of the number *391* in *pi*."

When Cadence lifted her face, it reflected the same surprise I'd felt at how unlikely such a combination of numbers was in light of the context of their first occurrence and their Biblical significance.

"You're sure this is the first occurrence of the Hebrew value of Yeshua's name in *pi*?" she asked.

"I am. You want to see?"

She shook her head but the glass she was using to cut out the biscuit dough stopped moving. "No, I believe you." She looked back at the pad and scratched her temple, unmindful of the flour on her hand. Then she met my gaze with a laugh of respect and a bit of awe.

"He's been leading us along this whole time. His first cipher gave us 26, the value of God's proper name in the Bible. The second cipher gave us 391, the value of Jesus's Old Testament namesake, Yeshua. Then he showed us how Yahweh, 26, made a covenant with Abraham, 41. That covenant promised that all the world would be blessed through Abraham's seed. He then showed us how the New Testament authors believed this was fulfilled in Yeshua, 391. Now he just happens to find the first occurrence of 391 in *pi*, one of the least quantifiable numbers in mathematics, surrounded by the very name values that make this redemptive story come alive in the Bible."

I gave a soft laugh. "That pretty much sums it up, Sis."

Cadence's hair fell from her ear as she stared at me. This time she pushed a handful of hair out of her face, giving herself premature white streaks. "How could this be a coincidence? I don't even know how you'd go about calculating the odds."

"I don't either. I'm a skeptic, and I can't come up with a reasonable explanation. Maybe Dad just got lucky."

Cadence looked at me like I was some special kind of idiot. "Yeah, that must be it."

I leaned a hip against the counter, cocking my head. "You really believe there is some kind of mathematical connection between the Hebrew Bible and *pi*? Really?"

"The best you can come up with was Dad got lucky." Cadence slid the tray of biscuits into the oven. She let the door slam unnecessarily.

I held up my hand. I didn't want to fight about this. Playing the devil's advocate wasn't as much fun as it used to be. I'd probably punish myself, anyway—more bad dreams about doors I couldn't or didn't want to open and endless strings of numbers I couldn't understand.

"Okay. In all seriousness, why? I see the numbers, and I agree they have real Biblical significance. But were they intentional? I mean, that's what you are implying, right? That God, that Yahweh, the living God of the Bible, ordered the digits of *pi* so that the value of His name and the value of Abraham's name in Hebrew would encompass the first occurrence of the Hebrew value of Jesus's name?"

I waited for her to answer. When she faced me, her jaw bulged. Was she clenching her teeth or biting her tongue? But her eyes held no anger. Maybe she was just preparing to express the profound thoughts in her mind.

"Why not?" she finally asked quietly.

"Why not, what?"

Cadence wiped loose pieces of biscuit dough and flour from the countertop. "Why wouldn't the God of the Bible, the Creator of this amazing world around us, leave little nuggets like this buried in the mathematical world of His? If you were a gold miner, would you expect to find all the gold sitting in one refined block right inside the opening of your mine? Nothing in this world works that way."

A pause in her cleaning efforts indicated that she wasn't finished. That she needed to get it out the way she saw it in her mind.

"Maybe God made it that way intentionally. Maybe He ordered this world so that those who were willing to make an effort might have the satisfaction and joy of the search and discovery. Maybe He didn't spell it all out in one place at one time. The Bible itself was composed by dozens of different authors over hundreds, maybe thousands, of years. Maybe He wants us to search for Him. Maybe He reveals things about His nature and purpose in bits and pieces so that it still requires faith for us to believe. Maybe He rewards those like our father who in faith search, expecting to find evidence of Him. Isn't that what King David hinted at in Psalm 19 when he said, '*The heavens declare the glory of God; and the firmament sheweth his handywork. Day unto day uttereth speech, and night unto night sheweth knowledge. There is no speech nor language, where their voice is not heard.*'?"

Cadence rested both hands on top of the wet rag which concealed the final residue of her baking. She searched my eyes, probably reading me better than I could myself.

Like a well without water, I felt an emptiness at her words. I had rejected God. I had stopped looking for Him. I no longer looked at the world through the eyes of faith. For the first time in my life, the thought scared me.

Cadence must have seen some evidence of my fears. She stepped over to me and grabbed my arm. "If you can't have faith right now in your heavenly father, at least have a little faith in our earthly one. If you must take this as a coincidence, fine. Just add it to that growing list of unaccountable things we've learned so far. But don't make a final judgment until you've seen all the evidence Dad has to offer. Let him reach out to you from the grave with his words and numbers that represent his faith. Take his hand, take mine. Let's walk these final steps together."

The living warmth in my sister's eyes reassured me. I nodded my head slowly. I could have faith in my earthly father, and I wanted to finish this journey Cadence and I had started. I patted my sister's hand that rested on my arm.

"Okay, Sis. Okay."

Cadence let go of my arm. She gave a quick tilt of her head. "Enough serious talk. Come on, let's set the table. We'll eat lunch, and then we'll see if we can solve Dad's *pi* cipher."

Chapter 93

Greatly Beloved

We sat beside each other at the kitchen table. Light from the afternoon sun illuminated the cabin through the window behind us. Internet was out of the question, so we didn't need the desk by the entrance. We left the shutters on the front window closed. No reason to advertise our presence.

A spreadsheet glowed from my laptop. We'd spent a good hour converting the Hebrew letters of my father's cipher to their numerical values. Now we studied the 418 digits of *pi* we believed our father had used as his cipher key. I'd underlined the first seven.

2639141992726042699227967823547816360093417216412
99245863150302861829745557067498385054945885869269
56909272107975093029553211653449872027559602364806
54991198818347977535663698074265425278625518184175
46728909777727938000816470600161452491921732172147
23501414419735685481613611573525521334757418494684
85233239073941433345477624168625189835694855620992
92221842725502542568876717904946016534668049886272
27917860857

Copying the entire 418, I placed each digit of *pi* under one of the Hebrew letter values of my father's cipher. I programmed the cells of the spreadsheet to keep matching values. Any combined values greater than 22 were subtracted instead of added.

When I pressed *enter*, the spreadsheet would recalculate the values and convert the numbers back into Hebrew text. At least, that was what I hoped it would do if I hadn't messed something up. Finger hovering in the air over the keyboard, I looked up at Cadence.

"Are you ready?

"Just do it already."

I pressed *enter*, and a new string of Hebrew text appeared. I recognized the first five letters—the Hebrew word *techillah,* for *beginning*. Slowly, I read the words to Cadence as I made them out.

"Beginning of thy supplications the commandment came forth, and I am come to shew thee; for thou art greatly beloved: therefore understand the matter, and consider the vision."

The words struck deep. I slid back from the table and stood. They shouldn't have affected me the way they did. They'd been written thousands of years earlier. But they spoke to me—right here, right now. Like my father was speaking to me from the grave. Like he was warning me, encouraging me to pay attention. It made no sense, but goosebumps prickled on my arms. They were real. Tremors started in my hands. They were real, too.

I rushed to the front door but hesitated as I reached for the handle, half expecting it not to open. For the number *391* to start glowing there in the wood panels. I flung open the door and shot Cadence a haunted look as I stumbled out. The words, *Thou are greatly beloved: therefore understand the matter, and consider the vision,* followed me to the edge of the clearing.

Chapter 94

100 Hebrew Words

I tore down the trail to Clover Creek like a mad man. Only after I waded in the crystal pools, picked my way over moss-covered granite boulders, and wandered among the ponderosa pines did composure return to my troubled mind. I sat on one of the slabs of rock that rested in the middle of the creek like a small island. In the water around me, small trout glided back and forth. Green moss swayed and rippled in the eddies of the stream.

Did my father really love me? After how poorly I had behaved? Was I greatly beloved by him? By anyone? I looked back down the hallway of my life, and I didn't see much that deserved love. I'd fallen so head over heels in love with myself, I hadn't had any left over to share with others.

"I'm sorry, Dad," I whispered, "so very sorry."

Part of me wished that I could turn over the hourglass of time so I could make better choices. That wasn't possible, though. What I could do was use the hard lessons I'd learned to make better choices in the future. One thing I was certain of—life wasn't worth living just to satisfy my own wants and ambitions. Companionship, service, and love, made life worth living.

Faith too. Faith was important, I realized with regret. Like a compass that could keep you on track, it provided a perspective that transcended the here and now and could carry you through the rough times without bitterness or regret. I understood now that faith itself was the evidence of things not seen, the substance of things hoped for.

It was a pity I had forfeited mine.

I returned at twilight wet and exhausted. But where I had left in a frantic, mad rush to escape, I returned with a sense of peace and sadness. Maybe even a new awareness.

Cadence looked up from our notes on the kitchen table and gave me a searching look. “You okay?”

“I’m good.”

She watched me as I slid off my soggy shoes.

“I’m going to take a shower.”

“Okay, but you are going to want to see this,” she said as she tapped the pad with the end of her pencil. “I figured out the riddle. It’s fascinating.”

Fifteen minutes later, clean and in fresh clothes, I stood over the table looking down at the final five verses of a Biblical prophecy that Cadence had copied into our notepad.

Daniel 9:23-27

At the beginning of thy supplications the commandment came forth, and I am come to shew thee; for thou art greatly beloved: therefore understand the matter, and consider the vision.

Seventy weeks are determined upon thy people and upon thy holy city, to finish the transgression, and to make an end of sins, and to make reconciliation for iniquity, and to bring in everlasting righteousness, and to seal up the vision and prophecy, and to anoint the most Holy.

Know therefore and understand, that from the going forth of the commandment to restore and to build Jerusalem unto the Messiah the Prince shall be seven weeks, and threescore and two weeks: the street shall be built again, and the wall, even in troublous times.

And after threescore and two weeks shall Messiah be cut off, but not for himself: and the people of the prince that shall come shall destroy the city and the sanctuary; and the end thereof shall be with a flood, and unto the end of the war desolations are determined.

And he shall confirm the covenant with many for one week: and in the midst of the week he shall cause the sacrifice and the oblation to cease, and for the overspreading of abominations he shall make it desolate, even until the consummation, and that determined shall be poured upon the desolate.

After my gaze reached the end of the page, Cadence sat forward. "According to the text, the prophecy was given by God to His dearly beloved servant Daniel. The prophecy talked about the coming of an anointed prince or messiah after a certain amount of time measured in what the Hebrew text called *shabuwa,* or sevens. This made me think of the Abraham cipher and Yahweh's oath of sevens made with Abraham. Remember, one of the verse clues that Dad provided in that ciphered riddle was Daniel 9:4."

"That was the verse about Yahweh's covenant and mercy, which Moses said originated in the oath of sevens Yahweh made with Abraham."

Cadence nodded. "An oath that promised in part that through Abraham's seed, all the world would be blessed. That blessing was Jesus, Yahweh's Salvation."

"So what does this have to do with 100 words written as 49-49-49?"

She rubbed her hands together. "Oh, you are going to love this." She pointed at the open interlinear Bible on the kitchen table. "We are looking for a passage of 100 Hebrew words." She flipped back through the notepad a few pages and read the riddle.

This enciphered Biblical passage of 100 words can be written numerically as 49-49-49.

Provide the 13th & 14th keywords of this passage.

She spread the fingers of one hand. "In Hebrew, Daniel 9:23-27 is exactly 100 words. At first, I couldn't figure out how a passage of 100 words could be written numerically as 49-49-49 like Dad's riddle claims. But then I started counting the words in the passage. If you take the first 49 Hebrew words of the passage and the last 49 words, you are left with just two words in the exact center."

"Hate to break it to you, Sis, but even in the most creative kind of math, two does not equal 49."

Cadence gave me a wide, sparkling grin. "True …"

I leaned on the table. "Why do I feel a 'but' coming?"

"But …" Cadence said, laughing, "In mathematics, two does not equal 49, but in the magic of words, they do. Do you remember our discussion about Casper Laubuschange?"

"The one who claimed the Biblical authors often numerically arranged the text to emphasize certain words or ideas?"

"Yeah, he's the one. So …" She stared with exaggeratedly widened eyes at the Hebrew text of Daniel 9.

"And …"

She slapped the table with her hands. "You can be so obtuse sometimes, Timbre."

Cadence circled two Hebrew words in the interlinear Bible. "These two words are at the exact numerical center of Daniel 9:23-27. There are 49 words before and 49 words after. What are the two words?"

"*Sheba* shabuwa," I read out loud in Hebrew. Then I nearly choked. Sheba shabuwa was seven sevens or 49.

She pointed at her scribbles on the notepad.

49 + 2 + 49 = 49 + sheba shabuwa + 49

I stared at the elegant equation and then at my sister. "Crud, I see it. That had to have been done on purpose."

Cadence pursed her lips but plowed ahead, anyway. "Hold on. Before you overwhelm me with your enthusiasm, there is more. Not only is the word count designed to be balanced around the seven sevens at the numerical center of the text, but so is the letter count."

I double-blinked at her. "Seriously?"

"Dead serious," Cadence replied. "There are two hundred and four letters before the ten letters of *sheba shabuwa* and two hundred and four letters afterward. This all but proves the passage was intentionally designed." She wrote the letter count equation out for me.

204 + 10 + 204 = 204 + sheba shabuwa + 204

I sat down at the table beside her. "So the author structured the passage to emphasize a central numerical theme. In other words, 7 sevens?"

"Or if you take the passage at face value, it was a prophetic message from Yahweh, delivered by His angelic messenger Gabriel."

I flexed my fingers. "You really believe that?"

Cadence sat back, her chin raising. "I do. Why not? Why not take the passage as a divine prophetic revelation that predicted the coming of the Messiah?"

"I don't know, Cadence. I'm not buying it. I'd need more than speculation."

She got a frustrated glint in her eye, but then she just laughed. "Brother of mine, you are an incredible cynic. You've just got to have a little faith."

I held up my arms. "Not cynical, Cadence. Skeptical. As for faith, I wish I had as much as you. But haven't we gotten off track here? What is the answer to Dad's riddle? What are the 13th and 14th keywords of the passage?"

"What do you think they are?"

"Sheba shabuwa?."

Cadence nodded. "*Sheba* and *shabuwa* are the 13th and 14th words of verse 25 and the exact center of the passage." She tapped another one of her notes.

Daniel 9:23-27

49+2+49 = 100 Words

204+10+204 = 418 Letters

"So when do you want to leave?" I asked.

Chapter 95

The Blessing of 222

"Leave?" Cadence asked.

"Yes, leave. We can't risk using the internet up here," I reminded her.

"You still don't want to log in from here even though we got rid of the tracking device?"

Turning my head to one side, I grimaced. "I don't think we should. What if you were right about someone else tracking us through the IP address? Maybe there are others. Maybe someone else knows that the Lazarus Ciphers will soon be open for the public to solve, and they are keeping track of us to get a head start. Who knows?"

"Maybe we will see Bigfoot when we leave the cabin," Cadence muttered.

I couldn't help the smile. "Let's just be extra careful, okay? We'll drive down to Tucson in the morning. We'll find a coffee shop with Wi-Fi, get a hot cup of joe, enter our answer, get the 7th cipher, and head back here by evening. "

"Okay." Cadence's bottom lip pouted. "I was hoping to get a glimpse of the 7th cipher tonight."

I stood up and slid my chair under the table. "It will be there tomorrow, Caden."

She remained seated. Her frown changed to a grin when she looked up at me. "You want to see something else pretty cool about this passage?"

Not really, but the enthusiasm in her eyes made me sit back down. “Why not? It’s not like I have anything else to do more pressing.”

Cadence rubbed her hands together again. “While you were outside moping or whatever you were doing, I decided to count the Hebrew words in the entire passage of Daniel 9. I wondered if there was a numerical signature that might indicate if the passage was a complete work or if the final five verses were the only part of the passage that was numerically sealed, so to speak.”

Counting the words in a whole chapter of the Bible? My outdoor ramble sounded much more relaxing. I put my elbows on the table and then my chin on my fists and leaned toward the notepad as Cadence circled the number *462*.

“There are four hundred and sixty-two words in Daniel chapter 9. The eighteen words of verse 15 are the exact numerical center of the passage. There are exactly 222 words before Daniel 9:15 and 222 words after.”

I lifted my brows. “You doubled-checked the word count?”

“No. I tripled-checked the word count. What’s more, you can break the passage down into four separate stanzas or themes centered around the eighteen words of verse 15. There are three 7-verse groupings, and the final five groupings contain the prophecy of seven sevens. Look at it this way.” Cadence did some quick scribbling.

Verse Groups: (7 + 7) + 1 + (7 + 5) = 27 Verses

Words: (222) + 18 + (222) = 462 Words

“While the verse groupings are different between the two halves of the prophecy, the word counts are exactly the same.” She pointed to her equation.

(222) + 18 + (222)

“If you look closely at each of the 7 verse groups, you’ll find that each has a theme with its own numerical center of 13 or 26 words.” She grinned at me. “In a way, it’s as if the author signed the chapter with the numerical value of Yahweh’s name. Did you know that Daniel 9 is the only chapter in the book of Daniel where Yahweh’s name is used?”

I held up my hand. “Wait a second.” Something had just bubbled to the surface of my mind. The bubble had popped before I identified it. It had something to do with the number *222*.

“What?”

“Can I see the notepad for a second?” I asked, reaching for it and turning pages. “Didn’t we have the number *222* in one of our other ciphers?”

She let her arm fall across the table. “I don’t remember.”

“I think we have. I’m almost certain of it. I just can’t remember where.” I kept flipping pages until I reached our notes on the fifth cipher, then I punched the spot where we had figured out the numerical value of Haggai 2:19 with my index finger. I looked at Cadence, and Cadence looked at the four Hebrew letters on the notepad.

אברכ

The hair on my arms stood up—an all-too-common occurrence lately.

“*Barak.*” I wrote the word out again with the number value next to it.

אברכ = 223

"The Hebrew word for *bless* or *blessing*?" Cadence placed her finger under the word value. "I hate to point out the obvious, genius, but the word value there is 223, not 222."

"Yes, exactly. That's why I didn't remember right away. The form of *barak* used here in Haggai is not the root form." I wrote the word out again in its root form.

ברכ = 222

A new sparkle ignited in Cadence's eyes. I had a hard time meeting her gaze as I guessed what she was thinking. My father's fifth cipher pointed to a blessing, a *barak*, that promised salvation. The blessing that my father and my dreams were telling me was Yeshua, 391. This two-thousand-five-hundred-year-old prophecy just happened to tell of a promised Messiah who would bring salvation and just happened to be designed so that its word count emphasized the numerical value of the word *barak,* or blessing. I turned back to our notes on Daniel 9.

Verse Groups: (7 + 7) + 1 + (7 + 5) = 27 Verses
Words: (222) + 18 + (222) = 462 Words

"A blessing that promised salvation," I said quietly to myself. I just shook my head. Brick by brick, my father's riddles were breaking down my skepticism. And hope was seeping in.

Cadence interrupted my thoughts by taking hold of the notepad. My hands were on it, and she gently tugged. "May I?"

I released the pad. It was Cadence's turn to start flipping through the pages.

"Remember the third cipher? Where Yahweh made a covenant with Abraham?" Cadence glanced at me while she kept turning pages.

"I do. So?"

"Do you remember what Yahweh promised Abraham because of his faith?"

I jerked my head up. "He promised Abraham that in his seed, all nations of the world would be …"

"Blessed!" we said together.

Cadence reached our notes on the third cipher. There it was. Another blessing that promised Salvation. At least, that was how the New Testament followers of Jesus understood the oath Yahweh swore with Abraham. Cadence read the New Testament passages that we had written in our notes.

Galatians 3:14-16

That the blessing of Abraham might come on the Gentiles through Jesus Christ; that we might receive the promise of the Spirit through faith. Brethren, I speak after the manner of men; Though *it be* but a man's covenant, yet *if it be* confirmed, no man disannulleth, or addeth thereto. Now to Abraham and his seed were the promises made. He saith not, And to seeds, as of many; but as of one, And to thy seed, which is Christ.

Acts 3:25-26

Ye are the children of the prophets, and of the covenant which God made with our fathers, saying unto Abraham, And in thy seed shall all the kindreds of the earth be blessed. Unto you first God, having raised up his Son Jesus, sent him to bless you, in turning away every one of you from his iniquities.

When she had finished, she asked, "What do you want to wager that blessing Yahweh promised Abraham in Genesis 22 is the word *barak*?"

I shook my head. "My betting days are over, Cadence," I said soberly. I reached for the interlinear Bible on the table and opened it to Genesis 22. I read the English version of verses 16-18 out loud.

Genesis 22:16-18

And said, By myself have I sworn, saith YHWH, for because thou hast done this thing, and hast not withheld thy son, thine only *son*: That in *blessing* I will *bless* thee, and in multiplying I will multiply thy seed as the stars of the heaven, and as the sand which *is* upon the sea shore; and thy seed shall possess the gate of his enemies; [18] And in thy seed shall all the nations of the earth be *blessed*; because thou hast obeyed my voice.

As I read, I underlined the word *barak/blessing* in both the Hebrew and English versions of the passage. Right there in verse 17 was the root form of the word *barak.* The blessing, the 222 promised to Abraham's seed. Out of curiosity, I got up and walked over to my father's bookshelf by the window. I pulled down a concordance. I opened it and searched for the word *barak.* I looked up when I'd read the results.

"Genesis 22:17 is the first occurrence of the root form of the Hebrew word *barak* in the Hebrew Bible."

"Uh-huh …"

I snapped the concordance shut and set it on my father's desk, then returned to the kitchen table and sat down my hands hanging at my side. "Okay, Okay," I said to my sister's tentative smile. "You were right. It couldn't be an accident. Whoever wrote and designed the word structure of Daniel 9 most likely had the promised blessing of Genesis 22 in mind." I held up my hand. "But that still doesn't prove that the Messiah of Daniel 9 is talking about Jesus."

"Fair enough," Cadence said with a knowing look. "Not yet, anyway."

I could only shake my head. "I wish I had your faith, Sis."

When I started to get up again, Cadence gave an apologetic wrinkle of her nose. "One more thing? Please?"

I laughed at her kid-like enthusiasm. "Okay, Sis, one more thing. That's it and then I'm going to bed. I'm wasted."

"Promise," she said. "Here, take a look at this."

Cadence pointed at the snippet of *pi* that our father had used as his cipher key. She'd underlined two additional places in the string of four hundred and eighteen digits.

I contained a sigh. "Shoot."

"I know this is stretching things a bit, but it is such a strange—call it—coincidence, I found it fascinating. We think Dad chose this section of *pi* because it was the first occurrence of the numerical value of Yeshua's name. But there are also at least two more first occurrences in this string of *pi*."

Cadence pointed at the *7777* she had underlined. "This 7777 is the first occurrence of a triple or quadruple 7 in *pi*. Just as there are two hundred and four Hebrew letters preceding the seven sevens of Daniel 9:23-27, there are two hundred and four digits of *pi* between 26-391-41 and 7777."

She indicated the places in the string of numbers where she'd underlined the groupings.

2639141992726042699227967823547816360093417216412199
924586315030286182974555706749838505494588586926995
690927210797509302955321165344987202755960236480665
499119881834797753566369807426542527862551818417574
672890977727938000816470600161452491921732172147723
501414419735685481613611573525521334757418494684385
233239073941433345477624168625189835694855620992192
221842725502542568876717904946016534668049886272327
917860857

Cadence raised her face. “Makes you wonder just a little bit, doesn’t it? How about this?” She touched the pad where she had underlined *222*. “This triple 2 is also the first occurrence of the number in *pi*. So what do you think? Pretty cool, isn’t it?”

“Looks like Dad chose the best piece of pie.”

Cadence laughed and punched me in the arm. “I’m serious, Timbre. What do you think?”

My smile faded. “I don’t know what to think. Neat coincidence? Dad got lucky? Intentional? I don’t know? I’ll admit it is cool, even if it wasn’t intentional. If God exists, maybe He has a good sense of humor, and He just threw those numbers in there to give us pause. To see if anyone was paying attention. Not trying to give definitive proof but, you know, just a wake-up call. You know, like … ‘Hey, you, crazy creation of mine, *pay* attention!’”

Cadence laughed again at my pun.

I stood up and yawned. Cadence had gone back to searching the digits of *pi* for whatever mysteries they might hide, a look of pleasant concentration on her face. *More power to you, Sis. More power to you.*

It was a comforting idea to think that maybe there was a God out there who wanted to be found by those who searched for Him, a God who wanted to bless those who had faith like Abraham and my father. A blessing like my father had found stamped upon the Bible's greatest Messianic prophecy. A *barak*, a blessing, a 222.

I gently laid a hand on my sister's head as I started to turn. She placed a finger to mark her spot in the endless string of numbers and looked up. Her expression was one of understanding, of faith, of peace that had been tempered with wisdom in the forge of suffering. The words my grandmother had written in my father's Bible came cascading into my thoughts again. *I know in whom I believe ... may he bless and keep ...*

Based upon what we had learned from my father's ciphers, my grandmother's faith had been rewarded.

My hand was still on Cadence's head, and she was looking at me funny now.

"What?" she asked.

In a way I couldn't describe, I felt my grandmother's words reaching out to me. Flushing, I patted my sister's head gently. Quietly, I spoke the thoughts I didn't fully understand. Thoughts that I could not contain.

"If Yahweh does exist, Sis, may He bless and keep you. May His face shine upon you and bring peace."

As I turned away, Cadence glowed. She only spoke as my hand reached for the door to the bunkroom. She said the words I'd left out. She said them to me. She said them for me.

"*I know in whom I have believed*, Timbre Plummer. *And I am pursuaded that He is able to keep that which I've committed unto Him*."

My sister's words hung in the air, and her soft weeping chased me to my bed.

Chapter 96

Checkered Past

I stood on black-and-white tiles in an expanse without walls—one foot on a black tile, one foot on a white. I counted 37 tiles stretching away in front of me on a glowing, polished, checkered causeway six tiles wide. I froze in terror, for on my left and right yawned an empty void. Dropping onto shaking hands and knees, I started to crawl.

I marked my progress by counting in a hollow voice. "Six, twelve, eighteen, twenty-four …" I lost my sense of time. There was only the counting. Then I sensed the end. On bruised knees and tender palms, I reached it. My tongue was stiff and dry, my voice hoarse and raspy as I added the sums of the final four rows while my fingers curled over the edge.

"204, 210, 216, 222" I croaked.

Across the void I faced, the checkered path continued, but it was unattainable. I gazed down with dread, and my fingers came free of the edge as I recoiled. Nine steps led down to my hallway of dreams. I could see no steps leading back out.

Tile shattered behind me, and I whisked my head around. Row after row of the tiled causeway started to fall—each tile shattering on the unforgiving stones of the dark hallway below. The screeching cascade of sound assaulted me as tiles fell like dominos, row after row. I spun and, with my foot, felt blindly for the first narrow step. As the final row of tile tumbled, I crouched on the stone step on one leg, shaking. I clasped onto the step as the shattering roar finally stopped. Finding the edge of the next step with my free foot, I lowered my weight onto it, but I lost purchase and fell. Then it was a tumbling, sliding avalanche of muscle and bone down the final 7 steps.

I lay broken and paralyzed at the bottom, the only sight, a sliver of light outlining a door. Then a shadow passed in front of the light. Softly and hesitantly, bare knuckles rapped on hard wood. I couldn't call out. The knocking grew louder and more insistent. I fought for words. None came.

Relief swept over me as the sliver of light grew. The door opened. Light flooded the room. Cadence's cheerful expression turned to concern. My paralyzed limbs slowly regained their strength. I pulled myself off the floor and sat on the edge of my bunk.

"Rough night?" Cadence asked—more of a statement than a question.

I nodded. Even though my limbs worked, my tongue still stuck to the roof of my mouth. I stood up and leveled a stare at Cadence, who hovered in the doorway. "If hell is anything like my nightmares …"

A faraway look came over Cadence's face. With a nearly imperceptible shake of her head, she forced a sympathetic smile. "Breakfast is ready."

She left the door open, and soon the mouth-watering scents of bacon and a hint of floury biscuits flavored the air. The smells grounded me. Thank God I was not trapped in the world of my dreams.

We ate breakfast in a silence punctuated by frequent glances from Cadence. She was probably thinking I was cracking up. Maybe I was. The struggle between my skepticism and the faith and hope nurtured by my father's ciphers was taking a toll. Why was I fighting it so hard? My rejection of faith and the standards I had been taught had led me down a dead-end alley where only terror lurked. Seeing the world through my father's perspective these past several weeks had brought the first real peace and hope into my life in a long time. Even my troubles with Benito Silva didn't seem insurmountable anymore.

Most important of all, Cadence and I had rebuilt a relationship that seemed stronger and more real than anything we'd had growing up. Her companionship had given me a new sense of purpose, a renewed understanding of the importance of family, of relationships.

Part of me didn't want our quest to solve my father's ciphers to end. We were running out of time, but I wasn't ready. These dreams warned that the tension inside me was building to a breaking point.

Chapter 97

Redirection

The lawyer surveyed the scene of the nightclub fire with growing agitation. The smell of scorched wood, carbonized rubber, and melted plastic was so strong he could taste it. The charred remains lay in piles the fire department had left after extinguishing the last glowing ember. Only the steel-and-concrete emergency stairwell remained. Charred and black, it rose from the burned rubble like a lonely pier waiting for a ship that would never come. A burned-out Cadillac rested incongruously inside the ruins.

None of it made any sense. Why had his tracking device visited this location? Had the briefcase been stolen? Had Cadence and Timbre come here for some unaccountable reason? The newspaper he'd picked up in the airport coffee shop had not been much help either. All it said was that the building had burned, arson was suspected, there had been no fatalities, and the investigation was ongoing.

The lawyer turned to leave but stopped when a long narrow cylindrical object sticking out of a pile of debris near what had once been the front of the building caught his eye. He glanced around before lifting the caution tape and approaching the pile. Kneeling, he pulled a carbon-fiber arrow out of the ashes—a Carbon Express made by Feradyne Outdoors. Other than a partially melted feather, the arrow showed no other sign of heat damage. Now, how was that possible? How had investigators missed it? It couldn't have been in the building when it burned, so that meant … what? Was it left behind after?

The lawyer stood and tossed the arrow back on the pile. Maybe the front of the building had fallen after the fire had been mostly extinguished and had landed on top of the arrow. He brushed his hands off and turned back toward his car. The arrow told him one thing, though.

Back in the car, he checked the location of the tracking device he'd hidden in Timbre's briefcase. It was now outside Biloxi, Mississippi, heading east on I-10. Follow or wait? If he followed and it wasn't Timbre and Cadence, it might all be over before he got back here. If he waited, it might all be over before he got to them. He needed more information. Maybe he'd find it by going to where they'd been.

A half-hour later, the lawyer found the spray-painted message on the glass door to the patio. So Cadence had been taken by Benito Silva, and Timbre had gone after her. The Jeep was gone. The White Wolf had been burned to the ground. The carbon-fiber arrow discovered in the ruins was the same as those hanging in the quiver on the wall of the garage.

Timbre had faced the wolf in his den with a bow and arrow. The stern lines of his mouth cracked a bit. *Son of Gun.* That would have been something to see. The lawyer filed the thoughts away. Right now, he needed to figure out his next step.

Cadence and Timbre were driving the Jeep through Mississippi, or else something much worse and much more complicated was going on. How could he be sure? *Think.*

He left the window and returned to the garage. On the wall opposite the garage door, he pulled open the bottom drawer of the gray metal filing cabinet marked *manuals*. He riffled through it until he found what he was looking for. His lips turned up in a grim smile as he pulled out his phone and dialed the number on the piece of paper.

"Lojack. This is Terrance. How may I help you?"

"Hi, Terrance," the lawyer replied. "I'd like to turn on the Lojack tracking system for my Jeep Grand Cherokee."

Chapter 98

A Book Cipher

I waited for Cadence in the Jeep outside the Black Bean Coffee Company. We'd made the three-and-a-half-hour drive to Tucson with few words between us. We were both off today. My laptop sat open on my legs, the coffee shop's Wi-Fi login page displayed in my web browser.

Cadence came through the glass doors a minute later with two coffees. She slid into the car and handed me a piece of paper with the shop's Wi-Fi login. I set the paper above the keyboard and began typing. Cadence secured my coffee in the cup holder and sipped her brew as she watched.

When the Lazarus Cipher webpage came up, I looked over at her. "Ready?"

Cadence blew on her hot coffee, making creamy-white trails in her cup. She nodded once. I typed the Hebrew words *sheba shebuwa* into the answer spaces provided and pressed *enter*. Moments later, the page refreshed, and we were staring at our father's 7th cipher. I stuck my palm out flat. Cadence gave me a five and a smile.

This cipher differed from the others. It was not a grid of Hebrew letters but three columns. Cadence read the instructions.

In its original form, this enciphered passage is 13 Hebrew words. These words pose a Biblical riddle that has challenged some of the greatest minds in history. The key to the riddle is hidden in seven and its significance revealed by swear.

If you can decipher this passage and solve the riddle, the inheritance is yours.

Your answer will be the 5 numbers that lie between the א *and* ת.

אודה	הוה	ביה
אהבו	אבי	ונמצא
יהוה	ויבא	אתתי
ביה	ידא	ובטחת
גאו	יה	לתשועה
האב	זבחיהם	תתהללי
א	יהוה	ומהלל
א	באלם	תתהללי
הבו	אוהב	אבותיו
ויהוה	אב	הודו
באה	ואביו	ושאלתם
וביהוה	הא	הראית
ואהבהו	ואביו	סאים
ואב	אהי	תקשיב
הבה	אהבי	ביה
באהבה	ואב	ותאות
גאו	האב	וקדשת
יהוה	הבט	ותקופתו
ואהבה	כאב	וברכתיה
א	ואהב	נתעלסה
כבדו	ואביה	באמרתך
א	ואב	והמהללי
אביו	ב	תכבדני
אבא	אב	רזא
גבהא	כאב	אתותיו
אהבה	א	והאחת

Enter your answer in the spaces provided.
Only one attempt allowed per 24 hours.

א___ ___ ___ . ___ ___ת

I rubbed my jaw. "So … we are looking for a passage of Scripture that is 13 words long?"

"Not just any passage, but a Biblical riddle that has challenged generations of scholars." With that dramatic pronouncement, she raised her eyebrows.

"13 words? Intentional?"

"Intentional." As Cadence studied the cipher and its clues, she spoke softly to herself. "All the ciphers have had some connection to the number *13*. He sees some symbolism attached to it."

"What about his cryptic statement that the key to the riddle is hidden in seven and revealed by swear?"

"Other than what we already know from the Abraham cipher, I have no idea how it might apply here." Cadence pointed at the column of Hebrew letters and words. "I think we have a problem, though."

I started to ask what the problem was when a black Escalade pulled into the parking space next to us. I reached for the door lock and flipped the switch. Then I closed my laptop and slid it over onto Cadence's lap. Starting the car, I jerked the lever into reverse, my heart hammering. Cadence held onto my computer while plunking her coffee into the holder. When a soccer mom in spandex and a tank top stepped out of the vehicle, I relaxed my grip and let out a deep breath.

Cadence met my glance. “What was that about?”

“We need to get going,” I said. “If someone is watching the server, they know where we are right now. Let’s put some distance between us and this location.”

She raised her right eyebrow at me.

“What?”

“Don’t you think you are being a little too paranoid?”

“You are the one who suggested they might be tracing our IP.” I opened my hands in frustration. “ After what has happened each time we’ve entered an answer to one of these ciphers? In a word, no. Probably not being paranoid enough.”

Cadence sighed. “Just so you know, I’m tired of running.” She folded her arms across her chest.

“Me, too, okay?” I backed the Jeep out. “I’m sorry we have to run from my screw-ups, but I just don’t want to take any more chances. At least not until we solve this thing.”

“I know. I know you’re right,” Cadence said, letting out a long breath.

“Where to, then?”

“Doesn’t matter, I guess. We can drive across town and find a quiet place to work on the cipher. We might need internet access to track down some more information. I’d rather do what searching we need from here in Tucson rather than leave a possible digital trail back to the cabin.”

We settled on Reid Park next to the Reid Park Zoo. As I drove, Cadence talked.

“As I was saying earlier, Timbre, we’ve got a problem. I think this is a book cipher.”

“A what?” I gave her a glance. The guy in front of me was driving ten under the speed limit, and the guy behind me was right on my bumper, flashing his lights as if I was the problem.

“A book cipher,” she repeated.

"I heard you the first time. What is a book cipher?" I growled my frustration at the guy behind me, and Cadence gave me a dangerous look. If I wasn't careful, I'd have a way bigger problem on my hands than an impatient rich kid in a BMW riding my bumper. I took a deep breath. "Sorry. The punk behind me is starting to get on my nerves."

A long, blaring blast from the guy's horn pushed me over the edge. I slammed on my brakes and stopped in the middle of traffic. I started to reach for the door handle. Cadence grabbed my arm.

"Let it go," she said, her fingers like talons on my arm. "We don't have time for this."

I hesitated. The guy behind me was still laying on the horn. His hand gestures were getting more violent, and other cars now added their horns to the growing clamor. Cadence squeezed harder. Her piercing grasp brought me back to sanity. She let go, and I rubbed the marks on my arm. I took a deep breath and put the car back in gear.

As we started to move again, the guy behind me jerked out into a break in oncoming traffic, crossing the double yellow line. As he screamed by me, he released the wheel and saluted me with violent, vulgar gestures.

My jaw dropped. "Did you see that idiot?"

Cadence pressed her lips together.

Seconds later, blue and red lights flashed behind me. I pulled to the side, half expecting to get a ticket. The police cruiser raced by. I peeked over at Cadence, who gave me a *I told you so* look. I couldn't help the smile.

Half a mile farther up the road, my smile got even bigger when we saw the BMW on the side of the road with the cop behind him. I slowed as I went by and gave the BMW driver a thumbs up. He gave me more honking and hand gestures. This brought the police officer out of his car in a big rush. I laughed. Cadence didn't.

"What's wrong with you?" she asked after a long silence.

I did a double-take. "What you mean, what's wrong with me? The guy was a jerk."

"And you nearly escalated it because you can't keep your temper in check."

"The guy was a jerk, Sis."

"He's not the only one."

More silence. I was no mind reader, but Cadence's sharp breaths and lifted chin as she stared out her window practically shouted that I'd upset her. My anger receded. It left behind a gnawing hole in my stomach. I pulled off the road and eased the Jeep under a large elm tree in an empty parking lot at Reid Park.

"Come on, Caden. I'm sorry." I touched her arm, but she jerked away.

The action reminded me how far we'd come from our meeting in Pincer's office. Cadence had recoiled then, too. I put both hands on the steering wheel. I didn't want to lose what we'd rebuilt. Only Cadence could have kept me from jumping out of the car and yanking that impatient jerk through his window. I still had a taste for it. I breathed deep and then let it out very slowly. My sister was my anchor now. Without her, I was headed for crashing waves and rocky shores.

"What do you want from me?" I asked.

She said nothing for a painfully long time. Finally, she faced me, blinking back moisture. "I want you to stick around for a while. If you keep running into trouble like some mad berserker, you are going to get yourself killed."

"Cadence …"

She rested a shaking hand on my arm. "Putting a gun to your head and pulling the trigger is not the only way to commit suicide, Timbre. I lost Dad. You are the only family I have left. I'm afraid," she said haltingly.

"Afraid of what?"

"Afraid of going back."

"Back to rehab?"

Cadence shook her head violently and rolled her eyes. "I'm never going back to rehab." The dark certainty of her statement made me instantly tense.

"Afraid of going back where, then?"

"The dark, hopeless hell you've helped me crawl out of. I'm starting to see a way through this mess I've made of my life. Dad's ciphers are restoring my faith and giving me hope that I can live down the horrors." Cadence's breath caught. Her mask of enthusiasm and vitality slipped down for a moment. Pain and fear still lurked beneath, like two panthers waiting to spring upon their terrified prey.

The vinyl of the steering wheel creaked as my white-knuckled hands twisted it back and forth. My tendons felt like they would burst from my corded arms. Cadence wasn't the only one hanging by a strand of spider silk. One thing I knew. If I didn't control the burning inside of me, I would jeopardize my sister's future. That was a fate even worse than a life trapped in the hallway of my nightmares. I pressed my feet into the rubber mats as if I were pushing my demons out through the floorboard of the car. My seat strained with the pressure. My arms shook. I stared into my sister's eyes, and the truth hit me like a bullet train.

I didn't have what it would take to see my sister safely through. That realization terrified me like nothing in my life ever had. I needed help, and I had no one I could turn to. I laid my head against the steering wheel, closed my eyes, and rocked my forehead back and forth. I was saying the words even before my conscious mind realized the effort.

Dear God, I need your help. If you are out there somewhere, please hear me. Father, I plead for my sister's life. Help her, Father. I know it is not worth much, but I gladly give you mine in exchange.

I stopped moving and opened my eyes. Cadence's furrowed brow and the downturned ends of her mouth told me I hadn't spoken out loud. There was no obvious miracle in my prayer. None that I could see or feel, anyway. I had nothing else left to hang on to, so I took this snail's leap of faith, hoping my despairing cry reached the ears of Someone who cared.

Slowly, the tension in my body bled away.

"Okay, Sis, we can pull through this together. I'm sorry for losing control. I'll try to keep that dungeon door closed from now on. We can do this, right? You and me?"

Cadence brushed her eyes with her sleeve. "We can do this, Timmy. We three."

I searched her face. Had I spoken out loud, after all? I shook it off with a laugh. We were back on track.

"So … you want to tell me what I need to know about a book cipher?"

Chapter 99

The Book

“A book cipher is a style of encryption that uses a specific book known only to the cryptographer and the intended recipient of his message. The book is the means by which the message is encrypted and decrypted,” Cadence said, warming to the subject as she opened my laptop farther and tilted it toward me.

“How’s that?”

“Typically, a book cipher is a series of numbers which represent the page number, sentence number, and word or even a letter. For example, if I wanted to say camels are hairy, I would pick a book and look for a page with the word *camel* on it.” Cadence pointed at the Hebrew word in the first column of the cipher. “Because Dad has been using the value of Hebrew letters to represent numbers, it’s likely that the value of the Hebrew word in the first column represents the page number.”

“That makes sense.” I took the moment to grab my first swig of lukewarm coffee.

She pointed at the first word in the second column. “This column might represent the sentence or the paragraph where the word is located. And the final column would most likely give us where the word or letter is located in the sentence.”

"That doesn’t sound too difficult to solve."

"It's not. Solving it is the easy part. Knowing which book to use is the hard part."

I took another swig of coffee. "I don't see what's so hard about that."

Cadence lifted her brows and gave a slow blink. “Really?” "Yeah, really. The book will undoubtedly be the Bible. What other book would Dad use?"

Cadence laughed outright. She rolled her eyes at me. "Okay, genius. Which Bible do we use to solve this?"

"What do you mean, which one?” I scoffed. "Can't we just use any one we find?

"How many versions of the Bible are there, Timbre?"

"I don't know—a lot, I guess."

"Are they all formatted the same? Do all have the same type size? Will all of these different Bibles have the same page numbering system?”

I deflated with a sigh. "I guess that could be a problem."

"It's more than a problem, Timbre. In the past, Dad has made it so that we can either solve the riddle or the cipher to get the answer. Not anymore. We have to solve this cipher. We can’t sidestep it or work around it because the cipher is the only way to get to the riddle. Once we have the riddle, only then can we complete the 7th cipher. To do all that, we must first determine the exact version of the Bible Dad used to encrypt his message. Without that book, all our efforts to date have been for nothing.”

Well, that was grim. "Any ideas?" I asked finally.

She pointed just below the cipher. "Dad must have left us the answer in these verses.”

I blew out a breath. "How could any of these verses tell us what Bible Dad used?"

"I don't know, Timbre. That is what we will have to find out."

She grabbed her coffee, and we both started reading at the same time.

Genesis 1:14
And God said, Let there be lights in the firmament of the heaven to divide the day from the night; and let them be for signs, and for seasons, and for days, and years:

Hebrews 4:14
Seeing then that we have a great high priest, that is passed into the heavens, Jesus the Son of God, let us hold fast *our* profession.

Ephesians 2:13-14
But now in Christ Jesus ye who sometimes were far off are made nigh by the blood of Christ. For he is our peace, who hath made both one, and hath broken down the middle wall of partition *between us*;

Numbers 29:13
And ye shall offer a burnt offering, a sacrifice made by fire, of a sweet savour unto YHWH; 13 young bullocks, 2 rams, *and 14* lambs of the first year; they shall be without blemish:

2nd Timothy 1:12
... I know in who I have believed and am persuaded that he is able to keep that which I've committed unto him against that day.

My breath caught as I started reading the final verse. Our eyes met. These were the words that had left Cadence weeping several nights before.

I laid my head back against the headrest and closed my eyes. Righteous defeat. It was a punishment that fit the crime.

"I know the Bible Dad used," I murmured turning to Cadence.

Her eyes widened. But there was more in her look than surprise. Was it relief, nervousness, or something else? "How do you know that?" That same undercurrent of tension pierced her voice.

I inclined my head to one side. "You okay?"

Cadence couldn't meet my gaze. "I'm fine," she said, looking down at the laptop on her knees. "How do you know which Bible Dad used?" she repeated softly.

"It was the verse I quoted to you the other night. The verse Grandmother Plummer wrote in Dad's Bible. He kept his Bible in the briefcase."

Cadence nodded sadly like she already knew the answer. "Where is it now?"

"I don't know."

"You don't know?"

"I took it out. It made me uncomfortable." There it was—the awful truth. Our father had left us an inheritance, and the final key was his Bible. The very Bible I had once possessed and then discarded.

Cadence was silent then.

I turned away from my sister's intent stare. That night came back to me like it happened yesterday. "It was my birthday," I began. "My dorm buddies threw a surprise party for me in Kevin's room down the hall. It was a poker party with lots of booze … and women." My face flushed. "Lots of alcohol. Poker chips were stacked all over the table. It was a hot night, and all us guys were in our boxer shorts. Some of the girls had even less clothes on than the guys. It was a typical raunchy dorm room party." I opened my eyes and looked at Cadence. There was no judgment in her expression, just realization and curiosity.

"So what happened?" she asked.

"There was a hard knock on the door. Several of us hollered for whoever it was to come on it. The door opened. Dad stood there straight and proud with a smile on his face. I rose when I saw him. He dropped his briefcase. His smile disappeared. It was like he was rooted to the floor. What he saw clearly embarrassed him, but he could not turn away. Veronica, my girlfriend at the time, recognized my father right away. We could have been twins if it wasn't for the age difference. Anyway, she said something about needing another plumber. Dad fled." I cringed. "Our proud, Special Forces Dad, who'd never run from anything or anyone in his life, turned and ran from a half-naked, vulgar young woman."

Cadence gasped and put her hand over her mouth.

I forced the rest out. "He literally ran down the dorm hall like he was being chased by an enemy horde. I followed, his briefcase in my hand. He was at the stairs before I made it halfway down the hall. He wouldn't stop when I called." I tugged the case sitting between our seats onto my lap and ran my hands over its familiar seams and worn leather sides. "He never asked for it back, Cadence. All those treasures of his hidden inside," I said in almost a whisper. "And he never came back."

"Oh, Timmy. I'm so sorry." Cadence laid her hand on my arm.

I nodded, swallowing hard as I touched the briefcase's latches. "It took me weeks to figure out the combo. It was our birthdays. I saw his Bible the first time I opened the case. I didn't find the hidden panel and his treasures till much later.

After that, I kept the briefcase by my side wherever I went. I don't know if I hoped he'd show up someday and I'd have it waiting for him, or maybe I just needed to drag my kryptonite along with me wherever I went as some sort of penance. But the briefcase has been the one constant in my life for the past eight years. Eventually, I took Dad's Bible out—partially out of respect and partly because it … well, it bothered my conscience. Especially considering some of the places I started to frequent."

"Where did you put it?"

I took another long breath and let it out slowly. "In my dorm room closet. After college, after I married Jenny, I put it on a bookshelf in my office at home. That was three years and one divorce ago. I didn't take Dad's Bible when I left."

After that, I just sat there staring at my father's briefcase. Tears and bitter laughter came at the same time. This was the richest kind of irony. Exactly what I deserved.

I looked at my sister with wet eyes. "An ungrateful, shameful son does not deserve an inheritance. I'm sorry, Cadence. So sorry that my shame will cost you too."

Cadence put her hand on mine where it rested on the briefcase. Regret shadowed her eyes as well. Regret and understanding that was not judgmental. "I …" Her face flushed, but she didn't finish the thought. When she spoke again, I could barely hear her. "A shameful daughter doesn't deserve an inheritance either."

We sat in silence then for a long time. If Cadence's thoughts were anything like mine, it was a sad and discouraging journey. Where did we go from here? Would we have the strength and character to continue to rebuild our lives?

"What about Jenny?" Cadence asked finally. "Could she still have the Bible?"

"I doubt it, but I guess it is possible. When we got divorced, she wasn't a very religious person. I doubt she kept it. If it had anything to do with me, she probably burned it."

Cadence went pale, her hands twisting in her lap. "Don't say that," she whispered. "don't say that." She didn't look up when she spoke again. She got as far as, "I …" and stopped again. When she finally faced me, the wrinkles on her lips and at the corners of her eyes aged her. "Maybe she kept it? You never know."

Why such desperation in her voice? It put me in a terrible position.

I didn't want to call Jenny, this I knew for sure. My stomach knotted even thinking about talking to her. Our divorce had been brutal and mean. She'd gotten the house and my 401K. She'd proven that I'd gambled a large portion of our income away, so the judge had also awarded her our liquid assets. Truth was, our problems had been my fault. She shouldn't have married me. She'd tried to make it work for a while. And I played poker and left her alone at night. What a freaking jerk I'd been. Still was, I corrected myself after remembering my sister's words from earlier.

My fingers tightened around the briefcase. "You want me to call?"

"It's worth a try, don't you think?"

"Okay." I pulled my last prepaid phone out of the briefcase, took a deep breath, and let it out slowly as I punched in the number. Then I closed my eyes and laid my head back against the soft fabric of the headrest.

"Hello?" It was the soft, beautiful voice I remembered.

Chapter 100

Lost and Found

The voice brought back a crushing wave of memories. Some good. Many bad. My throat closed up, and Jenny gave a cheery "hello" again. I started to lower the phone. I'd rather talk to Benito Silva with a gun to my head than my ex-wife. The look I got from Cadence made me place the cell back to my ear.

"Jenny?" I said. This time, it was she who was silent. Had she hung up? "Hello, Jenny, this is Timbre." Still silence. "Are you there?"

"What do you want?" The cheer had faded to lifelessness.

Cadence started to roll her hands like I should say something. I gave her a pleading look. This was too painful, too difficult. Years of resentment and anger had eroded any common ground Jenny and I might have stood on. I exhaled into the phone slowly.

"How are you doing?" I finally asked.

"Better, now that you are no longer around."

I bit my tongue to stop the caustic reply that came all too easy. This was the mother of my child. In the beginning, we'd had good times. I loved her once. Maybe I still did a little. Maybe that was why it was so hard to talk to her now.

"What do you want, Timbre? I'm sure you didn't call me after all these years just to ask how I was doing." Besides the animosity in her tone, curiosity lilted. How strange. Almost as if she expected my call.

"Sorry to bother you, Jenny. I wouldn't have called, but I'm looking for my father's Bible. I left it on the bookshelf in my office. Do you by any chance know where it might be?"

Her mocking laugh stabbed like a burning knife in the gut. After a moment of silence and a muffled sob, Jenny spoke. "Bit late to get religion, isn't it, Timbre? A broken marriage and dead daughter, and now you want to talk to God? After all this time, you call me up and you ask for a Bible? Really? You son of a …" More muffled sobs kept her from continuing.

Why didn't she hang up? Anger, bitterness, and resentment I could understand, even expect, but her soft weeping broke my heart. I should have been a more attentive husband.

Before I realized it, words flowed out of my mouth. "I'm truly sorry, Jenny. I'm sorry for forgetting to treat you like the amazing person I married. For not being there for you when Lucy died. Sorry for all the late nights playing poker when I should have been home with you. And I am sorry I upset you with my call. Most of all, I'm sorry that I didn't realize until too late that you were the best thing that ever happened to me."

I took the phone away from my ear and pressed the *end* button. After a long silence, staring straight ahead, I muttered, "Sorry you had to hear that, Cadence."

Starting my father's Jeep and pulling out of the parking lot, I turned north. It was over. I still had a few thousand dollars in my pocket. If we were careful, we could make it last a while. I didn't want to think about the future. I just wanted to get back to the peace of our grandfather's homestead.

"The cabin?" I asked Cadence.

She nodded.

We were on the outskirts of Tucson when my phone vibrated on my lap. I picked it up and read the text.

I donated all your books to Mohave Salvation Army.

I handed Cadence the phone. "We are going through Phoenix, anyway. It's a long shot, but you want to go look?"

"I do."

As I pulled onto I-10, my phone vibrated again. Cadence held it up, and my breath caught as I read the words.

I'm sorry too.

Chapter 101

I Know In Whom I have Believed

Five hours and ten Salvation Army stores later, Cadence and I climbed back into my father's Jeep. It was evening. We were both hot and discouraged. I started the Jeep and cranked up the air conditioner.

We'd started the search with hopeful enthusiasm. After each unsuccessful search, Cadence had withdrawn a little more. We'd combed through every Salvation Army store in the metropolitan Phoenix area and a couple of used bookstores as well. We'd both known it was a long shot, but we'd stuck to it doggedly. Now she sat in the passenger seat with her head down, looking at the floor.

"You okay?" I asked.

She said nothing.

"I'm sorry, Cadence. I know it's my fault. Don't worry about the money, Sis. I'll get a job or start a law practice in Payson. I'll find a way, even if I have to dig ditches. We'll camp out at Dad's cabin until they throw us out. Then we'll find someplace else. I'm not going to leave you until you're ready to make it on your own again. I promise. We'll pull through this. We are still young. This isn't the end. This is …" My breath clogged in my throat. How desperate and trite my words sounded.

"It's my fault, not yours." Cadence glanced at me with tears in her eyes.

"How could it be your fault? I was the one who—"

Cadence held her hand up. The muscles of her jaw moved, but no words came. She swiped at her eyes. "It was my Bible that was the key to the cipher."

I made a scoffing sound. "What do you mean, it was your Bible?"

"I mean, Dad wrote those words in my Bible."

"He wrote the words of 2nd Timothy in your Bible like Grandmother did in his?"

Cadence nodded. She twisted her hands in her lap and looked at me with pleading eyes, willing me to understand.

"That's terrific," I said with new hope. "But why didn't you say something earlier? We could have just gone and gotten yours instead of wasting time looking for Dad's." In response to that, Cadence's lips trembled. Then it hit me. "You don't have it anymore, either, do you?"

Cadence shook her head and studied her fingers.

"What happened to it?"

More silence. Heavy, unbroken silence.

Finally, she spoke so softly I almost couldn't hear her. "I burned it."

"Burned it?" I blurted out before I could stop myself.

Now I understood the regret and shame I'd seen earlier when we'd read the verse together. The weeping back at the cabin when I'd recited the words from our father's Bible. The silence and growing discouragement with each failed attempt to find it. What could I say? I certainly couldn't judge her. I'd done no better.

I reached for her hand that now hung limply at her side. "I'm sorry, Cadence."

"What do you have to be sorry for?" She jerked her head toward me. "You didn't burn it. I did," she cried, her voice brittle.

I shrugged. “I’m sorry for both of us, I guess.”

“He loved us, you know,” Cadence said with conviction. “He loved both of us even though we didn’t deserve it. After all our failures, our disrespect, our disgrace, he still wanted to give us an inheritance.”

“He gave us an inheritance, Sis. His ciphers are the inheritance. They reminded us of what’s really important. They’ve restored our bond as brother and sister. We may have lost our way in this race of life, but we can still finish strong. Can’t we?”

Cadence gave me a weak smile. “We can.” She was quiet again for a while, then she smiled softly.

“He was so happy when he gave me the Bible. It was my 21st birthday. He took me out to dinner. Fancy restaurant. We both got dressed up. He looked dashing in his suit, and I wore a red dress. He didn’t make an elaborate speech, but his simple, humble enthusiasm just shone. Like he was giving me the greatest treasure in the world. I remember opening the front cover and reading the words he’d written, part of 2nd Timothy 1:12 that Grandmother had written in his. I could see in his eyes that those words were meant for me. That he had committed me to God and that he believed God was able to keep me no matter what path my life took. It was the best birthday present I’ve ever gotten.”

“Why did you burn it?”

Cadence studied me. Assessing why I wanted to know? She must have seen what she wanted because she continued.

“One year later...” She paused and took a breath. “You remember I told you that I didn’t get out much. I lived in my own little bubble and spent all of my time buried in books, learning and absorbing like a dry sponge. I loved college. I was at the top of my class. I guess my friends thought I was a study snob. So, they threw me a party. I felt obligated to go. There was lots of alcohol. I didn't want to drink, but they pressured me into trying some. I got a buzz right away."

I averted my gaze. What was coming could not be good.

"The party was at someone's house off-campus. I don't even remember whose. There was a big bonfire in the backyard. I was sitting in front of the fire by myself with a wine cooler. At that time, I carried a backpack with me everywhere I went. I was always writing down new ideas in my notebooks. One of the kids got into my backpack and pulled out my Bible. He held it up in the air and shouted, 'Looks like Cadence is a religious wacko!'" She waved her hand in demonstration, then dropped it abruptly. "I can still remember all eyes turning toward me. I wanted the ground to swallow me. To this day, I don't know why I was so embarrassed. I should have stood up and owned it. But I was already nearly drunk, and I felt like a hypocrite for being there and being wasted."

I could relate. I nodded and gave her a sympathetic expression.

"Then they all started chanting it. 'Cadence is a wacko! Cadence is a wacko.' The kid with my Bible threw it to me. 'Why don't you preach to us, Cadence, on the sins of drunkenness and debauchery?' I can still remember the Bible there at my feet, my most precious possession dirty, tarnished, and dishonored, not by the dirt in which it was laying, but by my actions. I knew I wasn't worthy of it."

I waited for Cadence to continue. I could guess now what was coming, and reliving it with her made my heart ache. Her big tears started falling onto the cover of my laptop.

"So I picked it up and threw it into the fire. They all cheered." Cadence choked out the words. She looked at me with a tear-stained face. "I was a traitor to the things that I cherished and believed, and they cheered me like I was some kind of hero."

I squeezed her hand, but Cadence seemed to gain some kind of strength in sharing.

"I got really drunk after that. I woke up the next day in my dorm room bed. My head felt like it was cleaved in two, and my heart was broken. That day marked the beginning of my demise at college. It was as if God turned a switch in my mind. Where once I excelled, I now struggled. I felt like Samson must have when his hair was cut. Before, I could do wonderful things with my mind that most people couldn't even imagine. After that night, I had trouble focusing on the easy stuff. I never drank another drop of alcohol. But I started taking amphetamines to try and keep up. I started popping Adderall like they were breath mints. That led to harder drugs, and before I realized it, I was a coke addict. Then it all came crashing down when I failed my finals that year. I overdosed, and Dad sent me to rehab. That helped for a while. But my mind no longer worked like it once did, and I knew it."

I made a small, compassionate sound. Her gaze returned to me, sharper.

"I can't tell you how painful and paralyzing it is to have a gift like that and have it taken away. That, and I was still consumed with guilt. So I fell back into my old habits. Then I returned to rehab. Each stint in rehab got longer, and my clean days got shorter. I knew Dad was at his wit's end trying to figure out what to do with me. He'd tried everything he could think of. I was so twisted up inside. My guilt turned to anger. For some crazy, horrible reason, I took out my anger on Dad. Dear God, I was awful to him."

Cadence angled her body to face me, her expression vulnerable but lighter. Her shoulders straightened. Like telling it to me had been cathartic.

"So that's my story. That's why you found your sister lying on the floor in a pool of her own vomit. If you hadn't come, I would have killed myself. Learning that Dad was gone with no hope of coming back broke the final thread that held me to this world."

"Did you ever tell Dad about the Bible?"

Cadence shook her head. "No, I've never told anyone but you. And I only told you because I knew you'd understand." She placed her hand on the briefcase between us. "I've carried around my broken mind like you've been carrying Dad's briefcase."

I nodded and looked at the old leather case. I'd held onto the symbol of the sins of my past, of eight years of terrible decisions, of regrets, of anger and remorse. I knew exactly how she felt. "We make a fine pair, you and I."

"Yep. Birthdays and Bibles," she muttered almost reverently. The words hung in the air.

How strange that both of us could trace the turning points in our lives to our birthdays and, in Cadence's case, a Bible. Now here we were, years later, sitting at another turning point, and the very things we had discarded were the keys to our future. A future we could no longer grasp.

My hand started to tremble. I grabbed Cadence's arm.

"Birthdays and Bibles! Dad gave you your Bible on your twenty-first birthday. His surprise visit to my dorm room was on my twenty-first birthday," I nearly shouted.

"Yeah? So? What in the world are you talking about, Timbre?"

“I never opened the present. I felt too guilty, too angry. I just carried it around—in this case. If I’d thought it was a Bible, I probably would have gotten rid of it too.”

We both stared at the briefcase. I let go of my sister’s arm, but facing my guilt and fears paralyzed me.

“You open it,” I said.

“No way.” She lifted both hands. “You carried this thing around with you for all those years. I’m not touching it.”

“What if it’s not …”

“It is. We both know that it is. Dad left both of us a key to our inheritance. Yours is still in there, unopened.”

I reached for the briefcase and slid it around so that I could unlock it. With shaky thumbs, I rolled our birthdates into the little brass tumblers—first 514, then 314. I pushed the lever, and the locks unsnapped. I looked at Cadence and then opened the lid.

Carefully, I raised the false bottom of the case. There, nestled in its hiding spot, was my twenty-first birthday present. I removed it, opened the note stuck to the green-and-white striped paper, and read it like I had countless times before.

To Timbre,

Happy Birthday my son.

Love Dad

We both stared at it. My eyes blurred. With unsteady fingers, I tore the striped paper. Beneath was a plain brown cardboard box. Removing the lid, I looked inside. It was a Bible just like the one my father had carried. Reverently, I cradled the book and turned the leather cover to read the words written inside—the same ones I remembered from my father's Bible but written by a different hand.

Dear Timbre,

I know in whom I have believed, and am persuaded that he is able to keep that which I have committed unto him against that day.

May God bless you and keep you.

Love Dad

Cadence watched as I ran my finger over the words my father had written to me eight years ago. We had found our key to the 7th cipher. I took a deep breath and looked at her.

"Well, shall we see what mysteries Dad has—"

The Jeep's back window shattered.

Chapter 102

Shots Fired

Cadence and I ducked. My rear-view mirror revealed a yellow truck parked sideways in the center of the lot twenty feet behind us. A man with dark shades and a baseball cap pointed a pistol in our direction through the drivers side window. It looked like the muscle-bound jerk I'd thrown out of Cadence's apartment.

"Get out of the car," he yelled.

I hissed at Cadence. "Get on the floor."

Cadence slid down onto the floorboard, pulling the briefcase with her. I put the Jeep in reverse and stomped on the gas. The tires spun. Rubber melted. More shots rang out.

We hit the yellow truck with a crashing roar. Our airbags deployed. I clawed and yanked at mine until I had it out of the way. I put the Jeep in drive and floored it. Tires squealing, rubber smoking, I flew out of the parking lot and onto 22nd Street. I smiled with grim satisfaction at the yellow truck's caved-in driver's side and hanging front wheel. The drug-dealing jerk who'd taken advantage of my sister scrambled out the passenger side, gun in hand, but I turned the corner, and a building blocked my view. The next block over, I hung a left and slowed.

Cadence still crouched in front of the seat. I nudged her shoulder.

"You can get up now. He won't be following us."

She eased back into her seat. "Who was it?"

"Your old buddy. Mr. Muscle Man."

"Bobby Joe?"

"If that's the guy who was camped out in your bedroom when I found you on the floor, then yes, it was Bobby Joe." I kept checking my mirror as we drove through the residential neighborhood.

"Where are we going, Timbre?" Cadence asked after I'd made another turn.

"Back to Dad's house. We've got to get rid of the Jeep. We can't make it to the cabin with missing taillights and a bashed-in rear end. If they don't already, the police will have a description of this vehicle, and there will be a manhunt for the car involved in a shooting."

"Shouldn't we go to the police and tell them what happened?"

"Probably." I glanced over as we idled at a stoplight, my foot poised above the gas pedal. "But we only have a few more days to solve the cipher. If we go to the police, they'll have more questions than we have answers. They will surely find out about the assault on Grandfather's cabin. It won't take Perry Mason for them to put two and two together and realize I might have had something to do with burning down Benito Silva's nightclub. Then I or possibly even both of us would be stuck in jail until they decide whether to charge us or give us a medal of honor."

Cadence gave me a sideways glance. "I doubt you are going to get a medal, even if they secretly applauded your efforts."

"I'll turn myself in, and they can throw away the key once we've solved the cipher. As long as you are taken care of and we've saved Grandfather's cabin, I'll face my sins."

Chapter 103

The 7th Cipher

Half an hour later, we were back on the road in my father's four-wheel-drive Dodge Ram 2500, the wrecked Jeep safely parked in his garage. Cadence was driving now, and I had my laptop on the seat. My Bible lay open on the legal pad that rested on my knees. I peered at the 7th cipher in the glow of my screen and read the instructions loud enough for Cadence to hear them.

In its original form, this enciphered passage is 13 Hebrew words. These words pose a Biblical riddle that has challenged some of the greatest minds in history. The key to the riddle is hidden in seven and its significance revealed by swear.

If you can decipher this passage and solve the riddle, the inheritance is yours.

Your answer will be the 5 numbers that lie between the א and ת.

אודה	הוה	ביה
אהבו	אבי	ונמצא
יהוה	ויבא	אתתי
ביה	ידא	ובטחת
גאו	יה	לתשועה
האב	זבחיהם	תתהללי
א	יהוה	ומהלל
א	באלם	תתהללי
הבו	אוהב	אבותיו
ויהוה	אב	הודו
באה	ואביו	ושאלתם
וביהוה	הא	הראית
ואהבהו	ואביו	סאים
ואב	אהי	תקשיב
הבה	אהבי	ביה
באהבה	ואב	ותאות
גאו	האב	וקדשת
יהוה	הבט	ותקופתו
ואהבה	כאב	וברכתיה
א	ואהב	נתעלסה
כבדו	ואביה	באמרתך
א	ואב	והמהללי
אביו	ב	תכבדני
אבא	אב	רזא
גבהא	כאב	אתותיו
אהבה	א	והאחת

Enter your answer in the spaces provided.
Only one attempt allowed per 24 hours.

ת__ __ . __ __ __א

"So you're telling me that if this is a book cipher, the first column is likely the page number?" I asked, picking up where we'd left off when Bobby Joe had shot out our window.

Cadence didn't answer right away. We were on a particularly winding stretch of 87 this side of Payson. She had both hands on the wheel. She kept her eyes on the road when she responded.

"Yes, the first column should represent the page number, the next column the verse number, and the final column the word or letter in that verse. The third column is probably the word, though. If we were looking for the individual letters for the 13 words Dad ciphered, the column would be a lot longer."

"Got it." Out loud, I read the first three keywords in the top row. "*YA be praise* is a rough translation of the first row. The Hebrew letter value of each of those words is 17, 16, 16."

Cadence nodded. "In your Bible, look for page 17, verse 16, and word 16."

I flipped through the first few pages of the Bible. Page 17 was Genesis 22. If the second column was the verse number, then the verse was Genesis 22:16.

"You were right about this being a book cipher, Sis. Dad used Genesis 22:16 for the location of his first word."

Cadence gave me a quick smile. "This is the final cipher. If Dad is true to form, this one will be special. By using Genesis 22:16, he's reminding us about the oath Yahweh swore with Abraham. I'll bet you, each of the verses Dad uses in this cipher will have significance to his overall theme."

She was probably right. This cipher was the final prize, his magnum opus. I copied the verse onto my notepad with an anticipatory smile.

"Can you drive and count at the same time?" I asked.

"Sure, just as long as you don't expect me to count and read at the same time. What am I counting?"

"I'll read the verse, and you count the words as I say them. We are looking for the sixteenth word."

"Got it."

I read Genesis 22:16 slowly. Cadence stopped me on the word and. I underlined it and then wrote in my legal pad.

Genesis 22:16

And said, By myself have I sworn, saith YHWH, because thou hast done this thing, and hast not withheld thy son, thine only son:

"This is kind of cool. I get now why you and Dad enjoyed your refrigerator war so much. You know, it is hard to imagine the effort and knowledge that went into just one of these ciphers, let alone all 7 of them. Each is a work of art in its own right. But it is the manner in which he strung them together that is most compelling. Maybe compelling is not the right word."

"Intriguing?" Cadence suggested.

"Yeah, that too. But it is more than that. It's congruent in a way that makes the Bible or the Biblical story, rather, seem intentional. Like it wasn't written by the hand of many authors but the mind of one. Each of these ciphers has taught us something about the Bible we hadn't known before. Together, though, they are …"

"Majestic," Cadence offered.

"Yeah, that sounds about right."

"I wish Dad was sharing this with us himself."

"Would we have been ready to listen?"

"Probably not," Cadence said softly.

Considering the journey it had taken both of us to get to this point, definitely not.

I tapped my finger on the edge of my screen, staring out at nothing. "Well, I'm grateful he didn't give up on us. That he cared enough to make one last, desperate effort."

"You mean that?" Cadence tilted her head to one side.

"I do. I'm also thankful he didn't just give us all his money."

She nodded. "That would have been the final nail in my coffin, for sure."

"Mine too. Question is, can we, money or not, start over and do something with our lives that will honor the faith Dad had in God and us?"

"I believe I can," Cadence replied sincerely. "With God's help, that is. After all, Dad's love is really about his faith in God to keep you and me, no matter how far we'd wandered away from our faith."

I know in whom I have believed and am persuaded that he is able to keep that which I've committed unto him against that day.

Seeing the words in my Bible like Cadence did—as my father's testimony to his faith in God's ability to keep us—was profoundly moving to me in a way I couldn't describe. Was that the essence of faith? Was that comforting knowledge evidence of an unseen world? The knowledge of my father's faith brought me a sense of peace and comfort that I'd felt few times in the last decade. I no longer doubted if my father loved me. It may not have come in the package I was looking for, but right here, spread around me, was tangible evidence of that love.

"Okay. Let's keep going." I refocused on the next row of Hebrew keywords. "'Find father love,'" I read out loud. I shook my head, and Cadence glanced over at me. "It's like he's speaking directly to me. Like he's reading my thoughts."

"Maybe he is."

"You really believe Dad is reading my thoughts and communicating with me from the grave? That's ridiculous, Cadence."

"I didn't say Dad."

If it wasn't my earthly father, then could it be my heavenly one? The only other two options were coincidence or my own imagination. Both of those were looking less likely by the day. I shook my head again and did a quick calculation of the word values in the second row of the cipher.

"The second row's word values work out to be page 187, verse 13, word 14," I said, flipping pages in my Bible. The book cipher gave me Deuteronomy 29:13. I read the verse out loud as I copied it onto my notepad.

This time Cadence stopped me at the word *that*. I underlined it and finished copying the verse. I read the two words we'd gotten so far.

Deuteronomy 29:13

That he may establish thee to day for a people unto himself, and <u>*that*</u> *he may be unto thee a God, as he hath said unto thee, and as he hath sworn unto thy fathers, to Abraham, to Isaac, and to Jacob.*

"'And that.' Not much to go on."

"Well, get with it then." Cadence winked. "At this rate, we'll be in Montana by the time you get the cipher solved."

I laughed. "I'm working on it."

For the next hour, we solved the 7th cipher word by word. Cadence turned out to be correct. Many of the verses related to other ciphers or the redemptive theme Dad was sharing. Nearly all the keywords had something to do with father, Yahweh, or God. The third row of the book cipher was *signs come Yahweh*. The fourth, *trust hand Yah*. The fifth, *salvation Ya triumph*. And so it went.

But I frowned at the results so far. Dad had said that the Biblical riddle was 13 Hebrew words, yet he used twenty-six words to describe it. The only thing that made any sense was that the English translation of the original Hebrew was twice the words. Since we were using my father's Bible as the cipher key, and not a Hebrew Bible, the cipher had to use English.

When I wrote the final word of the book cipher on my pad, I read all twenty-six words out loud.

> and that from the and to unto the of the going Prince shall Jerusalem be seven build to return therefore sevens know anointed understand forth word

"Any of that ring a bell?" I asked.

"Some of the words sound familiar, but it doesn't make any sense. Dad probably randomized the words so that it would be more difficult to solve. If he'd left the verse in order, we wouldn't have had to solve the entire cipher to know what verse he was talking about."

"Hold on a second." I quickly turned back several pages to the sixth cipher. I slapped the pad and looked up at Cadence. "We already know the verse."

Chapter 104

13 Words

"We know the verse?" Cadence brushed back her hair to glance my way.

"Yes, it was part of our last cipher. It is Daniel 9:25 and the prophecy about the coming messiah." I read it to her.

Daniel 9:25

Know therefore and understand, that from the going forth of the commandment to restore and to build Jerusalem unto the Anointed Prince shall be seven sevens ...

I looked up as the truck turned. The headlights played across the asphalt and then a narrow track of dirt road. We were already at the forest service road that led to the cabin. Bracing my notes from the sixth cipher as we bumped along, I counted the Hebrew words of Daniel 9:25. My heart quickened.

"That's it. In Hebrew, the first part of Daniel 9:25 is 13 words."

"How many words in the entire verse?" Cadence turned her headlights on bright.

I counted out the rest of the words in Daniel 9:25. "Twenty-two."

"Why did Dad only use the first 13 words, then?"

"I'm not sure." I turned back a page in my notes. After a minute, I looked up. "Oh, you are going to love this. Remember in the last cipher, we had to figure out how 100 Hebrew words could be described as 49-49-49?"

"I do. So?" Cadence said, glancing at me.

"Well, that middle 49 turned out to be a play on words? Right? The middle 49 was not the number of words in the passage but the center two words' implied value. The author designed the passage to focus on seven sevens, the Hebrew *sheba shabuwa*. There were 49 words before the seven sevens and 49 words after."

"What's your point?"

"Well, look at this."

Cadence leaned over to assess the writing on my pad. A second later, she jerked the wheel to avoid a pine tree.

"Okay, don't look. I'll try to explain."

"No, hold on, I want to see." Cadence slowed down and pulled to the side of the road, her headlights shining into the ponderosa pines. The glow from my computer screen was not enough for her, so she turned on the dome light.

I cleared my throat. "Okay, I'm going to read all of Daniel 9:25, and you tell me where a natural break in the passage might be."

Know therefore and understand, that from the going forth of the commandment to restore and to build Jerusalem unto the Messiah the Prince shall be seven sevens, and threescore and two sevens the street shall be built again, and the wall, even in troublous times.

Cadence was silent for a moment after I finished reading. She pointed at the seven sevens in the middle of the passage. "It sounds like the passage could be divided between seven sevens and sixty-two sevens."

"Exactly right. In Hebrew, the first 13 words of Daniel 9:25 end with the Hebrew words *sheba shabuwa*, or *seven sevens*." I illustrated my point by writing out the verse in English, but this time, I divided it at the end of the 13th Hebrew word.

Know therefore and understand, that from the going forth of the commandment to restore and to build Jerusalem unto the Messiah the Prince shall be seven sevens,...

and threescore and two sevens: the street shall be built again, and the wall, even in troublous times.

"In Hebrew, the twelfth and 13th words are *shabuwa sheba* or *seven sevens*. In other words, 7 is the 50th or final word of the first half of the 100-word passage and the natural dividing point of Daniel 9:23-27. Up to this point, the passage tells us about the coming of his messianic figure and his purpose."

Cadence read the rest of the passage from our notes. She looked up. "I see what you mean. The word *7* marks the climax of the passage. After that point, the rest turns decidedly more somber."

"Right." I grinned. "The final eight Hebrew words of verse 25 describe troublesome times. But here is the point. If this is indeed a prophecy about the coming of this messianic figure, then the 13 Hebrew words of verse 25 give us the specific parameters of his coming. In essence, the passage tells us that from a commandment until the coming of the Messiah Prince, there would be seven sevens."

Cadence put the truck back in drive. "So, in order for us to solve this riddle, we need to figure out what commandment the passage is talking about. This will give us our starting point." She looked at me with her brows raised.

"Correct. Then we need to figure out the length of time intended by seven sevens."

Cadence lifted an index finger from the wheel. "And if we do that, we might end up finding evidence that proves Jesus was the Messiah."

Cadence gave me one of her you-know-where-this-is-going looks. I just shook my head at her. She laughed. I continued, nonplused.

"Theoretically, yes. If we can determine the starting point and the length of time the author intends. And if we can tie that to a legitimate historical date and then further connect that to what we know about the historical Jesus, we might actually have reasonable evidence that might compel a skeptic like me to reconsider some of my conclusions about the nature and significance of the Biblical record."

Cadence's ringing laugh filled the cab of the truck. "That's just lawyer-speak for you are going to have to reconsider your lack of faith in the Bible."

I chuckled along with her. "Don't get ahead of yourself, Sis. My skepticism might be on the ropes, but I'm not yet convinced."

"For goodness sake, Timbre. If I were you, I'd be careful. Dad has already claimed you for the kingdom of God. You keep fighting this, and Yahweh might just have to whack you upside the head with a proverbial two-by-four. You know, like the apostle Paul on the road to Damascus. Or like Jonah and the whale. You can't run fast enough to escape God's purpose for your life. Dad has committed you to God. You are treading on holy ground, brother of mine."

"I'm not running from God, Cadence," I said defensively. "I just need something more tangible, more intellectual, than what I have." I looked at my hands thinking about Doubting Thomas.

Cadence drove the last few miles in silence. As we pulled up to the gate of Grandfather's cabin, she looked at me with a certainty. Her intensity was like a guard tower's spotlight at midnight. She swept her hands in an all-encompassing gesture.

"The evidence is all around you, Timbre. If you want to see it, God will show it to you."

Chapter 105

Evidence of Faith

The next morning, I woke to the smell of coffee. I'd slept like a dead man. Cadence stood in the kitchen humming a tune I didn't recognize. The front door was open, and sunshine was spilling its welcome into the room like a golden river. Cadence had found new boldness in her last biscuit-making adventure because she was up to her elbows in flour again and her face had spots and streaks of white. Even groggy, I could sense her enthusiasm and energy.

"You're chipper this morning," I croaked out in a voice still heavy with sleep.

"Good morning, Arizona!" She sang out the greeting and extended her hands wide as if to embrace the sunshine. "Good morning to you, too, my dear brother," she added with the glowing warmth of the sun reflected in her eyes.

I sat down at the kitchen table, and Cadence wiped her hands and brought me a cup of coffee. "Thank you," I mumbled. It was still a little too early to appreciate so much enthusiasm. "What's got you so stoked this morning?"

She attacked the sizzling scrambled eggs with a wooden spoon, then lifted it and pointed it at me. "Today is the day, Timbre Plummer," she said mysteriously.

"The day for what?"

Accentuating the words with the spoon, she declared, "Today is the day that Yahweh hath made, I will rejoice and be glad in it."

She gave me one of those rare smiles that one might be lucky to see a few times in their life. It was as if all of Arizona's sunshine, all of my sister's enthusiasm, and all of her joy were distilled and then reflected in her face.. You couldn't say it was the way the corners of her eyes turned up or the perfect wrinkles around her lips. Nor was it the white of her teeth that showed between the curve of her lips. It was all of that but something more. Something almost intangible. Like the pull of gravity you felt but couldn't see.

Her words from last night came back to me.

The evidence is all around you, Timbre. If you want to see it, God will show it to you.

As we ate breakfast, Cadence still radiated that … I was still struggling to even describe it. An energy, power, spirit? None of the words I could think of really captured it. But I could see it in her animation. Her enthusiasm. That was it, wasn't it? She had enthusiasm from the Greek *en theos,* or *God within.* The spirit of God shone through Cadence. My logical mind wanted to deny it, but I couldn't.

Cadence looked up from the last piece of scrambled egg she'd speared with her fork. "What?"

I almost joked about her being high on something but managed to assassinate the thought before it became words. What kind of person could see what I saw and then come up with a sacrilegious joke about it? I pushed my food around on my plate before looking up. Cadence watched me curiously.

"You … you seem different this morning," I finally managed.

Her eyes shone. "It's back, Timmy."

It's back? Fear sparked an alarm in me. She wasn't losing it, was she? "What's back?"

"The gift," she said, beaming.

I took a long sip of coffee. It burned my tongue, but I hardly noticed. What was she talking about? The look on my face must have been equal parts confusion and concern because she laughed richly and explained.

"Timmy, my gift is back. My mind works again like it used to. God gave me back the gift I lost the night I burned my Bible."

When I just stared, Cadence got up from the table. She walked over to the bookshelf and pulled down the 8-inch thick, 2200 page *Webster's Unabridged Dictionary*. She returned to the table and dropped it next to my plate. The dishes rattled, and silverware jumped.

"Pick any page you like."

Who knew where she was going with this, but I grabbed an inch and a half of the book and flipped it open. Page 391. The word at the top of the page was *conspicuously*. I tried to steady my shaking hand, but. Cadence's rich, enthusiastic laugh filled the cabin.

"You can run but you can't hide, Timbre Plummer," she said, stepping around to the other side of the table. She turned her back to me. "Timbre Plummer's hand is shaking Con-spic'u-ous-ly. It is an adverb which means *in a conspicuous manner*. The next word, Con-spic'u-ous-ness, is a noun which means *the state or quality of being conspicuous*."

For the next several minutes, I listened in awe as Cadence recited all fifty-two words, their usage, and definitions on page 391. After she finished page 391, she started reciting page 390 backward. After just a few words, I raised my hand.

"I believe you." I looked down at the words and then back up at her. "You have a photographic memory?"

Cadence nodded.

"Was it always like that?"

"Until I lost it after the bonfire. Now it is back again."

"Why did I never know?"

Cadence shrugged. "Only Dad knew. I didn't want people thinking I was a freak or something, so I tried to hide it when I was around others. Dad also told me it was good not to show all your neurons. Let people think you are just a bit dumber than you are."

I scratched my head. "I can see how losing that would have been a game-changer. Like Superman becoming paralyzed."

"Like I said, I think I understood how Samson might have felt."

"So what changed? Why did your gift come back?"

Cadence plunked down and pushed a piece of her biscuit around her plate. Whatever she was thinking, she must have come to some conclusions because she stopped playing with her food and looked at me, a look of sincere conviction where doubt had been banished.

"I asked Yahweh for it back."

"That's it? You didn't have to dance in circles and beat yourself with sticks or something?"

Her expression clouded at my poor attempt at humor. She picked up her fork and continued to eat. My irreverent comment didn't hold her attention long because a moment later, she was smiling and finishing her final bites with gusto. It was as if she'd stepped out of my world and into her own. Panic twisted my stomach. It was as if I'd been left behind.

"Seriously, Cadence. That was it? You just asked God to give you back your gift, and He said yes?"

My words pulled Cadence from her world into mine once more. She shook her head sadly. "No, Timbre, that wasn't all. I got down on my knees. I folded my hands, and I poured my heart out to God. All the hurt, anger, and bitterness I let go of. I pleaded with Him to forgive me. To forgive my selfishness, my lack of character, and my weakness. I promised that if He gave me back the gift that I had taken for granted, I would spend the rest of my life using that gift to bring honor to Him and His holy words. Then I went to bed."

I searched my sister's face. Like an ancient parchment marked in symbols of a lost language, it was indecipherable. There was no doubt in my mind that she was sincere about her experience. Nor could I doubt the result. But … I still wasn't whole-heartedly looking for God, but rather looking for reasons to doubt Him.

If I was being honest with myself, I'd already seen evidence of Him in my office when I'd had a gun to my head and my finger was a fraction of a second away from blowing my brains out. I'd seen Him when I'd been left unconscious and broken in that alley and woken up in my own bed. I'd seen Him when I'd gone to my sister's house just when she needed me most. I'd seen Him in my metamorphosis from a selfish jerk to a man who now found hope and peace in helping someone else. I saw Him in my dreams. I saw Him in my father's ciphers. I saw Him in my twenty-first birthday present. Most of all, I saw God's presence shining through my transformed sister.

I knew then that I no longer needed convincing. I had enough evidence to have faith. What I still needed to do was humble myself, answer the knocking, and open the door to my heart.

Chapter 106

Swearing Sevens

Cadence stood and surveyed the kitchen. "I'm going take a walk. I'll clean this mess up when I get back."

"You want some company?"

"Not really," she said apologetically. "I'll be back in a while. Just need to clear my head."

After she stepped onto the porch, I sat at the table brooding. The room felt colder and gloomy without Cadence. I tried to fight the depressing feelings that started creeping up on me. With a soft growl, I stood.

For the next half hour, I kept busy cleaning the kitchen. When I finished, I sat down to work on the 13-word riddle of Daniel 9:25a. From my notepad, I read my father's instructions one more time.

In its original form, this enciphered passage is 13 Hebrew words. These words pose a Biblical riddle that has challenged some of the greatest minds in history.

The key to the riddle is hidden in seven and its significance revealed by swear.

Your answer will be the 5 numbers that lie between the א *and* ת.

I flipped back to the page in my notes where I'd written out the English translation of the 13 Hebrew words.

Know therefore and understand, that from the going forth of the commandment to restore and to build Jerusalem unto the Messiah the Prince shall be seven sevens …

I kept revisiting my father's cryptic instructions.

"'The key to the riddle is hidden in seven and its significance revealed by swear. The key is hidden in seven and revealed by swear,'" I mumbled.

I knew from my father's Abraham cipher that *swear* and *seven* shared the same Hebrew root word. But here in this cryptic clue, he ascribed a function to both its meanings. It was overwhelming, trying to think about all the pieces of the puzzle at once. Maybe if I had Cadence's mind, I could do that. Since I did not, I'd have to tackle just one piece at a time.

So how could the key be hidden in seven? *Seven* in the context of Daniel 9:25 was a Hebrew word that functioned as a number. If a key was hidden in 7, maybe the key had something to do with the numerical value of the Hebrew word *seven*, *sheba*. I retrieved the interlinear Bible from the bookshelf, sat down at the kitchen table, and opened it to Daniel 9. Slowly, I read through the entire chapter.

The Hebrew word *sheba* or *seven* was only used once. This key word happened to be the 13th word of Daniel 9:25. This word also was the fiftieth of the 100 words of Daniel 9:23-27, marking the halfway point of the passage.

Shabuwa, the Hebrew word for sevens, was used multiple times, as well as *shibiym,* or *seventy*. Even *shebuw'ah,* or *oath*, was used once.

If there was a key in the word *seven*, then verse 25 was it. Carefully, I added up the numerical value of *sheba* in my head and wrote *377* on my notepad. I added it one more time to be sure and came up with the same answer. 377 had no significance that I knew of.

I needed to figure out its factors. Without access to the internet, I had to do it manually, starting with two. I was beginning to think it was a prime number until I tried 13. That was it. I didn't need to look any further because 377 was the product of the prime factors 13 x 29. But other than 13 being one of the factors of 377, nothing else stood out. It certainly didn't look like a key to anything. Perhaps this was a dead end.

Something about the numbers tickled my memory. I flipped back through my notes to the first pages of the 7th cipher and—aha!—clicked my pen against the page. Numbers 29:13. It wasn't 377, but the reference used its factors. Was this a coincidence or intentional? I recopied the verse, but this time under my notes for 377.

> *Numbers 29:13*
> *And ye shall offer a burnt offering, a sacrifice made by fire, of a sweet savour unto YHWH; 13 young bullocks*, 2 rams, *and* 14 lambs of the first year; they shall be without blemish:

Apparently, 13 bullocks, two rams, and fourteen lambs created a sum of 29. Another coincidence? This was beginning to stretch the limits of my coincidence theory.

My interest roused, I kept reading through my 7th cipher notes. The numbers *29 and 13* were used as one of the book cipher keys. This time, though, the passage referenced an implied oath sworn to Abraham and his descendants.

> Deuteronomy 29:13
> *That he may establish thee to day for a people unto himself, and <u>that</u> he may be unto thee a God, as he hath said unto*

thee, and as he hath sworn unto thy fathers, to Abraham, to Isaac, and to Jacob.

We knew from reading all the book cipher verse clues that Dad had chosen them carefully. In that case, 29:13 had significance, but what?

Footsteps echoed on the porch steps, and a shadow slid into the room. I turned toward the door, where Cadence's silhouette blocked the mid-morning light.

"Back so soon?"

Cadence laughed. "It's been nearly two hours, Timmy."

I looked at my watch and scratched my head. "I don't know where the time went."

Cadence walked over to the kitchen table where I had my books and papers scattered. "Make any progress?

"Not really." I pointed at my notes. "Dad's key may have something to do with the numerical value of the Hebrew word *7*. In Hebrew, *sheba* has a value of 377. It could have something to do with its factors as well. At least two of Dad's verse clues used 29:13."

Cadence pulled over a chair and sat down beside me. She reached for my notepad. "Mind if I take a look?"

I sat back and gestured with my hand for her to go ahead. Cadence picked up the nearly full legal pad and flipped it back to the beginning. Then, page by page, she went through the notes. Her eyelids fluttered slightly as she read. *Read* was probably not the correct word. *Photographed* would probably be more accurate. She didn't spend more than a few seconds on each page.

A few minutes later, she set the pad down and closed her eyes. They moved under her lids, and her cheeks twitched slightly. Her eyes stopped moving and she opened them.

She gave me a mysterious smile and then picked up the interlinear Bible. At first, it appeared as if she was randomly searching for verses, but then I realized that she was looking up each reference we'd written down in the notes. I grabbed my notepad and flipped back to the first page. Sure enough, she was recalling each reference from memory and then reading the larger context from which it came.

Like a treasure hunter following a map to buried treasure, Cadence followed the clues my father left. Though her expression remained impassive, several times her breath caught for a second, undoubtedly a reaction to something surprising. Not once did she look at me or anything else in the room. Her attention focused totally and solely on what she was reading.

When she got to the 7th cipher, she started through the twenty-six verses Dad had used to encrypt his book cipher. Most of the time, she only read the chapter from which the verse came, but when she got to Deuteronomy 7:9, she read the entire book. Before she moved on to the final four verses of the book cipher, she also read the entire book of Genesis. She polished off her morning meal of words with another perusal of Daniel 9 before closing her eyes again. I looked at my watch. It was now past lunchtime. Where had three hours gone?

"Would you grab me Dad's Bible dictionary off his bookshelf?" she asked without opening her eyes. I stood. "Third shelf, eleventh book from the end. It's the thick one with a brown leather cover."

The book was exactly where she said it would be. I returned to the table with it and set it down. Cadence opened the book to the Calendars heading. A few seconds later, she turned to the subject of Time, and finally Years. She closed the book and then her lashes fluttered shut. Her cheek didn't twitch anymore, and her eyes didn't move, but if the pulsing vein in her neck was any indication, her mind must have been as active as the surface of the sun during a coronal mass ejection.

With a gasp, Cadence grabbed the edge of the table and opened her eyes—unfocused at first. Gradually, though, they brightened, and she turned to me. She drew a breath, and her lips and throat moved, but nothing came out. It appeared as if she had forgotten how to speak. In what I could only describe as amazed wonder, Cadence managed to whisper.

"Yahweh is awesome!"

I don't know what I had expected her to say, but that wasn't it. I just waited. There had to be more coming. Perhaps her trouble was not with what she knew or saw in her mind but in how to explain it to me in a way that my brain could handle.

Cadence reached for the pen lying on the table. "Do you have another notepad?" she asked finally. I opened my briefcase and handed her a new pad. She took it and wrote a number at the top, then underlined it. "This is the answer to the second riddle."

Chapter 107

515.02

515.02

My sister tapped the number with the end of her pen. I waited for her to say more. She looked at me. Or, more accurately, she looked through me like she was in some far-off place.

“Earth to Cadence. I need more information.”

“I know,” she said softly.

“So?” I rolled my arm like I was trying to crank start a Model-T Ford. “Talk to me. Just tell me what you are thinking, and if I don’t understand, I’ll tell you.”

Cadence gave me a funny look like I wouldn’t have a chance understanding her thoughts right now. She took a deep breath and let it out slowly, then reached for the pad with our cipher notes. Turning to the sixth cipher, she pointed at my rendering of Daniel 9:23-27 and its 100 words which I had arranged in 49+2+49 blocks of text. This cryptogram was the answer to Dad’s sixth ciphered riddle of 100 words that he had expressed as 49-49-49.

להגיד to speak	באתי I came	ואני and I	דבר word	יצא went out	תחנוניך thy supplication	בתחלת [23] Beginning
במראה the vision.	והבן and consider	בדבר the word	ובין understand	אתה thou	חמודות beloved	כי because
עיר city	ועל and upon	עמך thy people	על upon	נחתך determined	שבעים seventy	שבעים [24] Sevens
עון iniquity	ולכפר and to atone	חטאות sin	ולחתם and to end	הפשע the transgression	לכלא to finish	קדשך thy holy
ולמשח and to anoint	ונביא and prophecy	חזון vision	ולחתם and to seal	עלמים everlasting	צדק justice	ולהביא and to bring
דבר word	מצא going out	מן from	ותשכל and understand	ותדע [25] And know	קדשים holies.	קדש holy of
שבעים sevens	נגיד prince	משיח anointed one	עד unto	ירושלם Jerusalem	ולבנות and to build	להשיב to restore

ושבעים sevens	שבעה seven

ובצוק and in distress of	וחרוץ and wall	רחוב street	ונבנתה and.	תשוב again	ושנים and two	ששים sixty
משיח anointed one	יכרת will be cut off	ושנים and two	ששים sixty	השבעים the sevens	ואחרי [26] And after	העתים the times.
נגיד prince	עם people of	ישחית will destroy	והקדש and the sanctuary	והעיר and the city	לו to him	ואין and there is not
נחרצת determined	מלחמה war	קץ end of	ועד and unto	בשטף in the flood	וקצו and end of it	הבא coming
וחצי and midst of	אחד one	שבוע sevens	לרבים for many	ברית covenant	והגביר [27] & strengthen	שממות desolations.
שקוצים abominations	כנף wing of	ועל and upon	ומנחה and offering	זבח sacrifice	ישבית cause to cease	השבוע the sevens
שמם desolate	על unto	תתך poured out	ונחרצה and determined	כלה end	ועד and unto	משמם desolator

Cadence angled the drawing toward me. "All this time, scholars have been arguing about the meaning of Daniel 9, and they've missed the real genius of the prophecy. This prophecy is written as a genuine Hebrew numerical word riddle. This riddle and its solution were then locked by the author's organization of the passage into 7-by-7 blocks of text. Those require the reader to understand that two words, *sheba shebuwa',* seven sevens, are the literal and figurative focal point of the prophecy.

"Okay …" I drummed my fingers on the table.

"Daniel 9:23-27 talks about the coming of a Messiah Prince and His—what can only be described as—redemptive purpose. But the passage does so in cryptic numerical units. All the units of measure are derivatives of Hebrew word *sheba*/seven and its cognate, *shaba*/swear. In this prophecy, the derivatives of this root word are seventy, sevens, and oath." On the new notepad, Cadence wrote this out for me to see.

ROOT = שבע = *Sheba' / Shaba* = Seven / Swear

Derivatives = שבעום = *Sheb'iym, Shabuwa'* = Seventy, Sevens

"You following me so far?"

I nodded. "I hear what you are saying, but I don't understand where you are going with this."

"Just hear me out, okay?"

"I'm listening, Sis. But try to just give me the Cliff's Notes version, please."

"Okay," she said, plowing ahead. "We've already realized that we need at least three pieces of information to solve this riddle. We need a starting point, and we need to know the units of 'time'"—she made quote symbols around the word—"used by the author to calculate the units of 7. When Dad said this prophecy challenged some of the greatest minds in history, this was what he referred to."

I rubbed my face with my hands. "No kidding," I mumbled

"Pretend for a moment that Dad wrote this prophecy. It's pretty obvious now that all of his other ciphered riddles were conceived in light of the genius of Daniel 9:25. If he wanted to ensure that we would be able to find the missing 'time' key to this prophecy, where do you think he would hide it?"

When I just stared at her, waiting for a clue, she nodded to my drawing of the 49 + 2 + 49. "I guess I'd look for it here in the center, where Daniel purposely focuses our attention on the two words *seven sevens*."

"In Dad's instructions, where did he say the key was hidden?"

"In seven," I pointed at the fiftieth word of the passage.

Cadence turned back to the other pad. "You found that this Hebrew word has a numerical value of 377, and its factors are 13x29, correct?"

"Yes, so what's your point?" I ran my hand through my hair.

"Did you know that when Daniel 9 was written, Israel used a lunar/solar calendar?"

"I guess. That sounds kind of familiar." I shrugged, suppressing a groan. "Sis, can you please just cut to your point?"

Cadence frowned but continued. "Because Israel's calendar was lunar/solar, its months were 29.53 days long. Because twelve lunar cycles of 29.53 days do not fit perfectly into a solar year of 365.24 days, the Hebrew calendar required intercalation. Kind of like us adding an extra day or 'leap year' every three or four years, the Hebrew calendar requires an extra lunar month.

This way, the lunar part of the calendar stays in numerical balance with the solar calendar. The bottom line is that the ancient Hebrew calendar year at the time of Daniel was based upon a certain number of lunar cycles. More often than not, it was twelve lunar cycles of 29.53 days each. But once every three years or so, an extra month was added, which made the year 13 months long." Cadence leaned towards me, willing me to come up with the connection on my own. When I didn't say anything, she added, "A lunar month is 29.53 days in length … and the key is found in seven …"

I looked down at the Hebrew riddle. What Cadence was driving at hit me when I finally stopped trying so hard to understand. It was obvious. The author of Daniel 9 hid the time key in the root word upon which the entire prophecy was built. "Daniel 9 uses a lunar year of 13 months as its time key?"

"Bingo! Now look at this." Cadence circled the twelfth and 13th words of the Daniel 9:25 riddle. "These two Hebrew words, שבעים שבעה , are seven sevens and give us the units of measure between the commandment and the coming of this Messianic Prince. In Hebrew, these two words describe what?"

"The twelfth word is *shib'yim* and means *seventy*, but in some cases, it also spells the Hebrew word *shabuwa,* or *sevens*. It depends on the context. The 13th word, of course, is sheba and means *seven*." I indicated the word at the center of my drawing.

"So, the twelfth word of verse 25 offers us one of two possible combinations, correct?"

"Yes. We have either 7x70 or 7x7. Both are legitimate translations of שבעים. Basically, it's the same root number, only one is a magnitude larger than the other. In a way, it's kind of like sheba and shaba. Both have the same Hebrew spelling, but depending on context, they can take on the meaning of *seven* or *swear*. Probably back in the obscure past of antiquity, the number *7* was associated with making an oath, and those words came to have two meanings wrapped up in the same spelling."

"Okay." Cadence clicked her pen on the table, focusing my attention. "The bottom line, then, is that 7x70 units of time using a 13-month lunar cycle year give us 188,106.1 days," she said, writing down the number.

My mouth hung open, and my brows knitted into a crazy line.

"What?" Cadence opened one hand.

"Where did you pull that number from?"

Cadence tapped her head with the pen. "Up here."

"Really?"

"Yes, really." She smiled tolerantly at my doubt.

Doggedly, I wrote out the equation on the pad.

13 x 29.53 = 383.89
383.89 x 490 = 187106.1

Cadence cleared her throat. When I ignored it, she did it again.

"What?" I snapped.

"You made a mistake. You should have carried the one, which would have made 8, not 7."

I looked down at my addition columns, and sure enough, I'd made a mistake. I shook my head. "I couldn't even get it correct with a pen and paper, and you multiplied and added it all in your head?"

"If it's any consolation, it's not really like that. I don't multiply and add in my head. I just know the answer. I don't have to work it out.'"

"Seriously? You are not yanking my chain?" And that was supposed to make me feel better?

"No, I'm not." Cadence wrote a multiplication problem on the pad. "Do you have to write out all the math when you multiply 12x12?"

"Of course not. I just memorized the answer. But that is not the same as 383.89 x 490."

"Sure, it is. It's the same, just a bigger number."

I scratched my head. Theoretically, it might be possible, but it would take me several lifetimes.

"May I continue now, Sir Doubting Thomas?" The corners of her mouth twitched.

I threw my pen down. "Sure, Sis. Go ahead. Dumb Doubting Thomas over here will keep his mouth shut until you are finished."

Cadence made a funny noise in her throat, probably swallowing her laugh. "So 188,106.1 days equal 515.02 solar years. 515.02 years is the length of time from the commandment to the coming of the Messiah. Now, all we need to find out is when the 'commandment to restore and build Jerusalem' went forth, and we will have our starting point."

"Which by default will give us the ending point."

"Exactly." Cadence beamed.

I leaned back, eliciting a squeak of protest from my chair. "And the starting point?"

Chapter 108

A Light, A Word, A Door

Cadence straightened, just as eager to answer this question as the last. "Did you know that the English word *commandment* used in Daniel 9:25 comes from the Hebrew word *dabar,* which means *word, speech*, or *utterance*? *Commandment* as used in this English version of Daniel 9 is an outlier. *Dabar* appears several times in Daniel 9, and nearly all of them refer to the word, speech, or utterance of Yahweh. In fact, *dabar* is used over fourteen hundred times in the Bible, and the vast majority of those refer to the word of Yahweh."

I blew out a breath and opened my hands. "Are you saying we are looking for the word of Yahweh to start the countdown in Daniel 9:25 and not necessarily a commandment?"

"Yes. Keep in mind that Daniel 9 opens within the context of Jerusalem's destruction and Daniel realizing that the seventy-year desolation of Jerusalem as prophesied by Jeremiah was almost over." Cadence started to recite the passage from memory but stopped. "You want the context?" she asked and then reached for my Bible.

I put my hand over hers. "Just tell it to me, Cadence. I know you don't need to read it. You don't need to pretend you are normal around me anymore. Just cut me a little slack if I do or say something stupid, okay? It's kind of hard to wrap my mind around the fact that you have superpowers."

Her hesitant, vulnerable look softened in relief. A new enthusiasm burned in her eyes. Cadence closed the Bible and started reciting the opening verses of Daniel 9.

In the first year of Darius the son of Ahasuerus, of the seed of the Medes, which was made king over the realm of the Chaldeans; 2 In the first year of his reign I Daniel understood by books the number of the years, whereof the word of YHWH came to Jeremiah the prophet, that he would accomplish seventy years in the desolations of Jerusalem.

Then she continued, "From what I've read, it was Cyrus of Persia who at the prompting of Yahweh first allowed the Jewish people to return to Jerusalem and rebuild the city and the temple at the end of the seventy years. For nearly sixteen years, the repatriated captives didn't get much further than laying some of the temple foundation stones before their building efforts were interrupted. It wasn't until the second year of Darius in 520 BC that Yahweh, through the prophets Haggai and Zechariah, gave His word, or *dabar*, for the people to restart construction."

"Sounds familiar."

Cadence slid my old notepad across to me and turned the pages to the Jefferson cipher. Her eyes were sparkling with excitement. "Remember this?"

I read through our notes and jerked my chin up. "Is this what I think it is?"

Cadence nodded. "13 letters that have hidden within them the value of 391, the value of Yeshua's name in Hebrew."

"Dad used the Jefferson cipher to give us the starting point of the coming of Yeshua?" I said incredulously.

"Yes, old Doubting Thomas himself." Cadence's excited laugh rang out. "Dad used one of America's greatest doubters of the divinity of Christ to provide us proof that Jesus, that Yeshua, was the Messiah prophesied in the Scriptures."

"Does the math work?"

Cadence rolled her eyes at that. "Really? You think Dad would go to all this trouble, and the math wouldn't work?"

Warmth crept into my cheeks. "I'm not questioning Dad's ability here, Cadence. I would just like to see for myself." She tucked her chin and searched my eyes. I finally said, "I just want to put my hands in those nail holes. I want to see it for myself."

Cadence gave an understanding tilt of her head. "Okay. These events in Haggai 2:18-20 take place in the second year of Darius, in the twenty-fourth day of the ninth month." She watched me as she explained.

"I'm with you, Cadence. This was the eve of what would someday be Hanukkah. We learned it was at Hanukkah or the Feast of Dedication, a.k.a. the Festival of Lights, where Jesus stood up in the temple and said that He was the light of the world."

My memory of the context must have proved sufficient, for Cadence gave a nod and went on. "It wasn't just Haggai who gave the word or dabar of Yahweh to the Jewish people, telling them to return and build His house. The very same dabar was given through Zechariah, also in the second year of Darius. Here's an excerpted part of Zechariah 1:7-14, which tells of those events.

> *Upon the four and twentieth day of the eleventh month, which is the month Sebat, in the second year of Darius, came the word—dabar—of Yahweh unto Zechariah, the son of Berechiah, the son of Iddo the prophet, saying, ...*
>
> *... Then the angel of Yahweh answered and said, O Yahweh of hosts, how long wilt thou not have mercy on Jerusalem and on the cities of Judah, against which thou*

hast had indignation these threescore and ten years? [13] *And Yahweh answered the angel that talked with me with good words and comfortable words.* [14] *So the angel that communed with me said unto me, Cry thou, saying, Thus saith Yahweh of hosts; I am jealous for Jerusalem and for Zion with a great jealousy ...*

... Therefore thus saith Yahweh; I am returned to Jerusalem with mercies: my house shall be built in it, saith Yahweh of hosts, and a line shall be stretched forth upon Jerusalem.

"Still with me?" Cadence asked after she finished reciting the passage from Zechariah.

I gave her a thumbs up. "So we have two passages which tell of the dabar or word of Yahweh commanding the Jewish people to return and build."

Cadence gave a quick nod of her head as she opened my Bible and turned to Ezra 6:14-15. "Here is confirmation. Read it for yourself."

And the elders of the Jews builded, and they prospered through the prophesying of Haggai the prophet and Zechariah the son of Iddo. And they builded, and finished it, according to the commandment of the God of Israel, and according to the commandment of Cyrus, and Darius, and Artaxerxes king of Persia. [15] *And this house was finished on the third day of the month Adar, which was in the sixth year of the reign of Darius the king.*

I looked up from the passage. "If I understand all this correctly, between the passages of Haggai and Zechariah, we have kind of a prophetic window between the sixth and eleventh months during which Yahweh commanded the Jewish people to return and build His house. His house, of course, was the very beating heart of the city of Jerusalem." I pushed back from the desk and faced my sister. "During this window of time, we have the passage of Haggai 2:19 telling of the laying of the temple foundation and a reminder by Yahweh for them to consider that from this day forward, He would bless them—those 13 letters also equaling 391, the value of the Hebrew name *Yeshua*."

I paused, and Cadence waited for me to work my way through it.

"Daniel 9:25 tells us that from Yahweh's word or *dabar* to restore and build Jerusalem, there would be four hundred and ninety periods of time, which we've worked out to be 515.02 years. If the Haggai passage begins on the eve of Hanukkah in 520 BC, then the time of the Messiah's coming would be 515.02 years after that." I scratched my head. "How many days is .02 of a year?"

"Roughly 7.48 days."

I laughed at her. *Roughly*. I bet she could have given me a dozen-decimal-place answer if I had asked. "Okay, then, the coming of the Messiah, according to this criteria, should have taken place sometime during Hanukkah in the year 5 BC. His birth would have followed nine months later in September or October, during the Feast of Tabernacles in 4 BC."

Cadence rolled her clenched fist in the air in celebration. "And 4 BC is one of the dates many scholars give for the birth of Jesus."

I rubbed my jaw. "What would it have been? Roughly thirty years later that Jesus stood up in the temple during the Festival of Lights on the anniversary of his conception and proclaimed to those listening, 'I am the light of the world'? Knowing that backstory, I sure would have liked to have been there to witness that."

"Me, too."

I smiled at my sister. "The key to the Daniel 9 riddle really was hidden in the number *7*."

Here was reasonable evidence that the Bible predicted the coming of Jesus hundreds of years before the event. Here was a scar I could feel with my hands. I was running out of reasons not to believe. Cadence's eyes were shining. Clearly, she wanted me to take that next step of faith.

I closed my eyes and saw the door in the hallway of my dreams. Light glowed behind it. All I had to do was open it. I reached for the handle. A thump brought my eyes open. I had pushed over my father's briefcase.

Cadence drew back and screwed her face up.

I shook my head and laughed. "You don't want to know." I pointed at the instructions for the 7th cipher. "We solved the key hidden in seven, but what about the significance of *swear*?"

Chapter 109

The Oath

"What is the underlying theme of Dad's riddles?" Cadence watched me think it through.

"They point to Jesus."

"Who is Jesus?" she leaned forward.

"The son of God?"

"True, but that's not the answer I'm looking for."

"Okay, what then?" I exhaled and I sat back in my chair giving myself a little more space.

"What did Dad's second cipher tell us about Jesus?"

"Come on, Cadence. I know I'm several steps behind you on this. Just spill it."

"Just answer the question, Timbre. What did Dad's second cipher tell us about Jesus?"

I sighed and closed my eyes. Sometimes she was impossible. The second cipher had been about Moses changing Hosea's name to Joshua or the Hebrew Yeshua. I opened my eyes. "Dad's second cipher told us that Jesus was the name of the Old Testament Joshua or Yeshua, which means *Yahweh's salvation*."

"Okay. In light of this information, what might we say is the theme or idea behind Dad's ciphers?"

"They are the story of Yahweh's salvation?"

"Yes …" She rolled her hand. "To whom is this salvation directed?"

"The Jewish people."

"And …"

A note of exasperation crept into her voice. The tapping of her pencil came harder and slower, like the drum of an ancient galley. My mind, like the slaves of that ancient ship, struggled to keep an obedient pace. When Cadence threw down the pencil with a soft grunt, my cognitive functions died in the water, just as they had every time Jenny had said those magic words, “Talk to me.” They had been like an eraser on my mind.

Cadence’s eyes were closed, and she was rubbing her temple. Maybe being a genius wasn’t all glory and roses. I imagined her thoughts traveling like a starship at warp speed. Here I was, moseying along in my beat-up old Chevy as she tried to toss bits of paper into my window as she passed.

I put my hand on her shoulder. “I’m drawing a blank here, Cadence. I’m just a bit overwhelmed with all this.”

Cadence nodded like she understood but kept her eyes closed. After a while, she opened them with a new look of determination on her face. She picked the pencil back up and started scribbling bullet points on the notepad.

- 7 - seven = *sheba* = 377 = 13x29
- 7 - sware = *shaba* = 377 = 13x29
- Yahweh (26=13x2) *shaba* (sware) an oath of sevens with Abraham (41)
- Oath of Seven = Yahweh’s blessing on <u>all</u> nations of the earth.
- The Blessing = Jesus = Yeshua, which is literally “Yahweh’s Salvation.”
- The prophecy of Daniel 9:25 predicted that from the word or dabar of Yahweh until the Messiah would be a period of 70 sevens. (Seventy and sevens come from the root sheba/shaba = seven/sware)

- The prophecy tells that during this 70 sevens an Anointed One will:
    - Finish the transgression
    - Make an end to sins
    - Make reconciliation for iniquity
    - Bring in everlasting righteousness
    - Seal up the vision and prophecy
    - Anoint the Most Holy

Cadence stopped after writing out the sixth messianic goal of the prophecy of seventy sevens. "You following me?" she asked gently.

"Yes, just my speed." I gave her a wry smile.

"Good. If we take Daniel 9 at face value, the prophecy was given near the end of the seventy years of captivity of the Jewish people in Babylon. Daniel 9 opens with Daniel acknowledging this context, and then he petitions Yahweh to remember His people, His city, and His desolate sanctuary." Cadence slid my Bible across the table in front of me. She flipped the pages until Daniel 9 lay open. "Now, tell me, what does Daniel open his pleadings to Yahweh with? What does Daniel ask Yahweh to remember?"

I scanned the first few verses of Daniel 9 and put my finger on the page when I got to verse 4. I read it out loud.

And I prayed unto YHWH my God, and made my confession, and said, O Lord, the great and dreadful God, keeping the covenant and mercy to them that love him, and to them that keep his commandments;

When I finished, our eyes met. The frustration that had wrinkled her brow and the corners of her eyes had been replaced with sparkling intensity. She grabbed my wrist.

"One of the verses Dad included in his clues was Deuteronomy 7:9. That verse also talked about the 'covenant and mercy to them that love him and keep his commandments.' What Dad must have realized was that this quote by Moses about the 'covenant and mercy' of Yahweh was an allusion to the oath of sevens Yahweh made with Abraham. Here, take a look." Cadence flipped to Deuteronomy 7 and started reading excerpts.

YHWH did not set his love upon you, nor choose you, because ye were more in number than any people; for ye were the fewest of all people: [8] *But because Yahweh loved you, and because he would keep the oath which he had sworn unto your fathers, hath Yahweh brought you out with a mighty hand, and redeemed you out of the house of bondmen, from the hand of Pharaoh king of Egypt.*

Cadence pointed to the word *oath* in the passage. "See that? Moses is telling Israel that Yahweh loved them in part because of the oath, shabuwa, He swore, shaba, with their fathers." She continued reading.

Know therefore that Yahweh thy God, he is God, the faithful God, which keepeth covenant and mercy with them that love him and keep his commandments to a thousand generations;...

Wherefore it shall come to pass, if ye hearken to these judgments, and keep, and do them, that YHWH thy <u>God shall keep unto thee the covenant and the mercy which he sware unto thy fathers:</u> [13] *And he will love thee, and bless thee, and multiply thee: he will also bless the fruit of thy womb, and the fruit of thy land, thy corn, and thy wine, and thine oil, the* *increase of thy kine, and the flocks of thy sheep, in the land which he sware unto thy fathers to give thee.*

Cadence paused again. “You catch that? Daniel 9:4 is a quote taken from right here.” She gently patted the Bible with her open hand. “Right here where Moses is talking about the oath of sevens Yahweh swore with the fathers. In this same context, Moses talks about the blessings, the barak, the 222, that will result. But look at this. The passage goes on to talk about the ‘mighty arm’ of Yahweh that delivered Israel from Egyptian bondage.” She widened her eyes, unable to hide her enthusiasm. “You recognize that phrase?”

“Didn’t Daniel 9:15 talk about the mighty hand of Yahweh in the context of Egypt?”

My words galvanized her. “Exactly! Daniel 9:15, those eighteen words that are the numerical focus of the entire chapter, with 222 words before verse 15 and 222 words after, are taken from the theme of Israel’s deliverance right here in Deuteronomy 7, where it also talks about Yahweh’s oath of sevens with Abraham.” Cadence wrote out the numerical word configuration of Daniel 9.

222 + 18 + 222.

She swept her hand in an all-encompassing gesture. “Yahweh’s oath of sevens made with Abraham, the promised blessing, and Yahweh’s deliverance from bondage are the themes of the Song of Moses that Daniel uses in chapter 9 when he sets out to petition Yahweh to deliver his people from Babylonian captivity.” Cadence looked at me, her eyes glistening.

"Timbre, do you see how beautiful this is? Because of Abraham's faith in Yahweh regarding Isaac, his promised heir, Abraham knew that he and Isaac, no matter what transpired on that mountain, would be returning. Yahweh, in honor of that faith, made an oath of sevens with Abraham and promised through Isaac's seed that all of the nations of the earth would be blessed." She placed her hand reverently on my open Bible. "Here in Daniel 9, Daniel petitions Yahweh, by way of Moses in Deuteronomy 7, to remember that oath of sevens Yahweh made with Abraham. That so-called 'covenant and mercy to them that love Him and keep His commandments.' Then, in answer to Daniel's petition, Yahweh sends him a prophetic vision that tells exactly when that promised oath of sevens, that blessing, would come to pass. He answers with a prophecy of seventy sevens that finds its spiritual, numerical, and phonetic roots in that ancient oath of sevens."

"I see it, Cadence." It was like watching a black-and-white movie and all of a sudden, a switch was flipped, and I was looking at high-definition, 3D color. Exquisite. Daniel 9 was a numerical and literary work of art right down to its word and letter structure—its purpose was to showcase the promise of Yahweh's Salvation, his Yeshua.

Cadence turned the pages of my Bible once more, this time to the New Testament. She stopped in the Book of Acts, chapter 3, and put her finger on verse 25. She looked at me. "Tell me that these words of Peter to his Jewish brethren don't just jump out at you now with their significance and symbolism."

Ye are the children of the prophets, and of the covenant which God made with our fathers, saying unto Abraham, And in thy seed shall all the kindreds of the earth be blessed. Unto you first God, having raised up his Son Jesus, sent him to bless you, in turning away every one of you from his iniquities.

Cadence underlined the words *sent him to bless you.*

Well there it was. Jesus was the blessing, the promised salvation. "Sent him to bless you ..." I repeated solemnly. I bowed my head. Tomorrow morning, we'd make one more trip to civilization to enter the last answer to my father's ciphers. What then?

Chapter 110

The Final Answer

We got an early start for Tucson. As we wound our way out of the final turns of the Tonto National Forest, the sun burst forth over the Phoenix skyline, warming my fingers on the steering wheel. A soft gasp from Cadence made me turn. My sister's face glowed in the first golden blush of the smoky desert sun. In just a few weeks, the craven creature I hadn't recognized in Eric Pincer's office had been transformed. The sparkling intensity in her violet eyes had dispelled sunken, stagnant pools of pain. Smooth, full, tan skin had supervened the shriveled emaciation of a drug addict. And the confident, swinging stride of an athlete had usurped the stuttering steps of a person with one foot in the grave. But it was her voice that seemed to capture the full measure of her transformation. In just her gasp, vibrant, compelling, living wonder burst from a transformed soul.

"Glorious, isn't it, Timbre?" she said as she held up her hands as if to capture the life-giving warmth.

I glanced at her again and said, "A marvelous metamorphosis, indeed."

Cadence inclined her head, then shrugged. "Never thought of the sunrise as a metamorphosis, but I guess I could see it that way." After a moment, she asked with a mischievous smile, "If you were a larva that metamorphosed into a beautiful butterfly, what kind would you choose to be?"

I responded without hesitation. "A *Cadenceus danaus plexippus Linnaeus*."

Cadence's warm, rich laugh filled the truck. "Never heard of a Cadence Monarch Butterfly before," she said, smiling warmly at me.

I laughed with her. "Rather rare, from what I hear. Only one known to exist."

Two hours later, we were sitting outside a Tucson Starbucks. Two steaming cups of bitter, brown liquid filled the truck's cab with the musky scent of roasted coffee beans.

Cadence had my laptop on her knees. We both read the instructions a final time.

In its original form this enciphered passage is 13 Hebrew words. These words pose a Biblical riddle that has challenged some of the greatest minds in history. The key to the riddle is hidden in seven and its significance revealed by swear. If you can decipher this passage and solve the riddle, the inheritance is yours.

Your answer will be the 5 numbers that lie between the א and ת.

Enter your answer in the spaces provided.
Only one attempt allowed per 24 hours.

ת__ __ . __ __ __א

The five blank spaces between the Hebrew alaph and *tav* were our father's way of representing the beginning and the end, the starting and ending point.

Cadence looked over at me. "You want to do the honors?"

"No, go ahead. You are the one who figured out the answer. This is your inheritance, anyway."

Cadence frowned at me. "Our inheritance, brother. Plus, I've already got the real inheritance," she said, typing *515.02* in the blanks. Cadence slowly pushed the enter key with her index finger. The screen went blank. We glanced at each other.

A few seconds later, a new screen appeared. We read the words together.

I knew in whom I had believed and was persuaded that He was able to keep the two of you whom I have committed unto Him against that day. Though all my worldly possessions are now yours, I hope you understand that the love and faith these ciphers and riddles concealed are your real inheritance, the only one that matters.

I hope to see you both again someday on the other side of eternity.

Love, Dad.

He believed we would find our way back," Cadence whispered.

Yes. He had acted in faith, believing we'd not only start on this journey, but we'd also finish it. Like Abraham believed that he and Isaac would come back down off that mountain together, our father believed that Cadence and I would climb out of the valley of death we had wandered into. What was it like to have that kind of faith? Was it a single decision or a lifetime of small steps that comprised a life of faithfulness? I wanted to have that kind of faith—that kind of confidence in God.

Sensing Cadence's eyes on me, I turned to her. She reached across the seat for my hand, her eyes misty.

"He loved us, both of us."

I nodded. I knew that now for sure. I guess I'd known that all along. His Lazarus Ciphers were a demonstration of his love for God and us. "No doubt."

I read the final line on the webpage.

Contact my attorney, Eric Pi*ncer, for final instructions on the distribution of my estate.*

I reached for my briefcase and took out the burner phone. It was still early, but with the East Coast time difference, our father's lawyer or someone at the firm would be available. Time to finish this and move on with our lives. I punched in the number and extended the phone to Cadence. "You talk to him," Cadence said, withdrawing her hand.

"It's your inheritance, Caden."

She pointed to our father's message. "He knew we would both be here at the finish."

"I know, but I forfeited my share by taking the twenty thousand."

Cadence stomped her foot. "This is our inheritance, Timmy."

"I appreciate that, Cadence, but we solved these ciphers using your account. You need to talk to Eric. This is a legal matter now, and he has to talk to you." Raising my brows, I extended the phone.

Cadence flattened her mouth, then took the cell and punched the green button. After it started ringing, she pushed the speaker button. On the third ring, I recognized the voice that answered.

"Layton, Barrett, and Stowe. This is Alex. How may I help you?"

"Hello, Alex. This is Cadence Plummer. May I talk to Eric Pincer, please?"

"May I ask what this is regarding, Miss Plummer?"

"My father's estate."

"One moment, please."

A moment later, a cool voice came on the line. "Hello. This is Eric Pincer." When Cadence shot me a nervous glance instead of responding, Eric spoke again. "Miss Plummer, are you there?"

"Hello, Mr. Pincer. This is Cadence," my sister said, grasping the edge of the phone so hard her fingers turned white.

"I was expecting your call, Cadence. I've been following your progress. Based upon the electronic notification I just received, you have completed all seven of your father's ciphers."

Cadence looked at me. I could read her thoughts. She wanted to tell him that we had solved the ciphers together. I shook my head.

"You got this," I mouthed.

"Yes, sir," she said after an uncomfortable pause. "The ciphers are finished. What is our next step?"

I gave Cadence a *be careful* look. She should have said *my next step*.

"We need to meet. There are papers for you to sign."

Cadence raised her eyebrow and gave me a wicked little grin. "Will I need an attorney?" For my benefit, she added a wink.

Eric Pincer didn't reply right away. When he did, his voice was tight. "I don't think that will be necessary, Miss Plummer. I'm your father's lawyer, and I can walk you through the process. But if you prefer to have another set of eyes, why don't you ask your brother to be present? Estate law is not his area of expertise.—he's more a lights-and-sirens kind of guy—but he might understand the concepts enough to represent your interests."

My ears burned at the insult. The look on Cadence's face, though, more than made up for the slight. A fire ignited in her eyes. The muscles in her jaw bunched. I pushed my hands downward in a damping motion and shook my head. Her jaw unclenched slightly.

Cadence gave a brittle laugh. "Indeed. Reminds me of one of my father's favorite quotes about estate lawyers. Maybe you've heard it. It was by Lord Henry Brougham. He said that a lawyer is 'a learned gentleman who rescues your estate from your enemies and keeps it himself.'" She let her words hang for a moment. "Surely, you understand my concern well enough to appreciate why I would like to have my brother present."

The laugh that came back over the phone had a wild, strident ring to it. "Touché, Miss Plummer. Your father was a smart man for a lawyer." Eric laughed again at his joke.

"My dad was a genius," she shot back.

Silence. Cadence and I looked at each other. I mouthed, "Where to meet?"

She nodded and turned back to the phone. "When would be a convenient time for us to meet?"

"Let me check my schedule," Eric replied, all warmth gone from his voice. After he returned—"How about the day after tomorrow? I can fly out late tomorrow night, and we can meet in the late morning or early afternoon."

"At your offices in Phoenix?" Cadence asked.

"Sure, if you want. But if you like, I'll come to wherever you are staying. There is not much to the paperwork. A few signatures are all I'll need for now. I have a packet of keys for your father's homes and vehicles. There will be some deed transfers, and we will have to talk about what you want to do with your father's stock and bond portfolios. We'll take care of all that from this end after the formalities are completed."

Cadence held her hand over the phone and asked me, "Meet at the cabin?"

I shrugged. "It's probably safer there than Dad's office in Phoenix. Benito Silva might have someone watching for us there. Yeah, let's do it at the cabin."

Cadence beamed. "Seems fitting in a way, don't you think?"

"It does, Sis."

Cadence turned back to the phone. "Would you mind coming up to Dad's cabin in Payson? I think he would appreciate us settling it there. He loved the place so much."

"That would be fine. I'd like to see the place again. Your father often talked about it. Noon then, day after tomorrow."

Cadence handed me the phone.

"Now what?" Cadence sighed. "I've been so focused on solving Dad's ciphers, now that we are finished, honestly, I'm a little lost."

"Me too." I took a deep breath and slapped my knees with my hands. "Well, one thing is for sure. I'm not going back to where I've been."

"I'm not going back, either," Cadence said with conviction.

"For starters, then, let's head back up to the cabin. If Silva is still tracking our location through Dad's IP, then we need to get away from this place."

"Yeah, I forgot about him." Her brow wrinkled. "What are you going to do about him once we've got the inheritance? You can't run forever, you know."

"I know that, Sis. I'm tired of running." "If you'll loan me the money, I'll try and pay my debt. If that doesn't work, and he wants his pound of flesh, too, I'll find a safe place for you, and I'll go to war. I don't want to look over my shoulder for the rest of my life. And I don't want to move too far away from you."

"Loan nothing." Her hair came loose from its clip with the vehemently shake of her head. "How many times do I have to tell you? This is our inheritance. You can have whatever you like as long as we can share Grandpa's cabin. That's where I want to spend the rest of my days."

I put the truck in reverse and backed out of the parking space. "You can't live like a hermit the rest of your life."

"Why not?"

I accelerated out of the parking lot. "Well, for one, it's not healthy for you. You are still young and beautiful. Find yourself a good man and raise a family. Pass along your life lessons and wisdom to the next generation. And second, if I remember correctly, didn't you make a promise to use your special gifts to share the story of Yeshua as Dad's shared his with us?"

A long silence fell. "I did," Cadence admitted.

"Well, don't you intend to keep your promise?"

The equivocation on Cadence's face disappeared in a smile of resolve. "I do intend to keep that promise, Timmy."

There was an undefinable certainty to her expression that told me my sister would be okay. With or without me, her faith would find a way. About my future I still had apprehension. Like an ink stain spreading on a white tablecloth, I felt a growing unease.

Chapter 111

Ripples in Time

I worked feverishly by the dim light that glimmered around the edges of the door. Thick, dusty air left an earthy, chalky taste in my mouth. My breath came in ragged, panting gasps. With grim determination, I pried and levered another brick out of the wall. My stiff fingers released their hold on the cold crowbar, and it fell to the stone floor with a clanking ring.

My hand moved toward the dislodged brick as if I were reaching through honey. As my fingers closed around it, scratching and growling rushed toward me from the darkness of the hallway. My hair prickled over every inch of my body. I willed myself to throw the brick but watched in horror as my arm moved with the sluggishness of a sloth. I screamed in voiceless loathing as glowing eyes appeared out of the darkness, and the fetid, sulfurous breath of the creatures stung my nose. In panic, I threw the brick. Slowly, like an insect swallowed by the golden amber of tree sap, the brick fell through the air and noiselessly landed at my feet.

Recoiling from the wretched sounds, I fell backward and landed with my back to the door and my feet hanging over the two layers that remained of the brick wall. The hot breath of the creatures fanned my bare feet. I wrapped my arms around my legs in a tight, protective grasp. Yellow fangs and glowing eyes advanced.

Urgent knocking sounded on the door behind me. With a whimpering whine, the phantoms withdrew. I sagged against the door as it vibrated under the earnest assault.

"I'm trying to get to the door," I sobbed. "Please don't leave."

A soft, warm hand touched my shoulder. Then a gentle voice called. I opened my eyes and blinked several times. Cadence stood over me. I released my arms from around my legs and swung my feet to the floor. My nose still burned with the terrible smell. I sat on my hands to try and stop the shaking. The vein in my neck pulsed like a trip hammer.

Cadence's concerned gaze assessed me as she sat down beside me on the bunk.

"Did you hear me?" I asked in a shaky, groggy voice.

Cadence nodded, and tears filled her eyes. "Tell me about it?"

"It was so real, Sis. I was trying to get the final bricks out of the way so I could get to the door. Those terrible creatures were trying to get me, and I couldn't throw the bricks to scare them off. You know, like those slow-motion dreams where you are trying to run away from a bad guy, but you can't seem to move fast enough?"

"Yeah. How'd you get away from them?"

"The knocking on the door scared them away. Then you woke me up."

Cadence stood and put on a smile. "How about we get some breakfast and then take a walk down to the creek? Some fresh air and sun will do us both good. I don't want to hang around the cabin all day waiting for Eric Pincer."

I rose, too, and grabbed the bunk post to steady myself. "Give me a minute to brush my teeth and pull myself together, and I'll help you make breakfast."

An hour later, the sun warmed the backs of our heads as we gazed down at the edge of the trail to Clover Creek. A layer of clouds hung in the canyon, like foamy cream on a piping-hot latte. With the first streaks of sun tinging the far edge of this cloudy blanket, it began to move. The stirring grew as more of the sun's energy found its way through the stately ponderosas picketing the canyon edge.

"Magnificent!" Cadence threw her arms open in a wide embrace. She tilted her head toward the trail. "Ready?"

"Sure. Just as long as you don't run."

She laughed, but her lack of reply hinted that she'd thought about it.

We started down the steep trail like two kids on a secret rendezvous, entering the vaporous layer just as bars of burning light set the misty veil on fire. As if in reverent tribute, all living sounds of the canyon stilled. The only disturbance to this homage was the drip of dew from trees and plants around us.

The shimmering began to lighten. Then, as suddenly as it had been set on fire, our gleaming velarium disappeared, as if its golden cords had been cut and it had floated away, leaving behind the pale blue of the early-morning sky. On cue, the canyon sounds returned.

Twenty minutes later, we sat on granite boulders as the gurgling waters of Clover Creek eddied and swirled around us. We faced the west wall of the canyon and watched the morning sun trace its way down the sheer cliffs.

"After today, this place will be safe." I cupped a handful of the cool water and let it trickle through my hand. I glanced at my sister.

The dreamy look on Cadence's face faded. "What do you mean? You don't think we are safe right now?"

I shook my head. "No, I mean after today, after you sign the paperwork, you'll own the homestead. No one can take it away from you then."

"You know the first thing I'm going to do when this is all settled?" Cadence leaned her head against her right shoulder.

"I have no idea, Sis."

"I'm going to have Eric add your name to the deed of this place."

I said nothing for some time, then I murmured, "Thank you, Caden. I'd like that."

"So would I," she replied. "This place will always be special. It is where God honored our father's faith and returned us to ours."

I picked a flat pebble out of the sparkling water. With a flick of my wrist, I sent it skipping across the water, leaving behind little circular ripples that expanded and then merged with each other and the other currents of the water. My life, our lives, resembled those ripples. For just a fraction of a second in the eternal waters of time, we made our own ripples. Those ripples added energy and a subtle influence to the currents of the surrounding water. Then the irresistible river of time overwhelmed and merged them in some unfathomable purpose that only the mind of God could comprehend.

I gazed at my sister until she turned her head. "Thanks for having faith in me, Cadence. And …" As I searched for words, she waited, silent, expectant. "Thank you for your faith in God's purpose for me. Your faith has sparked the dormant seeds of my own—seeds I didn't even know I still had buried in the garden of my heart. I'm ready to believe again. I can feel it in my soul. It's like I have a different kind of fire burning there now. Does that make any sense?"

Cadence wiped the corner of her eye. She tried to speak, but it only came out as a half-choking gasp of deep emotion. She nodded, tears streaming down her face now. She clenched her teeth and swallowed several times before speaking, her voice husky. "Your love and care gave me a second chance too."

"But I … my motivation wasn't …"

Cadence shook her head and raised her hand. "No buts, Timbre. It's all been part of a divine purpose to bring us into our inheritance."

"Guess I can accept that." The sun, not quite halfway across the canyon, split a passing cloud. I glanced at my watch. "Speaking of inheritances, Sis, we'd better get going. Eric should be here in an hour."

She sighed and looked around one last time. "I suppose we'd better."

I led the way back up the trail, setting a brutal pace, and we were both panting by the time we'd climbed the last set of stepped switchbacks. Hands behind our head, we paused and caught our breath.

Cadence flashed me one of her mischievous smiles. She took off running. Over her shoulder, she called, "Last one to the cabin gets to do the dishes tonight."

I leapt into motion. She was fast but not as fast as she had once been. Her laugh rang out as I gained on her. Then I tripped. I managed to keep from plowing the dirt with my face, but I skidded some skin off both elbows.

I picked myself up while Cadence disappeared into the cabin with a triumphant laugh. The rest of the way to the cabin, I picked sand and bits of debris from my hands and elbows. I crossed the porch, a rueful smile on my face.

"You cheated, Cadence," I called out as I stepped through the door. I looked up as I removed the final grains of sand from my hands and froze.

In a split second, I took it all in. A bald man stood behind my sister, his face cold and impassive. One of his hairy arms encircled her neck, and his hand covered her mouth. Cadence struggled, eyes bulging, making small grunting sounds.

"So nice of you to join us, Mr. Plummer," a soft, slurred voice called from the shadows.

Benito Silva perched on the kitchen counter like a white gargoyle. His weak lips split in a crooked smile broken spasmodically by the twitching of his left cheek. The incongruent blinking of his swollen eyes resembled that of a deranged Morse code operator. Across his black-and-purple forehead, a gash stretched from eye to eye, courtesy of my trip rope and the stairwell of the White Wolf. The stapling on the gash looked like a stainless-steel zipper on a swollen blue plum. One leg, from toe to ankle, dangled with an alabaster cast.

The blinking stopped as I launched myself at the disgusting man. Benito Silva howled like a wild animal. The man holding my sister released his hand over her mouth and reached for something behind his back. Cadence screamed. My world turned black.

Chapter 112

Backup

A scream from the cabin rent the quiet mountain air. The lawyer edged from the forest and slid behind one of the giant ponderosas encircling the clearing near the barn. A second later, a pickup truck and two Cadillac Escalades emerged from the wooded drive and lined up in front of the cabin. Three muscled men in black pants and button-down gray shirts got out of the black Escalades. Each man had an assault rifle slung over his shoulder. The pickup truck turned around and backed up to the porch. The lawyer stiffened as another scream came from the cabin. It was cut off by a meaty slap and then the thud of a body falling onto a wood floor.

Four men unloaded a fifty-gallon metal barrel from the truck. With grunts and curses, they carried it to the porch. One of the men adjusted his rifle, then grabbed the top edge of the barrel and carefully rolled it into the cabin. The cabin door closed. One man stayed on the porch, and the others spread out around the clearing, two heading his way. The lawyer slid back behind the tree as they approached the front of the barn. He gave them a couple more seconds and then looked around the tree. They were no longer in sight.

He didn't know how many men were in the cabin, so a direct approach was out of the question. Only a couple of the men in sight moved with any military bearing. The rest joked and looked around like they were bored. The 1WOLFE license plate of one of the black Cadillac Escalades told him it belonged to Benito Silva. The little mobster had come to collect his pound of flesh from Timbre. Cadence would suffer too. He pushed the thought of what was in store for them out of his mind.

Reaching into his waistband at the small of this back, he slid out a Heckler & Koch 45. He checked the pistol and chambered a round. From his left pocket, he removed a key, placed it between his teeth, and bit down hard. He would have to move fast. No need to waste time looking for it later. He felt the pouches on his camouflaged pants to make sure the spare magazines were where they needed to be, then took two deep breaths through clenched teeth and stepped from behind the tree.

He walked toward the barn with unhurried steps, his pistol beside his right leg. When he was halfway to the side door of the barn, the man on the porch finally saw him. The man's rifle started to come up. The lawyer let loose a quick shot in his direction and ran for the side barn door. As he reached it, the man on the porch opened up with his assault rifle. Rounds peppered the side of the barn.

The man on the porch ceased firing as his two comrades came around the corner at a run. The lawyer shot the first man in the chest, and he went down in a heap. The second man got off a round before the lawyer dropped him with a shot to the head. The lawyer ignored the burning in his arm as he removed the key from his mouth and inserted it into the locked door. The man on the porch fired again. The lock turned, the lawyer opened the door and stepped through.

He closed and locked the steel door and leaned against it for a moment. He set down his HK45 and peeled off his woodlands camouflage jacket. Yanking the Velcro straps of his Kevlar vest, he dropped that to the floor as well. Sweat soaked his tan T-shirt. Blood dripped off his fingers from the wound in his forearm. The lawyer inspected it closely. Thankfully, the bullet had passed through the muscled part of his arm. It would hurt, but it was not a severe or incapacitating injury.

Loud, ringing impacts of bullets on the steel door told him he did not have much time. He cut his jacket with swift, sharp jerks to fashion a makeshift bandage for his arm and tied it over the wound with his teeth and free hand. Satisfied, he clipped the folding knife on the inside collar of his T-shirt where it would be out of the way and accessible in a hurry.

Pounding on the door with a heavy object brought his head up. Quickly, he emptied the pockets and pouches of his pants. He patted his pants one last time to make sure nothing was in them. He left everything on the floor in a pile except two clips for his HK45, then grabbed the pistol from the floor and ejected the spent clip. As he ran for the basement stairs, the lawyer inserted a fresh clip into his pistol and another into his pocket.

Time for a reckoning.

Chapter 113

Captivity

I regained consciousness with the splash of cold water on my face. My head ached, and my vision cleared slowly. I was sitting in the wooden kitchen table chair, my right hand secured to the chair, my left free. A steel barrel loomed close enough to touch with my free hand. My stomach churned—a result of the strong chemical smell in the room or the throbbing of my head? Nothing made much sense at first. Then I remembered Cadence. I turned my head in search of my sister, and the sharp movement brought darkness to my vision. Slowly, my sight returned.

She lay still on the bearskin rug in front of the fireplace, face down with her arms tied behind her back. A rope bound her feet. Connected to the rope between her ankles was a thin wire, strung from one of the logs in the ceiling. It glistened and sparkled. This didn't make any sense until my gaze fell on the fire in the fireplace. In front of the hearth, a childlike figure stood with arms extended to the heat. On each side of the fireplace, men waited in the darkness. Slowly, the ghostly figure turned to face me, but Benito's face remained hidden in the shadows. Involuntarily, I shivered. The outline of his small body glowed and flickered like some demon who'd stepped from the flames of hell.

I couldn't see Benito's lips move, but I heard his voice. "I once told you what I did to the last person who called me an albino runt, didn't I, Mr. Plummer?"

Nausea swept over me. A man soaked in bleach, hung from a bridge. And it hit me—the chemical smell was bleach. A terror I'd never felt before filled me. *Dear God, please no.*

I steeled myself for what was to come. One thing I wouldn't do today was show this man fear. That was what he wanted, but he wasn't going to get it from me. I said nothing. A new, calculating fire lit within me. Not the old, uncontrolled rage. A protective indignation that left me calm and ready. This wasn't going to end well, but I knew one thing. Today, Benito Silva would not be leaving this cabin alive. If I had to drag him back into hell to save my sister, I was going to do it.

Benito moved from in front of the fire and limped around the barrel, the thud … thud … thud … of his cast foot on the cabin's wood floor the only sound. The stuttering walk ended at my chair. Flickering firelight now clearly lit the contours of the man's face. I stared at the ghastly scar on his head. His left eye bulged with red veins and purple blotches, the lid unable to shield its grotesquely swollen member. A dark stain seeped from under his eye socket. Like cancer under his pale, cadaverous skin, the stain spread down his cheek. A cruel, demented smile split the pigment-less face. The stitches across his brow grew little buzzard's feet where the skin stretched from his hideous smile.

An unholy fire—a terrifying insanity—danced in Silva's eyes as his foot thudded again and he moved still closer. I fought to keep my own eyes open as his stale, tobacco-stained breath enveloped me. He leaned in close. His lips pulled further back in a cruel smile that revealed the tips of his yellow teeth.

I stared at him without flinching. That set him off because his mouth moved in voiceless, spastic grimaces. His jaw muscles corded and uncorded. Foam built at the corners of his thin lips.

"Don't you have anything to say, tough guy?" he hissed as white spittle spewed from his mouth and peppered my face. Benito glanced toward Cadence. "I've decided to cancel your debt because"—he gave a sick little laugh and poked the air in Cadence's direction—"after today, you won't be around for me to collect. I'll be transferring your debt to your sister. Shall I play a Cadence for you, Timbre?"

An anticipatory grunt from the shadows on the right side of the fireplace made me turn my head. It was the big guy who'd man-handled my sister. The old anger burst from its furnace. This time, though, instead of the consuming fury, my white-hot anger calmed and sharpened my focus. I knew what I had to do.

I turned back to Benito and smiled. "Not today, you little runt," I said, cold and deadly. "It's going to take a lot more than the two-and-a-quarter men in this room for you to play any music."

My words had their desired effect. He leaned away from me and swung his waxen hand at my face. If I had been in the boxing ring, I could have hit him twice in the time it took his open-handed slap to reach me. It stung but didn't even turn my head. I braced myself with aftershave with more force than that. I almost felt sorry for him. I couldn't help the laugh that escaped.

"I misjudged you, Silva. I thought there were two-and-a-quarter men here. Now I know there are, at most, two men and a boy."

He stood there, his swollen eye nearly popping out of the bruised lid. Then I hit him with my free hand. He slid across the floor and lay still.

The man on the left side of the room ran for the still form of his boss. The big man leaped over my sister and started pummeling me with his fists. I lowered my head and let them come. He was strong, but no skilled power lay behind his punches. Finally, he caught me with a hard right, my head snapped back, and the room went dark again.

When I came to with the shock of more cold water on my face, I saw a sight that would give me nightmares forever. My sister hung upside down over the barrel of bleach. She must have still been unconscious because she didn't move. Her body just slowly turned one way and then the other in the flickering light. Her hair, in a shimmering cascade, hung into the mouth of the barrel.

My gaze followed the piano wire from the rope around my sister's ankles, up through the beam in the ceiling, and down into the gloved hands of the muscled man. The hard, chiseled lines of his face had been replaced by wrinkles of anticipation. Benito stood at a safe distance on the other side of the barrel, his face once again in the shadows. Judging by the twitches and jerks of his silhouette, his agitation was extreme. The second man hovered on the other side of the barrel at the edge of the firelight.

I should have been terrified, but I was not, maybe partly because the white-hot resolve had burned away my fear. But some part of it was unaccountable because the berserk fury that normally consumed me was missing. I observed the room around me and the people in it with a slow-motion clarity. Maybe it was a bit of crazy hope or a whiff of faith, but I knew that my sister would not die in a barrel of bleach at the hand of a madman.

Part of my hope rested on something I'd seen just before the right hook knocked me unconscious. The idiot who'd tied me must have assumed there would be no resistance or was too stupid to know better, but he'd secured the zip ties to the lower portion of the chair's legs. All I had to do was jerk the chair up two inches, and my legs would be free. Battle lust mounted within me. I was going to stand up, yank my sister to safety with my free hand, then use my bound hand and the chair it was attached to as a weapon.

Chapter 114

One Conundrum, Two

I couldn't see Benito's face, but he must have seen mine because a gun appeared in his hand. He tried to speak, but his words came in stuttered, painful gasps. Had my earlier punch broken his jaw? My grim satisfaction faded as Benito pointed his gun at Cadence's head. Fear wormed its way through my anger. There was no way now I could whisk her to safety before he pulled the trigger.

"You ... will … pay …" Benito managed to get out. With a violent jerk, he threw a cup of water at my sister's face. Her eyes came open, and her head moved in short jerks as she tried to get her bearings. Her gaze finally found mine. There was confusion and terror there.

"Timbre, what's happe—" Cadence coughed and couldn't continue. After she managed to stop coughing, she didn't say anything more. Her sharp mind must have worked out our predicament because the next turn of her body brought her face to face with me, and she gave me a sad, resolved look.

I was speechless for a moment, then I said, "I am so sorry I got you into this, Sis."

She shook her head. "I'm not. I know in whom I have—" Again her words were cut off by coughing.

"No … more … talk," Benito gasped out. With a twitch of his head toward the man waiting in the shadows, he said, "Now." The second man moved around to help. Silva kept the pistol pointed at my sister.

The big guy spoke for the first time. "Hold out your hand." Before I realized what was happening, they had wrapped the piano wire around my hand. Instinctively, I grasped it as tight as I could. They let go, and searing pain lashed through my hand as the wire bit into it. Cadence dropped a few inches closer to the barrel, and my hand turned blue.

Benito's sick, rasping laugh was cut off by a gasp of pain. Now that my hand was fully occupied, he moved around the barrel to face me again, just inches from my face. I could see the crooked angle of his jaw and the sharp edge of bone just below the skin. He must have been in excruciating pain, but that didn't stop the wicked, broken smile that briefly crossed his face. Benito waited. He wanted me to beg, the one thing I wasn't going to do.

I looked away from those burning eyes and back at my hand. The pain was like nothing I'd ever felt. Blood had started to drip from just below my little finger, where the wire bit into the flesh, tendons, and bone. Even if I could have stood the pain, which was doubtful, the wire was going to cut through all the soft parts of my hand. Eventually, voluntary or involuntarily, I was going to let go of the wire.

Cadence spun slowly back to face me. Her gaze went to my bloody hand, then to my face. Something beautiful in her look gave me resolve. Faith. She accepted her fate, and she was not afraid to die. But there was more. Her look told me that this wasn't the end for either of us. It was, at worst, a painful but new beginning. Somehow, I felt she now knew I believed that too. I grunted and took a deep breath. I was ready to meet my maker, but I wasn't going to just let my sister die while my heart still beat a painful staccato in my chest. I called to her.

"I, too, know in whom I have believed, Cadence." Then I started counting. "One conundrum, two conundrum, three conundrum." Just as I lost sight of her face, her eyes closed, and she took a deep breath.

I let go of the wire, jerked my chair, and stood.

Chapter 115

Of Heroes, Hating & Heeling

Cadence plunged headfirst into the barrel of chlorine.

I kept counting. "Four conundrum, five …" It was a game we'd played as children. Every time we passed through a tunnel, Cadence and I would hold our breath, and our father would start counting, "One conundrum, Two conundrum …" Even after we emerged on the other side, he'd keep counting until one of us took a breath. I never figured out why he used the word *conundrum* instead of *potato* or *Mississip*pi like other parents, but that was our father.

The moment my ankles came loose from the chair, I grabbed Benito's white hair right where the gray streak cut his scalp. The anger I'd held in reserve came flooding out, and I slammed his head down against the edge of the metal barrel. His pistol fell from his hand and slid across the floor. As I let go of Silva's head, I grabbed my sister's pants at the waist and pulled her out of the barrel. Thankfully, she had doubled over as she fell so that only her head and shoulders had been submerged.

I gave Cadence a violent push toward the bearskin rug. Maybe she'd be able to use it to wipe or absorb some of the chemicals from her face before she had to take her first breath. But I couldn't worry about that now. I still had two bad guys to deal with.

I pivoted in a violent, swinging arch. The chair became my scythe. The big guy reacted first, his gun coming up. His first shot missed me as I spun. The look of surprise was still on his face as the chair hit him. The gun flew from his hand, and he crumpled to the floor.

The other guy reacted too slowly as well. He must not have had a weapon because he dove for Silva's gun. I landed on top of him as his hands closed around the weapon. Our bodies jerked with the muffled shot. The man screamed and went limp. The broken remnants of the chair hung from my left wrist as I straightened.

Cadence was rubbing her face on the bearskin rug and coughing in ragged gasps. Across the room, the big man now stood with the gun in his hand. I'd run out of time. He raised it until it was aligned with my chest. His finger tightened on the trigger. But he didn't shoot. His expression changed to a look of pure malevolence, and he lowered the pistol until it pointed at Cadence. He gave me one last evil grin. Then a small hole appeared in his forehead, and the back of his head exploded in a deafening roar.

I stared at the fallen thug, my mind grasping for an explanation. Hadn't everyone been accounted for? I turned, bracing for the impact of the next bullet. What I saw was incomprehensible. A man, a livid scar across his face, stood with his arm extended and a smoking pistol in his grasp. I raised my shaking, bloody hand. I tried to speak, but my tongue cleaved to the top of my mouth. Surprise, then respect, and finally love, flashed across the man's face—because the man was my father.

He stood in the pantry doorway like a ghost from the grave. A bloody bandage encircled his forearm, and long streaks of blood colored his tan T-shirt and camouflaged pants. It felt like I'd been staring at him for minutes, but it couldn't have been more than a few, precious seconds because the gun still trailed smoke. His curt nod and glance at Cadence brought me back to my present circumstances. With his free hand, my father pulled a knife from the collar of his T-shirt while he tucked his pistol against the small of his back. He tossed me the knife as he leaped past to attend to Cadence. I caught the knife, opened it, and slashed the zip tie that held the remnants of the chair to my left hand.

"We need to wash her down so she can breathe," I said.

Dad scooped Cadence up in his arms. I followed him toward the bathroom but stopped near the front door. It was cracked. There had to be more of Silva's men outside. I took several quick steps and slammed and bolted the door just as boots hit the porch. Both security shutters were closed. Benito must have closed them when I was unconscious, probably so he could do his gruesome work in the dark. I shuddered.

Dad had Cadence in the bathtub and was washing the chlorine from her face and hair. The room reeked. I coughed and sat down on the edge of the tub beside my father. With his knife, I cut the rope that bound my sister's feet, then bunched it and the wire in a tight bundle and threw it in the trash.

Cadence's eyelid still squeezed tight together. Dad smiled and raised his finger to his mouth. I nodded, my eyes wet. I still didn't believe what I was seeing. I couldn't imagine what Cadence's reaction would be when she opened her eyes.

When her coughing fit finally passed, her breaths came in shallow, panting rasps. But these gradually subsided as well.

"Timbre?" she asked when she could speak

"I'm here, Sis. It's all good now. You okay?"

Cadence coughed again but nodded. I reached for a towel as Dad turned off the water and passed it to him. He gently dried my sister's face and then put the towel over her head and blotted her wet hair.

From under the towel, in a muffled, husky rasp, Cadence asked, "Can I open my eyes now?"

I could barely answer past the tightness of my throat. "Sure, Sis, I wish you would."

Dad let go of the towel. Cadence reached up and pulled the towel off her head. She peered out from under her wet, stringy, bleached-blonde hair. Her arms froze, and she grasped the towel to her chest, the tendons of her hands standing out, raised and white. She gasped, and her hands came back up to cover her mouth. A broken, desperate cry escaped her lips. She came up out of the tub in a screaming, laughing rush and jumped into my father's arms as he stood. I will never forget the sight. And no matter how long I lived, it would always bring tears to my eyes.

They stood like that for minutes, my sister's soft weeping interrupted by coughing fits from her chlorine-burned lungs. The sound of a high-powered rifle interrupted their reunion. A second later a burst of semi-automatic fire answered. My father gently pushed Cadence back.

"Timbre and I have unfinished business out there." He tilted his head toward the living room. "Stay in here and get out of those clothes. We'll throw you some clean ones through the door in a few minutes. I'll come get you when it's safe."

Cadence clenched his arms, and a look of alarm crossed her face. Then she released him with an understanding nod. She looked at me for the first time, her expression filled with admiration. She pointed at herself, gave me the hand sign for love, and then pointed at me. My heart swelled, and I smiled. She turned away with more tears in her eyes. We left her alone and closed the door.

From the door to the living room, we surveyed the macabre scene. The crack of a rifle sounded again and our heads jerked toward the front door. This time a piercing scream and a thud on the porch followed the shot. Men yelled and more shots followed. "Sounds like a Winchester 300 magnum," Dad said his focus fixed on the front.

I glanced at my father. "Are they shooting at each other?"

His lips turned down in a frown. "I don't think so. Someone with a high-powered hunting rifle seems to be shooting at Benito's men. Doesn't make sense."

He let a long breath out through his nose, as if dismissing the outside threats and returned his attention to the room. His gaze settled on my damaged hand that still oozed blood. "We should bind that up and then contact law enforcement. I think it's best if we stay hunkered down in here until help arrives. I'll grab the first-aid kit."

Without waiting for my response, he walked toward the pantry, flipping on the kitchen light as he went. The moment Dad disappeared into the pantry, Benito Silva came off the floor like a jack-in-the-box in a haunted house. He didn't seem to see me as he wailed and screamed in a mix of Spanish and what sounded like German. The edge of the barrel had done fearful damage to his face. His nose twisted to one side, and a bloody curtain of flesh hung from his forehead.

The big man's pistol lay where it had fallen when he'd been shot, mere steps from where I stood. I jumped for the weapon, scooping it up. Benito turned toward me and extended his arms. He gave a blood-curdling scream that ended in a wailing whimper. This was the monster that had terrorized my sister and me for weeks now. I lifted the pistol, wrapping my finger around the trigger. A warm hard hand on my arm stopped me. I turned my head in anger.

My father stood there. His face was hard, but something softer flickered in his eyes. Sympathy. And pain? Why pain?

"Don't confuse a guilty conscience for justice," he said quietly.

I stared at him, uncomprehending. Fury still consumed my mind.

"If you pull that trigger, the guilt won't go away. It will only get worse."

"He tortured Cadence," I nearly yelled. "Didn't you see? He hung her upside down and was going to make me drown her in that barrel. He…"

I didn't finish because Benito started to sway like a drunken man, and he fell to his knees in front of me, his hands resting on the floor. Like a crimson waterfall, blood ran down his face and dripped onto the boards. The pistol in my hand followed him until it was pointed at the top of his snow-white head.

My father's hand squeezed my arm like a vise.

My face twisting, I shook my head. What was he thinking? "I have to end this now. I don't want to be looking over my shoulder forever."

"If you kill him in cold blood, you'll be no better than him. And he will haunt you for the rest of your life."

Better to battle a phantom of the mind, than a demon of flesh and blood. My finger curled around the trigger.

My father's hand squeezed even tighter. "It's our weakness that gives men like this the power that they have. Son, it was *your* weakness that brought him into our lives."

I clenched my teeth and steadied my arms. I looked down at the weeping, moaning monster at my feet.

"Timbre," my father said quietly. Finally, I shifted my gaze to him. "Do you know what he is saying?"

Benito was now repeating the same words over and over. I concentrated on the broken German.

"Papa, bitte schlag mich nicht mehr. Ich werde jetzt gut sein. Ich verspreche es, Papa. Ich verspreche es, Papa."

I shook my head.

"It means, 'Papa, please don't beat me anymore. I'll be a good boy, I promise, Papa. I promise, Papa.'"

A dark horror swept over me. Dad nodded sadly. I lowered the pistol. My father let go of my arm and extended his hand. I placed the pistol in it. I looked back down at Benito Silva, and the monster was gone. This time, I saw a broken and beaten little boy at my feet.

Dad walked over to the kitchen table, and the pistol and first-aid kit clunked down. "Come here, Timbre. Show me your hand," he said, his gentle voice belaying the hard look on his face. When he finished bandaging my hand, he handed me the first-aid kit. "Take care of his wounds." He indicated Benito still crouching on the floor. "We'll let the law mete out the justice he deserves."

I nodded, took the first-aid kit, and knelt in front of the man who I could no longer hate.

Chapter 116

Friend and Foe

Benito Silva's broken cries would forever haunt me. They would remind me that even men who acted like monsters were still human and that the line that separated the two was narrower than most of us realized.

When I'd finished dressing his injuries, I led him gently to the couch.

He grasped my arm as I sat him down. "*Lo siento*," he whispered in Spanish.

This I understood. *I am sorry*. I didn't know if he was still speaking to his father, to me, or to someone else. His apology made me think of my father's words, though. My weakness had given Benito Silva power. It had given him the power to hurt me, my sister, and others.

"I'm sorry, too," I said as I straightened.

While I attended Benito, my father had given Cadence fresh clothes. He'd gathered the dead men's guns and placed them on the kitchen counter along with their other belongings he found after quick a search. The shooting outside dwindled and finally stopped. Doors slammed and a car engine roared. Seconds later, the sound of spinning tires and flying gravel told us that someone had left in a hurry. It was deathly quiet then.

Of the cell phones Dad found on the intruders, one had been crushed, but the others appeared undamaged. Pressing the home button on one, Dad glanced up at me. "Had to empty my pockets to fit through the utility chase. Left my satellite phone in the barn." He stared at the screen a moment, then tossed it back on the table. "No service."

Benito had curled into a ball on the sofa, a staccato of soft moans mingled with guttural German escaping his broken lips. I headed for my laptop on the desk. "I'll send them an email. That's how Cadence and I contacted law enforcement before."

In my sent folder, while keeping an eye on Benito, I located the previous SOS from Cadence. A minute later, I sent two new emails requesting an ambulance and law enforcement. I also warned them there might be armed assailants in the vicinity. When I finished, I turned to my father.

"Okay to let Cadence out?"

"Yeah, just give me a second first." Dad walked to the bunkroom. He returned with a couple of sheets that he draped over the bodies.

I knocked on the bathroom door. "It's okay to come out now, Sis."

Cadence opened the door. She had on a fresh pair of blue jeans and a white t-shirt. She hugged me as she stepped out. "Oh, Timbre," she whispered in my ear.

I wrapped my arms tight around her. "He didn't die. God gave us a second chance to make things right." Then I held her at arm's length.

A radiant smile lit her face, and her lips quivered. "He did give us another chance. I hope I can live up to the opportunity."

Our arms around each other, we walked toward our father. The serious lines that etched his face transformed into a smile. He met our open arms halfway, and the three of us stood with our heads together in a tight circle.

"Thank you, Yahweh, for bringing us back together," our father said softly.

When we moved back from the embrace, all three of us wore big smiles, but we hesitated as if time and events had made us a bit like strangers.

Cadence broke the uncomfortable silence first and turned up her hands. “They told us you were dead. What happened?”

“It’s a long story,” he said and stepped over to the kitchen table. “You might want to sit down.” After we were all seated, he folded his hands in front of him. “My team and I were landing on the outskirts of the Libyan capital when I saw the missile launch. It streaked through the—”

At a knock on the cabin door, Cadence and I jumped. We looked at each other, and our father rose from the table. I followed him to the door. The knock was repeated. This time, a voice called out.

“Hello, Timber, Cadence? It’s Eric Pincer. Are you guys okay? … Hello? If you are in there, I’ve called the sheriff.”

My father looked at me.

I said quietly, “We solved the 7th cipher the day before yesterday. He agreed to come here to settle the will.”

My father’s face relaxed. He stepped closer to the door. “Are you alone, Eric?”

There was a long silence. “John?”

“Are you alone?” Dad repeated.

I heard a choking gasp through the door. “I’m alone. Is that you, John?”

“It’s me.” His rigid posture softening, Dad unbolted and then cracked the door. Peering out, he blinked several times in the bright light. “Eric.” The name held recognition. He opened the door farther—then stiffened.

Flame and a cracking roar exploded through the opening. My father stumbled backward and fell to the floor. Cadence screamed. Benito Silva whimpered.

A pistol barrel showed through the door, followed by Eric Pincer. He kicked the door the rest of the way open. A wild light gleamed in his eyes as he stepped into the room. "Well, isn't this a sweet reunion?"

Shock rooted me to the floor. As Cadence darted over and dropped to her knees beside my father, Benito jumped up from the couch. Eric blinked in the dark room, then his pistol bucked in his hand and Benito crumpled onto the rug.

Eric looked at me and gave a crazy laugh. "Another loose end that needed tidying up." He motioned with the pistol for me to join my father and sister. The muzzle of the weapon followed my progress as I knelt beside my father. Blood seeped from between my sister's white fingers where she held them over the wound in his upper right chest. Dad gathered himself as though he might stand.

Eric shook his head and clicked his tongue. He spoke to my father but pointed his pistol at Cadence. "Stay where you are, John, or this party will be over sooner than you expected."

Cadence looked at me, ignoring Eric and the gun. "We need to stop the bleeding. Do you have a knife?"

I glanced at Eric and the pistol pivoted to me as I retrieved my father's knife from my pocket. I handed it to Cadence. Carefully she cut off my father's bloody T-shirt. Then with swift sharp slices, she slit it into ribbons. Her hands shook. Some of the larger pieces she used for padding, and with the other, she tied the padding in place. The blood flow slowed. Deep lines on my father's face betrayed his pain, though he did not make a sound. Eric watched all this with macabre interest.

"So, it was you all along," Dad said with effort.

Eric nodded. "Yep, I had been siphoning off money for years until you stuck your nose in where it didn't belong."

"Then you sent me to Libya."

Eric waved the pistol in a sweeping gesture. "But you wouldn't die." He got a far-off look in his eyes and then said, "Just like Desert Storm. You led our platoon into a minefield. Rory stops to take a leak, and the next thing I know, I'm eating my best friend's brains."

Eric raised his stump of an arm. "And I lose my arm and my ability to ever have children. And you?" He swung his pistol back to Cadence and me. "You walked away without a scratch and fathered these two worthless pieces of trash."

I don't know what I expected to see on my father's face at Eric's words. Anger, for sure. Outrage, definitely. But the look of sadness and pity were unexpected. He placed his hand over my sister's as she fussed with his bandages. Gently, he pushed her hand away and shoved off the floor with his good arm. Cadence and I assisted him as we stood with him.

Dad faced his one-time friend. "I am sorry for what happened to you, Eric. I'm sorry for Rory. He was my friend too. If I could have traded places with him, I would have. You know as well as I do that the minefield wasn't marked. What you are doing here won't make any of that right again. If you want to kill me, fine. Just let my children go."

Eric shook his head violently. "No," he shouted. "I'm going to take from you everything you took from me."

My father took a step toward Eric. "You'll never get away with it, Eric. We've already called the sheriff. They are on the way."

Eric gave a wicked grin. "Oh, I think I will. But what you don't get, John, is that I don't care anymore." B*ang*! The defining roar shook the room and a high-pitched ring, like the scream of ten thousand mosquitos filled my ears.

Cadence cried out as my father collapsed. Blood spurted through a hole in his leg.

"Now be a good soldier and stay put." Eric rolled his eyes and addressed Cadence with a laugh. "Looks like you have more work to do. Get busy, girl, while your brother and I talk. Then I'll have another chore for you."

As Cadence knelt, she held my father's knife in a death-like grip. She was a hair's breadth from attacking Eric. She started to bandage Dad's leg.

Before I could react, Eric had tucked the automatic pistol in his waistband and pulled another revolver from the small of his back. I looked at the pistol and then up at Eric. The man was truly insane.

"Recognize it, don't you?"

I swallowed hard.

"I found it in your closet when I went looking for clues to where you and your druggy sister were hiding. I tried to get Benito to do my dirty work for me, but he obviously wasn't up to the job. Like always, your father screwed things up." Eric turned the revolver this way and that, admiring the weapon. "Nice little revolver. Thought about using it to make your and your sister's death look like a murder-suicide." Eric swung the revolver around the room. "This mess makes my romantic plan a bit superfluous, don't you think?"

When I still didn't answer, he laughed and twisted his neck violently to one side, producing a loud pop. "Ah, that's better. Back to business. I can't spend all day here." He looked down at my father. "How about I let you choose where I put the next hole?"

I had heard enough. Eric Pincer made Benito Silva look normal. If we played along with Eric's sick game, we'd all end up dead. As I stepped in front of Cadence, she glanced up. Our eyes locked. I gave her a grim smile, and the slightest nod indicated that she understood.

I turned to face Eric Pincer. The rage I had always depended on was gone, but in its place was a passionate love for my family. I hadn't been there for them for the past eight years. But I was here now. So help me, God, I was here now.

"So, the whelp is not a coward after all." Eric pointed the revolver at my forehead. I remembered the feel of that barrel there and the blood trickling down from where the gunsights had cut my face. I looked into Eric Pincer's crazy, cold eyes and said the first thing that came to mind.

"At least it's not my birthday."

The confusion on his face turned to surprise as I lunged. My words had bought me a fraction of a second, and my feint to the side caused the first bullet to miss. The next one did not. The shock of its impact stung my belly. I grunted but kept moving. Eric was three steps away, and I was going strong when the third bullet took me in the chest. The last shot exploded in my face, burning my scalp as I ran into him. My arms locked around his chest, and my momentum propelled us out the door.

Another pumping thrust of my legs, and we sailed off the porch in a twisted embrace. We landed on the ground a couple of feet past the first step. My forehead caught Eric on the bridge of his nose and I felt the brittle crunch and a gush of warm blood. Searing pain exploded through my hands as Eric's body went limp.

Chapter 117

The Door

The sound of Cadence's voice and the hobbling thump of my father's boots across the porch brought me back from the edge of unconsciousness. The pain from my broken hands nearly caused me to black out again. When my vision cleared, the big pine tree and the barn with a sliver of the blue sky above it came into focus. Cadence's face hovered over me as she knelt beside me. Her hands nervous and uncertain, she plucked at the sleeve of my shirt. Warm wetness spread underneath me.

Cadence groaned. "You crazy, brave man."

She tried to pull my arm out from where it was trapped. I screamed. The pain was exquisite. Now that the shock was wearing off, a blossoming ache spread through the rest of my body. It was difficult to breathe.

Dad appeared beside my sister. He was calm and certain. "We've got to roll him to get his hands free," he said to Cadence.

I steeled myself for what was coming, but I still wasn't prepared. I spent what seemed like an eternity on the brutal frontier of semi-consciousness as they untangled me from the body of Eric Pincer. They turned me to one side, and Cadence managed to roll Eric off my pinned arm. When I was free, Cadence took one look at my chest and ran back into the house.

Grim sorrow sank into my father's face as we stared into each other's eyes. I saw the truth. With clenched teeth, he managed to get his good arm underneath mine. Steely lines on his face betrayed the pain he ignored to draw me onto his lap.

He placed his hand on my head and smoothed back my hair like I was a child again. Tears ran down the livid scar on his face. "My dear brave son."

Cadence returned and opened my shirt. She placed a pad of gauze over the hole in my chest where pink foamy blood rasped and bubbled every time I took a shallow breath. She held her hand over the wound and looked at my father in desperation. Her fingers trembled. Dad placed his hand over hers and gently squeezed.

"I'll hold this one. Take care of the other one."

Cadence removed her hand and placed another gauze pad over the wound in my belly. This slowed the blood, but a lot had already soaked into the dirt around us. If the .22 hollow-points had done their job right, they had broken up and done all sorts of damage inside.

Far off, the faint, plaintiff wail of a siren could be heard.

Eyes widening, Cadence glanced at Dad. "What else can we do?"

"Nothing until the medics get here."

The pain had started to fade, and an unfamiliar cold seeped into my arms and legs. I felt my father's warm tears and heard my sister's soft crying. Cadence was on her knees in front of me. She pulled out the tail of her t-shirt and brushed the crimson froth from my lips. A strange happiness filled me, just to be here with both of them. I'd done one more thing to be proud of. A big thing. I looked into Cadence's violet eyes and smiled.

"It's … okay, Sis," I managed. Cadence sobbed. I lifted my arm and placed my broken hand on top of hers, wincing.

She stifled her sobs and said, "You are going to make it. You hear me? We still have unfinished business. You made me a promise, and I'm not letting you out of it. You understand me?" The sharp nod of her head showered me with tears.

I nodded my head weakly. I tried to laugh but only managed a rasping rattle that spewed more bloody foam over my sister and Dad's hands and arms. The cold crept farther up my legs and arms. I was running out of time. I could feel it, not in my extremities shutting down but in the clarity of mind that my imminent death seemed to energize. My father's face held the same look I'd seen when he found me facing Benito and his men with a broken chair hanging from my arm. Though not a word was spoken, my father and I shared an understanding in those few seconds. Once again, he gave me that slight nod of respect.

I looked at Cadence. I had one task to complete. I tried to speak again, but it was difficult to take a breath. "Brief … case," I said through bloody lips.

With her free hand, Cadence squeezed my arm in understanding. She jumped up and ran into the cabin. A moment later, she returned with my father's briefcase. I tried to get into a better position, but I didn't have the strength.

"Please help me up," I rasped.

Cadence shot Dad a questioning glance. He nodded. Between the two of them, they helped me sit up a bit straighter against my father. His right arm held me like a band of bronze. I reached for the case. I couldn't get my hand to work, so I just rested it on the handle and looked into my father's eyes. Closer to him now, I had to turn my head up and sideways.

"I … wanted … to give … this …" Cadence wiped my lips again as I willed myself to continue. "Back …" The tension in my father's arm and body relaxed slightly. "Too … long, wasted years," I whispered.

I closed my eyes. I saw a long lighted hallway. I saw the door. It was open. Instead of knocking, I heard my sister's weeping. I felt her soft hands shaking. I opened my eyes again.

It took several attempts to get the words out. My tongue was heavy now. A grayness dimmed the edges of my vision.

"I'm sorry, Dad." Those words felt like the sweetest thing I'd ever said.

My father squeezed my arm again, and he gave a shuddering sigh. "I'm sorry, too, Timbre."

I turned to look at my beautiful sister. Her tears flowed like the cool waters of Clear Creek. I grabbed the handle of my father's briefcase and tried to pull it toward me. "My … Bible."

Cadence gently laid my hand aside. She opened the briefcase and removed my Bible. When she made to lay it on my chest, I pushed it toward her.

"I give … to you." I smiled and closed my eyes.

Cadence sobbed, and my father's frame shook.

With a final effort, I started to whisper, "I know in whom I have …"—Cadence joined me—"believed, and I'm persuaded that he …"—our father's rich bass joined us—"… is able to keep that which I've committed unto him against that day."

I let go of my Bible and fumbled for Cadence's hand. "Walk me …" Cadence leaned close to hear. Her warm breath brushed my cheek. I studied her sorrowful face for a long moment. "I love you, Caden."

"I love you, too, Timmy."

I closed my eyes and pictured the long hallway again. I could no longer see the door of my dreams, but I knew without any doubt now that it was open. I tugged weakly on Cadence's hand.

"Walk me to the door, Sis?"

Epilogue

4-Caden

One Year later

The tension electrified the car as my father drove north out of Phoenix. The three of us sat in silence, each lost in our thoughts. This trip back to Grandfather's cabin stirred a powerful mix of emotions in all of us. My life had changed there. *Our* lives had changed there. Through all the horror and pain, my faith had been reborn.

I jiggled my leg and searched for a distraction. On the back seat next to me lay a copy of the *Phoenix Herald*. I unfolded the front page of the paper. The picture stopped me. My hands shook. But it was the number in the picture that made me gasp.

4 – 314514

The big, graffiti-like numerals had been spray-painted in black on the side of a yellow sports car. I read the headline, and the paper started to shake. My breath came in quick, short gasps as I read further.

HOUSE of HORRORS

Phoenix AZ, ------

Desert Healing Behavioral Health was closed by state authorities today as investigators look into claims of abuse.

According to sources close to the investigation, Wendel Grimes was arrested on multiple charges of abuse of DHBH clients. Witnesses tell the Herald *that Grimes was found handcuffed to the steering wheel of his car in DHBH's parking lot Friday morning. Unconfirmed accounts say that Grimes had substantial incriminating evidence inside his vehicle.*

The number spray-painted on the car also allegedly matched an empty file on Grimes's hard drive. At this time, it is unclear what, if any, connection the numbers have to Grimes, the crimes he is accused of committing, or the person responsible for bringing these horrible revelations to light.

I tried to still the shaking of my hands as I lowered the paper enough to look over the top. I met my father's eyes in the rear-view mirror. His lips trembled, and a single tear rolled down over the jagged scar on his face. Then his lips firmed, and he flicked the tear away with his thumb. His gaze returned to the road. I raised the paper again to hide my tears.

I hadn't planned on telling him what had happened to me at the rehab center, but four weeks earlier, he'd heard my screams at night. His touch had woken me, sweating and scared. He'd sat there with a bowed head as I told him. He said nothing for a long time after I finished. There had been no tears, just stony silence. But his face told me what his lips couldn't. That had been the closest I'd ever seen my father to being broken. And the clenched jaw and deep furrows across his forehead indicated that the Plummer rage smoldered just below the surface. Somehow, though, my father had beat it back and gently squeezed my shoulder.

"I'm so sorry, Cadence," he'd said. A tremor had passed through him like the shifting of some subterranean fault line just before a mega-quake. He'd let go of my shoulder and stood. His muscles in his jaw had worked, but still, no words had come.

"I'm okay, Dad," I'd told him. And when he searched my face—"I really am."

He must have seen what he wanted to because he gave me a convincing nod and spoke. "If you ever need to talk about it, I'm here, okay?"

Now those 7 black numbers spray-painted across the bright-yellow muscle car said it all. They were a cipher that hid an apology and a promise.

4 - Caden

Two hours later, the crunch of gravel and a slight jerk brought my eyes open. My heart beat heavy in my chest. My fingers closed around the door handle.

"I'll get it." I opened my door and stepped out, inhaling a deep breath of the heady ponderosa forest. As I walked around the front of the car, I ran my fingers across the eleven letters cut into the metal plate that had been hung on the gate. My father had finally named Grandfather's homestead.

Timbre's Rest

So fitting. Like my brother, the sign was rough, its letters cut into hard steel with the flame of a cutting torch. I smiled at that.

I swung the gate open, and they started through. I held out my hand and stopped my father. He rolled down the window.

"I'll walk from here," I said.

He nodded and drove on.

A few minutes later, I emerged from the wooded drive into the clearing. The cabin lay in front of me, its familiar yellow logs beckoning. My father's car was parked near the steps. No one was in sight. As I neared the porch, I saw them standing apart at the base of the old pine tree where Timbre and I had so many times competed with bows and arrows. I paused to take in the sight.

My father stood straight and tall at the foot of the long mound of earth. His hands were clasped in front, his head bowed. Because Arizona law allows for personal burial plots, we'd dug it together, my father and I. Six feet long and six feet deep. Then we'd lowered him into the grave with ropes, my tears showering the plain pine casket my father had built with his own hands.

Now, one year later, my mother knelt in front of that mound of dirt, her hands resting on top as her tears watered the earth between them.

I started walking again. My heart burst with hope as my eyes flooded with tears. What a strange, terrible, wonderful journey, this thing we call life. I no longer walked it in fear and desperation, but rather in hope upon that invisible bridge of faith that rested on the foundation of God's love and stretched between the dark shores of my past and the glorious promise of eternity.

I stopped between my parents and reached for my mother's hand, then my father's. I smiled as I softly read the words written on my brother's tombstone.

I know whom I have believed,
and am persuaded
that he is able to keep
that which I have committed
unto him against that day.
2 Timothy 1:12

Author's Note:

This story is a work of fiction, but the Biblical information upon which the Lazarus Ciphers are based is true. I hope this novel strengthened your faith and will inspire you with a new appreciation for Yeshua – Yahweh's Salvation.

If you would like to learn more about the Biblical history and facts woven into this story, I invite you to visit my website at www.the13thenumeration.com

My non-fiction Prophecies and Patterns books are free to for subscribers to my newsletter. Subscribers will receive advance notice on my next novel and periodically I'll share blog articles about Biblical history and Bible prophecy. I won't share your email nor will I spam with endless requests or advertisements.

Help Share the Good News of Yeshua:

Fifty percent of the royalties from the sale of this book will be donated to ONE FOR ISRAEL. To learn more about their ministry to share the good news of Yeshua with the Jewish and Arab peoples, please visit their website at: www.oneforisrael.org

Non-fiction by William Struse

- The 13th Enumeration:
  Key to the Bible's Messanic Symbolism
- Daniel's 70 Weeks:
  The Keystone of Bible Prophecy
- The Jubile Code:
  Prophetic Milestones in Yahweh's Redemptive Plan

Novels by William Struse

- The 13th Enumeration
- The 13th Prime
- The 13th Symbol
- The Lazarus Ciphers

Made in the USA
Middletown, DE
04 October 2022